HARD LIMITS

BLACKSTONE HOUSE
BOOK 3

ELISE NOBLE

Published by Undercover Publishing Limited

ISBN: 978-1-912888-65-8

Edited by Nikki Mentges, NAM Editorial

Cover design by Abigail Sins

www.undercover-publishing.com

www.elise-noble.com

Don't limit your challenges.
Challenge your limits.

CHAPTER 1
THE ASSISTANT

"Hey! Watch out!"

Too late. The side mirror of the SUV clipped my hand, and the coffee I was holding flew through the air. A second later, my cappuccino with caramel syrup splattered over a candy wrapper, a crinkled flyer advertising Dr. Jo's Therapy Services, and the sorry remains of a fancy beaded shoe. If that wasn't a metaphor for my life on this gloomy January day in Los Angeles, I didn't know what was.

At least the cup wasn't broken. The insulated travel mug had been a gift from my best friend, and although the lid bounced off, it had survived the fall with only a small dent. But the coffee... I'd *needed* that coffee, and I couldn't afford a refill.

The driver's tinted window rolled down smoothly. At first, I only saw dark hair, and my insides seized because my older brother drove the same vehicle—a dark-grey Porsche Cayenne—and I feared that my family had finally caught up with me. But the window continued its downward journey to reveal intense blue eyes, smooth white skin, high cheekbones, a straight nose, and a well-defined jaw that definitely didn't belong to any of the men I was related to.

"Maybe if you'd looked where you were going, you wouldn't have walked into my car."

Okay, he and Raj did have one thing in common—they were both assholes. And you know what? I'd had enough of jerks like them. They thought that having money gave them a licence to do as they pleased.

"And maybe if you hadn't been driving your gas-guzzling penis extension so fast in a parking lot, you would have seen me before you hit me."

"You just appeared from nowhere."

"What if I'd been a child, huh? Would you still be using that excuse?"

"I'd like to think a child's parents would have taught it to look both ways before crossing the road. And for the record, I don't need a penis extension."

"Screw you."

"Not an option, my darling." He held out a hundred-dollar bill between thumb and forefinger. "Here—get yourself another coffee and a pair of glasses."

"You can't just buy me off like that."

He let the bill fall to the damp asphalt. "Suit yourself."

A second later, he roared away in his dick-mobile, leaving me fuming. Were arrogance and condescension coded into the Y chromosome? If I'd been allowed to continue my medical career, I could have done a study on it.

The hundred-dollar bill fluttered in the breeze, and I trapped it under my foot. Much as I didn't want to take the stranger's money, a hundred bucks was a hundred bucks, and I *really* needed caffeine. These days, I was too poor to be proud. My pride had gone the same way as my designer shoe collection, my top-of-the-line Mercedes coupe, and my gold jewellery—I'd left it behind when I escaped Massachusetts.

I picked up the bill and clutched the cup Meera had given

me tightly as I hurried back to the coffee bar. The cup said "Not today, Satan," but nobody down there seemed to be listening. What was the time? Ten thirty-seven. Which gave me twenty-three minutes to refuel and walk the half mile to Dunnvale Holdings for my job interview.

And I needed the job almost as much as I needed the caffeine. My Toyota's fuel pump had stopped working, the tyres needed replacing, and last week, my landlord had announced he was putting up the rent on my shared apartment by twenty percent. Twenty percent! Even with the amount split four ways, I'd still have to find an extra two hundred bucks each month. When we'd questioned the increase, the landlord had merely shrugged and told us we were free to leave if we wanted to because there were plenty more people waiting to take our place, and he was right. The cost of living in LA was skyrocketing. If I couldn't find a good-paying job, my only option would be to move somewhere cheaper, but I liked the anonymity of a big city. The neighbours didn't know my name, and nobody cared about my business as long as I coughed up my share of the rent money.

The line for coffee took forever, and I scalded my tongue as I headed out into the parking lot for the second time this morning. I'd have to hustle to get to Dunnvale on time. The job was a personal assistant position, hardly my dream career, but it was better than tending to the every need of a man I didn't want to marry. At least in this role, I'd be able to do as I pleased in the evenings and—most importantly—sleep alone at night. I mean, I just wasn't wife material. I was a terrible cook, everything I ironed still ended up with creases, and the idea of submitting to a man the way my mother did made my skin crawl.

But in a professional capacity, I could deal with being told what to do, and this position paid better than most.

Dunnvale's headquarters came up on the right, a

sprawling Art Deco-style building that stood four storeys tall. The lady I'd spoken with on the phone said to use the side entrance, and the offices were on the third floor. So far, so good... This place looked far nicer than the last company I'd worked at. Clifton Packaging had been based in a soulless brick building in the Warehouse District, the air always filled with dust from the manufacturing processes and too hot because the AC rarely worked. Dunnvale Holdings was closer to Beverly Hills. Farther to commute to but safer, and as an added bonus, the building would look great on Meera's Instagram page.

I buzzed the intercom, and somebody answered almost immediately.

"How may I help you?" a female voice asked.

"Meera Adams to see Braxton Vale. I have an interview."

"Come on up. The staircase is on your right."

The lock clicked, and I found myself in a small lobby. A coffee table and couch sat to the left, shaded from a twinkling chandelier by a potted palm. I tucked the empty cup into my purse and took the staircase to the third floor, my footsteps soft on the thick carpet. I'd long since given up wearing heels. Now that I had to rely on bus rides and my own two feet to travel anywhere, ballet pumps were far more comfortable.

This office... It wasn't like an office. Granted, my experience was limited—I'd only worked for two other companies since I moved to LA, and one of them was a gym, but I'd spent time at my father's business. Regular offices had rows of desks and filing cabinets with noisy printers providing a soundtrack, cubicles decorated with drooping plants and pictures of pets and kids as their occupants desperately tried to pretend they were elsewhere. Sad employees gathered around water coolers, and people sometimes cried in the bathrooms. Okay, that was me. I cried in the bathroom.

But this was more like a luxury hotel, minus the bellhop

and the noisy tourists. Gilded mirrors gave the place an airy feel, the velvet Chesterfield opposite the ornately carved reception desk was richly padded, and there was a bowl of chocolate truffles on the coffee table. Paintings decorated the walls, not corporate propaganda and health-and-safety posters.

"You must be Meera?" The lady behind the desk was my mother's age, dressed in a burgundy shift dress and a pearl necklace. Her hair was cut into a sleek bob, a shorter version of the style I currently sported. My waist-length hair had been the first sacrifice I'd made before coming to the West Coast.

"That's right."

"It's lovely to meet you. Can I get you coffee? Tea? A glass of water?"

Coffee? That fight in the parking lot had been for nothing? Well, not nothing—I'd come out of it ninety-six dollars richer, which made the bruised hand worth it. That cash would pay for two weeks' worth of groceries, although I was *so* sick of eating rice. One of my roommates had suggested ramen, but that didn't taste much better.

"Coffee would be wonderful."

"Do you take milk? Sugar?"

Low-calorie caramel syrup with foam was probably out of the question.

"Just milk, thank you."

I was one minute early, and Braxton Vale was ten minutes late. A power play to prove that his time was more important than mine? Probably. My father used the trick regularly. Meera called it a dick move, but at least I had time to drink my coffee and use the bathroom. The bathroom that was stocked with expensive perfume and unused Chanel make-up, just in case I got the urge to go back to my old ways. Would the receptionist think it strange if I came out with scarlet lips when they'd previously been pale pink? I left them as they were.

"Mr. Vale will see you now. Take the hallway to your left and go through the double doors at the end."

"Thank you for the coffee."

The hallway was lined with photos, artful black-and-white shots of the Los Angeles skyline, the ocean, Sunset Boulevard. Santa Monica Pier. The Hollywood sign. A naked woman staring out across the city.

Wait.

What?

I paused to stare, and apart from the barely there panties, she wasn't wearing a stitch of clothing. I mean, the picture was certainly artistic, and I was no stranger to nudity, but was it really suitable for the workplace? The taut ass of the man in the next print was no less risqué. What sort of company was this? I'd googled, of course, but little had come up, just a vague paragraph on some business website noting that Dunnvale Holdings had backed a new indie movie starring Violet Miller, this year's hottest Hollywood property. Did she know about this objectification? I stepped closer. The pictures weren't tasteless—quite the opposite, in fact—just…unexpected.

Maybe Violet did know? After all, she *had* filmed a gloriously dirty movie last year, an erotic thriller with Kane Sanders. I'd seen it in the movie theatre with Meera on one of our final nights out together in Boston, and I'd had to fan myself on more than one occasion. My father would have lost his mind if he'd found out what I'd been watching.

There's something strange about this place…

A part of me wanted to spin around and run out of the building. There was an odd vibe in the air, an undercurrent of energy that left me twitchy. But the rent wouldn't pay itself, and nobody else would even give me an interview. So many employers wanted ten years of experience in return for minimum wage these days, and I lacked the first and couldn't afford to live on the second. Not with no support network whatsoever. Living alone was every bit as hard as I'd feared it would be, but despite the constant setbacks, I knew I'd made the right decision in leaving my old world.

I might have been tired, and poor, and a little bit scared, but I was free.

And freedom was worth more than a healthy bank balance.

Silence reigned as I approached Braxton Vale's office. The doors ahead of me were as opulent as the rest of the building, carved wood with gold handles. Should I knock? The receptionist hadn't said anything about knocking, but if anyone walked into my father's office unannounced, even at home, his annoyance was all too evident.

I knocked.

"Come in."

The doors were as heavy as they looked, but when I pushed on the left-hand one, it swung open silently on well-oiled hinges. I took one step forward and nearly threw up.

Why?

Because the man sitting at the desk in front of me was the same man whose penis I'd insulted in the parking lot less than an hour earlier.

CHAPTER 2
BRAX

Braxton Vale sifted through the stack of résumés on his desk. Dozens and dozens of them. Getting applicants was never a problem—he paid well over the market rate—but finding the right person for the job always presented a challenge. Some of the candidates had included headshots, and he weeded out all the pretty ones and filed them in the trash. Too tempting. They definitely had to go.

Perhaps he should try hiring a male assistant again? Although that was a minefield too—the first one had tried hitting on a married chef, so Brax had picked out a gay guy as his replacement. Scottie rearranged everything in Brax's office, his home, and even his car, then started redecorating. Emails went unanswered. The phone kept ringing. Interior design had been Scottie's passion, not admin. Two years later, Brax was still finding miscellaneous items in strange places. Who stored Scotch in a white wine refrigerator? Horizontally?

Hmm, what about an older candidate? A possibility, but in Brax's experience, they rarely lasted long. Jealous husbands, family commitments, a dislike of last-minute travel... Although he'd once hired a terrific lady in her sixties, fun yet quietly efficient, a former actress with an adventurous streak and a deliciously warped sense of humour. But Luisa had suffered a heart attack when one of the shows in the basement —the space nicknamed The Dark—got a little wild, and after she recovered, she'd retired to Acapulco.

Brax had adored Luisa.

He missed Luisa.

Today's candidate was twenty-four, but she'd passed the telephone interview, and Rhonda, his HR manager, thought she had potential. Brax scanned through her résumé. Meera Adams had been educated at Harvard with a concentration in environmental science and public policy and a secondary in European history, politics, and societies. Since she graduated, she'd held two positions in LA, the first as a receptionist at a gym and the second as a PA at a packaging company. She'd lasted two months at the first, four months at the second. Brax's assistants averaged two and a half months. The record was thirteen months—Luisa—and one girl had quit within five hours.

Rhonda had tagged the corner of the résumé with a sticky note.

Well-spoken, uptight, would turn her nose up at a man like you. A possible?

Bless Rhonda's heart. She knew exactly what he was looking for in an assistant, and she was Team Brax all the way. Loyalty was invaluable, especially in Brax's unfortunate situation. Every so often, one of Carissa's stooges slipped through the net, so he had to remain constantly vigilant, watching for any signs of betrayal.

A sigh escaped. How had it come to this?

Because you let your guard down, asshole.

Eight years ago, Brax had gotten distracted and fallen victim to an ambition greater than his own. When he married Carissa Dunn, signing a prenup with a vicious adultery clause hadn't seemed like such a problem. Just a mere formality. They'd been young and in love, and she'd appeared as eager to make a success of Dunnvale Holdings as he was.

Appeared as eager…

It turned out that Carissa was allergic to latex, costume jewellery, shellfish, and work. Possibly dogs too, although Brax suspected they just didn't like her very much.

Fast-forward the better part of a decade, and Brax had come to realise that Carissa had one love in life, and it wasn't him. No, it was money. Shopping came second, and luxury vacations took third place. He wanted a divorce. So did she, but only if she got the lion's share of the spoils. And therein lay the problem. Clause eight of the prenup said that if one party to the marriage cheated, they were entitled to one million dollars or ten percent of the joint assets, whichever was smaller. Brax hadn't spent his adult life building an empire just for Carissa to take ninety-nine point eight percent of it.

Mediation had failed, as had couples counselling, so now they were engaged in a game of sexual chicken—no bestiality involved because even he wouldn't stoop that low—and Carissa had a definite advantage. Her sex drive had never been as high as his, which had been yet another problem in their marriage.

Brax had taken cold showers, swallowed pills, bought every sex toy known to man, and even spent two weeks in a Peruvian monastery, but he was still trapped in his worst nightmare. Some of the most beautiful women in America worked in his clubs, women who were up for anything, and he wasn't allowed to touch any of them. And if he hired an assistant who was in any way attracted to him, it would be game over. Hell, she didn't even have to be beautiful. He could just close his eyes and sink into that warm—

A soft knock stopped him from going down that hole.

"Come in."

The door opened, and all his prayers were answered.

Halle-fucking-lujah.

Because Meera Adams and the woman he'd nearly run over this morning were one and the same person. In truth, he'd been feeling slightly guilty about that—yes, she'd walked out from between two stationary cars, but he probably shouldn't have been checking his phone behind the wheel, even in a parking lot.

This was perfect.

He wanted to ask her to start right away, but if he made things too easy, that might soften her attitude toward him. So he leaned back in his obscenely expensive swivel chair and studied her. Stared long enough to make her fidget.

Funny, she wasn't so talkative now.

Meera was slender, with shoulder-length black hair and light brown skin that suggested South Asian heritage. Luckily, Brax preferred blondes. Her features were fine, dainty, but her big brown eyes still held a flash of fire. Good. The ballet flats were another check in the "pros" column. Brax liked his women in heels, the higher the better. At home, Carissa had started wearing Crocs just to spite him, even though they made her feet sweat. No, Meera definitely wasn't his type. Although somehow, she still managed to appear regal while at the same time looking as if she wanted to vomit onto his Persian rug.

"So, you majored in environmental science? Now I understand the 'gas-guzzling' comment. Why aren't you busy measuring ice in the Arctic?"

She hesitated for a moment. Surprised he hadn't kicked her out right away?

"I'm actually more interested in ecosystem restoration."

"From restoring ecosystems to office work—that's quite a change."

"There are more jobs available in offices."

"And yet you only lasted four months in your last position. Why did you quit?"

Her hands balled into fists at her sides, and she glared for a second before she caught herself.

"Do you want the real reason or the one they gave me?"

"Let's hear both."

"Officially, I was fired after I called in sick."

"I see. And the real reason?"

"My boss exposed himself to me in his office."

"And that was a problem for you?"

"Of course it was a freaking problem! I reported him to HR, but he was the CEO's son, so guess who took the fall."

She objected to seeing her boss's cock? This got better and better. That jackass's loss was Brax's gain.

"An entirely predictable result. If a man raises his son to believe that non-consensual sexual activity is acceptable, he's going to protect him when he harasses a woman."

Brax's father had done the opposite—punished him for every indiscretion, real or imaginary. His mother suffered too. Brax had turned twenty by the time she finally left him, and by then, her psyche had been damaged beyond repair. Vernon Dupré might have been a pious son of a bitch, but the devil lived inside him.

The backbone of Brax's business portfolio, his sex clubs, had been born out of that troubled childhood. When he escaped to college, he'd wanted to experience all the sins his father deemed abhorrent, in private, with no judgment. And later, as he explored the darker side of Washington, DC, he'd discovered that there were plenty of wealthy individuals who shared the same desire. Each branch of Nyx—there were eight now—made Brax a lot of money and gave others a lot of pleasure.

"So you're saying it was my fault?" Meera asked. "That I shouldn't have reported him to HR?"

"If you'd thought things through, you would have realised that introducing his genitals to a paperweight would have led to a similar result with infinitely more satisfaction." Brax took another glance at her résumé. Strong academic record, little in the way of extracurricular activities. A good work ethic. "Do you make a habit of shouting at strangers?"

"Only when they deserve it."

A fair answer. The woman tried to smother a yawn, not very successfully.

"Am I keeping you up?"

"One of my neighbours had a party last night. All night."

"Then you should go back to bed and get some rest. I don't tolerate laziness here. See Rhonda in HR on your way out, and she'll provide you with a contract, a non-disclosure agreement, and details of our working arrangements."

"I'm sorry? A non-disclosure agreement?"

"Many of our clients are high profile. We need to ensure their privacy."

"Wait, are you offering me the job?"

"Unless you don't want it anymore. In which case, what are you doing here?"

"I…"

"I'm sure a smart girl like you can work out how to pick up my dry cleaning."

Those pretty brown eyes narrowed. "But—"

"That'll be all. You can start tomorrow morning."

For a moment, Meera just stood there. Despite the fact that there was a chair positioned in front of Brax's desk, she'd remained on her feet, fidgeting. No doubt she hadn't been expecting to stay long. Another moment, and she turned on her heel and marched out, leaving the door open behind her. Book smart but a tad ditzy, Brax assessed. Hopefully, she wouldn't get lost running errands. One time, an assistant had collected several shirts from the tailor, and he'd never seen

13

her again. He'd begun to suspect something nefarious, been on the verge of reporting her missing, when he'd received the shirts in the mail, cut into tiny pieces with a note telling him to go fuck himself.

Brax rose to close the door himself, his mind on the future as he strolled across his office. How long would Meera last? If past form was anything to go by, he gave her three weeks.

What the…?

His new assistant walked right into him, and he grabbed her arm as she stumbled. Why had she come back?

"You need to learn to look where you're going."

"You just appeared from nowhere."

"Isn't that my line?" he asked, referring to the earlier parking lot incident.

She bit her bottom lip as she looked up at him, and somewhere deep inside, Brax began to wonder if he might have made a terrible mistake in hiring her. Later, he'd wish that he'd paid more attention to his subconscious, to that little voice telling him to wake the fuck up. Maybe *he* was the one who needed more coffee?

"I thought the door would close by itself."

When Meera tried to take a step back, Brax realised he was still holding onto her arm. He released her, and one step turned into a dozen.

"We start work at eleven a.m. tomorrow," Brax called after her. "Don't be late."

He didn't wait for an answer, just closed the door and headed back to his desk. His laptop was open, and he typed out an email, copied to five of his oldest friends and one new one.

From: Brax
 To: Dawson, Zach, Justin, Nolan, Alexa, Ari
 Subject: Assistant #27

Her name is Meera. So far, she's told me to go screw myself and called my car a gas-guzzling penis extension. Place your bets, folks.
B

The first response came from Alexa. As far as Brax could work out, she never slept.

Two weeks. And I'm going to need her surname, date of birth, and social security number.

Brax could get those from Rhonda. He hadn't asked Alexa to start running background checks, but three or four years ago, she'd taken it upon herself to help and discovered that his former finance director was embezzling funds, so Brax wasn't going to stop her. She also read all his emails. Some might have resented the intrusion, but short of disconnecting from the internet entirely, there was no way to keep her out, and in her own strange way, she cared.

Dawson's answer came next. *Ten days. If she doesn't like your car, she'll hate your boat.*

Quickly followed by a message from Justin: *Three weeks. Did she see your dick already? I thought that was against the rules?*

Brax tapped out a quick reply. *Ha-ha. Very funny.*

And the boat was only a small cabin cruiser, not a super yacht. He needed a hobby to distract him from the Carissa nightmare, so he'd begun escaping to the water.

Nolan: Five weeks. Why don't you grow some willpower and hire an assistant who doesn't hate you?

Willpower? He thought Brax hadn't tried that? Even the hypnotherapist had given up on him.

Ari: One month. Women are tough, but should we really be betting on them this way? Why don't you look for a guy like Chase instead? P.S. Zach says six weeks.

Ah, Chase. Alexa's assistant was a true unicorn. If there was the slightest chance he might be looking for a new job, Brax would offer the man any salary he asked for. But Chase would never leave Alexa. Their arrangement had grown from employer-employee into a deep friendship that had withstood the test of time. Plus there was the fact that Alexa would erase every last byte from Dunnvale's network if he tried to mess with her.

Brax: If you stumble across Chase's twin, let me know. I've given up hope.

CHAPTER 3
THE ASSISTANT

I got a new job! Call me when you can x

Most of the day, Meera didn't have a phone signal. She was living her dream in Portugal, working on a farm and planting trees in deforested areas to increase carbon uptake and encourage the return of wildlife, all while spending time with the man she loved. She also taught the occasional yoga class, plus she was learning to play the guitar. Meanwhile, I was living the life her family wanted her to have. The life they thought she had.

When she first suggested the arrangement, I thought she'd lost her mind. I'd pretend to be her while she went backpacking around Europe? That was crazy, right? But as the date of my marriage approached, the idea had become less wishful thinking and more my only chance of escape. And after the engagement party, I knew. I knew I couldn't marry Karam Joshi. He was self-centred, opinionated, and lazy, plus his idea of a wife's role was very different from mine. If we tied the knot, I'd become my mother, forever destined to rise at five a.m., ready to clean the house and make breakfast *precisely* the way my husband liked it. Basically, I'd be an unpaid housekeeper, nanny, and cook, but also be expected to keep in shape and look lovely on his arm at parties.

The day our engagement was formally announced, I'd been on my way back from the bathroom in the lavish hotel when I overheard Karam asking his father whether it would be acceptable to ask me to have a boob job before the wedding. Or should he wait until afterward? That was the moment I'd texted Meera and told her I'd do whatever it took. Whatever it took to not become Mrs. Indali Joshi.

In the end, it had been quite simple. Meera and I spent our last seven months at Harvard plotting. She and Alfie, her fiancé, planned their trip overseas while I figured out my half of the guest list for an event that was never going to happen, agreed on a venue, hired a wedding planner, and bided my time. Then, the night after my final exam, she'd cut my hair to look like hers, and I'd slipped away in the early hours with one carefully packed suitcase to catch a bus. Destination? As far from Massachusetts as possible.

I'd made it all the way to California.

Today, I took a picture of Dunnvale's beautiful Art Deco building before I left, the outside giving no hints as to what lay beyond. Why was there no signage? Maybe the clients weren't the only folks who liked privacy, and judging by the decor, business was booming. There was a restaurant and a spa on the first floor, Rhonda had told me as we went over the paperwork, and since it was lunchtime, she'd asked the chef to send up a few snacks. The food was as good as anything I'd eaten with Papa, and he only went to high-end establishments. One time, he'd seen a charge from McDonald's on my credit card statement and called to lecture me on the danger of saturated fats. Did he think I wasn't aware of that? I'd been in my second year at Harvard Medical School at the time.

Medical school. I should have been halfway through my

first year of residency by now—overworked, underpaid, and enjoying my job—but Karam believed a woman's place was in the kitchen, not the hospital. Although if he tried eating my masala dosas, he might change his mind. On the plus side, at least I'd be able to treat him for food poisoning.

Was I bitter about having to abandon the career I'd worked so hard for? Of course. Who wouldn't be? But I couldn't change my father's mind, and the second place he'd send the private investigators that he'd hired would be hospitals. At least there were plenty of medical facilities in the United States, so they'd take a while to not find me there. How did I know he'd hired investigators? Because the first place they'd gone had been Meera's family home. Her mom had given the PI Meera's number, and Meera told him that she hadn't heard from me since I left Massachusetts, but she'd noticed me researching rental properties in New York and so maybe I'd headed there?

A sigh escaped. Life in Los Angeles was miserable, but far better than the alternative. And at least I had a temporary job now. That was how I thought of it—temporary. Braxton Vale was a rude, cocky, abrasive, pushy, hot jerk. No, no, no, not hot. Objectively handsome, possibly. Definitely not hot.

Looks didn't matter to me anyway. If they did, I'd be marrying Karam and spending his money on expensive clothes. Oh, and cosmetic surgery, apparently. C-cups weren't enough for him. He wanted watermelons.

Anyhow, I had a job, and if I lasted one month, I could fix my car. I missed my dented old Toyota in a way I'd never thought possible. Not only did riding the bus cost more than buying gas, but the journey to work took twice as long. Until I moved to LA, I hadn't realised how incredibly expensive it was to be poor.

Should I add a picture to Meera's Instagram now? I had one ready to go—a close-up of the geometric stonework above the entrance to the Dunnvale building that was pretty without giving anything away. No, better to speak with her first. While I waited, I flipped through the file Rhonda had given me. She'd called it Braxton's Bible. Except according to page one, I wasn't allowed to call him Braxton or Brax or anything other than Mr. Vale. He liked his coffee made with Hawaiian Kona beans and served at 140 degrees Fahrenheit, no more, no less. A note said the beans and the thermometer were in the cupboard beside the refrigerator in his kitchenette. The instructions went on and on and on... The type of car air freshener he liked (nothing pine scented), his favourite cologne (Hugo Boss), his preferred kind of underwear (briefs, not boxers, and certainly not thongs). I had to buy his freaking underwear?

Working at Dunnvale Holdings promised to be an ordeal, but if I'd known just how dramatically it would change my life, perhaps I'd have taken the bus to Santa Monica Pier, jumped off the end, and kept on swimming.

I woke with a start as Frank Sinatra sang "My Way." The song had been Meera's little joke because that was what we'd chosen—to do things our way. What time was it? Five in the afternoon, which meant it was...one a.m. in Portugal. Why was Meera calling me at that time?

"Hey, you're up late." I heard a sniffle. "Is everything okay?"

"We had a fight."

"You and Alfie?"

"He says he's sick of digging swales and chopping down trees."

"What's a swale? And I thought you were planting trees, not removing them?"

"Swales are shallow channels that help to prevent

flooding. And we're getting rid of the eucalyptus trees because they're harmful to the environment. In springtime, we'll replace them with native species."

In truth, I did understand Alfie's point, but he *had* volunteered to go on this trip. Enthusiastically, as I recalled. This was the first issue Meera had mentioned, so hopefully any problems would soon blow over.

"Maybe he just had a long day? What was the weather like?"

"It poured again. That's six days in a row."

"He'll mellow out when the sun's shining. Anyone would be miserable after nearly a week of rain."

"I'm not. The swales are working so well."

"Okay, almost anyone. You're just weird."

Meera didn't argue with that. "So, you got a new job? Grandpa's gonna be happy."

"You'll need to manage his expectations—I don't think it'll last long."

"Why not?"

"Well, first my new boss hit me with his car…"

"*What?*"

I filled Meera in on the day's events, starting with the coffee incident and ending with the salary offer that put my expected earnings as a new doctor to shame. Although I realised now why Mr. Vale paid so much—the extra was for putting up with his obnoxious temperament.

"So I just need to stick it out there for a month," I said. "That's all."

"I'm telling you, the guy at the auto shop is ripping you off."

"I tried three different ones."

"Want me to ask Alfie to call? He speaks fluent mechanic. His brother used to race motorcycles."

"You think he would? If he's in a foul mood…"

"The weather's meant to be better tomorrow. And if your

new boss is nasty, you should quit. Life's too short for shitty men."

That phrase had become our mantra in those last months of college, much to Alfie's amusement. Although Meera's family definitely disagreed with her taste in boyfriends, which was another reason for our subterfuge. So many lies... They thought she was single now, while she'd actually gotten engaged to Alfie before we graduated. He'd gone down on one knee after her final exam, and of course she'd said yes.

Meanwhile, her grandfather spent way too much time watching British crime dramas, and he thought that Englishmen in general and Alfie in particular were ignorant yobs. The fact that Alfie had no ambitions beyond working as a barista and hanging out with his friends didn't help matters. Work to live, not live to work, that was his ethos. Didn't Grandpa Adams understand that not everyone needed a high-powered career to be happy? Clearly not. Meera could do better, he said, and if she chose not to, he was going to leave his home to the local cat sanctuary instead of her when he died. No—and I quote—lazy little pillock was going to get his hands on the cash.

Given Grandpa Adams's penchant for fried food, that bequest would come sooner rather than later. I suspected he was only one partially blocked artery away from a heart attack, but he refused to have his cholesterol measured. Or his blood pressure. And Meera loved cats, she really did, but do you realise how hard it is to get on the property ladder? A year ago, I'd had no idea, but now I knew the difficulties all too well. My dream was to own a tiny apartment, but at this rate, I'd have roommates for the rest of my life.

Meera's parents weren't keen on Alfie either, although they hadn't been quite as outspoken as her grandpa. I'd overheard her dad telling her mom that Alfie was a bum, and while it was true that barista work paid minimum wage, he did well with tips, and his folks—who both taught at Harvard

—were happy to support him. Wealth wasn't measured in money, I knew that better than most. Happiness was priceless.

"'Nasty' is the wrong word," I told Meera. "I think Mr. Vale will be demanding."

"Not a pervert like Clifton junior?"

"I don't get that vibe from him."

Although in that awkward moment when he stopped me from overbalancing, he *had* held onto my arm for longer than was strictly necessary. Or had I imagined it? Dealing with men wasn't exactly my forte. My father scared most of them off. Or paid them off. Did it really matter which? They never stuck around.

"If he starts to unzip his fly in front of you, run. Don't hang around to look this time."

Meera made it sound as if I'd peeked out of curiosity, when the truth was, I'd been stunned. Until Lance Clifton whipped out his genitalia, I'd assumed he was just scratching his balls the way his father always did.

"Believe me, I'm out of there."

CHAPTER 4
THE ASSISTANT

"This is cold."

I'd gotten to work at a quarter to eleven. Braxton Vale had shown up at ten past. By then, his coffee had cooled to 135 degrees, and of course he noticed.

"Sorry, Mr. Vale. I'll reheat it."

He pulled a face. "No, make it again."

If he hadn't been paying me so well, he would have ended up wearing it.

"Right away, Mr. Vale."

Even my father didn't complain about microwaved coffee.

"And pick me up a croissant. And the new shoes I ordered from Lewis Jefferson. Plus I need more moisturiser."

Moisturiser? Well, he did have a smooth complexion. "Uh, which brand?"

"Make a dinner reservation—a table for six—on Thursday evening at the place I like on North Cannon Drive. I forget the name... The one with the blue sign outside. A private table, nothing near the window. Send a bouquet to my mother, and get Herve Weisberger on the phone."

"How do you spell—"

"And find me strawberries. I fancy having strawberries. Don't forget to ensure they're organic."

Croissant, shoes, moisturiser... Crap, what was the fourth thing? This was like one of those game shows where you had to memorise the items on the conveyor, except I wouldn't be going home with any prizes at the end of the day. If I was lucky—or perhaps unlucky, depending on how you looked at it—I'd manage to keep my job. I should have brought a notepad and pen with me. Or better yet, recorded my new boss, although that would probably be in contravention of the NDA I'd signed.

"Could you just—"

Mr. Vale turned his chair away from me. "That's all, Meena."

"Actually, it's Meera."

He didn't bother to answer, and I stood there like a fool until I finally realised I'd been dismissed and ran for the door. Not the heavy set of double doors I'd come in yesterday, but the regular door to the left of Mr. Vale's giant desk—another sign of tiny-dick syndrome. My own workstation was in a smaller anteroom that came with a luxurious couch, a kitchenette, and a large closet. According to the manual, I should put Mr. Vale's dry cleaning and any new clothes he purchased into the closet, and he'd take them upstairs later. Apparently, he lived on the fourth floor, but I wasn't to enter his apartment unless specifically requested. That suited me just fine. He'd probably modelled his penthouse on a dungeon, and it wouldn't have surprised me if he had a refrigerator full of blood bags and slept in a coffin.

A notepad, I needed a notepad. And a pen. My desk was a smaller version of Mr. Vale's, an ornate thing carved from dark wood, and I pulled open the top drawer. It was empty except for a greeting card decorated with a shiny four-leaf clover. Curiosity got the better of me.

To his new PA,
Good luck—you'll need it.
Monique (#26)

Was the message meant for me? Was Monique my predecessor? What did the number twenty-six mean? Was I the twenty-seventh assistant? Surely not—Mr. Vale couldn't have been more than thirty, and even my father had only gotten through nine assistants in the last decade. I knew that because I'd spent more time talking with them than I had with him. He, on the other hand, barely remembered their names—when I'd tried to include them all on my wedding guest list, he'd asked who they were and then vetoed that plan.

I opened the second drawer and hit pay dirt—a brand-new Moleskine notebook and an expensive-looking silver pen nestled in a velvet-lined box. I turned to the first page and began scribbling frantically.

Croissant.
Shoes.
Moisturiser.
Dinner.
Bouquet.

Had he asked for strawberries or raspberries? And *bhains ki aankh*, who was that person he'd wanted me to call?

I thumbed through the manual, looking for key words. Where should I buy the croissant from? Did it matter? Mr. Vale had a favourite brand for everything, it seemed—what about pastries? The "food" section gave me my answer. Pastries came from the kitchen downstairs or the patisserie half a mile along the road. Guess I'd better get used to walking. At least the exercise might help me to shift the six pounds I'd gained during my time at Clifton Packaging. Boredom had given me a cookie habit.

Since I didn't know how to call the kitchen, I took twenty dollars from the petty cash box (located in bottom desk drawer, keep receipts, email spreadsheet to finance department monthly detailing expenditure) and headed to Bakeology. Croissants came plain, garnished with almonds, or filled with ham and Gruyère. I sucked in a calming breath. *Just ask for one of each, Indi.* If Mr. Vale had a problem with that, then he should have been more specific, shouldn't he?

A grocery store nearby sold organic fruit, so I bought strawberries and raspberries to cover all bases. Back in the office, I arranged three croissants on a china plate I found in the kitchenette, put the fruit in a matching bowl, and knocked on the connecting door.

"Come in."

"Here's your breakfast."

Should I have added a "sir" at the end? The manual didn't specify.

"Put it on the desk. Why haven't I spoken with Herve Weisberger yet?"

Herve Weisberger. That was the name I'd forgotten.

"I'll get right onto that. Would you like more coffee?"

"No, but I'll have water."

Sparkling, three ice cubes—I knew that already.

"I'll bring it in a moment."

"Meena, why do I have raspberries?"

"Because they looked nice, and it's important to eat healthily."

I hurried out before he could complain, although I felt his gaze searing into me as I closed the door. The raspberries were sweet and delicious—I'd tried one—so maybe they'd take the edge off his sourness.

Or maybe I'd get a lecture later.

Herve Weisberger's number was in the contact list on the computer, and he had an assistant too. She promised to have Herve call Mr. Vale as soon as he finished his meeting. I figured I should probably inform Mr. Vale of that, but the raspberries hadn't had time to work their magic yet, so I sent him an email instead. My email address was *BValeOffice@dunnvalecorp* rather than my actual name, which was yet another indication of the transient nature of Mr. Vale's assistants.

Joyfully, I crossed three items off my to-do list. What was next? Shoes?

Shoes were easy as the file contained the address of Lewis Jefferson, a high-end shoe boutique in Beverly Hills. I could head there after lunch. Moisturiser? What type of moisturiser did he use? I scanned the "personal grooming" section three times, but all it listed was shampoo, conditioner, shower gel, and beard balm. He didn't even have a beard.

Why couldn't men just say what they meant?

My father was the same—he'd give a vague instruction, then grow upset if it was interpreted incorrectly. Moisturiser... Okay, Mr. Vale had a private bathroom attached to his office, so the manual said. All I needed to do was sneak in and take a look at the products he used, then update the manual so the next poor schmuck who ended up with this job didn't have to go through the same process. Mr. Vale's schedule was computerised, and I studied the entries. Lunch was scheduled for two thirty today, so maybe he'd leave the office then? Or was I expected to bring him lunch? The "food" section didn't specify, although I did find three restaurants located on North Cannon Drive listed as "favourites." Should I call each one and ask if they had a blue sign? Wait, wait... Google was my friend here. I typed in the first address and switched to street view. No blue sign on that one, but I found it on the third attempt. Mr. Vale wanted to go to Aperitivo for Italian cuisine with a twist.

What time did he want the table? Of course he hadn't said. I checked his schedule, and he was free from six, so I booked the table for seven and blocked the extra hour out as travel time. LA traffic was a nightmare.

Once the booking was confirmed, I breathed a sigh of relief. Four tasks complete, three to go.

I flipped to the "family" section of the manual, which seemed thinner than the others. Mr. Vale's mother was listed on the first page, Leonora Vale, with an address in Virginia. *The Cardinal Center.* What was that? It didn't sound like a private residence. So I googled—I had a feeling that in this job, Dr. Google and I were about to become the best of friends —and oh my gosh. She lived in a psychiatric facility? *The Cardinal Center offers the highest standards of care in a luxurious and private setting. Five-star service from an internationally renowned team of doctors.* One of my predecessors had added a note—*Leonora likes freesias, lilies, and carnations. Avoid roses.*

The numbers of three local florists followed, and one of them had an asterisk. What did that mean? Use it or don't use it? This was the most frustrating job I'd ever had. At least Lance Clifton had been straightforward in his vulgarity.

Out of curiosity, I flipped the page, and my jaw dropped. Mr. Vale was married? But...but...who would marry a man like him? Had her parents made the decision for her? Or had she tied the knot voluntarily? A gold digger, perhaps? Marrying for money, I could understand—it was a valid choice, just not one I would make—and she sure couldn't have chosen him for his sparkling personality.

Carissa Dunn. She'd kept her own surname, and now I understood where the name of the company came from. Dunnvale Holdings. Had the marriage been an extension of a business arrangement? She lived in New York, on the Upper East Side. A handwritten note said not to call her under ANY circumstances, underlined in triplicate.

This job got stranger and stranger.

A message popped up from Mr. Vale. *Where is lunch?*

Oh, crap. What time was it? Two thirty-one, and I didn't even know what to bring him.

What would you like to eat?

His reply was almost instant. Was it weird, emailing each other when he was in the next room? Yes, but also preferable.

The chef makes lunch. You have to collect it.

Collect it from where? Downstairs?

Gingerly, I exited my office and headed along the hallway. Rhonda had given me a whistle-stop tour this morning (finance, facilities, operations, legal, oh here's your office, good luck) before she abandoned me to the big bad wolf. The finance department was closest, and I poked my head around the door. The theme for this room seemed to be silver and turquoise with plenty of fan palms. They didn't have filing cabinets; they had padded ottomans.

"Excuse me?"

The four people working there all turned to stare. Two more desks were empty.

A petite blonde my age spoke first. "Are you lost?"

In every way possible.

"I'm looking for the chef."

"You're on the wrong floor. Are you Brax's new assistant?"

Unfortunately. "That's right."

Two women sitting behind her exchanged a look. Pity mixed with "Boy, she's an idiot."

"Good luck."

"You're not the first person to say that. Which floor is the kitchen on?"

"The first floor. Want me to show you?"

At that tiny kindness, my eyes began to prickle. My emotions had been all over the place since I left Massachusetts.

"If you have the time, I'd be grateful."

"Follow me. I'm Charlotte, by the way."

"Meera." I rolled my eyes. "Or Meena, according to Mr. Vale."

Charlotte giggled. "Oh, he always gets his assistants' names wrong. He called Terri 'Kerri' for a whole month."

"And then he started getting it right?"

"No, then she quit. Come on, I'll show you where to find the chef."

Charlotte led me to the stairs rather than the elevator, and we headed down to the kitchen. I'd expected something far more modest, but the expanse of stainless steel and industrial appliances wouldn't have looked out of place on one of those TV chef shows. It was quieter, though. People talked rather than shouting over the whirr of a mixer, the hum of an oven, and the hiss of food frying.

I counted four staff—three men, one woman—all wearing white tunics and blue-and-white checked pants. Charlotte pointed out the tallest of the men.

"That's Fabien."

"He's the chef?"

"Yes, and his food is divine."

She waved, but he didn't smile, just put down the bowl he was holding and strode over.

"This is the new assistant? She's late."

"Give her a break. It's her first day."

"The caramelised onions are dry," Fabien grumbled. "The dish has been sitting on the pass for ten minutes."

"Just stir them or whatever."

Muttering ensued, in French, not English. Stirring clearly wasn't an acceptable suggestion.

"*Je suis vraiment désolé, je suis toujours en train de trouver mon chemin,*" I said.

When in doubt, apologise.

Fabien stopped dead. "*Vouz parlez français?*"

"*Oui, un petit peu.*"

When I was fifteen, I'd been offered the chance to join a French exchange program, and I'd taken the blessed opportunity to get away from my parents for a while. In Paris, I'd learned how life could be if your father acted like a dad instead of CEO of his own family and if your mother wasn't a little mouse who never stood up to him. Celeste, my French sister from another mister, was the only person apart from Meera who knew how to contact me in an emergency. And like Meera, she'd been sworn to secrecy about my current circumstances.

Now Fabien beamed at me. "*C'est merveilleux!* I will fix the onions."

A minute later, he handed me a tray with two plated caramelised onion tarts served with vegetables, plus two crème brûlées. Either Mr. Vale had a big appetite, or I was missing something.

"Who is the second portion for?"

And, more importantly, where did I find them?

"For you. You need to eat, *non*? If you have allergies, you should tell me so we avoid those foods."

I could get lunch at work? On a scale of one to a hundred, with a hundred being head of the ER and one being head toilet unblocker (bare hands only, no gloves), I'd rated this job as a solid six. But with the addition of five-star food, it might just inch up to a seven. French cuisine certainly beat the leftover pasta I'd planned to microwave.

Upstairs, Mr. Vale barely acknowledged me when I placed the tray on his desk, but the instant I returned to my own workstation, an email arrived. A dinner party? I had to organise a dinner party? In the middle of March, for nine people, which was a weird number. I also needed to procure him a bow tie for a charity gala being held on behalf of the Finlay Foundation this Friday. Something "fun." Really? Mr. Vale didn't strike me as a man who knew how to have fun. Oh, and Floss's birthday was next week—I had to buy her a gift (budget three hundred bucks) and send it care of the San Francisco office. Who was Floss? There were no clues, and Dunnvale Holdings didn't have a staff directory, at least not one that I'd managed to find. Floss could have been a seven-year-old child or a seventy-year-old woman or anything in between. Or even a pet?

Mr. Vale's Porsche needed a service (and possibly a new side mirror), plus his dishwasher was leaving streaks on the flatware. The tree in his living room had yellowing leaves—why? A man named Joe Fulton was coming in for a preliminary meeting, and I should book a room and arrange refreshments. Senator Gold's wife had passed away, so I needed to find out the details of the funeral, schedule Mr. Vale to attend if he was free, and send flowers and a sympathy card if not.

Okay.

Okay, I could do this.

For years, I'd watched my mother catering to my father's unreasonable demands, so I understood the strategy. Stay out of the way whenever possible, smile and say very little when crossing paths was unavoidable. *Don't antagonise him.* No more outbursts like the one outside the coffee bar. I still couldn't believe Mr. Vale had hired me after that.

In one month, maybe two, I could quit and find a less stressful job. Yes, leaving three positions within a year would look bad on my résumé, but if I had a nervous breakdown, that would look worse. I just needed to get through the next year or three. In time, Karam would marry somebody else, and I'd slip off my father's radar.

Short-term, survival was my only goal. As time stretched, I hoped for financial stability and possibly companionship, but right now, they seemed so far out of reach. And as for the happiness I craved, I was beginning to think it wasn't a part of my destiny.

CHAPTER 5
BRAX

voidance. An interesting strategy. Brax read Meera's fifth message of the day and caught himself smiling. The dishwasher was fixed—it had needed a new pump, apparently—and did he want more coffee? So far, nearly all of their communication had been by email. She went out of her way to avoid him, which was a welcome relief after previous assistants had spent half the day traipsing in and out of his office, asking inane questions. *How do I contact the chef? What colour shirts should I order? Where do I take the car to be serviced?*

In fact, he hadn't seen Meera at all today. His coffee had been waiting, probably at the right temperature—he didn't really care, but ridiculous demands like that weeded out the lackadaisical newbies who didn't care enough to be fastidious—and the reports he'd asked her to print and bind last night had been sitting beside the cup.

But she couldn't lie low forever. Tonight was the Finlay Foundation benefit, and Brax needed her with him in case there were any last-minute glitches. Something always went wrong at these things—an extra guest showing up, infighting among the band, an issue with the AV system—and he'd need an additional pair of hands to ensure everything ran smoothly while he spoke with the guests. Although the purpose of the evening was to raise money to support families affected by EAST Syndrome, nobody attended these events out of the goodness of their hearts. Politicians, celebrities, and businessmen were there to network, to see and be seen, Brax included.

Plus at some point, the new assistant would need to find out what actually went on downstairs. No, not *that* downstairs—the restaurant, the spa, the members' lounge, they were all perfectly innocent, much like Meera herself. But descend a little further into The Dark, and the place took on a whole different tone.

The phone rang.

"Floss for you, Mr. Vale."

Floss, of course, knew all about what happened in the basement. She practically lived down there, by choice, obviously. She was a lady who loved her job.

"Braaaaaax." She dragged out the vowel. "I love the gift. Did you pick it out yourself?"

"Of course not."

"So you finally hired an assistant with a brain? I only ask because this year, I got a gorgeous purse that matches my hair, and last year, I got a Barbie Dreamhouse."

"A what?"

"A dollhouse, Brax. For kids."

What the hell? "Why did someone send you that?"

"Probably because you told your previous girl nothing about me, and she didn't bother to find out. Women aren't psychic."

Brax's wife was. She found out about everything.

"Why didn't you mention it sooner? I'd have asked her to buy something else."

"Because I heard Carissa was being even more of a bitch than usual, and I figured you had enough on your plate."

Floss was a darling, and Brax wasn't the only man to think so. If not for Carissa's roving spies, he might have said to hell with his "no fucking the club girls" rule and sunk into her wet centre. The woman's tongue was legendary, and if she wrapped those plump pink lips around his cock... *Enough!* He forced the image out of his mind and focused on the conversation.

"If Meera lasts through the weekend, I'll get her to buy you a matching set of luggage."

"You don't think she'll stay?"

"She hasn't found out what happens in The Dark yet, and she seems...I don't know...sheltered?"

Floss gave a low whistle. "You didn't mention the spanking bench in the job interview?"

"What do you think?"

"Forget about the luggage. I gave the Barbie house to my cousin, and she loved it. Hope Meera doesn't screw your balls into a crusher when she finds out what you've been hiding."

Brax's testicles shrank just from thinking about it.

"Maybe I'll leave it for another week."

"Rip the Band-Aid off, baby. Talk later—I have to go tell a Supreme Court judge that he's been a bad boy."

"Justice Walden?"

"Who else?"

"He *has* been a bad boy. His dissent in the Rybacker case was obscene."

Not to mention hypocritical. After Samson Rybacker's prudish, holier-than-thou neighbour filmed Rybacker and his mistress in a compromising position and posted the resulting clip on the HOA's online discussion forum, Rybacker had argued that he'd had a reasonable expectation of privacy during the act because the balcony where the dick-sucking took place was part of his private residence. Justice Walden had sided with the neighbour. However, Justice Walden also liked to have his ass spanked in front of an audience, and if footage ever became public, he'd be the first person to complain about it.

Just as well electronics were banned in The Dark.

And discretion was guaranteed.

Eight years ago, after his name had been dragged through the mud, Brax had spotted a gap in the market that was just begging to be filled. Folks, especially those with money, didn't like to have their private affairs splashed all over the gossip columns, but some of them—more than you might think—also craved kink. So he'd created Nyx, a private members' club in northern Virginia, to cater to their needs and desires. Membership was only granted to those with something to lose. Celebrities, politicians, more millionaires than Brax could count. Even minor royalty, a foreign prince who flew in to get his kicks every other month and paid handsomely for the privilege.

Over the years, as members became more comfortable with each other, the basement offering had expanded upward into the light, with a restaurant, a spa, and rooms that rivalled any five-star hotel's for those who wanted to stay overnight. The one constant? Secrecy. In eight years, there hadn't been a single leak. Dunnvale Holdings had no marketing department. The club operated by word of mouth only, and new members had to be sponsored by an existing client or by Brax himself.

Of course he'd never ask Meera to go into The Dark, not when clients were present, but at some point, it was inevitable that she'd realise what went on there. And then there was a fifty-fifty chance she'd quit, based on past experience. A shame. Brax decided that he liked her hands-off style. She kept herself to herself, and the work got done.

In short, Meera Adams was his perfect woman.

"We'll be leaving at six, no sooner, no later. You did arrange the car?"

"Yes, it'll be waiting in the parking garage. Wait… What do you mean, 'we'll' be leaving at six?"

"For the benefit. Your predecessor made the arrangements, but you'll need to be on hand to fix any issues that crop up."

And knowing Monique's work ethic, or rather the lack of it, it would be a miracle if the evening went off without a hitch. Yes, she'd hired a planner to take care of the food, the music, and the furniture, and Finlay's parents would be co-hosting the event, but Monique had once tried serving cashews to a visitor with a severe nut allergy. Paying attention to detail hadn't been her strong suit.

"I already checked on everything. The chef couldn't source pheasant eggs for the appetiser, so he swapped them for quail eggs, and the florist replaced the chrysanthemums with dahlias, but everything else is going according to plan."

"You still need to attend. This is an important event for Finlay's parents, but it's also a reminder of their son's condition, so they don't need to be burdened with any unexpected problems."

"I… Okay, fine." Meera smiled, but she was gritting those perfect white teeth, and her eyes were mutinous. "Fine, I'll be there."

"If you need to take an extra break this afternoon to change, then do so."

"Change? Into what?"

"Nobody wears pants to a charity benefit."

"So you're planning to wear a dress?" Meera quickly covered her mouth with both hands. "Sorry! I didn't mean to say that, sir."

Sir? Fuck. Brax struggled to maintain a blank expression as his cock twitched under his desk, and he almost walked back the request. Meera in pants was distracting. Meera in a dress would be trouble. He much preferred emailing her from the other side of a wall, but he had to stick to his guns. What if they had a repeat of the JJ Wardle incident? Five years ago, JJ had accidentally texted his wife instead of his mistress just as dinner was about to begin, and the former had locked herself into a bathroom stall, sobbing inconsolably. Luisa had sat with her for over an hour, talking through the options. The last Brax had heard, Mrs. Wardle was driving a new top-of-the-line Audi and screwing her tennis coach.

Plus Debra Finlay would need someone to hold her hand. She put her heart and soul into raising money to support other parents with EAST Syndrome kids in addition to working as a housekeeper on the second floor, but event planning wasn't her area of expertise. If a speaker showed up late or one of the guests changed their menu choice at the last minute, she'd get stressed. Somebody needed to support her.

"You already picked up my suit." Brax motioned to the tux he'd retrieved from the closet and draped over a visitor chair. When his next videoconference was over, he'd take it upstairs to his apartment. "Don't you remember? And yes, you need to wear appropriate attire. I expect you to be at my side for most of the evening."

"Most of the evening? How late will this event finish?"

"Eleven? Midnight? Does it matter? Your contract specifies that your hours are flexible and overtime is required."

"Well, my contract says nothing about dresses, and I don't own one."

Either she was a liar, or her closet had befallen a recent tragedy—a fire, a flood, an ex with scissors… Meera was made to wear beautiful dresses. Brax might have been avoiding her for the entire week, but he wasn't blind. Far from it, when it came to checking out women's assets. That was part of his job. His clients expected their drinks mixed to perfection, their food delectable, and their hostesses—and hosts, because The Dark was all about equal opportunities—

sexy as hell. In terms of looks, Meera would fit right in, but he couldn't imagine a firebrand like her handcuffed to a bed.

Not downstairs, anyway.

Maybe upstairs.

"If you're incapable of finding a dress yourself, speak to Teresa in Operations. Lose those shoes as well."

Now she put her hands on her hips. Then she realised what she'd done and dropped them to her sides again, fists balled.

"What's wrong with my shoes?"

What wasn't wrong with them?

"They're plain, frumpy, and scuffed."

The door slammed behind her as she marched out, and Brax sighed. Meera was angry again.

Which was probably for the best.

CHAPTER 6
THE ASSISTANT

My new job came with health insurance, but did it come with dental? Because I was about to crack a tooth.

Frumpy? *Frumpy?* Braxton Vale thought I was frumpy?

I caught sight of myself in the gilded mirror opposite my desk and took in the low ponytail, shapeless white shirt, and pants a size too big. Thrift store shoppers couldn't be fussy. Okay, he was probably right, but he didn't have to say it out loud, did he? That was just rude. And my shoes were only scuffed because I'd tripped over a step when I collected his tuxedo from the cleaner earlier. At least he hadn't commented on the novelty bow tie. I'd chosen an abstract pattern that reminded me of Van Gogh's *The Starry Night*, but now I wished I'd bought the one covered in tiny dicks instead.

Who was Teresa? Why would she have a spare evening dress on hand? And where was I meant to find more shoes? Friday afternoon, and I felt like crying. By tiptoeing around Mr. Vale, I thought I'd survived my first week, but now he'd pulled the rug out from under me. I never used to be this fragile. But my father's ultimatum—marry Karam or else—coupled with Meera moving overseas and three horrible jobs in a row had left me riddled with tiny cracks that were just waiting to break wide open.

I'd also promised to call Meera at eleven tonight. She left for work at seven a.m., and this weekend, she was digging more swales because a storm was forecast for Monday. If I went to the benefit, I'd miss speaking with her, and I needed to hear her voice. Plus I wanted to check she was okay after the fight with Alfie. He'd come back home, at least. Meera had messaged me on Wednesday to say things were still awkward, but he'd apologised and claimed he'd snapped because he was tired.

I knew the feeling.

Why had I asked Mr. Vale if he was planning to wear a freaking dress? The comment had just slipped out, and I needed to remember I wasn't at college anymore. The freedom to speak my mind was a luxury I couldn't afford, plus there was the fact that Mr. Vale had undergone a sense-of-humour bypass, if his stony expression was anything to go by.

"Hey!" Charlotte waved from the doorway. "It's Selena's birthday, and a group of us are going out for drinks tonight. Wanna come?"

"I can't."

"Hot date?"

A snort escaped. "Not unless you count being at Mr. Vale's beck and call all evening."

"He's making you stay here late?"

"No, he's going to a charity benefit, and I have to—quote —fix any issues that crop up. I need an evening dress, better shoes, and a magic wand. Know any fairy godmothers?"

"Oh, sure, you need to see Teresa."

"Mr. Vale mentioned her."

"It's twisted the way he makes his PAs call him 'Mr. Vale.' Nobody else does."

"Really?"

"Selena figures he has some weird *Fifty Shades of Grey* thing going on." Charlotte tilted her head to one side, appearing to expect an answer even though she hadn't asked a question.

"No way. I'm not playing that game."

She laughed, her eyes twinkling with amusement. "I thought you'd say that. If you want my opinion, the 'mister' is an instruction from his wife. She's a bitch."

I was about to opt for diplomacy, the card I'd been taught to play my whole life, when I reconsidered. Instead, I lowered my voice. The door between my office and Brax's was solid wood, but a girl couldn't be too careful.

"She'd need the spirit of an Amazon and the patience of a saint to stay married to a man like that. If she's a bitch, it's probably a match made in heaven."

"Brax isn't that bad."

"You think? He's been through twenty-six assistants. Twenty-six! And he can't be much older than me."

"He just turned thirty. At least, I'm almost sure he did. There was no party, but someone delivered balloons and a cake, and the balloons were shaped like a three and a zero. The cake was real good—he only ate one slice and put the rest in the staff kitchen. And the assistant thing isn't entirely his fault. I mean, it sort of is because he must be terrible at interviewing candidates, but half of the people he hires are psychos. No offence."

"None taken, I think?"

"Number twenty-two, or it might have been twenty-one, she was, like, this raging feminist. John in legal held the door open for her one time, and she totally chewed him out. Didn't he realise she was capable of opening a door herself, equality was her right, men like him belonged in the nineteenth century, blah blah blah. The poor guy holds the door open for everyone. It's polite. Don't you think it's polite?"

"Absolutely."

"And then Brax held a door open for her, and she threw a Mooncup at him."

"A...Mooncup?"

"You know, one of those—"

"I know what it is," I added hastily. "She *threw* it at him?"

"Yup. Fished it out of her purse, wound back an arm, and *bam*. It hit him right on the forehead. And number eighteen crashed his Porsche in the parking garage."

"Are you joking?"

"She got confused between the gas and the brake. Then there was number twenty-three, who spent the whole day bitching about all the work she wasn't doing and then quit to become an Instagram influencer."

Wow. "Has he ever hired a competent assistant?"

"One, I think. She had a heart attack in the basement and left before I started here."

A heart attack in the basement? I hadn't even realised there *was* a basement. Did they use the space for storage or something?

"My cholesterol levels are good and I do yoga on the weekends, so hopefully I won't follow in her footsteps. And speaking of footsteps, is there a shoe store around here?"

"Just ask Teresa. She'll have spare shoes."

Perhaps Teresa looked after lost property?

"Where do I find her?"

"She's on the first floor. Go past the entrance to the spa, and her office is through the next door. Your pass should work."

Teresa didn't look after lost property. My eyes bugged out as I took in the rows of dresses in the room beside her office, plus the dressing tables surrounded by lights, theatre-style, and what could have been a professional hair salon. Shelves held rows of wigs on mannequin heads, everything from Marilyn Monroe to disco alien. Beyond the wigs were the shoes, high-heeled pumps in every colour of the rainbow by Jimmy Choo, Christian Louboutin, Manolo Blahnik. What was this place?

"I didn't realise there was a boutique here. Is it only for members?"

Teresa herself was an older woman, her steel-grey hair styled into a long pixie cut that she had the bone structure to pull off. She looked as if she sampled the merchandise, dressed as she was in an emerald shift dress and towering pumps. Her peal of laughter was unexpected.

"Oh, my sweet summer child, Brax has left *another* of his assistants in the dark?" Another laugh. "Or rather, out of The Dark."

Out of the dark? What did she mean? How could I know what I didn't know?

"Maybe?" Although a lack of communication had certainly been a central theme of our working relationship so far. "Probably."

"These clothes are for the staff."

"Which staff?"

My colleagues on the third floor wore slightly more fashionable versions of my own outfits, and the waitstaff in the restaurant had a black-and-white uniform. I couldn't imagine Fabien the chef in an evening gown. What if a bead dropped into the soup?

"The staff who work downstairs."

But we were already downstairs? Wait, hadn't Charlotte mentioned something about a basement? Why would people wear designer dresses in the basement? Unless... Unless there was an entertainment space? In Boston, Meera and I had once gone to a nightclub in a basement, and the lack of air left me feeling suffocated.

No, this place wouldn't have a nightclub. The clientele was all wrong. Possibly a cabaret show? Burlesque?

"What happens downstairs? Some kind of performances?"

"Performances? I suppose you could say that. We're in the business of wish fulfilment here."

Wish fulfilment? My wish was to become an emergency medical specialist, but that couldn't be done in the basement of an office building-slash-restaurant. And my fallback, to sip cocktails on a quiet beach with a man I'd married for love rather than out of obligation, also didn't fit with the whole "underground" concept.

I recalled a kid I'd met during my paediatric rotation. His dream of flying a plane had come true—at least, he'd gotten to sit in the cockpit and hold the controls. Was that what Teresa meant by wish fulfilment? Matching sick patients with people who could make them smile? Why would Mr. Vale keep that a secret? And how did the dresses come into it?

"Like the Make-A-Wish Foundation?"

"No, no, these wishes are for grown-ups. Maybe 'fantasies' is a better word? Say a man wants to have his toes sucked by three women dressed as Marilyn Monroe…" Teresa waved a hand toward the collection of wigs. "We can make that happen."

Realisation dawned, along with horror and nausea. Sucking toes? Gross.

"Are you talking about sexual fantasies?"

"That's right, dear. Although, as I recall, Brax did lend his boat to a young boy with cancer last year. He wanted to see dolphins."

I sank onto a padded velvet banquette. Suddenly, it all made sense. The sexy-luxury vibe on the first floor. The secrecy. The gorgeous clothes. The risqué prints in the hallway outside Mr. Vale's office. The pretty women I saw coming and going when I ran errands for my new boss. I'd assumed Mr. Vale was merely filthy rich, but now I realised he was filthy-filthy too.

"So what is this place? A high-class brothel?"

"Heavens, no. We don't take walk-ins. Clients are paying for access, privacy, and the freedom to express themselves, not sex. Many of them bring their wives. Or their mistresses—we don't judge here."

"Then who are the dresses for?"

"The hosts and hostesses."

"They don't sleep with the customers?"

"Sometimes they do." Oh my goodness. I'd ended up working for a pimp. "Their job is to keep the clientele happy, whether that's facilitating interaction between members, serving drinks, or participating in the activities. Everything is consensual." Teresa studied me. "It makes you uncomfortable."

"Of course it makes me uncomfortable!" The words tumbled out before I could stop them. "I thought this was an investment company with a restaurant on the side, not... not...a whorehouse."

Too late, I realised somebody else had entered the room behind me. The newcomer was blonde and slender with legs a mile long, and she walked with a confidence I could only dream of. Even without make-up, she was stunningly beautiful, and I had an awful feeling she might be one of the hostesses.

"Sorry, I'm so sorry. I didn't mean to suggest... I mean, if you're..."

She just grinned. "Call me whatever you want, hun. I'm laughing all the way to the bank. Teresa, I need a schoolgirl outfit and a lollipop."

"White cotton panties or lingerie?"

"White cotton and white socks too, the knee-high kind." The blonde turned to me. "You must be new, huh? Let me guess—assistant number twenty-six."

"Twenty-seven."

"Hmm. Guess twenty-six didn't last long. Who won the pool?"

"Tawny," Teresa told her.

"That's twice in a row."

"She always goes for the low numbers."

"Twenty-seven, if you can last five weeks and three days, I'll forgive you for the whorehouse comment. How's about that?"

"I...I don't know."

"Aw, you're trying to decide whether to suck it up and be polite, cry, or burn rubber on your way out of here, am I right?"

There was no point in lying, not this time.

"It's that obvious?"

"Written all over your face, hun. Plus I'm a psychology major at UCLA. Jayme." She held out a hand, and I shook it automatically, admiring her manicure—bubblegum pink with tiny yellow flowers. "What's your name, twenty-seven?"

"Meera."

"Well, Meera, I bet Brax invests in stuff too, so forget about what goes on downstairs, do your job, and I'll do mine." Jayme found a giant jar of lollipops and began rummaging through it. "Teresa, do we have any of the cola ones left?"

"Only whatever's in there," Teresa called from behind a rail of clothing.

"Well, that sucks." Jayme giggled, her laughter musical. "And so do I, if that's what the client wants."

"You don't mind?" I blurted.

"Hell no. Letting old guys spank me with a ruler means I'll graduate debt free, and how else would I get my kicks? Fuck a frat boy?"

Teresa reappeared with a clear garment bag over one arm, plus the requested underwear.

"These should be your size."

"Thanks." Jayme unwrapped one lollipop and stuck it in her mouth, then pocketed two more and took the garments. "See ya tomorrow. And maybe I'll see you next week, twenty-seven. Depends whether you're a quitter or not."

She pulled the door open and strode into the hallway, humming "Baby One More Time" to herself, and even if I'd wanted to run out of there, I couldn't have. Jayme thought I was a quitter—I'd heard it in her voice—and perhaps she was right. My legs turned into overcooked noodles as the plan I'd made for myself fell apart. I'd assumed Braxton Vale was a secretive—yet respected—businessman, but he hired out women for money. I didn't want to work in the sex industry. What if somebody found out? What if *my family* found out? They'd shame me forever.

"Were you sent here to collect something, or are you lost?" Teresa asked.

I was lost, all right. What was I meant to do? Good-paying jobs were hard to come by in this city, especially when you had to stay under the radar, and if I left, I'd struggle to pay the rent this month, let alone get my car fixed. And despite Mr. Vale's den of sin, he'd remained fully clothed at all times, which was more than could be said for Lance Clifton.

"He told me to ask you for a dress."

"Who? Brax?"

I nodded. "And shoes. He hates my shoes, and there's a benefit I'm meant to attend tonight, although now I'm not even sure whether I should go or not."

"Only you can make that decision, my dear. A cocktail dress or an evening gown?"

"A cocktail dress."

I'd seen pictures online from last year's event, and most of the guests had opted for the shorter length, so I wouldn't look out of place. One lady had even worn sequined pants.

"And you're a size six? 34C?" Teresa's gaze dropped to my feet. "Size eight shoe?"

"How did you know?"

"It's my job. Do you have a favourite colour?"

"Uh, purple?"

"Let me see what we have."

Ten minutes later, I had two dress options, one plum and one black, with matching pumps, appropriate underwear, and even a pretty gold necklace. Teresa really was the fairy godmother. Now I just needed the carriage and the horses to get me home later because the last bus came at eleven thirty, and if I missed it, I'd have a long walk.

"You can keep the lingerie. Just return the rest when you're finished with it." A pause. "You still haven't made your mind up about staying?"

"Not yet. The whole basement thing freaks me out."

And I only had half an hour to decide. Then I'd be expected to climb into a car with a man I knew both nothing and too much about. A man who made me sweat, and not in a good way. An enigma in a designer suit.

"At least you're honest, dear," Teresa said.

Oh, if only she knew.

CHAPTER 7
BRAX

She knew.

The instant Brax saw Meera walking stiffly toward the limo in the parking garage, he knew that she knew. Had Teresa spilled the beans? Most likely. It wouldn't be the first time. She didn't agree with Brax's "break them in gently" approach.

"You look lovely."

She didn't answer, not in words anyway. Her rigid expression said "I don't want to be here."

The driver held the door, and Brax motioned her into the car.

"Ladies first."

Silence.

She climbed in hesitantly and clipped her seat belt into place, staring straight ahead. It could have been worse. Fifty percent of her predecessors had quit at this point. Brax slid in beside her and took in the folded arms, the teeth worrying her bottom lip, and the way her thighs pressed together. He made her uncomfortable. Usually, he saw that as a good thing, but this woman... Despite the fireworks at their initial meeting, she wasn't the antagonistic type. There was a hint of a spine under that flawless skin, but it only showed when her back was against the wall. Otherwise, she preferred to use those avoidance tactics. And sometimes, like tonight, she simply gave in. She knew how to pick her battles. Yes, Meera Adams was smart.

And poor. Was that why she hadn't walked out? Despite looking like a model and being on the high end of competent as a PA, she lived paycheck to paycheck. Alexa had obtained her bank details from the payroll department and sent him a data dump of her recent transactions. And when he said "obtained," he meant "stolen." He'd given up trying to keep her out of the system. She saw every new firewall as a challenge, and besides, she had her uses. Like eight years ago, when, after a nightmare of a year when their former roommate, Levi Sykes, was convicted of murder and Levi's parents tried to blame Ruby's death on anyone but their darling son, Brax included, Alexa had stolen most of the Sykes family's money and disappeared.

Poof.

Gone.

Her foster family had lived miles from the nearest town, and she'd vanished in the middle of the night, only to reappear several years later in digital form and tell him that a member of Dunnvale's finance team was a crook.

Anyhow, back to Meera. Alexa's checks covered the basics—Meera had indeed graduated from Harvard, and her former boss had been charged with indecent exposure several years ago, although the case was dropped when the main witness declined to testify in court. In an amazing coincidence, that same witness had obtained a brand-new car shortly afterward, despite having worse finances than Meera. A little more digging, and Alexa had discovered that the vehicle was purchased by one Robert Clifton, who just happened to be Lance Clifton's father. Meera should have gotten herself a lawyer, and then she could have replaced the ageing Toyota registered in her name with a newer model.

"How much did Teresa tell you?" Brax asked.

"Enough. Prostitution is illegal in California, you know. I checked."

"The women who work downstairs are hostesses, not prostitutes."

"That's just semantics."

"Some don't even sleep with clients."

"But others do. I don't think the cops would care about the technicalities."

"The chief of police is a member here—I'll be sure to ask him the next time he swings by to fuck Britney's ass." Meera flinched at the comment, leading Brax to conclude that she'd led a somewhat sheltered life. Missionary position all the way. "Which part do you have a problem with? Women owning their sexuality and making money out of it, or men enjoying themselves?"

"I—"

"Did you know we have female members too? One fellow bought his wife a membership after medical treatment left him impotent. He likes to watch."

"But—"

"And what about our gay members who don't yet feel ready to come out of the closet? We provide a safe place for them to shed their inhibitions. A new offering for us, and only in LA so far, but it's proving to be successful."

"I just—"

"We have some members who want to experience sexual satisfaction without the commitment of a relationship and others who make lasting friendships based on shared experiences—I believe we've had two weddings and an engagement so far. Many more clients just want to explore their kinks with willing partners who know what they're doing. Every member and host submits to regular health screening, and privacy is guaranteed." Brax twisted in his seat to face her. "So, what upsets you about the activities downstairs?"

"I...I don't know. I guess... I guess I thought it was an investment company."

"I also invest, in commodities mainly. And I can tell you for certain that hedge fund managers screw people for money more often than my staff do."

Silence.

What was going on in that pretty head of hers? Brax wasn't a fool—he understood that his job was unconventional —but he also had a healthy disrespect for authority that had only been exacerbated by the events that followed Ruby's death. He'd seen the way people bowed down to Levi Sykes's father just because he had money, but instead of becoming bitter, Brax had followed the old adage: if you can't beat 'em, join 'em.

Besides, the current fashion for prudism was only temporary, he was convinced of that. Prostitution was the oldest profession in the world, older than the Bible, widespread in Ancient Rome, Ancient Greece, and indeed in the United States of America until a group of religious zealots had gained influence in the early twentieth century. Those killjoys were determined that if they couldn't have fun, then nobody else could either.

But the tide was turning.

Senators, congressmen, judges... They were all members of Nyx. There was a good reason Brax had opened the first branch a stone's throw from Washington, DC.

"Everything that takes place in the basement—we call it The Dark—happens by mutual consent. If you continue to work at Dunnvale, there's nothing in your job description that would require you to go down there."

And Brax was surprised to realise that he did want her to stay. Partly because he was sick of training new assistants, but mostly because she was exquisite. No, not exquisite. He gave himself a mental slap. *Competent.*

Finally, she spoke. "Where do the girls come from?"

"I poached the first ones from high-end escort agencies, but now it's mostly word of mouth."

"How? I mean, why? Sleeping with men is hardly a career, is it?"

"Nobody's pretending it is. Many of our girls—and guys —are in college, and they quit when they graduate. But before they quit, they scout out their replacements. And despite what you might think, it isn't a bad job. If they work one night a week in The Dark, they make more than they'd earn in a month waiting tables, plus the job is more pleasurable. How many college girls don't have sex?"

Meera looked away. It might have been dark outside, but the limo's interior light was still on, and Brax didn't miss the slight darkening of her cheeks.

"You were one of those girls?" he asked softly.

"What kind of a question is that? You're my boss. I should report you for harassment."

"Go right ahead. HR can send someone to spank me."

"That isn't funny."

"I apologise. Look, if you're ace, I'm the last person to judge. Just own it. Don't blush."

"Ace?"

"Asexual." When she looked blank, he clarified. "Little to no sexual desire, but as with so many things, that covers a broad spectrum."

"Oh, I'm not that. I mean, I don't think so." Meera grew more flustered. Cute. "I just... I just chose to focus on my studies, that's all. And this is a totally inappropriate conversation to be having."

When she eyed up the car door as if she was considering jumping out of it, Brax knew it was time to change the subject.

"When we get to the hotel, find Debra and help with anything she needs. She puts a significant amount of effort into organising this benefit each year, but her event-planning experience is limited, and she tends to panic if anything goes wrong."

"What about you? Don't I need to hold your used cocktail sticks and come up with an excuse to leave if you get stuck talking to somebody boring?"

Brax stifled a smile. "I don't believe canapés are being served, but if you see Congressman Drummond speaking to me, I'd appreciate being rescued. Does this mean you're not going to quit?"

"I need the weekend to think about it."

At least she was honest.

"Mr. Vale? I'm afraid there's an issue with one of the auction lots. Would you mind helping? So sorry to interrupt."

Brax hadn't actually expected Meera to rescue him. But five minutes into the congressman's monologue about lawn care, she'd tapped him on the shoulder. Thank fuck for that.

"Of course. Max, I do apologise."

"Sure, sure, catch you later."

Meera sashayed across the bar, looking more comfortable than he'd expected in the heels Teresa had found for her. And the dress… He couldn't decide whether to give Teresa a pay raise or a reprimand. The thing had no back. Nothing from shoulders to waist. Meera clearly wasn't wearing a bra, and Brax's gaze dropped to her perfect ass as he followed her to the door.

"Is there really an issue with an auction lot?"

A flicker of uncertainty appeared in those expressive umber eyes of hers.

56

"You said I should excuse you from Congressman Drummond."

"Yes, but I didn't realise you even knew who he was."

"I googled him, although the pictures on his website make him look fifty pounds lighter."

"The right camera angle can work wonders. Excellent timing, by the way. Dinner's just about to start."

"Oh, well, in that case, I'll leave you to eat."

She veered to the left, and without thinking, Brax grabbed her hand. She tugged it free and faced him, hands on her hips.

"Don't manhandle me."

"I apologise." He seemed to be doing a lot of that lately. "Where are you going?"

"Out of the way?"

"Why?"

"So you can eat?"

"And when are you planning to eat?"

"I guess...after I get home?"

"Is there something wrong with the food here that you're not telling me about?"

"No, but—"

"Did you expect me to send you to eat in the kitchen like Cinderella?"

Nail. Head. That was exactly what Meera had expected. Brax touched a hand to the small of her back, and she jolted as if he were wearing an Electro-Sex massage mitten, then bit that damn lip again. At that moment, he half hoped she would quit because this...this could be a problem. Meera was a hot mess of nerves, fire, and intellect, all wrapped up in satiny skin and a purple sequined cocktail dress.

"You're eating with me, Meera."

Be still his twitching cock.

CHAPTER 8
THE ASSISTANT

"**M**ore wine, ma'am?"

"No, thank you. Just water."

I hadn't intended to drink any wine at all, but I'd figured one glass with food wouldn't hurt. Okay, two. Wine had been out of my budget for months, and while my father forbade me to consume alcohol, I'd developed a taste for Chardonnay at college.

Beside me, Mr. Vale was talking to yet another boring politician, a grey-haired Texan who loved both golf and the sound of his own voice. My father played golf, which was enough of a reason for me to hate it. My back still burned from my bossy boss's touch, and I was afraid to check in the mirror in case he was the devil and his palm print had been branded onto my skin. I mean, it was possible. He sure did know how to sin.

I took a sip of ice water, but it did nothing to cool me down. Was I sick? My belly felt fluttery, and I pressed my thighs together to ease the throbbing in my core, all the time racking my brain for something, anything from my medical textbooks that might explain these symptoms. Low blood sugar? Food poisoning?

And why had I worn this freaking dress? Both of the choices Teresa had offered fit perfectly, but the black Versace number had a deep slash between my breasts that made me uncomfortable. I mean, what if everyone stared? So I'd chosen the backless option, only for Mr. Vale and his wandering hands to come along.

Discreetly, I glanced at my watch. Nearly nine p.m., and we still had the dessert, the auction, and half of the speeches to go. Hell, some folks hadn't even finished their entrée. I'd have to spend precious money on a cab, and I'd miss my call with Meera, and what was I even doing here? Mr. Vale half expected me to quit—he'd said as much. So why didn't I? He had a sex den in his basement, plus he was dangerous. No, not "serial killer" dangerous, but "tear out your heart, stomp it into wet sand, and flambé the soggy remains" dangerous. Prior to starting this job, I'd had zero involvement with men like him, but after the Lance Clifton experience, I was learning to trust my intuition.

And my intuition told me that while Mr. Vale was an asshole with kinks I couldn't even begin to understand, he was unlikely to wave his schlong at me in his office and expect my undying admiration. Plus he was married. That had to count for something, right?

So why was I beside him and not his wife?

His whole life was weird.

He'd also remembered my name tonight. What did that mean?

Decisions, decisions… The job paid well, and his other staff seemed happy. Even Jayme with her lollipops and schoolgirl outfit. And although the schoolgirl fantasy was kind of gross, at least her client was indulging his desires with a willing partner over the age of eighteen instead of hanging around the gates of the local high school or grooming teenagers online. Or worse, flying them to a private island to give his friends massages.

"Holy crap!"

Someone swore at the table behind us, and the curse was closely followed by the tinkle of a glass shattering as it hit the polished wooden floor. On instinct, I swivelled in my seat to look, then chided myself because staring was rude and whoever had dropped the glass would be embarrassed enough already. I was about to turn back when I realised one of the guests was clutching her throat, an older lady wearing pearls and a demure dress I'd have sold my soul for.

Oh, shit. She was choking!

Nobody else seemed to be moving, so I shoved my chair back and ran around the table. I might have been relatively clueless when it came to office politics and sex and fathoming out what Mr. Vale was thinking, but I was well-versed in how to perform abdominal thrusts, formerly known as the Heimlich manoeuvre.

First, I gave her five back blows, and when nothing dislodged, I wrapped my arms around her, grasped my fist, and pressed hard into her abdomen, once, twice, three times, before a lump of what looked like chicken flew across the table and she began coughing.

"Is there anything still stuck?"

She shook her head no, clutching at the hand of the man next to her, presumably her husband. Her skin was pale, which was hardly surprising—choking in front of two hundred people must have been quite a shock.

"When you feel ready, take some small sips of water. Do you have medical coverage?"

Her husband answered for her. "We have great insurance."

"It might not seem necessary, but it's always a good idea to get checked out after choking. Aspiration pneumonia is a risk—tiny pieces of food that migrate to the lungs—and damage to the airway can lead to swelling. Abdominal thrusts can also cause bruising, and if you have the financial means, scans can rule out any small issues that might become bigger ones if left untreated." With rising horror, I realised the entire room had fallen silent and everyone was watching us with morbid fascination, including Mr. Vale. "Uh, or so I've heard. I'm not a doctor."

The man bobbed his head. "We'll do that. We'll do that right away. Thank you, Miss... I'm not sure I know your name."

"Meera. Just Meera."

My patient grasped both of my hands in hers. "Thank you, Meera."

Could everyone stop freaking staring?

"Glad I could help. Uh, I should go and sit down."

That damn hand seared my back again. Mr. Vale was just being polite—I'd seen him do the same with Charlotte and Selena and other ladies in the office—but my brain was frazzled enough already this evening without him adding to the problem.

"Stop it," I hissed under my breath.

"Stop what?"

"Touching me."

"Oh, uh..." He hadn't even realised he was doing it, had he? Those gentlemanly, borderline-intimate gestures came so naturally that he was completely oblivious. "I apologise."

People were applauding now, and my cheeks heated. I just wanted to eat dessert, help Debra to set up the auction items on the stage, and get the hell out of there. But, hey, at least my insanely expensive seven-year college education hadn't been completely wasted.

Back at the table, I brushed off congratulations and bolted dessert as soon as it was placed in front of me. I'd never enjoyed these kinds of events in the past, mainly because I was always on show (here's Indali, hasn't she grown, what a good wife she'll make for the right man) like a side of meat stuffed into a designer gown. This evening, I was being gawked at for the right reasons, but being the centre of attention still made me cringe.

The moment the plates were cleared, I excused myself.

"Don't you want coffee?" Mr. Vale asked.

"I promised Debra that I'd carry things. Isn't that what I'm here to do?"

It was a rhetorical question, and I didn't give him a chance to answer before I hurried away from the table. If the auctioneer went through his spiel fast enough, I might catch my bus, but it would be close. I loved the beautiful shoes I was wearing, but if I tried to run in them, I'd be joining the lady from the next table in the hospital.

And speaking of impracticality, Mr. Vale bid nearly five thousand dollars for a meal at The Treehouse, a hot new restaurant located in—you've guessed it—a tree. Or possibly several trees. The brochure was vague on that and gave no hints as to how diners were meant to climb up there either. Still, it was his problem, not mine. I just needed to get home.

"Do you need me for anything else?" I asked after the hammer came down on the final auction lot—a round of golf at a course I'd never heard of—desperately hoping the answer was no.

"Could you see if that Treehouse thing is transferable?"

"You don't want to go?"

"Not particularly."

"Then why did you bid on it?"

"Because it was the second-to-last item, and I like golf even less than I like heights."

"I'll ask." I checked my watch—the bus left in ten minutes, and the stop was almost half a mile away. Crap. "Or maybe I could email?"

"Is there a problem?"

I almost said "No, everything's fine," but if I did that, Mr. Vale would keep on expecting me to work in the evenings, wouldn't he? And I hated going home late. It wasn't only the bus ride; the walk from the bus stop to my apartment made me nervous. Most of the streetlights were out, and drug dealers used one corner as an office.

"Actually, there is. My bus leaves soon, and I don't want to miss it."

Blank look. "Why are you taking the bus? Your résumé says you have a driver's licence."

"My car needs repairs."

"Well, get it fixed."

"Oh, just like that? I have news for you, Mr. I-spent-five-thousand-bucks-to-sit-in-a-tree—repairs cost money, and I don't have any." I clapped a hand over my mouth. "Sorry. I'm so sorry. This is why I shouldn't drink alcohol at a work event."

"You honestly believe I'd leave you to make your own way home at this time of night? Do you really think that little of me?"

"Uh…"

"On second thought, don't answer that. My driver will take you. And assuming you decide to come into work on Monday, ask Rhonda to give you an advance on your salary so you can fix your car. I'll authorise it."

He had me. He knew he did. The smug smile gave it away. Now I'd have to work next week, and several weeks after that too, because if Mr. Vale paid me enough money up front to cover a fuel pump and four new tyres, I couldn't leave Dunnvale Holdings until I'd paid him back.

"I'll go ask about The Treehouse."

"Oh, wow. Do you get to keep the shoes?" Meera asked.

"I tell you my boss is running a sex club in the basement

of his office, and that's your question? Do I get to keep the shoes?"

I wasn't entirely sure I should have disclosed that snippet of information under the NDA, but the legal jargon seemed more concerned with protecting the clients' identities, and I'd definitely keep quiet about those. And technically, Meera Adams worked for Mr. Vale anyway.

"Okay, I'll ask a different question—do you get a free membership at the sex club?"

"Meera!"

"What? If you got laid, maybe you'd loosen up a bit."

"You know why I don't get laid."

"No, I know why you didn't get laid at college. You're not in Kansas anymore."

"Massachusetts."

"Whatever. Your dad isn't spying on you now. You have the freedom to sleep with whoever you want."

My father had made no secret of the fact that my future husband would expect me to be a virgin. I'd received several stern lectures on the subject before I left for college, all of which avoided the word "sex" and instead focused on sin, shame, and the importance of traditional values. Values I'd stopped sharing when I saw just how much of the world I was missing out on. My father hadn't even wanted me to go to Harvard. Only the influence of my grandfather had allowed me to pursue my dreams. I'd always known I was on a time limit, so I'd pushed myself to graduate high school early and headed straight to college, but after Daada had passed away in my final year of med school, I'd lost that layer of protection, and things had gone rapidly downhill.

Over the years I spent in Boston, I'd had the worst luck with men. I'd heard the "it's not you, it's me" speech twenty times, and after the tenth such episode, I began to suspect that it was in fact me who had the problem. Did my breath smell?

Was I a terrible kisser? Or had my refusal to jump into bed on the first date been the source of the problem?

No.

No, it hadn't.

Potential suitor twenty-one at least had the guts to tell me the truth. That my father's spies watched me, and if I got too close to a man, he paid them to break it off. And while twenty-one had spilled the beans, he'd still taken the cash. Two thousand bucks. That's how much I was worth. In those days, I'd owned purses that cost more.

Meera told me I should just pick up a guy in a bar and have a one-night stand, get it over with, but that idea didn't sit right with me either. While I didn't view marriage as a necessity, there had to be feelings involved. To me, sex was a meeting of hearts and minds, not simply a set of instructions from a biology textbook.

"At the moment, my choice is to sleep with no one." Which reminded me... "How are things going with Alfie?"

"Better, I think. The sun was shining today, and he didn't complain so much. But now he's gone out to a bar with a group of others from the project, so who knows what time he'll be back?"

"You didn't want to go with them?"

"And miss talking to my bestie?"

Meera's words were upbeat, but there was an underlying tension that made me think the situation with Alfie wasn't quite as rosy as she made out. At least I hadn't skipped the call. Mr. Vale had still been talking with other guests, but he'd told the driver to take me home and come back for him afterward. Moments like that made me realise the job wasn't as awful as it could be. Yes, Mr. Vale could be rude and demanding, and then there was the basement harem, but at least he didn't hide who he was. Lance Clifton had been nice to my face, then morphed into a total sleaze the moment I let my guard down.

"What do you think I should do about the job?"

"Honestly? I think it has more pros than cons right now. And if you quit another job so soon, it'll start to look as if you're the problem, not your sucky employers. What if you ended up with another Lance?"

"That would be worse."

"And it's not as if Mr. Vale— He seriously makes you call him that?"

"Yes."

"What a snob. Anyhow, it's not as if Mr. Vale's asking you to go in the basement, is it?"

"He said I'd never have to do that."

"Although maybe you should? You're way overdue for some action with a hot man."

"I'm going to hang up now. Enjoy your digging."

"Hope the job works out."

"Fingers crossed."

"But not your legs."

"Oh, go fall in a hole."

Meera was laughing as I hung up, but I definitely wouldn't be taking her last piece of advice.

CHAPTER 9
BRAX

C arissa Dunn might have considered the Finlay Foundation benefit beneath her, but no such luck with the Alford Gala. Held in Maryland at the Alford family's private art museum and just a hop, skip, and jump from the seat of power, the event attracted a host of politicians as well as entrepreneurs keen to hobnob with the influential, celebrities looking to shed the "nouveau riche" tag, and a handful of representatives from old-money families. A number of attendees were already members of Nyx, and Brax would bet his recently purchased Ulysse Nardin timepiece that other guests would become clients in the future. That was the reason for his presence—it was never too early to start the vetting process. As for Carissa, she just wanted to be seen among the great and the good. And the politicians.

"Gregorio," she cooed beside him. "I loved your last movie."

Had she even watched it? Brax hadn't, but he'd asked Meera to do so as part of her research into tonight's attendees, and she'd noted that the 2.2 rating it achieved on Rotten Tomatoes had been overly generous. Which figured—

Gregorio Phillippé was a poseur with a brain the size of a walnut. That he'd remembered his lines was a miracle.

Phillippé kissed Carissa on both cheeks, his lips lingering longer than was polite but not long enough for Brax's liking. He just needed her to sleep with one dumb asshole, that was all. The problem? Carissa was too smart. Brax had hired investigators, even sent in a number of eligible men with the sole intention of fucking her. She'd turned down every one of them. The stalemate continued. At this rate, they'd spend half of the contested money on private investigators—Brax had a team of three following her at all times, and he knew damn well she returned the favour. Occasionally, he spotted one of the watchers—a car in the wrong place, a dawdling passer-by, or a restaurant patron who paid a little too much attention. And those were the obvious ones. The double agents worried Brax more. Those who pretended to be friends and then reported snippets of information back to Carissa. There weren't many, but Brax had no doubt there were a few.

"Sometimes, one has to take risks and step outside the comfort zone," Phillippé said. "The script for *Sink or Swim* was written by a true visionary, a genius, and the director brought his masterpiece to life. The first day I walked on set, I knew that movie would change my life."

For goodness' sake. *Sink or Swim* was a romcom set in a hot-tub showroom, not a contender for this year's Golden Globes. Carissa could talk to this jackass if she wanted to—they deserved each other—but Brax was done with the conversation. He checked his watch—not his new Ulysse Nardin, of course. If Carissa realised he'd bought it, she'd try to take that too. Eight thirty. He'd stay for another hour or two. Senator Jansen was rumoured to be making an appearance at some point, and a member had nominated him as a possible future addition to the client list. Carissa didn't know that, thankfully. After the first year, she'd stepped back from the business, preferring to spend her time squandering the fruits of Brax's labours instead of assisting in any way.

"Well, if it isn't Braxton Dupré."

A hand clapped Brax on the back, and although he hadn't heard the voice in years, not in person anyway, he recognised the speaker immediately. His former friend and roommate, Greyson Meyer.

"You're right; it isn't Braxton Dupré."

"Braxton Vale. I do apologise; old habits die hard."

That part was true—Grey never missed an opportunity to remind people that he knew where the bodies were buried. His apology was as sincere as his smile to Brax's hopefully soon-to-be ex-wife.

"Ah, and the lovely Carissa. You look radiant tonight. New dress?"

"Naturally."

"The colour suits you." Red, just like the blood she was out for. Grey winked at her. "I bet it cost Brax a fortune."

Carissa's heavily made up eyes narrowed, and her smile slipped, as if she wasn't entirely certain whether Grey was getting a dig in or merely making small talk. It was definitely the former. She linked her arm through Phillippé's, and the band of tension around Brax's gut eased when she took a step away.

"Let's take a look at the paintings. I hear the Alfords recently acquired a Picasso. Do you paint, Gregorio?"

Paint? Crayons were probably a challenge.

Phillippé shook his head. "Not on canvas, but some say that acting is like painting with words."

"What an ass," Grey said as the pair moved out of earshot. "So, you're still hitched?"

How much should Brax tell him? On many occasions in the past several years, he wished they'd kept in touch, that he'd said he was sorry instead of letting the wound Carissa had inflicted on their friendship fester and grow.

"Yes, we're still together. Unfortunately."

Grey raised an eyebrow. "Trouble in paradise? Don't say I didn't warn you."

He had, repeatedly. Grey might have come across as glib and a touch too smooth, but he'd always been good at reading people, Levi Sykes excepted. But they'd all messed up there. Anyhow, he'd told Brax on more than one occasion that underneath the pretty co-ed with the striking blue eyes who acted as if Brax were the centre of her world lay a closeted gold digger. At the time, Grey's assessment had strained their friendship because how could Carissa be out for Brax's money when he didn't have any?

The answer?

He'd had potential. She'd seen it, and so had Grey. Brax had told Grey he was full of shit, then graduated Georgetown summa cum laude with a degree in management, leadership, and innovation; a wild business idea; and the ambition to make his first million before he hit thirty. Turned out he'd been underestimating himself.

"I won't say it." Brax sighed. "The divorce is on hold until we can agree on a financial settlement."

He'd filed the initial paperwork over a year ago, well in excess of California's minimum six-month waiting period. Now they'd moved on to lying about their assets.

"Divorce? I'd say I'm sorry to hear that, but I'd be lying."

"Isn't lying your job, Congressman?"

"Touché." Grey glanced across the room to where Carissa and Phillippé were looking at paintings. "And yet you came here with her tonight?"

Carissa still had her arm looped through Phillippé's, and Brax knew she was only doing it to annoy him. To give him false hope that she might break the infidelity clause in the prenup first.

"The invitation was a joint one, and we were both too stubborn to turn it down."

"Some things change, some things stay the same." Grey glanced sideways. "I need to get some air."

Air? Grey had never been a fan of the great outdoors.

"See someone that you want to avoid?"

"Margaret Ravensberger is heading in this direction. Every time we cross paths, she wants to know why the government hasn't done more to ban handguns. Other countries have managed it, so why can't we?" Another glance. "She lost her husband to gun violence."

"He was shot?"

"No, he got incarcerated for blowing his mistress's brains out with a Colt .45. I realise there's a lot to unpack there. Don't even try. Margaret's cuckoo for cocoa puffs."

Then she'd probably get along with Carissa like a house on fire. Someone should introduce them. But Grey was leaving, and before he disappeared for another seven and a half years, Brax had to get something off his chest.

"Before you go, I need to apologise for everything that happened between us over Carissa. You were right, and I was wrong. I only wish I'd listened."

Grey set off toward the door that led to the terrace, nodding for Brax to follow. On a normal day, visitors bought drinks and snacks from the small café to eat at bistro tables scattered between topiary bushes and fragrant flowers, but tonight, the caterers had set up a champagne fountain and platters of hors d'oeuvres.

"I always knew you'd regret marrying her. That's why I refused to be your best man, not because I was an asshole or jealous or stuck in the past, which I believe were all things you accused me of."

Although Carissa had barely spent any time at Blackstone House—she'd said the place was creepy and had too many spiders—she'd studied for her MBA at Georgetown, so the three of them knew each other from business school. Grey had disliked her from the get-go.

"I wasn't entirely wrong on the 'asshole' part."

A shrug. "Perhaps. I realise now that I could have been more diplomatic." Grey accepted two glasses of champagne from a passing waiter and handed one to Brax. "And I take no satisfaction from being right."

"You're lying again."

"Maybe. Send me an invite to the divorce party. I'll be at your side for that one."

"It might be a long wait."

"You need a good lawyer?"

He was referring to himself, of course. After they finished their bachelor's degrees, Grey had stayed at Georgetown for law school and then passed the bar exam on the first attempt, but following work on several high-profile cases, he'd decided that his future lay in politics. A week ago, he'd been sworn in as congressman for the tenth district of Virginia.

"I should have gotten you to read the prenup before I signed it. Congratulations on the new job, by the way."

"Thanks. The prenup—how bad is it?"

Nearly eight years had passed since they'd spoken properly, but Brax remembered why he'd once considered Grey to be among his closest friends. Blackstone House had been an oversized hovel full of strangers brought together by one thing—desperation—and they'd grown into allies. Okay, so Jerry had mostly kept to herself, and Alexa wasn't really a people person, but everyone had gotten along. And Brax had fucked up. He owed Grey a proper explanation, even if it was too late to repair the friendship they'd once had.

"It's bad." Brax summarised the agreement, his enforced celibacy, and the fact that the trio of PIs tailing Carissa couldn't catch her out. Ditto for the men he'd hired to seduce her—a masseur, a tennis coach, and a fake entrepreneur so far. "I'm basically fucked."

"Quite the opposite, I would say. But you're right. You

should have gotten me to read that agreement. I'd have put it in the shredder where it belonged."

"When you're in love, you do stupid things, not that you'd know anything about that."

"Bachelorhood suits me. If I decide to run for president, then I might consider getting married."

"Because it looks better for the voters?"

"Exactly. Polls show the majority are more likely to trust a family man."

"A family man? You're saying you'd bring kids into your charade?"

"If that's what it takes."

"And you think *my* sex life is messed up?"

"What sex life?"

"Touché. My only consolation is that Carissa's not getting screwed either. With her impossibly high standards, she wouldn't go for a nameless hookup."

"Actually, she would."

Brax looked at his old friend sharply. "Do you know something I don't?"

"Many, many things. In this instance, I know that Carissa once hooked up with some guy named Tony in a bar and left before morning."

Brax nearly spat his drink across the terrace. "What? When?"

"Before you got married, so no luck there."

"I need the details."

"I'm afraid I don't have them. Ruby told me. In our last conversation before I left Blackstone House, we were lamenting your terrible taste in women, and she said Carissa wasn't the demure little angel she wanted everyone to believe. Tony was an acquaintance of Ruby's."

"Why the hell didn't you say anything?"

"Because I went out of town, and two days later, Ruby was dead. I'm not even certain when the encounter took place. Maybe it happened before you and Carissa were dating? And then all the fighting began, and that business with Linus and Mary Sykes and their slander, and by the time things settled down, you were married. I figured it would last about three months."

"For the first year, things were good. She helped with the company, acted as a sounding board, supported me. After we started making money, she changed. I guess we both did."

Grey nodded. "Indeed. You both became successful in your own ways. Achieved your goals. You created a profitable business and made money; she hooked her talons into a human cash machine." Another of those sideways glances Grey had become so proficient at. "Speak of the devil."

"So this is where you disappeared to." Carissa scowled at Grey, no attempt at a fake smile this time, then turned to Brax. "I thought you might have crept off somewhere with that pretty new assistant of yours."

She kept her tone light as if she were making a joke, but they all understood that she wasn't. That Carissa was aware of Meera's existence was no surprise. She harvested information from her spies, then slipped those little tidbits into conversation to make sure Brax knew that she knew. In the beginning, she'd stayed quiet about her intelligence-gathering operation, they both had, but as months of frustration became years, it had turned into a sick, twisted game.

But the mention of Meera was also a problem. Because Meera was different from the legion of assistants who'd come before her. If Brax had been asked *why* she was different, he'd have struggled to articulate the reason, but he wanted to keep her. Maybe it was the intoxicating mix of grit and vulnerability? Maybe it was the beauty she didn't seem to realise she possessed? Or maybe it was the care she showed for those around her? He'd never thought watching a woman perform the Heimlich manoeuvre would be a turn-on, but a man lived and learned.

And tonight, he'd also learned that he needed to put more space between himself and the goddess who sat outside his office every day. Plus he'd need to fire Teresa if she ever put Meera in a backless dress again. He could still feel the silky, warm skin of her lower back on his palm. Fuck, he'd dreamed about it last night. This was what Carissa had done to him.

"Rest assured, I can resist the temptation. Have you finished eye-fucking Gregorio yet? Or do you want to go back for a second round?"

Carissa's mouth formed an O of shock. Yes, they jabbed at each other this way in private, but never before had Brax landed such a barb with an audience. Grey merely smirked.

"I might have known he'd take your side."

She turned on her heel and stormed off, much to Brax's relief. Grey raised his glass in a mock toast.

"Here's to your future divorce. Good luck, buddy. You'll need it."

CHAPTER 10
THE ASSISTANT

"Happy birthday to you, happy birthday to you, happy birthday dear Meera, happy birthday to you!"

Charlotte was carrying a cake with a glittery "25" on it, and what seemed like everyone from the third floor had squashed into my office along with Teresa, several waitstaff, and a few girls I recognised as being from downstairs. My eyes began to sting—this was the nicest thing to happen since I'd left Massachusetts, and it sure made me smile on a Monday morning.

"But...but I didn't even tell anyone it was my birthday."

Mainly because it wasn't. I hoped Alfie was treating Meera to a nice dinner in Portugal, but I had my doubts, and I hadn't even sent her a gift because we'd agreed at the beginning that mailing items was too risky. The fewer links between us, the better. Meanwhile, I'd turn twenty-six next month to zero fanfare whatsoever. Maybe I'd buy myself a cookie.

Rhonda held up a box wrapped in shiny gold paper. "Dunnvale rules—everyone gets a cake and a gift on their birthday."

"Open it, open it," Charlotte squealed.

With everyone watching expectantly, I tore away the paper and thanked my new colleagues for the orange-blossom-scented candle and matching hand cream. Despite the unorthodox nature of the business, there was a sense of camaraderie here that had been missing at Clifton Packaging and Silver's Gym.

"Thank you so much."

"And it's Becky's birthday on Wednesday, so we're going out for drinks. Why don't we make it a joint celebration?"

"Any excuse for a party," Selena muttered.

"What's wrong with that?" Charlotte asked.

"Absolutely nothing." Selena turned to me. "So you'll come?"

I'd been working for Mr. Vale for a month now, and my first paycheck was in my bank account. Well, Meera's bank account. She had several, and I'd taken over a rarely used one for our pretence. Plus my car was running again. Although this week, it had started making a weird vibration when I drove over fifty, so it would need further attention soon, but I could afford a drink or two as long as I avoided expensive cocktails.

"I suppose."

"Careful, don't sound too enthusiastic."

"I'd love to."

"Better."

Charlotte beamed at me. "We're meeting in the Pink Panda at seven."

Notable by his absence this morning was Mr. Vale. He was in the adjoining office, I knew that for certain, but I guess he didn't believe birthdays were important. Or he didn't believe I was important. Or both. Probably both.

Not that I saw much of him. He sent emails, usually vague emails that required several rounds of clarification before I could act on his instructions. Those clarifications came with varying degrees of rudeness. But the job was bearable, and the work was well within my capabilities. And if I got stuck with anything, my other colleagues helped however they could. For the first time since I became Meera, I didn't feel as if I'd made some horrible mistake.

But I suspected the real Meera might. Alfie was being a jerk. Yesterday, she'd been in tears as she told me he'd quit the ecological project to work evenings in a bar, which meant they'd hardly see each other now since she worked during the day. Personally, I thought a little space might not be such a bad thing, and I desperately hoped they'd resolve their issues quickly because we couldn't have two Meera Adamses in the United States using the same social security number and the same driver's licence.

Rhonda began cutting the cake and handing slices around with plastic forks and napkins. Meera would have had a fit about the forks, and the disposable plates too. China was infinitely reusable. Except in my family—my father had thrown more dinnerware than I cared to think about. Whenever he got annoyed...*smash*.

And when Mr. Vale got annoyed? He just sent an email, all caps.

I'M ON THE PHONE.

"Shhh, shhh, shhh. We're being too loud, and Mr. Vale's trying to make a call."

"Oops." Selena giggled and forked another piece of cake into her mouth. "Sorry."

Charlotte picked up an extra slice and headed for the adjoining door.

"Wait, wait! What are you doing?"

"I'm telling Brax to stop being a party pooper."

"No!"

But it was too late. Charlotte was already through the door, and I put my head in my hands. Should I attempt to do damage control? The call light blinked out, along with any hope of salvaging the situation. All I could do was herd my colleagues out of the room and back to their desks so they couldn't annoy our boss any further. The email came the moment everyone had left.

USE THE KITCHEN IF YOU WANT TO THROW A PARTY, NOT YOUR OFFICE.

Happy fake birthday to me.

The Pink Panda was a Japanese-themed wine bar two blocks from Dunnvale's headquarters. I'd walked past it several times while I was running errands for Mr. Vale, and it was the type of place I might have ventured into with Meera, but never on my own. The cool kids hung out there, and I'd always been the nerd in the library. The second-floor reading room, to be precise. But with Charlotte on one side of me and Selena on the other, I worked up the courage to walk through the door of the bar on Wednesday night, trying to look as if I belonged. Charlotte had reserved a trio of tables at the rear, and they were already full. Some of the girls I recognised from the office, but others were strangers.

"Do all of these people work for Dunnvale?" I whispered to Charlotte.

"If they don't now, then they used to."

Which of them came from The Dark? I could take a guess —the long-legged blonde with the perfect posture, the striking redhead with the hourglass figure, the brunette with the million-dollar smile, the Black woman with skin like silk and eye-catching earrings. All of them looked so confident. A handful of men had shown up too, including a guy who looked like a cover model from one of Meera's romance novels. She'd tried to get me to read them, but they only depressed me. Romance was out of the question in this messed-up life I'd ended up with, so why torture myself?

Becky threw her arms around me. "Hey, it's the other birthday girl!"

"Careful," the hot guy told her. "I got told off for saying 'girl' last week."

"By who?"

"A woman at Whole Foods."

"Well, screw her. The song is 'Girls Just Want to Have Fun,' not 'Women Just Want to Have Fun.'"

"Or 'Females Just Want to Have Fun,'" the long-legged blonde said. "And we're no ladies, not tonight anyway."

Becky had been here for at least half an hour already, and judging by her high-pitched giggle, she'd gotten through several drinks.

"'Bitches Just Want to Have Fun' is also acceptable. Who wants to go to a karaoke bar later?"

Everyone groaned. Yes, quite. I'd die a painful death if I ever had to sing in front of an audience.

"No singing, Bex. Nobody brought earplugs tonight."

The brunette held up a small package. "Actually, one of us did. Hearing Becky murder 'I Kissed a Girl' once was quite enough."

Carole-Ann from housekeeping passed me a drink, something pink with fruit around the rim. I knew everyone on the third floor now, by sight if not by name, plus I'd spoken with a few people on the first and second floors too. Nobody had a bad word to say about working at Dunnvale, which was one reason I'd decided to stay for now.

"Aw, I love your necklace," she said. "It's so pretty."

"Thank you."

The necklace? That was the other reason. I thought Mr. Vale had forgotten my birthday, but he hadn't. After I returned from my final errand on Monday, a trip to pick up a new suitcase because baggage handlers at LAX had destroyed the last one when he flew back from Maryland two weeks ago, I'd found a small box on my desk, gift-wrapped with a bow on top. Real ribbon, not the plastic kind. There was no card, only a note. *Happy Birthday, Meera.*

Mr. Vale had bought me jewellery. A beautiful ruby-and-diamond key on a gold chain. I recognised the name of the jeweller, and I knew this little trinket would have cost him more than he paid me in a month. I'd leapt up to tell him it was too much, that I couldn't accept it, but he wasn't in his office. Nor had he shown up yesterday, or today. But after I'd received several grouchy emails, including one that had kept me in the office until nine p.m. last night, fighting with the printer, and another that sent me all over LA looking for a "silk scarf with peonies" for his mom, I figured I'd earned the damn necklace.

And Carole-Ann was right—it really was pretty.

Charlotte put another drink in front of me, this one green.

"Oh, thank you, but I'm only having one."

"What? But it's your birthday."

"I need to drive home."

"Take a cab. Is your car in the parking garage at Dunnvale?"

"Yes."

"It'll be fine there overnight. The security guys are good."

"But—" Cabs were expensive, yes, and I didn't love riding the bus with strangers either, but I couldn't hide away my whole life. I was meant to be having fun tonight. "Okay, okay, I'll have another drink."

"That's more like it. There's a tab, and birthday girls don't pay for their own cocktails—order anything you want."

One more drink turned into three, and the Pink Panda served food too, rice dishes shaped into cute little animals, pandas and kittens and teddy bears, so I wouldn't have to eat dinner tonight. Three drinks turned into four, possibly five. They were so sweet and fruity—they couldn't have that much alcohol in them, right?

More girls appeared, dainty cocktails turned into pitchers of margaritas, and Selena climbed onto the table and began singing an out-of-tune version of "Drunk in Love" to a guy she'd met at the bar five minutes previously. I hadn't had fun like this in a year, maybe even in forever. I used to go out with Meera, but we'd never let our hair down too much in case my father's spies were watching. He'd have been furious if he heard I was indulging in liquor.

Oh, how the angel has fallen.

Hmm… That was a great song—"The Angel has Fallen" by Indigo Rain, Meera's favourite band. And there was a microphone…

"Selena?"

"Yeah?"

"Can I share your table?"

"Oh, of *course*."

By eleven, euphoria had turned into nausea, I'd slurred my way through several songs with Selena on backup, my ankle throbbed where I'd twisted it climbing off the table, and I'd begun to wonder if perhaps my father had been right about one tiny thing.

Alcohol sure did have a lot to answer for.

I stumbled into the ladies' bathroom and puked into the nearest toilet. Hell, that tasted gross. My throat burned, and some of the vomit got on my hair. With a hideous reflection in the mirror as my witness, I was never drinking again. I tried to wipe the mess away with a paper towel, but I mostly just smeared it around. Dammit. Dammit!

I needed to go home.

Take a shower.

Why did my mouth still taste so bad?

I rummaged in my purse for gum, mints, any kind of food, but something was wrong. What? What was wrong? My phone was there, my wallet, my... Where were my keys? When I shook my bag, there was no comforting jingle.

Couldn't shower if I couldn't get inside my apartment.

The keys...

Had I dropped them?

No.

No, they were on my desk.

I'd used them to score open the tape on a package earlier when I couldn't find the scissors.

Which meant...

Which meant I'd have to go back to the office.

Maybe I could just sleep there tonight? There was a couch. A bathroom. Four kinds of toothpaste I'd bought for Mr. Vale because that tight-lipped jackass found it too difficult to simply tell me which brand he liked to use.

But that would be weird.

No, I couldn't sleep in the office like a dishevelled Goldilocks, and I wasn't even fond of porridge.

I'd get my key, and then I'd get an Uber, and then I'd go home.

The bar's side door was wedged open, probably to let some air in or let smokers out. There was a group of them standing in the alley, puffing away. The doctor in me wanted to give them a lecture on lung cancer, but I had to deal with my own...situation first. Alcohol poisoning...alcohol poisoning... I checked off the symptoms in my head, the ones I was able to remember, anyway. Yup, had most of those.

Boy, did my feet hurt. I kicked off my shoes, and ooh, that was better. The office... The big, fancy building... I had to turn right. No, the other right.

"Hey, do you need a ride?" a guy asked. Was he with Uber?

"Uh, yes, but not yet."

"My car's just over there."

"No, I have to go this way."

One foot in front of the other. You can do it, Indi.

The man fell into step alongside me. "Are you okay? You look a little unsteady."

"I'm fine."

"A pretty lady like you shouldn't be walking home alone."

"I'm not… I'm not…"

"That's right. I'll keep you company."

Really? That was nice of him, but Alfie had told me not to talk to strangers outside bars. I distinctly remembered him saying that one night in Boston, right after I talked to a stranger outside a bar. I stumbled over a bump in the sidewalk, and my new friend caught me. Wow, I'd almost ended up on my ass.

"Easy, babe."

His arm wrapped around my waist, and I wasn't sure I liked that. Being touched in that manner. I tried to push his hand away, but he gripped me tighter.

"I just don't want you to fall, babe. Look, my car's right here. I'll drive you anywhere you want to go."

Everything was dark. So dark. The old station wagon, the quiet street, the man's eyes. Eyes that weren't so friendly anymore. I didn't want to go with him, but he opened the rear door and tried to push me inside. This…this was bad. Very bad. I grabbed the edge of the door and hung on as he unpeeled my fingers, and this was why Alfie had warned me, wasn't it?

"No, no, no. Get off me!"

"It's okay, babe."

It wasn't okay. Nothing was okay. I tried to kick him, but

my shoes were gone and he just laughed a creepy laugh that made me shudder.

Then he groaned.

And disappeared.

Wait.

Where did he go?

A sickening *thud* was followed by the *crack* of glass as somebody slammed him against the car, again, again, again, each *crunch* punctuated with angry words.

"She said no."

Crunch.

Another groan.

"And she meant it."

Crunch.

"She's mine."

Crunch.

Someone began whimpering. Was that sound coming from my throat? Or the stranger's?

"Nobody touches her but me, do you understand?"

Crunch.

More whimpering, and the rustle of clothing.

"I have your driver's licence, and by morning, I'll know everything about you."

Crunch.

"If you try this shit with any other lady, I'll find you, and I'll break every fucking bone in your body. Have I made myself clear?"

"Y-y-yes."

The whimpering turned to full-on sobbing, and the man's limp form slithered to the ground beside me, blood trickling from his broken nose. He'd need to get that reset. Maybe he'd even need surgery, and then there was a risk of septal haematoma or a deviated— I leaned forward and puked again, this time onto distinctive black laceless Oxfords. And through my alcohol-induced stupor and hazy memories of medical school, one thing became startlingly clear.

I knew those shoes.

I'd ordered those shoes online a week ago, size eleven point five, express delivery.

Fuck.

I looked up and met Mr. Vale's furious gaze.

And then I passed out.

CHAPTER 11
THE ASSISTANT

Firecrackers went off behind my eyes as I rolled over in bed. *The pain.* I'd never had a headache like it. My memory returned in flashes—the cocktails, the rice pandas, duetting with Selena... Oh, hell. How much had I drunk?

At least it wasn't light. I wasn't late for work, not yet, but I'd have to drag myself out of bed as soon as Kamal turned his music on. I had three roommates, and we got along okay, mainly because we all worked long hours and never spoke to each other. But Kamal liked to listen to rock, and at some dim and distant household meeting in the past, eight o'clock had been deemed an appropriate hour for him to crank up Spotify. I didn't mind. I just took it as my cue to get up.

But today, there was only silence and darkness, which meant I could close my eyes for another hour or two and pray my head stopped throbbing. I shifted on the mattress, reaching for my phone on the nightstand, but my hand hit smooth cotton. What the...? I only had a single bed. My mattress wasn't that wide. Heart pounding as well now, I stretched out the other arm and found pillows, a whole mound of them.

Then the real panic hit.

This wasn't my bed.

Another memory—a man walking beside me, talking, trying to push me into his car. Had I been kidnapped? A scream bubbled up in my throat, but the alcohol had worn off now, and the rational part of my brain told me that if I'd been kidnapped and put into a king-sized bed, then I should just relax and enjoy the experience.

Wait.

What experience?

I'd changed into a skirt after work yesterday, and a quick check under the covers revealed I was still wearing it, my top too, although that smelled a bit funky. Underwear was all present and correct. So I hadn't been molested, but where was I?

As my eyes adjusted to the darkness, I saw I wasn't just in a king-sized bed, I was in a king-sized four-poster bed, and the room was huge. Faint cracks of light on the far wall suggested the windows were covered with blackout blinds. What if it was later than I thought? Mr. Vale would probably send me to the torture dungeon if his coffee wasn't ready when he arrived.

Mr. Vale...

Mr. Vale...

Shiny black Oxfords...

Oh, fuck!

No, no, no, no, no, no, no. I'd thrown up on my freaking boss. Had he called the security team? Made them stash me in one of the beautiful bedrooms on the second floor until he could fire me this morning? I mean, where else could I be?

I groaned louder than that awful man who wouldn't take no for an answer last night. Had Mr. Vale really broken his nose? Fragments of conversation came back... *She's mine, nobody touches her but me, I'll break every fucking bone in your body.* He hadn't really meant any of that, had he? No, of course not. He'd been angry, that was all. And I was angry too. If that scumbag had cost me a well-paid job I was starting to like, I'd knock his damn teeth out.

But first, I had to find my boss and apologise. Actually, no, I had to take a shower, then find my boss and apologise. If I walked into his office with vomit in my hair, breath that made a cadaver smell good, and armpits that could collapse a man's lungs at ten paces, he'd fire me on the spot.

I felt my way around the room, fingertips outstretched, until I located the light switch. Each room on the second floor was decorated in a different style, but they had commonalities. The luxurious padded furniture, the high-end electronics, the perfectly matched colour scheme. This one was fifty shades of teal with silver accents. The bathroom had a swimming pool for a tub plus a separate shower stall, two sinks in the vanity, and a basketful of expensive toiletries. If I'd had more time, I'd have delighted in my first bath since I came to LA—my apartment only had a tiny shared shower room, usually with somebody else's hair in the plug hole— but Mr. Vale's anger was no doubt simmering already. I grabbed the necessities out of the basket and jumped into the shower.

My choices of attire were a fluffy towel, a silk robe, or my yucky clothes. With little other option, I shimmied into last night's outfit and sprayed it with perfume. Now to do the walk of shame to the elevator. What if I bumped into a guest? I wasn't meant to mix with clients, and if any of them said hello, I wouldn't know where to look.

The bedroom door didn't lock, which I thought was a little odd, but I gathered from Mr. Vale's (vague) explanations of Nyx that a lot of emphasis was placed on trust, so perhaps the members considered the lack of security normal? Or maybe they went wife-swapping after hours and pesky keys got in the way? I cracked open the door, peered out to check the coast was clear, and found a reading nook lined with books in the hallway outside. Memoirs, thrillers, leatherbound classics. I didn't remember those, but I'd only been to the second floor a couple of times, so maybe the building was bigger than I thought?

I tiptoed along, my bare feet sinking into plush grey carpet. And found myself in a vast living room. A grand piano sat in one corner, and a horseshoe of pale grey couches surrounded a coffee table, overlooking the park in the distance.

Wait.

If we were on the second floor, we shouldn't be able to see into the park. There was a row of tall evergreens blocking the view. Deliberately, Charlotte had told me. Mr. Vale had sponsored the planting. Which meant... Oh no.

"It wakes."

If one of the windows had been open, I'd have jumped right out of it. But I just wasn't that lucky. I didn't want to turn around, so I sure took my time doing it, and there he was. Mr. Vale. Large as life and wearing a disapproving scowl.

"Why am I in your apartment?"

"I was going to take you home, but I couldn't find a key to get in." He stopped ten feet away and perched on the back of a couch, coffee in hand. This was as casual as I'd ever seen him clothing-wise—suit pants, white shirt but no tie, bare feet —but he radiated tension. "And you weren't providing much assistance."

"I'm sorry. I'm so sorry. I didn't realise how much I'd had to drink, and that man... He was just *there*, and he started following me."

"Why were you walking the streets alone, Meera?"

"Because I left my key on my desk. Why were *you* there?"

"I was coming to pay the bar tab. Something I sorely regret offering to do if this was the result."

"I'll replace your shoes." I caught sight of his bruised

knuckles and gasped. "Your hands! You should go to the hospital. Have them X-rayed and get anti-inflammatories for the swelling."

"I don't give a shit about the shoes, and my hands will be fine. *You* need to be more careful. Next time you go out, you'll book a car and have the driver wait outside the venue to take you home."

"But I can't afford—"

"On the company account, Meera."

"You mean I'm not fired?"

"I can replace shoes. I can't replace an assistant."

"Uh, hello? Assistant number twenty-seven right here." I clapped a hand over my mouth. "Sorry, that just popped out."

"Go home and get some sleep." He took a sip of coffee, then sighed. "And if my wife asks about this little episode, you need to tell her nothing happened between us."

"Nothing *did* happen."

"Then it shouldn't be a problem for you."

"No. No, of course not. I'll just go home and change, and then I'll come right back."

"Take the day off."

"But—"

"Take the day off, Meera." He pointed behind me. "The door's over there."

"And he just kicked you out and told you to take the day off? Wow. That's so…so…"

"Weird?"

"I was going to say 'sweet.'"

Meera always saw the silver lining in every cloud. She was the optimist to my pessimist, the sunshine to my drizzle.

"Trust me, Braxton Vale is anything but sweet."

"And yet he beat up another man to save you. Then took you to his luxury apartment instead of leaving you on the sidewalk."

"He was probably worried nobody would make his 140-degree coffee otherwise."

"No, he totally likes you."

I'd thrown up on his freaking shoes.

"Oh, please. He won't even let me call him by his first name."

"I bet he has some weird *Fifty Shades of Grey* thing going on. Has he mentioned his palm twitching?"

"What? No!"

"But he does have a sex dungeon, so there's that."

"It's not *his* sex dungeon. It's for the clients. I can't believe we're even having this conversation." And it was time to change the subject. "How are things going with Alfie?"

Her silence told me what her words didn't. That the situation hadn't improved, but she was trying to put a brave face on things.

"Getting better, I think? He said he'd help me to move some rocks tomorrow."

"That's great news!" Did I sound enthusiastic enough? I hoped so. "Maybe you could both take a day off and do something fun together? An indoor activity? Alfie's a good guy, but you've both been under a lot of stress lately."

In Boston, he hadn't spent much time outdoors, so I could imagine that working on a farm every day was somewhat of a culture shock for him. And Meera got so enthusiastic about the project that she tended to forget he wasn't actually an ecologist. Alfie had put his own plans on hold so she could follow her dream, and there had to be a little give and take.

"I guess that's a good idea," Meera said.

"Let me know how it goes?"

"Always. Update me on the hot boss?"

"Of course."

"So you're not denying he's hot?"

"I'm going to hang up now."

I was laughing as I did so, but no, I couldn't deny it. Braxton Vale might have been a world-class asshole, but he was also incendiary.

CHAPTER 12
BRAX

"She drank herself into a stupor, almost got abducted, and then passed out. What did you expect me to do, Carissa? Leave her there on the sidewalk?"

"You could have taken her home."

"I couldn't find her keys, and she was incapable of telling me where they were."

"Ever heard of calling a locksmith?"

"At one o'clock in the morning? You're really reaching now."

"Why didn't you put her in one of the rooms on the second floor?"

"Because she'd already vomited at least once, and I didn't want her to ruin the soft furnishings. We were fully booked the next night. For fuck's sake, Carissa, haven't you ever heard of altruism?"

"My lawyer might want to speak with her."

"Fine. Call her in for a deposition. I'll give her the morning off, but I'm deducting the cost from your settlement."

The bitch hung up, and Brax raised his hand to hurl the phone against the wall. Stopped himself just in time. Carissa had cost him three phones this year already, and it was only February. She just had that effect on people.

Brax took a calming breath instead. Carissa wouldn't depose Meera, not at the moment, but her poking around still left him with a problem. It was becoming harder and harder to deny the effect his new assistant had on him. Not only was she smart and beautiful, but the magic combination of submissive with a hint of feistiness that she struggled to control made his cock stand to attention. If Meera had been compos mentis and willing last night, Carissa might very well have won the divorce war.

But Brax didn't take advantage of inebriated women, so he'd gotten a reprieve. And Meera herself wasn't the only issue. Carissa had known that she'd spent the night in his apartment, not in a guest room downstairs, which meant his darling wife had a mole inside the building. In a business that involved so many secrets, a breach of trust was of great concern.

He emailed Alexa.

Call me.

Two seconds later…

You forgot the "please."

Alexa called anyway—the lack of a "please" was an old joke between them. But she didn't call on a regular phone. No, she used an app that had suddenly appeared on his cell one morning. He suspected the app gave her access to everything on the device, but even if he removed it, she'd find another way to dig through his life. Alexa didn't give up. A quality he intended to utilise for his own purposes.

"What's the problem?" she asked. "Did you accidentally sleep with your new assistant?"

"Why would you think that?"

"Because you got a call from Carissa and then emailed me right after. And then Carissa called her lawyer."

"Well, I didn't sleep with Meera, but she stayed in my

apartment last night. The one in LA. And Carissa found out about it."

"Ah."

"Exactly. She has a source here feeding her information, and I need to know who it is."

"Let me check a few things…" A full minute passed as Brax paced the great room. "She's only received six calls today: two from her friend Danielle, one from her mother, one from Saks Fifth Avenue, one from the Elements Spa, and another from Bruce. That's her tennis coach, right? He's one of yours?"

"Yes, he's one of mine."

"Zilch in her emails. Either she's using a burner phone, or Danielle is involved. Or her mother."

"Her mother probably called to give her a pep talk. *Why is this taking so long?*"

If Carissa Dunn was a gold digger, then Madeleine Dunn drove the backhoe. She'd been married six times and divorced five, including twice in the years Brax had known her, trading her way up into an Upper East Side penthouse. Husband number six was a retired investment banker, and according to Alexa, he'd been suffering from heart problems. Perhaps Madeleine had decided to give widowhood a try this time? That wouldn't have surprised Brax one bit.

During the early days of his relationship with Carissa, he hadn't realised just how often the two women spoke. Carissa had barely mentioned her mother at all. But after the wedding, suddenly there she was, sticking her nose into their business at every possible opportunity.

"Bet Carissa's asking the same thing about her new stepfather. If Madeleine orders rat poison, we'll know what's coming. Hmm. Maybe I should check her credit card statements?"

"Can we focus on the Dunnvale issue first? I don't like

having a traitor in our midst. And besides, Madeleine will need a year or so to jack up her new hubby's life insurance."

"Yeah, I'll take a look."

"I'll send funds to the usual place."

"You don't have to."

This was another dance they did every time. Alexa always refused payment, but for Brax, that wasn't an option. He'd feel guilty for requesting these favours otherwise. So they'd agreed on a compromise: Alexa did the work, and Brax made a donation to Project AVA, an organisation that helped young people running from violence and abuse. It was a cause close to Alexa's heart.

"Yes, I do have to."

"Zach's gonna win the pool on Meera, isn't he?"

As Brax recalled, Zach had made the longest guess with six weeks. At the time, it seemed like a long shot, but now? If Meera failed to last that long… The hitch in Brax's chest told him that he didn't like the idea one bit.

"I hope so," he said, half to himself.

"Fuck my life, you have to get rid of Carissa."

"Believe me, I'm trying. I bumped into Grey two weeks ago, and he thinks Carissa had at least one hookup. I'm going to try a different approach—have someone run into her at an event and make a no-strings offer. I doubt she'll bite, but I'd be remiss if I didn't attempt it."

"Grey? As in Greyson Meyer?"

"Yes."

"After the whole 'best man' fiasco?"

"I apologised."

"Well, I still think Grey was a dick. Even if your friend's marrying a total bitch, you should support them. I mean, I couldn't stand the conniving shrew, and I still managed to send a wedding present."

"She's allergic to shellfish, and you sent a gift certificate for the Grand Banks Oyster Bar."

"It's the thought that counts. And speaking of shellfish, have you considered slipping a piece of lobster into her dinner?"

"It's only a mild allergy. She just comes out in hives."

"Shame. How did Grey know about the hookup? It wasn't with him, was it? I can imagine him having hate sex if he's in a particularly shitty mood."

"No, it wasn't with him. It was some friend of Ruby's."

"Interesting. Ruby told him about it? Or did Grey know the guy personally?"

"Ruby told him, which means it happened before we got married."

"Okay, well, good luck with the one-night-stand thing."

Alexa hung up, abrupt as always. Now Brax needed to find yet another man willing to have sex with a woman for money and report on the sordid details. There should be an agency for this kind of thing. If Brax ended up giving in to his baser instincts and losing Nyx, then maybe that was a business idea for the future.

But in the meantime, he'd just have to distance himself further from Meera. Make her stay out of his way. Of all the women who'd crossed his path in recent years, she was the one who gave him sleepless nights.

CHAPTER 13
THE ASSISTANT

Yesterday, I'd been picking up birthday gifts for two members of the housekeeping team, making arrangements for Mr. Vale to travel to a board meeting in San Francisco for a tech startup he'd invested in, and finalising the details of the dinner party he planned to hold next weekend.

Today? Today, he wanted me to research the gem trade in Colombia. Just a high-level paper, he said, and if he needed more, he'd engage a specialist to prepare a detailed report. But where should I start? With the logistics? The ethics? The finances? Last week, he'd wanted details of the wheat trade in Eastern Europe, and when I'd emailed him the facts I'd pulled together, he'd given me no feedback whatsoever. Had it been mediocre? Good? Were there improvements I could make? At times, I felt as if I was shouting into the void with this job.

After the shoe-vomit incident, I'd spent two full weeks keeping out of Mr. Vale's way, and he seemed content to communicate by email. But enough was enough. If I was going to do this job properly, we needed to have some kind of personal interaction. A short meeting each day, or even a phone call.

I read the brief again, as if somehow in the past five minutes it might have sprouted extra words, more helpful ones. But it was no good. I'd have to speak with him. Perhaps if I sweetened the deal with coffee? Usually, I just placed the mug on his desk and backed out of the room. At least he hadn't complained about the temperature recently, so I had to be doing something right.

When the drink reached 140 degrees exactly, I took a deep breath and knocked on the door.

"Yes?"

"Your coffee, Mr. Vale."

"I didn't ask for more coffee yet."

"I know, but I was hoping we could talk over the brief you just gave me."

He checked his screen. "Did you email me a question?"

"No, but I thought…"

"You thought what?"

"Sometimes it's easier to go over these things in person, face to face. And quicker, especially since I'm only sitting next door."

His scowl said he didn't agree, but he waved at the chair opposite his.

"Fine. Sit. What do you want to ask?"

"What's the focus of this report? What are your concerns?"

"Firstly, what would the benefits of an investment be? Not only in terms of money but for the people involved. And what are the negatives? Risks to capital, ethical considerations, and any environmental issues. With your background in environmental science, I would have thought that preparing a report like this was a piece of cake."

"Uh, yes." I'd been vaguely aware of Meera writing essays while I studied *Gray's Anatomy*, but I'd never worried too much about the content. Now I wished I'd paid more attention. Maybe she could email me some of her work? "I just want to ensure I meet your expectations."

"Are we done now?"

"Yes." *Now or never, Indi.* "I mean, no. Could we have a catch-up each day that you're here? After I, uh, threw up on you, I can understand if my presence makes you uncomfortable, but I really think that going over our plans each morning would be beneficial. And I realise I don't have much experience as a personal assistant, but I just figured it would be more, well, personal, and we have very little contact."

"That's the way it has to be at the moment."

"At the moment?"

Silence. Was I dismissed? Should I leave? Mr. Vale hadn't told me to, but he seemed to be staring right through me. I was on the verge of getting up and scuttling out the door when he let out the longest sigh.

"Your presence does make me uncomfortable, but not for the reasons you think. There are some ongoing issues with my wife."

"*She* doesn't like me being around?"

Was it because I'd spent the night in the apartment upstairs? No, he'd been weird before that, but sleeping in the guest room couldn't have helped matters.

"Quite the opposite, in fact. This doesn't go any farther than this room, is that clear?"

"Crystal."

I wouldn't even tell Meera if the secret was that big.

"My wife and I are in the process of getting a divorce."

Oh, wow. "I'm so sorry."

"Don't be. I'm not. The issue is that we signed a rather restrictive prenuptial agreement, one that later came back to bite me. If one of us is unfaithful prior to the divorce being finalised, the other automatically receives the bulk of our joint assets. Although Carissa isn't involved in the day-to-day

101

running of the business, on paper, Dunnvale Holdings belongs to both of us. So..." Mr. Vale gave a shrug. "We've spent the past three years trying to goad each other into making a mistake, and for me, it's easier if temptation remains out of reach."

His words sank in, and boy, that was some warped game they were playing. After I'd slept upstairs, he'd warned me that his wife might ask questions. At the time, I'd assumed she'd want assurance that nothing had happened, but now I understood the opposite was true. And what was that last part? Slowly, it dawned on me, and I swallowed hard.

"Are you saying that I'm...temptation?"

"I am."

His dark gaze locked onto mine, and I realised I'd been wrong. Totally wrong. This man was far, far more concerning than Lance Clifton. When Lance dropped his pants in front of me, I'd been afraid I wouldn't get out of the room fast enough. With Mr. Vale, I was afraid I might not want to leave at all. His eyes smouldered. He was the lion; I was the gazelle. But he was also an arrogant asshole. How dare he assume that I'd want to sleep with him just because he had no willpower? I mean, so what if he was handsome and magnetic and experienced and— *Keep it together, Indi.*

"Do you realise that consensual sex takes two people to participate? I'm assuming you like things consensual?"

The flash of horror that crossed his features told me I was safe in that respect, at least. Plus his previous actions spoke for themselves—he'd rescued me from a man who wouldn't take no for an answer. *And also told that man that I was his. That only he could touch me.*

Holy hotness. I mean, he was absolutely a jerk.

"I would never force myself on a woman."

"Good. Well, no matter how tempting I might be, I'm going to say no. So rest assured, we can have a five-minute meeting over coffee each morning without me ending up spreadeagled across your desk. Does that work for you?"

"Carissa got to assistant number seven. I don't know how much my scheming wife offered her, but she said we'd slept together and nearly cost me everything. Avoidance is definitely the best policy."

My turn to look horrified.

"She lied?"

"It's amazing what people will do for money."

"How did you prove her wrong?"

"Luckily, at the time in question, I was discussing an investment in a Japanese copper refinery, and my attorney was on the call. I provided phone records, and he gave a statement under oath."

"That's...that's so dirty."

"Welcome to my world. I'm also aware that someone in the building is feeding information back to Carissa, but I don't know who. Now do you see why I avoid being alone with women who aren't my wife?"

"Yes." And even though I'd never met Carissa Dunn, I already knew I'd hate her. "But I'm still finding it difficult to work without speaking to you, and I want to do the job to the best of my abilities. Could we meet if we record the sessions? Or even talk over Zoom?"

"We can do that. Add it to my schedule."

"Thank you. And I'm sorry your wife's so horrible."

"You and me both, Meera. You and me both."

CHAPTER 14
BRAX

B rax considered the Zoom suggestion, but with Meera sitting next door, the idea was ridiculous. Instead, he emailed Alexa to ask about a discreet security camera, then gritted his teeth as a hairy fellow named Bug climbed up a ladder in his office to install it. Bug's was the first ass crack that Brax had seen up close in months.

Meera scheduled a meeting for eleven the next morning, but at two minutes past, there was still no sign of her. Had she quit without notice? Brax couldn't have blamed her—she hadn't signed up to get tangled in the middle of somebody else's marital problems. Her desk was empty, and he was just wondering if he should risk Carissa's wrath and drive to Meera's apartment when he realised she was in the kitchenette. He leaned on the doorjamb and watched her for a moment before she realised he was there.

"Sorry, sorry, I know I'm late. Your coffee was too hot, so I added some chilled water, and now it's too cold."

"Shall I let you in on a secret?"

"Another one?" She sounded wary.

"I don't give a fuck how hot my coffee is. It's just easier when my assistants think I'm an asshole."

"Oh."

"You know why I hired you?"

"I'll admit I'm still baffled by that."

"Because you yelled at me."

"You were definitely an asshole that day."

"Not that I have any excuse, but I'd just gotten off the phone with Carissa that morning. She has a way of stretching my nerves to the snapping point."

"I guess I could have paid more attention to where I was walking."

"Let's draw a line under that day, shall we? We can start afresh, but there need to be rules in place to protect both of us."

"Okay."

"The camera in my office will be recording twenty-four-seven. If you want to speak with me elsewhere, you'll do so with a third party present. And if you need to visit my apartment again for any reason, make sure I'm not in it at the time."

"I understand."

Brax held the door open while Meera carried coffee for both of them into his office. She'd been to the deli too—there was a bag on her desk—and he waited while she slid two Danishes onto plates and brought those in as well. These meetings promised to be torture. But at the same time, he was glad she knew the truth now, that she understood. Being a jackass wasn't his default operating mode, or at least he liked to think it wasn't, and he'd hated having to be a jerk to her.

They both took a seat, and she'd worn a slightly tighter shirt today. With her excellent posture, her breasts pushed against the fabric, and his cock began to ache. Thank fuck his desk was made from wood and not glass. *Think of Carissa, Brax.* Better. His cock deflated instantly. If worst came to worst, he could ship Meera off to the admin department and hire a more appropriate assistant. A ball-breaker with poor hygiene habits and a love of kaftans.

"Was the format of the wheat report okay?" Meera asked.

"It was perfect."

"Are there any areas you need to be expanded?"

"No."

"So I should do something similar for the emerald report?"

"Yes." Brax swallowed. "Yes, please."

"I'll get a draft to you by the middle of the afternoon. What else would you like me to do today?"

Things that he couldn't possibly talk about under the beady eye of the camera.

"How are the arrangements for the dinner party coming along?"

"The caterer is booked, but they'll need access to your kitchen four hours in advance. Do you want me to hire a sommelier?"

"No need. Nolan will bring the wine. He owns a vineyard."

"And do you have enough seating? Nine people? That's definitely right?"

"Nine is correct. Three of us are single." Yes, Brax was counting himself in that number, no matter what a piece of paper said. "Maybe five. I have no idea what's going on with Chase and Alexa. In fact, Alexa probably won't show up."

Chase had RSVP'd and said Alexa was "ninety percent likely to attend virtually." Brax wasn't sure whether that meant there was a ten percent chance of her coming in person, or a ten percent chance that she wouldn't come at all. He'd make sure there was food for her, just in case.

"And the seating?"

"The table in my San Francisco apartment seats fourteen, sixteen if elbow room isn't a consideration."

"Do I need to do a seating plan? Place cards?"

"Don't worry about that. Everyone knows each other. It's kind of a reunion."

Six of the roommates from Blackstone House, together for the first time since the murder case that had ended with Levi's conviction. Brax considered inviting Grey as well, but it was too soon. And he had no idea how to contact Jerry. She'd dropped off the face of the earth before the verdict came in.

"Friends from high school?" She stilled. "Sorry, sorry, I shouldn't ask personal things like that. Uh, are there any specific dietary requirements or allergies that the caterers need to be aware of?"

Meera had a habit of veering into the unprofessional, and if she'd been any of her predecessors, he'd have snapped her back on track in a heartbeat. But she wasn't one of the others, and he found he didn't mind her questions.

"Old college roommates. Justin can't stand celery, I'm not fond of liquorice, and Nolan was vegan for about three months before he cracked and ate a steak."

For a moment, she looked adorably confused. "In the manual, it says you love liquorice. Who wrote that?"

"Someone who hates me. You have twenty-five names to pick from."

"Twenty-five? There was one assistant you didn't manage to antagonise?"

"Luisa retired for health reasons. Oh, and Violet doesn't eat invertebrates, but I don't suppose the chef will serve those."

"Invertebrates? Like bugs?" Meera stopped writing notes and shuddered. "Who would eat those?"

"Alexa."

"Are you serious?"

"She'll try anything once."

"Uh, so the chef's suggestion was grilled scallops for the appetiser, then roasted duck for the entrée and raspberry soufflé for dessert. Plus cheese and coffee, of course."

"That all sounds fine."

"Phew. I was going to order flowers as a table centrepiece?"

"Keep the arrangements low. We want to be able to see each other."

"Of course."

"And get extra flowers for the ladies."

"Okay." Meera sucked the pen. Did she even realise she was doing it? Brax only just managed to stop himself from groaning out loud. "Is there anything else you need?" she asked.

He almost invited her to be the tenth guest at the dinner party, but that would be a bad idea. Terrible. Truly dumb. He absolutely couldn't do that.

"We can discuss the rest over lunch."

"Lunch?" Her eyes widened, those thick lashes blinking in surprise. "With you?"

"Now that we have a camera in here, there's no reason not to make an attempt at social niceties, is there?"

If Meera was smart, she'd say yes, there was every reason not to spend a moment longer in Brax's company than was strictly necessary. Did she feel it? The pull? As if she were the sun and he were a doomed planet orbiting closer and closer, on a collision course for a fiery end?

"Uh, no. No, I guess there isn't. I'll see you at two thirty, Mr. Vale."

Fuck, this woman was going to turn his life upside down.

CHAPTER 15
THE ASSISTANT

"What's this?"

Charlotte tiptoed into my office carrying a cupcake on a plate. The cupcake had two candles stuck into the middle, and Selena was behind her, holding out an individual-sized bottle of champagne. I'd turned twenty-six three days ago, but I hadn't told a soul.

"I know Brax said no parties in here, but it's your two-month anniversary, and none of us thought you'd make it this far, so…"

"Except me!" Selena squeaked, putting the bottle down on my desk. "I won the pool for the very first time."

The pool? I'd forgotten about the freaking pool. I quickly moved the bottle to a coaster and stood.

"You all thought I'd quit that soon?"

"Well, yes." Charlotte nodded. "After you accused Brax of driving a penis extension, I bet on three days."

A gasp escaped. "You heard about that?"

"Tawny's brother works in the coffee bar where it happened. And you're still here, so I guess Brax didn't hold it against you."

Selena got a dreamy look in her eyes. "He could hold it against me any day."

"Shhhh!" I told her.

"Relax, the door's closed. Coraya's sister has a friend who did the deed with him in college—they both went to Georgetown—and she says he has nothing to be ashamed of in the showers."

I really didn't need to hear any of this. "So, thanks for the cake and the champagne, but I have emails to finish."

"Me too," Charlotte said, and pushed the plate into my hands. "Happy work anniversary!"

"Are you working downstairs tonight?" Selena asked her, and my eyes bugged.

"Downstairs?" Was she moonlighting as a server or something? "In the restaurant?"

"No, *down-downstairs*." She pointed with a finger. "That's where I started, but then I met a guy I liked, and I figured I should get a more respectable job and, you know, do the monogamy thing, so Brax found me a role here in the office."

I stared at Charlotte in a whole new light. It was obvious she was pretty, but she worked *downstairs*? She wasn't joking?

"Your face." She began laughing. "Don't look so shocked. The guy dumped me for a cheerleader from UCLA, and I missed all the fun I used to have. So now I fill in on the weekends."

"I…I…"

"You're shocked?"

"Well, yes? It doesn't…" I lowered my voice to a whisper. "Creep you out?"

"I enjoy my job, Meera. Both of them. This evening, one of my regulars is coming, and he's…" She fanned herself. "He's hot in a 'daddy' kind of way. And he has a kink that's also my kink, so I'm gonna sleep *very* well tonight." Charlotte took a step back. "I need to go finish the management accounts, then find an outfit."

"See you on Monday!"

Selena waved as they both hurried out of the room, and I closed the door behind them and leaned my forehead against it, trying to recover from yet another Dunnvale surprise. I knew I shouldn't judge, but when you'd been brought up to believe that sex was for procreation, not for pleasure, and that all pleasure was dirty, it was hard to adjust.

"Blow out your candles, Meera. We don't want an unscheduled fire drill."

My breath hitched, and I whirled to find Mr. Vale standing in the doorway between our offices, watching me with his hands in his pants pockets.

"Sorry, sorry."

"Just for your information, this door isn't as soundproof as it might appear." All I could do was groan. "Although now I'm curious who Coraya's sister's friend is." He gave a weighty sigh. "Those were the days."

Before I could regain my faculties, my gaze dropped to Mr. Vale's package, and although I snapped it back up to his face in one stuttering heartbeat, I knew he'd noticed. That smirk was *filthy*.

"I'm sorry," I muttered again, because staring at the CEO's genitals was probably forbidden in the company handbook. "I just need to…" Need to what? *Think, Indi.* "Uh, there's a package at the desk downstairs."

Mr. Vale was chuckling as I ran out of my office. When I came back, ten long, long minutes later, the candles were out, and there was a small box with a note sitting by the cupcake. *Happy work anniversary, Meera.*

Now I had the earrings to go with my necklace.

111

"You sound happier," Meera commented on Saturday evening. "Has your new boss stopped acting like a douche now?"

Yes. Yes, he had.

Which should have been a good thing. I mean, hadn't I longed for a friendly, approachable boss who didn't molest me? But now I was confused. Mr. Vale was a mercurial mix of taskmaster and testosterone. I'd asked for the morning meetings, but every day they were taking longer, and I kept getting distracted. By his sly smiles, by the way his shirt stretched across his chest when he leaned back in his chair, by the glasses he'd worn instead of contacts this morning. The lunches were worse. They didn't happen every day, but when they did, they were always three courses with no wine. I was very insistent on the no-wine part.

And Mr. Vale was surprisingly easy to talk with when he relaxed. Both about business—I was learning more details of his various investments—and life in general. Although every conversation seemed to involve a game of innuendo tennis where he hit ace after ace and all of my serves ended up in the net. He didn't mean anything by it. Did he? Charlotte said he was naturally charming, and he also owned a sex club. That was probably just the way he spoke with everyone.

"He's mellowed out in the past few weeks."

"That's *great*."

But if I sounded happy, then Meera sounded sad. I asked the question I'd been dreading.

"How are things with Alfie?"

She burst into tears.

All I wanted to do was reach through the phone and give her a hug. Meera had been my rock, my confidante for the past four and a half years. She was hurting, and there was nothing I could do about it.

"What happened?"

"He says he's sick of working outside in the rain, and he's not coming back to the project. He wants us to go to Lisbon for the rest of the winter because bar work's better paid there. What am I meant to do? I tried waitressing in a bar when we were in college, and I hated it."

Alfie was an extrovert; Meera was an introvert. I'd always thought their different personalities complemented each other, but now I wasn't so sure.

"Is it the weather that's the big problem? Will he come back to the project when it's drier?"

"I...I don't know."

"Because if he'd agree to that, why not suggest a compromise? You both head to Lisbon for a few months and then return to Fundão in the spring?"

"But I want to get the permaculture project up and running, and there are all the trees to plant, and the waterway to clear, and a chicken house to build..."

"Relationships are about give and take. You don't like Lisbon, but Alfie's fallen out of love with farming for the moment, and the weather *has* been awful. Maybe the two of you just need a break?"

"You think? You've never even *had* a relationship."

"Ouch."

"Shit, I'm sorry. I just meant that...that it's hard loving someone when you don't like them very much at the moment."

"You should talk to Alfie. Tell him how you feel. He might consider going somewhere quieter than Lisbon but busier than Fundão. A town in the Algarve? Or north near Porto?"

"I guess I could ask him. *If* he ever comes home."

"He's still out? What time is it over there?"

"Two a.m."

Two a.m., and Meera sounded a tiny bit scared. Hell. "Talk to him, okay? Talk to him, and call me back."

"I will."

"Give and take, remember?"

"I guess Porto might be okay."

"You've got this. Live the dream."

She managed a teary laugh. "Live the dream."

CHAPTER 16
BRAX

"This is our first vintage. Not every wine gets better with age, but this one has."

Nolan wasn't lying. Brax had drunk a bottle of the inaugural Dionysus Estate Syrah every year since Nolan bottled it, and it was smoother now. Gentler, with notes of leather and tobacco. Damn, he missed those cigarettes he used to sneak as a teenager. There were so few pleasures left in life now. Although that would have to change, and soon.

At least he could spend an enjoyable evening with friends, some old, some new. Violet and Dawson had flown in from Canada, where Violet was wrapping up filming on her new movie. Zach and Ari had driven up from Santa Cruz, Nolan had come from the Sierra Nevada foothills, Justin had journeyed cross-country from Virginia, and Chase had materialised from fuck knew where. As predicted, Alexa hadn't shown up in person, but she'd sent a box of French cheese and made an appearance as a cartoon avatar on Chase's tablet.

That had lasted through the appetiser and part of the entrée, then she'd left, citing work pressures. Again, not a surprise. Alexa had different priorities than everyone else. If there was an emergency, she'd drop everything to help, but her job—hacking, sometimes legal and sometimes not—would always take precedence over a dinner party. Alexa wasn't a social creature. She didn't do well in crowds. At Blackstone House, she'd emerged from her basement lair to eat, and that was about all. As for venturing outside, she only did that when absolutely necessary. Alexa was also a certifiable genius. Brax had long suspected she was somewhere on the autism spectrum, Asperger's maybe, but there was no way Alexa would ever consent to being tested.

Chase was her one companion, the man who travelled everywhere with her. Brax didn't think they were romantically involved, but Chase remained tight-lipped about their relationship, and Alexa never elaborated either. In Blackstone House, she'd managed to get along with everyone most of the time, although occasionally, she would perform an act so outrageously audacious that they wanted to throttle her. Such as installing electronic door locks so secure that nobody could enter or leave the house for two days unless they climbed through a window. And hiring some psycho from the dark web to break a neighbour's arm after she saw the man slapping his teenage daughter. And stealing several million dollars from Linus Sykes, depositing it in equal portions in offshore bank accounts, and gifting one set of account numbers to each of the six other housemates present at the last dinner they'd shared. That was the last time Brax had physically seen her.

Justin swirled the red wine in his glass, sniffed, and sipped. "I'll have to take your word for that. I still don't have the first damn clue about wine."

"You should come and stay at the vineyard sometime. We have the first guest cottage finished now."

"Maybe I will if work ever lets up. Finding four days for this trip was hard enough."

"Business is going well?" Brax asked.

"Too many buyers, not enough homes. Property prices are through the roof, land prices too. Diversifying to add a line of tiny homes alongside our regular developments is paying off."

"But you're still driving the same three-hundred-year-old pickup?" Dawson asked.

"If it ain't broke, why fix it? At the moment, I'm putting most of the profits back into the business. It's a long-term plan. We can't all make millions before we're thirty, like Brax."

Brax swallowed a spoonful of raspberry soufflé. Meera had made excellent menu choices.

"Yes, well, I'll probably lose the millions before I hit thirty-one."

"I thought the sex industry was booming?" Zach said.

"It is. And it'll make Carissa a very rich woman."

"What the fuck?" Justin put everyone's expressions into words. "You're not honestly considering giving her that exorbitant divorce settlement?"

"I'm starting to believe I don't have a choice. And money isn't everything. I used to think it was, but now I know otherwise. We only get one shot at life, and I keep asking myself: do I really want to waste another five years being utterly miserable?"

Carissa wasn't going to give in; he understood that. In the past two weeks, he'd sent three charming, handsome, and very different men into various situations to tempt her. They'd even tried luring her into a bar just in case old habits died hard. She hadn't bitten. Not even a nibble.

"Is this about the woman you asked Vi to buy the jewellery for?" Dawson asked.

Since Brax was monitoring Carissa's spending habits—via Alexa—he had to assume that Carissa was doing the same with him. And where Meera was concerned, he was taking no chances.

"I can't get her out of my head."

"Wait, who is this?" Zach asked. "What have we missed?"

"Assistant number twenty-seven. You win the pool, by the way."

"This is the one who insulted your car and your dick?"

"She was having a bad day."

"Damn."

They all stared at him, and Justin shook his head, incredulous.

"You're actually serious, aren't you? You'd give up, what, half a billion bucks for a woman?"

Something like that. It wasn't half a billion in cash, of course. Roughly a quarter of the investments could be readily liquidated; others were tied up for years.

"Yes and no. Carissa would run Nyx into the ground pretty quickly. She might have an MBA, but she doesn't have the experience or the personality to carry it. The relationships with the clients, those are all mine. I could start up a rival enterprise. One thing that isn't in that fucking prenup is a non-compete clause."

It would take several years, but he'd already built one business from scratch in less than a decade. He could do it again. Losing the commodity investments would hurt—he'd had some luck with timing that would be impossible to replicate —but he didn't need hundreds of millions to be happy. These past several weeks had taught him that he only needed Meera. He'd never felt like this about a woman before. Last year, he'd been sceptical when it came to Zach's feelings for Ari, that love could trump all the lies she'd told him, but now he understood. Once you felt it, you'd do anything to keep that high.

"I'll still get a million bucks as part of the settlement," Brax continued. "And I'll push Carissa to set up a trust to cover my mother's medical care. I think she'd budge that much."

And besides, if it hadn't been for Carissa, Brax's mom might not even be in the Cardinal Center. Yes, her first trip had been very necessary—Brax's father had seen to that—but not the second.

Three decades with Vernon Dupré had left Leonora Vale with layers of psychological damage—depression, anxiety, an eating disorder—and her first suicide attempt had almost been successful. A neighbour had found her after she wouldn't answer the phone, unconscious in bed from an overdose of sleeping pills. But she'd gotten better. The doctors had cleared her to go home, home being a guest room in Brax and Carissa's New York apartment.

The relapse was partly his fault, he realised that. He'd been busy with work, and both women said everything was fine. But Brax had forgotten just how good his mom was at wearing a mask. At pretending. The second time, he'd been the one to find her. Bleeding out in the shower, scarlet trails spreading from her wrists to the drain. Only in the safety of the Cardinal Center had she admitted just how inadequate Carissa made her feel with her snide comments. That she was a failure as a mother and as a human being. The following month, Brax had moved to LA. Things had been bad with Carissa before his mother attempted to take her own life, but afterward, they'd become unbearable.

"Are you sure about this?" Dawson asked. "You barely know the woman. Have you even…?"

"No, of course not. Because that would breach the terms of the fucking agreement. In fact, Meera specifically said she wouldn't sleep with me."

"You told her about Carissa?"

"Yes."

"But you like each other?"

"I think so."

"You *think* so?"

"Well, I like her, clearly. And she hasn't called me an asshole for at least a week, so that's progress."

"Damn."

"It's only money. I can make more money, but if Carissa's poison keeps running through my veins, I'll have no life at all."

"He does have a point," Zach said. "And the sooner he cuts his losses, the more time he'll have left to enjoy everything the world has to offer."

But Justin was shaking his head. "Don't do anything hasty."

"Meera might not be the one," Nolan put in. "But we know Carissa definitely isn't either, so Brax has to get away from her."

"Couldn't you negotiate a better settlement?" Ari suggested.

"Nothing like fifty-fifty. Carissa knows she can hold out longer than me. And unlike yours truly, she wouldn't be able to start over. She might be competent at setting up an accounting system and running an admin team, but she doesn't have an entrepreneurial spirit or the ability to lead. And although she can spot a Gucci purse at a hundred yards, she wouldn't know a good investment opportunity if it bit her on the ass."

And while she waited, while she bided her time, Brax was only making more money for her. As part owner of Dunnvale Holdings, she had veto power over any salary increases, so he couldn't drain cash from the business that way, and for every dividend he took, she got one too because they owned the same class of shares. He worked, she lunched. He networked, she shopped. He dealt with any issues that cropped up in the clubs, she relaxed at the spa.

And yes, in his blacker moments, he'd even considered going down Alexa's dark-web route, but knowing his luck, he'd hire an undercover FBI agent, and he couldn't enjoy life from jail either.

Violet reached across the table and squeezed his hand. "I think that if you truly love this woman, then you should tell her how you feel, and if she feels the same, you should take the plunge. Love beats everything."

"But leave it a few more weeks," Justin added. "You need to be certain."

They were right. They were all right. Brax had a lot to think about before he made the biggest decision of his life.

CHAPTER 17
THE ASSISTANT

I felt him before I saw him. A presence behind me as I climbed out of my car and speed-walked to my shared apartment. You know that odd prickle you get when you're being watched? Logic told me to turn around, to check for danger, but what you can't see won't hurt you, right? My walk became a run—screw decorum—and I sprinted for the door of my building. I didn't live in a great area. Being mugged was a very real possibility, especially now that I was wearing jewellery worth thousands.

I'd considered leaving Mr. Vale's necklace and earrings in my apartment, but although I had a lock on my bedroom door, I didn't entirely trust my housemates. And even if they were honest, our apartment was on the ground floor and my window didn't close properly. Keeping the gifts in my desk drawer was an option, but what if I had to run on short notice? My oversized purse held emergency supplies—Meera's debit card and driver's licence, my phone, a small amount of cash, clean underwear and a change of clothes, shower gel, a toothbrush—plus I'd sewn my own passport into the lining. I could pawn the jewellery if necessary.

When I reached the building, I risked a look around,

which was dumb because the lock on the exterior door was broken, so if someone *was* following me, they could easily come inside. But the only man in sight was in a black car on the other side of the street, and when I focused on him, he looked away.

A chill ran through me.

Was it all some big coincidence? Was he truly watching me? Or did I just have an overactive imagination? Could he be a cop waiting for a drug deal to happen? Or a drug dealer waiting for a customer? Or had my father finally found me?

Inside, I considered my options. Should I move on tonight? Climb into my car and keep driving until I found a new hiding place? I'd always known this might happen, planned for it, but life would become infinitely more difficult if Meera's identity was compromised.

An hour later, I peeped outside, and he was still there. Just sitting in his car, checking his phone. Was he contacting my family? Telling them that the hunter had spotted his prey? How had he found me?

No, no, he *couldn't* have found me. I'd been so careful. Indali Vadera was gone, and I'd used Meera's name for everything.

But if the car was still there in the morning, I'd climb out of the window and vanish again.

I barely slept that night.

In the morning, the car was gone.

"Here, have this." Mr. Vale used one elegant forefinger to push his coffee across the desk toward me on Monday morning. "You look as if you need it more than I do."

"Really, I'm—" Another yawn came before I could stop it,

and Mr. Vale folded his arms in a "see, I'm right" gesture. "Thank you."

I took a sip, and the beverage was a little on the cool side, but he hadn't complained once since his confession about Carissa Dunn two weeks ago. Now we only spoke with either a camera or a witness watching over us, and I'd actually begun to enjoy my job. It wasn't the emergency department, but it was a million times better than being chained to Karam's kitchen sink.

I'd also begun wearing make-up again. If video of me was going to be used in a court case, I at least wanted to look pretty while I gave Mr. Vale's wife the metaphorical finger.

"Are you okay?" he asked.

"Just tired, that's all."

"Busy weekend?"

On Saturday, I'd done the grocery shopping, and yesterday, I'd visited the laundromat and then gone out to catch a movie by myself because the occupant of the apartment next door was using power tools and I couldn't hear myself think. *Rules of Play* had just won an award, so the theatre put on a special showing with themed snacks, which had seemed like a good deal, but I hadn't expected the movie to be quite so scary. I'd jumped right alongside Violet Miller and spilled most of my popcorn, and maybe the residual fear was why I'd been so nervous about that man in the car last night?

Or maybe not.

It wasn't as if I could call the cops, was it?

While my big brother, Raj, had followed my father into the family business, my younger brother had joined the Springfield PD. Not only would I be on the missing persons list, but Vimal would also be monitoring every available channel for any sign of me. If I popped up on his radar, then he and Raj would be dispatched to bring me home.

This morning, I'd packed extra clothes into a backpack

and put them in the trunk of my car. If the watcher was there again this evening, I'd keep on driving.

"I didn't sleep very well last night."

"Is something worrying you?"

Everything was worrying me. The stranger outside my apartment, Meera's relationship difficulties, the thought that this new life I was building could fall apart in a heartbeat.

The fear that I might have to leave and never see this man again.

In hindsight, Mr. Vale had been absolutely right. Things had been much easier when there was space between us.

"No?"

"Liar."

His tone was mild, but his assertion was confident. He knew I wasn't being truthful with him.

"It's probably nothing. There was a man in a car outside my apartment last night, and it felt like he was watching me. But I went to see a horror movie yesterday evening, so I was probably overreacting, and—"

Mr. Vale already had the desk phone cradled against his shoulder, his mouth set in a hard line as he stabbed at a button. *Speed dial one.*

"Carissa, do you have a man monitoring Meera?"

I couldn't hear the response, but anger clouded those blue eyes of his, and they turned a shade darker.

"Was he outside her apartment last night?"

A pause.

"Stop wasting my money and call him off. He's scaring her."

Mr. Vale slammed the phone down and took two deep breaths, then forced a smile. I knew it was forced because he couldn't hide the turbulence in his gaze.

"If it happens again, tell me right away. Carissa's behaviour is unacceptable."

She'd sent the man? Boy, this divorce really was acrimonious.

"I will."

"The work can wait. Take a nap on your couch or ask housekeeping to prepare a room on the second floor."

"No, no, that's not necessary." I held up his mug, hating the way my hand trembled as adrenaline left my body. *My father hasn't found me.* "This is enough."

"Make sure you take a lunch break."

Mr. Vale's phone rang, and his work day began. I backed out of the office, still exhausted but limp with relief. Life could carry on as normal.

But not for long.

The call came the next morning, before I'd even made Mr. Vale's coffee. A New York number flashed up on the screen. I hated receiving calls from New York because Carissa Dunn lived there and her presence tainted the whole city in my eyes, but there was a branch of Nyx in NYC, the second one Mr. Vale had opened, and occasionally the manager would call to request that I schedule a Zoom chat or ask me to pass on a message. Another second, and I recognised the digits.

"Good morning, Jarrod. Actually, it's already afternoon on the East Coast, isn't it?"

"Is Brax there?"

"He's with somebody right now." A woman. A potential new basement girl. Teresa was acting as chaperone for Carissa's benefit. "An early meeting."

"Can you interrupt? I need to speak with him urgently. There's… Well, there's been a fire. Not a big one, and the fire department put it out, but there's water everywhere."

"Was anybody injured?"

"Everyone's fine, but we're gonna have a lot of unhappy clients."

"I'll get Mr. Vale right away."

But how? He was in The Dark, and I didn't go into The Dark.

First, I tried his phone, just in case there was a signal down there, but it rang on his desk—he was right, the soundproofing between our offices really wasn't that good.

There would be somebody downstairs who could help me, wouldn't there? The front-of-house staff didn't arrive until twelve, but maybe Teresa... No, Teresa was with Mr. Vale. Did the housekeeping staff go into The Dark?

The elevator wasn't on the third floor, so rather than waiting, I ran down the stairs, cursing the fact that I'd begun wearing heels again. The first floor was empty apart from the kitchen staff, and they didn't venture downstairs either. Dammit, I'd have to go myself. There wouldn't be clients present at this time, so what harm would it do?

If I'd known the answer, I'd have sprinted away along the street instead of heaving open the heavy door to the basement.

The first thing that struck me was the near silence as the door closed behind me. Soundproofing wasn't a concern down here. As I descended the stairs, my footsteps muffled by thick carpet the colour of deoxygenated blood, I heard the faint strains of classical music, heavy on the strings. Four beats, four beats, four beats. A dirty tango. The lights were dim, and it felt as if I were walking through a tunnel. Perhaps that was intentional? The stairs turned, and I saw a bar ahead of me, bottles of spirits on glass shelves, a mirror behind. An ornate metal arch spanned the polished wooden counter, reminiscent of the windows outside, and a row of empty velvet stools stood sentry in front. The colour theme was red and black, dark and moody. Sumptuous. Dramatic. Curved leather banquettes wrapped around tables for two, four, six, and this really wasn't so bad. Sexy chic. I'd been imagining a dungeon with ropes and chains and—

A gasp escaped as I caught sight of the stage at the far end of the room. A woman stood there, as tall and slender as a supermodel, her pale skin smooth, her small breasts high and firm. She wore nothing but spike heels, leather panties, and an ornate Venetian mask, and when she turned to stare at me, her expression was one of mild confusion for a second before her scarlet lips pursed into a hard smile. The man beside her didn't look up. That would have been difficult, seeing as he was tied to some kind of leather bench with his ass in the air. And while I'd come across plenty of interesting things in men's anuses during my rotation in the emergency room, I'd never seen a jewelled butt plug attached to a set of handcuffs before.

Mr. Vale was sitting on a velvet chair, legs crossed at the ankles, his arms folded as he studied the scene critically with Teresa at his side. I began backing away, horrified. Horrified at invading these people's privacy. Horrified at the ache between my legs. Horrified at being caught watching. But it was too late. My boss turned around, and he didn't look happy in the slightest.

"Excuse me for a moment."

He crossed the room in six long strides, wrapped an arm around my waist, and half carried me out to the stairs.

"What the fuck are you doing here, Meera?" he hissed.

"I-I-I'm sorry. I didn't mean… There's a problem in New York."

"What problem?"

"A fire. Everyone's okay, but the fire department… Water damage…"

"Shit." Mr. Vale scrubbed a hand through his dark hair. "Cancel the rest of today's meetings and book us plane tickets while I finish up here. A car to the airport too."

"Okay, I'll—" Wait a second. "Us?"

"All hands on deck, Meera." He smiled grimly. "Don't worry about packing. You can buy clothes in New York."

I didn't want to go. I didn't want to travel with Mr. Vale. I didn't want to risk running into the Wicked Witch of the East Coast. And I needed time to process what I'd just seen.

But this was my job.

I had to go.

"Yes, Mr. Vale."

CHAPTER 18
BRAX

As if Brax's life wasn't complicated enough right now…

Preliminary indications were that one of the clothes dryers had malfunctioned, and a pile of bedsheets had caught fire. Although the sprinkler system did its job, an overzealous passer-by had called the fire department when they saw smoke, and the fire crew had wanted to be absolutely certain the blaze was extinguished. The laundry room was out of commission, the kitchen had smoke damage, and just for good measure, water had gone through the floor and damaged some of the rooms downstairs.

And that wasn't even the worst part of Brax's day.

No, that had come when he turned to see Meera watching Roxanne and Michael, her expression a mix of shock and horror.

He needed to speak with her about it, to make sure she understood that they were only doing their jobs, that everything was consensual, but she was steadfastly refusing to look at him as she studied the airline website. And when he moved closer, she flinched.

Fuck.

"What are you doing?"

"Booking flights, as you asked."

"Why is one ticket business class and the other economy? Are they short of seats?"

"I just thought—"

Hell, she really did have a low opinion of herself, didn't she?

"Book two seats in business, Meera."

"Okay." She swallowed and clicked with the mouse. "There are only two left, and they're next to each other. Is that all right?"

No. "Yes."

At least if there were no more seats, Carissa couldn't have a spy hop onto the plane alongside them, but spending six hours sitting next to Meera promised to be torture.

"The car will be here in twenty minutes."

"Good. Pack our laptops, and don't forget the chargers. I need to brief the staff here before we leave."

Meera was already in the limo when Brax jogged out of the front door five minutes late. She'd carefully placed a backpack, her purse, and both laptop bags on the back seat between them, and his heart sank. The Dark thing had really upset her, hadn't it?

"You have everything?" he asked.

A nod.

He had to do it. He had to roll up the privacy screen and talk to her. If the driver was one of Carissa's spies, Brax was fucked, but the risk was worth taking, the odds low. When his previous driver had retired, instead of hiring a replacement, he'd contracted with a service Dawson had recommended that would provide security-trained drivers "as required."

There was no guarantee they'd send the same person each time, and that suited Brax just fine.

Meera didn't say a word as the screen closed.

And for once in his life, Brax didn't know where to start.

The silence stretched out, an uncomfortable, tangible thing that wrapped its fingers around his throat and squeezed. Kind of like Roxanne had done to Michael earlier, but minus the leather and other accessories.

"I'm sorry," she whispered finally.

He'd noticed that she apologised a lot. It was almost a default setting. What had happened in her past to make her that way?

"What are you sorry for, Meera?"

"That I went into the basement. That I saw...that."

"It made you uncomfortable."

"Yes."

"Which part made you uncomfortable?"

"Do we have to talk about this?"

"Yes, we do."

"Now you're making me even more uncomfortable."

"That's not my wish. But I do want to understand you. Because..." Brax tried without success to swallow the lump in his throat. "Because I don't want to lose you."

"I...I don't want to quit." That wasn't entirely what he'd meant, but okay. "I guess... I guess I was embarrassed for the people on the stage. I walked in on a private moment, and they were in such a vulnerable position. And also I was afraid that you'd be angry with me for interrupting you in a place where you'd told me not to go."

At least she was talking now, even if her concerns were ungrounded.

"I wasn't angry. The reason I told you to avoid The Dark was that I wanted to protect you."

"Protect me?"

"You're a candle in the wind, Meera, and The Dark is a

hurricane." At least she hadn't run from the building screaming. "You did the right thing when you came downstairs to fetch me."

"I should apologise to those people."

"There's no need. Roxanne is a dominatrix. Part of her role involves performing for a crowd. If she'd been upset by your presence, she wouldn't have been suitable for the role she was applying for, and I wouldn't have hired her. As for Michael, he gets off on being humiliated in front of an audience."

"He does? That's..." Meera crinkled her dainty nose. "That's weird."

"People have different sexual preferences. To Michael, quiet sex in bed with the TV on to cover up the noise while two kids sleep in the next room is like watching paint dry, and yet half of Americans find that a perfectly pleasurable experience. And for maybe half of that fifty percent, vanilla sex is their number-one choice. But the other half? They enjoy the vanilla because they've never tried strawberry or chocolate or banana peanut butter chip. In The Dark, they can try anything they desire, and they can keep tasting new flavours until they decide on a favourite." He studied her for a moment, the quickened breathing, the slightly parted, pink-painted lips, and willed his dick to behave. "I'm guessing you haven't tried many flavours?"

Slowly, she shook her head. "Not even vanilla."

Holy fuck. "Not even a taste?"

It came out as a whisper. "No."

She'd spent five years in college. Had she locked herself in a dorm room the whole time? Brax had spent his college years sampling every concoction imaginable. Mint choc chip, butter pecan, and passion fruit sorbet all in one bowl? You bet. And when he'd finished with the ice cream, he'd moved on to the drinks menu. Sex on the Beach, Porn Star Martini, Slippery Nipple, Screaming Orgasm. But he'd never tried a virgin cocktail before.

A situation he very much wanted to rectify.

He might even have told her that if she hadn't spoken first.

"What's your favourite flavour?" she asked.

Choices, choices, so many choices. Smooth caramel, perhaps? He loved to watch a woman writhe languidly underneath him, filthy words dripping from her lips. Or wild berries? Outdoor sex had always been enjoyable. The moon, the stars, the added risk that they could be caught. Of course, that had all ended on his honeymoon with Carissa. While on safari in Kenya, he'd persuaded her to climb up onto the roof of the minibus for a little nighttime entertainment, and it turned out that their audience was a lion. They'd been stuck up there for hours. Brax lay back to enjoy the view, but Carissa had spent the night complaining. That she was cold, that she was bored, that his cum was running down her leg. After that, she'd become a bedroom-only woman.

Would Meera be the adventurous type?

Would she take risks?

Right now, it was a risk for Brax just to have a private conversation with a woman.

"Sorry, I'm so sorry," she said. "I shouldn't have asked that. What was I thinking?"

She covered her face with a hand, but Brax gently lifted it away. And no, he didn't let go as quickly as he should have.

"What's my favourite? I'm a gentleman. My partner gets to choose."

CHAPTER 19
THE ASSISTANT

Although Meera was a year younger than me, and I used to wear my hair much longer, we looked so similar that people at college had called us twins. Even *we* had gotten suspicious, but a DNA test revealed the truth. We weren't related, not even distantly; we were just doppelgangers. Think I'm joking? One day when I wore my hair in a bun, Meera's ex-boyfriend had snuck up and kissed me full on the mouth before he realised his mistake. The kiss was followed by red faces, a thousand apologies, and a promise never to speak of the incident again. And we didn't. Meera and I borrowed each other's clothes, laughed off the "seeing double" comments, and became the best of friends.

Plus there was the cross-race effect. I'd studied it briefly during psych classes. It had been scientifically proven that people recognised faces within their own racial group more easily. People of one ethnicity found it harder to notice subtle variations in skin tone, in lip size, in brow strength when it came to those with a different heritage, as well as being slower to recognise and interpret emotions. The phenomenon was also linked to implicit racial bias.

And I intended to use it to my advantage.

When we got to the airport, I made sure I picked a security line staffed by white people, and as predicted, they glanced at me, glanced at Meera's US driver's licence, made me remove half of my clothing and poked suspiciously through my carry-on, then waved me past.

To where Mr. Vale was waiting.

He was a gentleman, he said.

He was a liar.

My new boss was a wolf in a French-blue made-to-measure suit.

And I was Little Red Riding Hood, just waiting to be eaten.

But at least it would be a pleasurable death.

His hand touched mine as he took my bag without asking, and I felt the same rush of warmth I'd experienced in the car. He, of course, was totally unaffected. In return, he passed me his black Amex card.

"You have forty minutes to shop. I need to make some calls."

"What do you want me to purchase?"

"You're not shopping for me, Meera. You're shopping for yourself."

He strode off before I could ask for clarification on what exactly he expected me to buy. Toiletries? A snack? He'd told me not to worry about packing, but I'd left my "running away" bag in my trunk last night, so I had most of what I needed. But I could do with an extra bottle of shampoo, and we'd both skipped breakfast. I found a drugstore, then picked up bottled water and pastries in case we got delayed at the gate. Still fifteen minutes left, and I had no idea where Mr. Vale had gone, so I settled in to window-shop the row of boutiques. Once, I'd have been inside, buying those sparkly Louboutins or the gorgeous red Valentino purse with the gold studs, but now I was reduced to browsing. And in truth, I preferred it this way. All the designer accessories in the world couldn't have made me happy in Massachusetts. In LA, I was still constantly on edge, waiting for my new life to fall apart, but at least I wasn't so miserable anymore.

"You have five minutes left."

I jumped out of my skin.

"You did that on purpose."

Mr. Vale was unrepentant. "Did what?"

"Crept up behind me."

His playful grin made me smile too. Who knew he had a sense of humour? His expression quickly grew serious again, but I knew what I'd seen.

"Purse shopping?" he asked.

"Oh, no. Just looking."

"You like the red one?"

"Who wouldn't?"

"Buy it."

"No, no, it's far too expensive. And I already have a purse, see?"

"Are you disobeying a direct order, Miss Adams?"

"Uh…"

He leaned in close, so close that his lips brushed my ear. I wasn't prepared for the flood of heat between my legs, or for my knees to buckle the way they did.

"Buy the purse, Meera, and the shoes. Quickly. Then meet me at the gate."

Oh. My. Gosh.

The New York branch of Nyx occupied a row of four converted brownstones in the Upper East Side. From the outside, there was no hint as to what might lie within, just a discreet entrance flanked by two topiary bay trees and a small brass plaque with a number on it. The real estate alone must have been worth millions.

But inside, what a mess. The laundry room was blackened with soot, and the twisted, melted hulk of the faulty machine gaped in a silent scream. The kitchen next door was unusable, the walls stained, the air thick with the stink of smoke. A professional cleaning crew was on the way, an electrician too, but their work would take several days.

Downstairs in the basement, temporary lights illuminated the three flooded rooms. Dirty water had run through the ceiling ducts and poured onto the soft furnishings. Carpet squelched underfoot.

"At least it only hit three of the private rooms." Jarrod poked at a soggy mattress. "The bar escaped unscathed."

Mr. Vale surveyed the damage. He seemed remarkably calm, considering. I gawked at the remains of the furnishings themselves—the huge wooden X screwed to one wall with a leather cuff dangling from each arm, the weird swing hanging from the ceiling, the squat little seat that looked a bit like the commode chairs we used in the hospital but undoubtedly wasn't. I'd have to google that one.

Or perhaps not.

"We need to get everything dried out," Mr. Vale said.

"I've hired ten dehumidifiers. They'll be here"—Jarrod checked his watch—"in less than an hour. The guy's dropping them off this evening as a favour."

"And the dumpsters?"

"They're arriving tomorrow morning."

"How are the clients?"

"Okay, for the most part. One or two are unhappy. We've rerouted Congressman—" Jarrod glanced at me and raised an eyebrow, checking whether it was okay to mention names.

"It's fine," Mr. Vale told him.

"We've rerouted Congressman McCall to Virginia, and Bernie Mathis to Boston." There was a Boston branch? I'd have to avoid that one. "Ted Cutter's going to stay in LA and use the facilities there."

"What did you offer the others?"

"Complimentary dinner to everyone, a free visit for the more disgruntled. Think we'll be up and running by next week?"

"I hope so. Justin promised to send half a dozen guys from Norquist Construction to help out. They'll be here in the morning, and then we'll just need to arrange the materials and replace the furniture. Meera can help with that if you give her a list of what we need. She'll also require a room for the night."

"Here?"

"Yes."

"And you?"

"I'll stay at home with Carissa, but I'll be back early."

Mr. Vale planned to stay with Carissa? The thought shouldn't have made me feel nauseated, but it did. And worse, I knew why he had to go: because of me. If I was here, he couldn't be. I almost offered to stay in a hotel, but I stopped myself in the nick of time. Jarrod might not know about the problems between the Vales, and I wasn't going to spill the secret.

"Should I pick up breakfast for everyone in the morning?" I offered instead. "I mean, with the kitchen being out of use."

Mr. Vale flashed me a tight little smile. "Thank you, Meera. We'd appreciate it."

There she was. The dragon herself.

Carissa Dunn was a slender blonde, two inches taller than me with the heels she was wearing, two inches shorter without. Stylish and pretty in a polished way, but I already knew her beauty only went skin deep. What was she doing here? She picked her way across the wreckage of the laundry room to where I was holding a flashlight for the electrician. Mr. Vale had said it was all hands on deck, help where I could. So there I was—balanced on a stool while the man peered at melted wire. Thank goodness I'd worn pants and ballet pumps today.

Mr. Vale trailed behind Carissa, his expression black. Was that because of her? Or due to the extent of the repairs that were required?

"Why didn't someone put the fire out sooner?" she asked. "We have fire extinguishers, don't we?"

"It probably took hold inside the machine, my darling."

"Well, have you tried complaining to the manufacturer? They should be paying for this, not us."

"I'll raise it with them in due course. Our priority is to get the club up and running again."

"Why aren't there more people here? Everything's filthy."

"Because we're making sure the place is safe first."

She gave the electrician a once-over and clearly didn't like what she saw. Her nose wrinkled, and her mouth flattened in disgust. He must have picked up on the vibes because he shinned down the ladder, muttered an excuse, and practically ran out of the room. Then she turned her attention to me.

"And you must be Meena?"

"Meera."

"Lovely. I've heard all about you."

From who? I was certain Mr. Vale hadn't told her a thing. Which meant he'd been right—spies were reporting our every move back to her.

"Really? I think I saw your name on some paperwork. You're Clarissa, right?"

Behind her, Mr. Vale smirked.

"*Carissa.* No L."

"Oh, I'm so sorry." For once, I absolutely wasn't. "Are you here to help with the clean-up?"

"What? Good heavens, no. I'm on my way to brunch. But let me make it up to you this evening. We can all go out for dinner."

Mr. Vale's eyes widened. He clearly hadn't been expecting this.

"That won't be necessary, Carissa," he said.

"Oh, don't be silly. You both have to eat. I'll make reservations at Le Jardin for eight o'clock. Sophie can join us too."

"I think we were planning to work late," I tried.

"Don't let this slave driver push you around." She elbowed Mr. Vale in the side, and he glared at her. "There's a dress code. Wear something nice." Carissa turned on her heel and gave a little finger wave as she headed for the door. "See you later."

Mr. Vale sagged against the dirty wall and groaned. "It's fine. We just won't go. And don't ask why I married her, because right now, I couldn't tell you. I didn't even do drugs in college."

A clatter came from the hallway outside.

"Will someone move this damn bucket!"

"Sorry, Ms. Dunn."

Oops.

"If we don't go, won't she think we have something to hide?"

"Probably. But I'm not putting you through that."

"Who's Sophie?"

"Her assistant."

I didn't want to go, not remotely, but I also hated the thought of putting the spotlight on myself through our absence. And although I couldn't tell Mr. Vale, I'd dealt with a hundred Carissa Dunns back in Massachusetts. Every one of my father's friends seemed to be married to either a gold-digging bitch or a meek little clone of my mother. There was no in-between. Some of the women were only a few years older than me, and they didn't much care for a girl who went to Harvard. Meera said they felt threatened.

"I know it might not always seem like it, but I'm stronger than I look."

Carissa, I could cope with; it was Mr. Vale who left me off kilter.

"I'm beginning to realise that."

"So we'll go to Le Jardin and prove I'm nothing but a PA. That the prenup won't be broken by me. I took this job for the steady paycheck, not sexual favours from the boss."

"Am I allowed to be disappointed by that?"

I laughed at the joke.

Mr. Vale didn't.

My phone buzzed in my pocket, and I checked the messages. "The construction crew just arrived. Let's start work."

CHAPTER 20
BRAX

W hat the hell was Carissa playing at?

Actually, scratch that question. Brax knew exactly what she was doing. She wanted to get close to Meera, close enough to assess the likelihood of Brax slipping up and breaching the prenup. She'd played this game twice before, with assistants number eight and seventeen, both of whom had been young, blonde, and beautiful, everything Carissa felt threatened by. Number eight had been dumb as a box of dildos, vapid enough that Carissa eliminated her as a prospective fuck buddy for her husband. She knew Brax got turned off by stupidity. As for seventeen, Carissa had made a proposal, the girl had accepted, and Brax had fired her the next day. Thank goodness his investigator had overheard the conversation.

But Meera wasn't blonde, and based on his history, not Brax's type at all. So why this dinner? What did Carissa know?

The question preyed on his mind the whole day.

Le Jardin des Délices Terrestres, known colloquially as Le Jardin, was an esoteric vegetarian French restaurant—an oxymoron if there ever was one—and Carissa's current favourite if her credit card statement was any indication. She'd stopped eating meat five years ago, or six if one didn't count the last time she'd sucked cock.

"A vegetarian French restaurant?" Meera asked as they paused outside, steeling themselves. "What does it serve? Bread?"

That her reaction should be exactly the same as his had been the first time Carissa brought him here made Brax chuckle.

"Based on past experience, it's a bunch of dishes pretending to be something they're not. 'Escargots' made from mushrooms. 'Salmon' made from carrots. 'Steak' made from soy protein."

"I can see why Clarissa likes it, then."

"It's Carissa," he corrected out of habit. She hated that extra L.

"Yes, I know that. She pretends to be a loving wife and successful businesswoman when in reality, she's neither."

Brax was seeing a different side to Meera tonight. A sharper side, and he liked it. He held the door open and motioned her through.

"Let's get this over with."

"Le Jardin des Délices Terrestres," she murmured as she brushed past. "The Garden of Earthly Delights. Our very own Hieronymus Bosch horror story."

At least they hadn't hung a replica of the eponymous painting on the wall. That would have put anyone off their dinner, and Carissa did a good enough job of that on her own. She'd already arrived with Sophie, the copper-haired, elfin assistant she'd hired midway through last year. While Meera had a degree from Harvard, Sophie held qualifications in massage, hairdressing, and nail art. Nothing wrong with that, but they were hardly relevant to the global business empire Carissa claimed that she helped to run.

Carissa's hair was perfect, as usual, and her nails had

French tips today. One of Meera's nails was chipped, and until an hour ago, they'd been covered in paint. She'd twisted her hair into a messy bun and pinned it into place with a jewelled nipple clamp she'd found in the basement. Brax wasn't certain she knew what it was, and he wasn't about to tell her. He got a kick out of it. Of course, he'd prefer she used it for its intended purpose, but beggars couldn't be choosers.

Meera was wearing the jewellery he'd had Violet buy for her, the necklace and the earrings, plus the shoes and purse she'd picked up at the airport. If Brax couldn't touch her, then using gifts as a proxy was the alternative. A poor substitute, but he had no other option. She'd teamed the accessories with a plain black knee-length shift dress, and she'd never looked more magnificent.

Brax kissed Sophie on the cheek, then did the same to Carissa. Had to keep up appearances. Meera took a seat between Brax and Sophie, which left her directly opposite Carissa at the round table. At least if tonight turned into a bloodbath, Brax was close enough to stick a fork in his wife's thigh.

"How lovely that you could join us tonight," Carissa said to Meera.

"It's a pleasure," she lied.

"Where are you from, Meena?" Sophie asked.

"Massachusetts."

"No, I mean before that. Like, are you Indian?"

For fuck's sake. Had Carissa schooled her assistant in the art of microaggression, or did it come naturally?

"I was born and raised in the United States of America." Meera smiled, but not with her usual sweetness. "I love your hair. Did you know that redheads originated in Central Asia?"

"Uh, no?"

"The colour is down to a mutation on the MC1R gene.

Instead of protection from the sun, you got freckles and those stunning copper locks."

"Really?"

"Sometimes our flaws make us beautiful."

Sophie decided to keep her mouth shut at that point. A wise decision. But Carissa just had to carry on.

"Have you been to this restaurant before?" she asked Meera.

"No."

"I'm always trying to get Braxton to eat less meat. We all have to play our part in helping the environment."

"Yes, absolutely. So we'd better avoid the avocados. Did you know that a single avocado takes between thirty and sixty gallons of water to grow? And when they're cultivated in dry places like Chile, that leads to illegal extraction of water from rivers and damages the local ecosystem." Meera ran her finger down the menu. "We shouldn't have the lettuce either—that's another thirsty plant. The raspberries and blueberries are also a 'no.' At this time of year, they've been flown in from overseas, so they'll have a huge carbon footprint. Mushrooms require a considerable amount of energy to produce the warm temperatures they thrive in, plus they emit carbon dioxide. Cocoa contributes to deforestation, and as for cashews? Oh, dear. Not only are they a low-yield crop, but their hard shells contain a caustic oil that can burn the skin. If that leaks into the environment during processing, well, that's a bad thing. I'm going to have the Coquilles Saint-Jacques. How about you?"

"Did you know Meera has a degree in environmental science from Harvard?" Brax asked.

If Carissa did know, she'd clearly forgotten. Her lips pressed together in a thin line, and he knew she was annoyed. Good. She was the one who'd suggested this stupid dinner. He could have been eating takeout and painting another wall right now.

"I'll have the vegan beefsteak."

"I guess it's your choice, but do you know how many kilowatts go into processing mycoprotein? The fungus also feeds on sugar, which requires fertiliser to grow."

When the waiter came, Carissa ordered Coquilles Saint-Jacques in a terrible French accent. A long time had passed since Brax had seen her on the back foot, and it was a joy to behold. The waiter's smirk when Carissa told him he had a lovely ass instead of thanking him very much was the frosting on the cake. She always got the pronunciation of "*beaucoup*" and "*beau cul*" confused.

And then Meera, his beautiful Meera, surprised him again, but in a good way.

"*Ah, bonsoir. Je voudrais la Coquilles Saint-Jacques accompagnée de légumes, s'il vous plaît.*"

Her accent was perfect, her delivery flawless. She spoke French? The waiter gave her a warm smile as he noted down the order.

"*Vous parlez français?*" Brax asked Meera after the waiter had taken his order. "*Tu ne l'as jamais mentionné.*"

"*J'ai passé six mois à Paris dans le cadre d'un programme lycée 'études à l'étranger'. Et vous?*"

She'd spent six months in Paris? Brax had never participated in a "study abroad" programme, but he was a quarter French and fluent in the language, thanks to his paternal *grand-père*. That *bâtard* had refused to speak English to his young grandson, so Brax had been left with no choice but to learn. Carissa, on the other hand, could manage restaurant French and shopping French—badly—but that was all.

"*Je suis un quart français.*" And Carissa was getting more and more peeved because she couldn't understand the conversation. "*Ne vous inquiétez pas pour ma femme. Elle fait just semblant de parler français.*"

"*Ah, c'est pourquoi elle a complimenté l'arrière du serveur.*"

Brax barely kept the smile off his face. This woman was on his wavelength in a way he'd never felt before. He loved the new, feisty Meera. Unfortunately. If time travel existed, he'd sell his soul to turn back the clock and tear up that fucking prenup.

Finally, Carissa gave in. "What are you saying to her?"

"I'm just complimenting her menu choices. The Coquilles Saint-Jacques looks delicious."

Carissa had a face like thunder for the rest of the meal. Meera bested her in every verbal jousting match, and when she gave his bitch of a wife a faux hug at the end and said, "*Merci*, Clarissa, dinner was wonderful," he could have kissed her.

No, really.

Brax was in a colossal amount of trouble.

CHAPTER 21
THE ASSISTANT

I hadn't expected Mr. Vale to be quite so hands-on with the renovations, but there he was, sitting on the floor in a pair of faded jeans, repainting a baseboard. I put down the bag I was holding and took a moment to study him. He looked younger in casual clothes. The suit added five years.

"Did you get them?" he asked.

"I got them."

Several pieces of art had been ruined by the flood, erotic poses drawn in black ink. The artist lived in New York, and she'd spent the past four days recreating what had been lost. I'd just travelled across the city to collect them. The carpet fitters were due at two p.m., and then we'd need to put the furniture back. Upstairs, the kitchen was back in action, the refrigerators had been restocked, and the laundry was being sent to a service until the new washers and dryers arrived. The faulty dryer was back with the manufacturer for investigation.

"What do you think?" Mr. Vale asked. "Did you look?"

I'd looked. The drawings were *not* safe for work, unless you happened to work in a sex club. A woman being fucked from behind while a man wrapped his hand around her throat, a naked woman cuffed to a cross, a man wearing a collar and leash... I'd always been taught that sex was shameful, but now I knew differently. Everyone I met at Nyx was happy to be there. There was no shame in pleasure among consenting adults.

"I think they're beautiful."

The artist, a sweet sixty-something lady named Bettina who'd converted one room of her apartment into a studio, had managed to capture emotions on paper. Passion, lust, vulnerability. I knew that because, for the first time in my life, I was starting to feel those things too.

But for the wrong man.

An unattainable man.

He stood, stretched, and took the package from me, handling it with the care it deserved. The T-shirt he wore today was tight, showing off muscles normally hidden beneath a dark jacket. I knew he went to the gym every morning before work, and all that exercise had certainly paid off. The man had abs. I'd dreamed about him these past few nights, while I lay in a luxurious room upstairs and he headed home to his wife. Did they share a bed? He hadn't said either way, but I couldn't see it. Watching them together at dinner on Wednesday evening, it had been clear they detested each other. And now that I'd met Carissa, it was equally clear that money couldn't buy class. Their marriage showed that even with the freedom to pick your own suitor, the process could sometimes go very, very wrong.

Mr. Vale looked at the drawings one by one and nodded. "They're just as good as the originals."

"Do you have much more to do here?"

"Fifteen more minutes on the painting, and then I'll hang these. Don't worry; I'll be finished before the carpet fitters arrive."

"How did you become the king of DIY? Did they run classes at Georgetown?"

"No, but I spent my final two years there renovating an old house."

"As a job?"

"Not exactly. As long as we helped out, the owner gave us a good deal on the rent. I didn't have much cash in those days."

"Really? I always assumed you came from money."

"I did." He gave a rueful smile. "But things were difficult with my family."

Just for a second, I saw it. The trauma he tried to hide. Had he turned his back on his father the same way I had? He still cared for his mother; all the gifts, the calls, the visits told me that much. In so many ways, Mr. Vale felt like a kindred spirit, and I wished I could tell him everything, ask his advice, but I had to maintain a respectable distance between us. Plus I didn't want to burden him. He had enough on his mind with Carissa.

"I'm so sorry."

"It's all in the past."

But was it? Whatever had happened, it obviously still bothered him. And if he'd been fragile mentally back then, it might explain his involvement with Carissa. She was just the type of woman to take advantage that way.

I tried a smile, because what else could I do? "Well, if you ever need a second career, people would line up to hire you as a decorator."

"It might come to that."

I laughed, but he didn't. And as I curled up in bed that night, I recalled the tortured look on his face. Mr. Vale had a secret: he wasn't as strong as he liked to make out. And as his assistant, I wasn't about to let anyone exploit that weakness.

Including myself.

Sunday morning found us back at the airport. The crisis was over, and the New York branch of Nyx would reopen tomorrow. It was time to go home.

The trip had shown me different sides of Mr. Vale—the down-to-earth man who'd muck in to help with repairs, the reluctant husband who put on a mask for the world, the asshole with a wicked sense of humour.

When I'd finally given in yesterday and asked what the potty chair was for, he'd said it was a sample, and what did I think of the idea of a themed crèche? Only when I appeared suitably shocked did he crack a smile.

I shoved him before I could stop myself. "You jackass."

"You actually thought I was serious? We have rules here: no kids, no animals. Unless you count the leather sheep in room three."

"A leather sheep? Is this another joke?"

"No."

"It has to be."

"A very special guest requested it. Go take a look if you want to."

He wasn't kidding. Sheesh. Mr. Vale had let me meander around in the basement freely on our visit, so perhaps he'd decided I no longer needed protecting? Or maybe he realised I'd changed inside? I was no longer the same woman who'd left Clifton Packaging. I felt braver, more confident.

"That still doesn't answer my question about the potty," I said when I came back.

"Do you really want to know?"

"Yes."

Mr. Vale handed me his phone and stretched out on the floor, his face positioned directly under the— Oh! Now I understood, and my cheeks burned.

"Imagine you're sitting on it," he murmured.

I did. Last night, I'd dreamed of that chair, of lowering myself onto the padded leather, supporting myself on my hands as I leaned back and let him taste me. I'd been raised to believe that masturbation was a sin, a forbidden act, but I'd orgasmed so hard I'd jolted awake. And when I regained my senses, I'd found my hand between my thighs, my fingers dripping.

Now I could barely look at my boss.

He was studying the departure board with my backpack slung over his shoulder and our laptop bags in his hand. He didn't have luggage—because he often had to visit other branches of Nyx, he maintained an apartment in each location. They ranged from the huge penthouse in LA that he considered his home to a studio in Denver. The property was an investment, he said, and he preferred having his own space to hotel rooms.

His phone rang.

My phone rang.

Shit, it was Meera.

Mr. Vale was already talking to whoever had called him, so I slipped away, heading in the direction of the bathrooms.

"What is it? What's wrong?"

"He's gone. Alfie's gone."

"What do you mean, gone?"

"To Lisbon."

"On his own?"

"No." She practically howled the word, then broke down in tears. "With Beatriz."

"Who the hell is Beatriz?"

"A girl he met in the bar. I went there last night and saw him kissing her, and we had a massive fight, and this morning, he packed his suitcase and they left."

That *bastard*. If I ever saw him again, I'd cut his balls off with a scalpel. Actually, no, a scalpel was too good for that asshole. A rusty bone saw would be better.

"My grandpa was right," Meera wailed. "Alfie *is* a good-for-nothing scrote."

A scrote? What was a scrote? Some British thing? Like a scrotum?

"What are you going to do?" A prickle of fear ran through me. I had a new life now, and I wanted to keep it. "Are you coming home?"

"Do you think I should?"

In my heart of hearts, I did. She needed my support, and her family's. Even if they were angry at first, they'd forgive her deception. Unlike my parents, Meera's Mom and Pop were good people with her best interests at heart, although they could be overbearing at times.

"I think that maybe—" I started.

"You know what? Screw Alfie. If I leave Portugal, he wins. This is *my* dream, not his, and there are still so many trees to plant."

Relief surged through me. "So you're staying?"

"I'll have to find a cheaper place to live. The rent's due this week, and I can't afford it on my own."

"Do you need money? I can send you money."

"What if someone traces it?"

"I could wire it through one of those transfer places."

"Let me talk to a few people first. Pedro's brother rents rooms."

"Are you sure you'll be okay?"

A pause, and then a sniffle. "No?"

"I'm so sorry Alfie did that to you."

"I thought he was The One, you know? He said he loved me."

Well, he sure didn't show it. "At least you saw his true colours before you married him. Can you sell your engagement ring?"

"No, I threw it at him. There were bushes. I don't even know where it went."

Out of the corner of my eye, I saw Mr. Vale hang up the phone and look around for me. Shit. He wasn't happy either.

"Call me later, okay. Let me know how things go."

"I will. At least I don't have to feel guilty about spending so much time on the project now."

"Put yourself first. Make yourself happy. I have to catch a plane, but I'll be back in LA this afternoon."

"Love you, twinny."

"Love you too."

Mr. Vale was checking in boutique windows by the time I caught up with him, searching for me among the shoes and purses. As if I needed another purse. The one he'd made me buy was perfect.

"Sorry, I had to use the bathroom. Is everything okay? You look stressed."

"My mom had a fall. I need to go to Virginia."

"Is she okay? Was she injured? I'll book you a flight right away." Should I go to the desk? Or try calling the airline? We'd already passed through security screening, and the ticket counters were outside. "Can I have my laptop?"

He hung onto it for a long moment, then finally held out the bag.

"Change your flight as well."

Huh? "You want me to visit your mom with you?"

"Do you have a problem with that?"

He was the boss.

The sexy, demanding, sweet, unpredictable, mysterious boss.

I swallowed hard. "No, there's no problem."

CHAPTER 22
BRAX

"Do you spend a lot of time in the gardens, Leonora?"

"Call me Leon, darling. And yes, I love the outdoors. There's such beauty in nature." Brax's mom glanced at her swollen ankle. "At least, there is when you look where you're going."

"You'll be back in the sun in no time."

Brax watched the two women in his life, past and future. Meera was curled up on a floral couch beside his mother, a cup of tea in her hand. His mom's leg was propped on an ottoman, the ankle bandaged and flanked by ice packs.

Meera was handling the situation far better than he was. His mom had only tripped over a step, but when he looked at her black eye, he saw his father's handiwork and all the bad memories came rushing back. His mom crying in the bathroom, the endless apologies to a monster, her whispered claims that things were fine when they clearly weren't. Brax had seen today's injuries and felt anger, while Meera had stayed calm and businesslike, asking how long ago the accident had occurred, then requesting an aide fetch a fresh ice pack and a stool to elevate the leg.

And now they were chatting like old friends.

Call me Leon.

Throughout Brax's marriage, his mom had insisted that Carissa call her by her full name. Every time Carissa forgot, she called her Carri in return, which his wife hated. When they shared an apartment, the two women had sniped at each other behind closed doors without him realising until his mom had another breakdown, something he'd never forgive himself for.

This was why he'd brought Meera to Virginia.

If he was going to give up everything for her, then he needed to know that she'd get along with his mother. That she wouldn't upset the fragile equilibrium his mom had spent years regaining. Meera had passed the test with flying colours, and she didn't even realise it *was* a test.

"Will you be okay here if I make a few calls?" he asked her, his voice thick with emotion he had trouble hiding.

"Sure, we're doing great. Do you need help with anything?"

"No, just keep my mom company."

"I don't need a babysitter," his mother told him. Then to Meera, "Do you play bridge?"

"Is that a card game?"

His mom nodded. "We can play with Matthew and Elda."

"I've never played, but I'd love to learn."

Brax backed out the door to book Meera a hotel room for the night. He had an apartment nearby, and a part of him wanted to say "screw it all" and take her there, but it was a huge decision to make. Financially, he'd slide from the top of the board, all the way down the snake, right to the bottom. Would that be a deal-breaker for Meera? There was heat between them, that was undeniable, but what if his circumstances changed drastically? He'd have to spend long hours building up the business again, and she'd need to work too, at least for the first few years.

After he'd booked her a suite at the nearest five-star hotel, the next call he made was to his lawyer.

"She's more than your personal assistant, isn't she?"

"Why do you say that?"

"I'm your mother, Braxton. Just because I live in this place, it doesn't mean I'm stupid."

"I realise that."

"Then stop avoiding the question."

Brax glanced toward the door of the private dining room —the facilities at the Cardinal Center were second to none. Meera had gone to use the bathroom before they headed off for the night.

"I…I think I'm in love with her."

His mom's expression softened. "She's a good one. Meera's the type of woman you should have married, not that other opportunist."

"I know. I just… I guess that after Carissa stuck by me through the Blackstone House debacle, I thought she'd be a partner for life."

"She's a parasite. Everyone knew you didn't murder that girl."

"It was hard to think straight back then."

"I understand that. But it's time, Braxton. Get a divorce and move on."

"You know why I can't."

"Money isn't everything. Look at me and your father—all the money in the world couldn't buy us happiness."

"I need to make sure you're taken care of in the settlement. This place doesn't come cheap."

"You can't let that keep you chained to Carissa. I have a

little nest egg, and someday, I'd like to have a yard of my own before I'm too old to tend to it."

"You want to leave Cardinal? But you said you intended to stay here forever."

"That was three years ago. Carissa meddled with both of our heads. I was in a fragile state emotionally—do you know how much therapy it took for me to be able to say that? I was in a fragile state, and this is my place of safety. But maybe... maybe the time has come for me to have my own space again."

"Here in Virginia?"

"I have friends in the area. I'm not completely isolated here, you know. Or perhaps I could try living in Los Angeles? I can't say I hate the idea of more sunshine."

"Are you sure about this?"

"I'm as sure as you are about Meera."

"In that case..." Brax took a deep breath and let the unbearable weight of Carissa roll off his shoulders. "In that case, it's time. I'll get the divorce."

"When do you want to fly home?" Meera asked. "Will we still be here tomorrow? Because there's a botanical garden nearby, and most of it is wheelchair friendly. I called to check. The manager at the Cardinal Center said they could arrange transport, although your mom hates the idea of being wheeled around. She'd rather use crutches, but that's not a good idea at the moment. She should be resting her injured leg completely. Of course, if you need to get back to LA, that's no problem—I can book the flights right away."

"Go to the botanical garden."

"Are you sure? I feel kind of guilty doing fun things when I should be working."

"It's fine."

"What about the operations call in the morning? Should I dial in to take notes?"

"What operations call?"

"At ten a.m. You forgot?"

"I have other things on my mind right now."

"Of course. Your mom. I'm so sorry—I'll just… I'll be quiet."

Slowly, deliberately, Brax leaned forward and rolled up the privacy screen. They were nearly at Meera's hotel now, and he couldn't go another night without telling her how he felt. He wanted her in his bed, not sleeping alone ten miles away.

"Meera, look at me."

She did, those beautiful dark eyes focused on his. He'd practised a whole speech in his head, the reasoning, the justification, the laying bare of his soul, but when she bit that bottom lip, none of it mattered. He fisted one hand in her hair and tilted her head back, giving himself access to that delicate throat. Just a taste…

And that taste was exquisite. Her pulse fluttered as he trailed the tip of his tongue along smooth skin, and the little gasp she gave made his cock harden in an instant.

"Meera…" It was a prayer, a declaration, and a plea all in one.

He pressed with a thumb, feeling the tight little indentations left by her teeth, and when her lips parted, that was all the invitation he needed. She moaned into his mouth as he kissed her, their tongues tangling. With every breathy whimper, her legs fell open another inch as her subconscious gave Brax the answer to his unasked question.

Yes, she wanted him.

He moved a hand to her thigh, inching it upward as he deepened the kiss. Why had she worn pants today? Why did she ever wear pants? What a horrible garment they were. Too much fabric, too many fasteners.

He stroked her through the polyester—ugh, polyester, she should be in silk—and she writhed under his touch. So responsive, his Meera. His queen. His everything. Her hand came to his chest, and he wondered if she'd tear the buttons off his shirt. Hoped she would.

But then she pushed him.

Hard.

"I can't do this."

Fuck. "You can. The decision's final; I'm getting a divorce."

"Okay, I *won't* do this."

As the car slowed to a smooth halt outside the hotel, her jaw set, and there was that backbone he both loved and hated. The fiery determination.

"Meera, it's okay."

"No, it isn't. I'm not going to be responsible for you losing your business."

"I've come to terms with it."

"Maybe you think you have, but I've seen what the company means to you. In a few months, you'd regret giving up everything for me. I'm not worth it."

"Yes, you are."

"If you knew more about me, you'd change your mind."

"Then let me get to know you."

"This…this…it won't work."

"Tell me one thing—if Carissa wasn't in the picture, would you be in my bed tonight?"

She wanted to lie. He saw it in her eyes. But she couldn't, and as she snatched up her bags, she whispered one word.

"Yes."

Then she was shoving open the door, stumbling out of it, and fleeing toward the lobby. And Brax could do nothing but watch. As soon as she'd disappeared inside, he picked up his phone and texted three words to his lawyer.

BRAX

Get it done.

CHAPTER 23
THE ASSISTANT

"So let me get this straight..." Meera said. "You're in love with your boss, and he feels the same way, but you can't have wild monkey sex because his ex-wife will take all his money? Indi, that's seriously messed up."

"I don't know if he loves me. He didn't say anything about that."

"He stuck his tongue down your throat in a limo, and he's willing to give up everything to be with you. Trust me, that's love."

It was all so confusing. On Monday, Mr. Vale had spent the day in his apartment while I took his mother to the botanical garden, and the flight back to LA on Tuesday morning had been one of the most uncomfortable experiences of my life. And considering I'd suffered through an engagement party beside Karam Joshi, that was a pretty big statement to make. In the end, I'd put on a pair of headphones and pretended to watch an in-flight movie while Mr. Vale stared at his laptop screen. *Mr. Fucking Vale.* He'd had his hand between my legs, and I still didn't have permission to use his first name.

And now we were back to emails. He'd cancelled our

morning catch-ups—thank goodness—and the lunches I used to look forward to, and changed the settings on his inbox. I couldn't even read half of the messages now. How was I meant to do my job? But at least he hadn't fired me. Although it might not be a bad thing if he did, because catching glimpses of him as I delivered his coffee and his lunch was unbearable. This morning, I'd made the coffee cold just to see if he'd talk to me, but he didn't. He simply drank it without a word.

And those glimpses, they were also a drug. A fix to get me through the day. I was a love junkie, and I'd gotten hooked on the wrong man.

"Even if it *is* love, I can't let him lose everything he's worked for. He doesn't even know my freaking name, Meera. He thinks I'm you. And what if you decide to come home? I can't keep your identity forever. I mean, what would you tell your parents?"

"Oh, relax. I can just fly home for Christmas and Thanksgiving, borrow some of your fancy clothes—I still can't believe he bought you Louboutins; no, actually I can— and tell them all about my splendiferous job as an executive assistant in LA. And when you marry your boss and I marry a sexy eco-warrior who is definitely *not* Alfie, then we can come clean."

And that was another problem. The only way I could possibly convince my father to back off would be to get a ring on my finger. His mindset was conservative, his views uber-traditional and horribly misogynistic. A woman was the property of her father until she got married, and then she became the property of her husband. Just shacking up with a guy wouldn't cut it. And he'd do anything to get his way. Think I was exaggerating? He wasn't the only man who thought like that, and when his friend's daughter had refused the suitor chosen for her, she'd found herself on a private jet bound for India. I hadn't seen her for another five years, and by then she was married, mother to three young girls (much to her family's disappointment), and pregnant for a fourth time in the hope that she'd provide a boy. Another six months passed before I saw her again. Then she'd been in the morgue, dead from a self-inflicted gunshot wound. It was the only time I'd thrown up during an autopsy.

So, I needed a husband, or I needed to run.

And if by some miracle, Mr. Vale managed to free himself from Carissa's shackles, he'd have to be a sadomasochist if he wanted to get married again. I was fairly sure he wasn't into that particular kink.

Hell, why did he have to go and kiss me? Things had been going so well until he lost his damn mind.

"That won't work, twinny."

"Well, don't sweat it for now. One of Pedro's boarders is going back to Albania in two weeks, and he said I could have the room."

"Where are you staying at the moment? In the apartment?"

"I found a hostel in Fundão. It's horribly basic, but it's clean and super cheap, and I only have to sleep there."

"How will you get to the project?"

"Polina and her boyfriend are staying nearby. They'll give me a ride. Plus I found my engagement ring in a bush. Pedro knows a guy with a metal detector, and we looked for, like, three hours and you wouldn't believe how much trash people throw away. But that asshole told me it was a diamond!"

"Which asshole? Pedro?"

"No, Alfie. Pedro isn't an asshole. The stone was a cubic freaking zirconia. I got sixty euros for it, which is better than nothing, but if I ever see Alfie again, I'm gonna kick him in the nuts."

"You'll have to get in line. I can't believe he did that to you."

We'd been friends for two years in Boston, and he'd acted

so caring. Started out by giving Meera free caramel syrup in her coffee, then been a true gentleman on dates. He hadn't even kissed her for two months (she'd texted me right after it happened, swoon, swoon, swoon). And now he'd moved to Lisbon with some random girl he met in a bar?

"I swear I'll never get serious with a man again," she said.

"You just said you planned to marry an eco-warrior."

"Okay, I'm not gonna get serious with a man for at least six months. Maybe I'll have a rebound fling with a Portuguese stud."

"Why don't you focus on the swales for now?"

"Aw, don't be a killjoy. Go lose your V-card to your hot boss. Wait, does he know—"

"Yes."

"Wow. How did that come up in conversation?"

"Please, just stop."

Because I knew Mr. Vale would. I'd said no, and he respected no. He wouldn't catch me off guard and do a Lance Clifton. Although I wouldn't mind—

No!

"I'll call you tomorrow," Meera promised. "Hang in there."

"Love you, twinny."

"Love you too."

CHAPTER 24
BRAX

Brax read over the latest email from his lawyer. Carissa had agreed to a provision for his mother—and let's face it, she owed that much—but now they were haggling over the amount. Carissa had come up from one million to one point five, and Brax had come down from five to four point five. They'd end up settling for three, he knew it, but they still had to play this stupid legal dance first. Otherwise the divorce attorneys wouldn't be able to afford their golf club memberships, and that would never do.

Today, he was viewing properties around Los Angeles. In less time than it would take Carissa to redecorate Brax's former apartment, Nyx would be reborn as Phoenix, and he needed to find the club's new home. He'd have the million from the divorce settlement as start-up money, and Violet Miller had offered a two-million-dollar loan. The movie business was going well. Plus she'd first met Dawson in The Dark, and they still dropped by on occasion to use the facilities. She'd get a free lifetime membership in return.

The first property he'd looked at was smaller than the current one, but it benefitted from a good-sized basement, a private parking lot, and a secluded location. There'd be no room for an admin team, and he'd have to live out of a modest studio apartment, but he'd done that in Virginia and survived. Remote working was a possibility, or he could hire a smaller office space nearby when funds allowed. The second property was much larger, a former warehouse, but it would need complete redevelopment. A huge project, but he'd be able to put his own stamp on the place. And then there was the derelict mansion he'd agreed to see tomorrow—that was the most interesting of the three, but would he have time for a major renovation project? Once Brax had put together a shortlist, Justin had agreed to fly in and give his professional opinion, and he'd also oversee the construction project for a sensible fee.

Brax's phone rang, and his guts seized. The only person he wanted to speak to today was his lawyer, and "wanted" was doing a lot of heavy lifting. But it wasn't Jeff Benedict. No, it was Alexa.

As usual, she didn't waste time on pleasantries.

"What the hell are you doing?"

"At this moment? I'm drinking lukewarm coffee and contemplating the meaning of life."

"Okay, what are you doing with Carissa?"

"Nothing. She's in New York, thank fuck."

"Don't be flippant. You know exactly what I'm asking."

Brax gave a heavy sigh. "I'm waiting for the divorce paperwork to land on my desk, and then I'm going to sign it."

"Have you lost your mind?"

"Probably."

"Because of your assistant? Chase said you had a thing for her."

"Because I'm sick of living in purgatory. If I so much as talk to a woman, Carissa finds out and tries to twist it to her own ends."

"And the assistant?"

"Her name is Meera."

"Yes, I know that already. So you'd pick her over everything you've worked to build? You'd write off a decade, just like that? What if the thing with Meera doesn't work out?"

"It's a gamble, true, but at least Carissa will be out of my life."

"You should wait longer. She's a sneaky bitch, but she's gonna fuck up."

"I've waited for years already, and I don't want to lose my chance with Meera. This is a risk I have to take."

"It's a stupid move."

"Are you telling me you've never done anything stupid?"

"I've never fucked my assistant or thrown my entire business away for a dumb crush."

"I know that. Which is why Nolan's running a winery in the Sierra Foothills and you're sitting alone in a hotel room with a tub of caviar and a bunch of computers."

"Fuck you."

She hung up, and Brax sighed. He'd long suspected that Alexa had liked Nolan, but she'd always refused to admit it. Guess the secret was out now. Screw her too—just because she'd chosen money over love didn't mean he had to do the same. He took the bottle of Scotch out of his desk drawer and poured the last remaining drops down his throat, then typed out an email to Meera.

I need another bottle of whisky and a driver. Please.

Fuck, let this be over soon.

CHAPTER 25
THE ASSISTANT

"Leon? How lovely to hear from you."

I'd hoped it would be Meera. Our long-distance chats had been a lifeline over the past two weeks, but she hadn't called yesterday. I hoped she was just busy moving into her new place.

"How are you, darling?"

Until we visited, I hadn't realised Mr. Vale's mom was English, although he'd told me his father was an American citizen but half-French by birth. Mr Vale's parents had met in Paris while they were both working there.

"I'm okay."

"Only okay? Is that son of mine giving you the runaround?"

"Oh, he's keeping me busy with work."

"I'm not talking about work."

"I...I don't understand."

"If he hasn't made his feelings clear already, I'm sure he will in time."

Hell, what had he told his mom?

"Things are a little difficult right now."

"Because of Carissa? I never did like that girl."

"Me neither." The words just popped out. "Sorry. I'm sorry, I shouldn't speak badly of people."

"We'll make an exception for her, my love. You have to trust that Braxton will resolve the issue. But enough of those problems—I'm calling to invite both of you to my birthday celebration."

"B-both of us?"

"It's only a small get-together at Cardinal, but we can play bridge again."

What was I meant to say? "Could you tell me the date?"

"Friday, June thirtieth, and if I don't put the details in Braxton's diary, he forgets and starts scheduling other things."

"I'll make sure the day gets blocked out."

And travel time on either side of it. Mr. Vale would definitely want to attend his mother's party. I'd need to book flights—business class, not economy—but first, I'd have to check his whereabouts before and after. There would be no point in booking a ticket from LA if he was in New York that week. A sigh escaped. If things kept going the way they were, I wouldn't be going with him. Hell, I might not be in the picture at all. At the moment, he mostly seemed to be drinking too much and ignoring me. His office door stayed firmly closed. If he was still mainlining whisky next week, I'd be forced to intervene, but so far, I'd just been monitoring his daily alcohol intake and making sure he drank plenty of water.

And it was good to hear Leon sounding cheerful. From the snippets Mr. Vale had let slip, I'd pieced together fragments of her history, and I feared my own mother would end up in a similar situation down the line. And worse, I couldn't do anything to help her. Not physically and not financially.

"No need to worry about a gift," Leon said. "Just your company will be enough."

"I'll make sure to tell Mr. Vale."

"Mr. Vale? There's no need for such formalities."

"That's what he prefers me to call him."

"Tell him not to be so silly. Everyone calls him Braxton. Or Brax, although he'll always be Braxton to me."

"I'll be sure to do that," I promised, but I knew I wouldn't say a word. Life was difficult enough at the current time without rocking the boat. If it listed any farther, we'd all fall out.

Where was she? Four days had passed since I last heard from Meera. I'd expected the usual silly memes, an update on the swales, photos of her new place. But instead, there'd been radio silence.

Yesterday, I'd tried calling someone at the project, but I didn't have a whole lot of information about it. Sure, I knew it was on a farm, and it involved a lot of digging, and there was a guy called Pedro, but I'd never asked for contact details. The farm was called Quinta do Lago—at least, I thought it was—but the only person I managed to speak to was a woman who told me in broken English that Meera was "no here, not today."

In desperation, I'd attempted to contact Alfie, but when I called the number I had for him, a recorded message in what I assumed was Portuguese seemed to be telling me that the phone was out of service.

The only other person I could speak with was Celeste, currently on the Côte d'Azur, and she told me to try the Portuguese police. They refused to even take a report. She's backpacking, they told me. She's probably just moved on. But Meera wouldn't do that, not without letting me know.

And what about her parents? She checked in with them every few days, and if she didn't call, they'd start to worry too. Worse, they thought she was in freaking LA, working for Dunnvale Holdings. What the heck should I do? I could hardly call them up and ask questions. What if my brother was monitoring their phone? Or he'd begged them to get in touch when I called because the whole family was just so worried about dear Indali? I could post updates on her social media accounts. I had all the passwords. Would that hold them off? The problem was, if Meera truly was in trouble, my cover story could also stop the authorities from investigating, assuming that one of her Portuguese friends raised the alarm.

Today was Sunday. Tomorrow, I'd try contacting Quinta do Lago again—Lake Farm, according to an online translator. I could call from work. Maybe I'd get ahold of a different person? Someone who spoke better English? Or a close friend of Meera's? If that didn't work, then…then… I didn't have a plan B. I'd have to go to Portugal. That would be the only option, and I couldn't fly as Meera, not internationally. I didn't have her passport; she did. Could I somehow obtain a fake? No, no, that was out of the question. Flying domestically with Meera's REAL ID driver's licence was a risk I'd take, but overseas with a biometric passport? No way. I'd get arrested, if not in the US, then at immigration in Portugal. I'd have to call the US embassy, and— Wait. The embassy… Could I call the US embassy in Portugal? What about the Portuguese embassy in the US? Where was it? Washington, DC? Again, Dr. Google came to the rescue. Yes, the main embassy was in DC, but there was an honorary consulate in Los Angeles. I could visit tomorrow. Mr. Vale was either drunk or AWOL these days, so the chances of him noticing my absence were slim. I had a plan.

As morning approached in Portugal, I sent one more message to Meera—*call me, we need to talk*—and said a silent prayer. *Please let my twinny be okay.*

CHAPTER 26

BRAX

I t was done. A final agreement had been reached. On Sunday afternoon, Brax sent his confirmation of the deal —the lawyers had been working overtime this week, and they'd been paid handsomely for the privilege. Brax would receive one million dollars in cash, and his mom would get three million in a trust, accessible only for her personal use. He'd also negotiated the apartment in San Francisco—Carissa hated the city and wanted to make sure he stayed out of her way—plus he could keep his two Porsches and his boat. Affording the upkeep would be a challenge, but he could always sell them if need be. The handover of Dunnvale would be completed over the next month. One thing Brax had insisted upon was the opportunity to visit each site and tell the staff in person. To warn them. They deserved that much. Plus he could start laying the groundwork to poach them in the future.

He took one more sip of whisky, then poured the rest into the plant pot beside his desk. At least now, he had a chance at a future with Meera. He'd been neglecting her these past three weeks, too busy with property issues and alcoholism to pay her the attention she deserved. Although some space wasn't necessarily a bad thing. Judging by her reaction to their one and only kiss—the kiss that had kept him going through the gruelling discussions—she wouldn't be happy about the divorce terms. She thought she wasn't worth enough? She was worth everything.

In two days, he'd make it up to her. He only hoped that his love was as good as his money. Meera wasn't materialistic, but he was glad he'd asked Violet to pick up a few more trinkets before the divorce went through. He wanted Meera to look like the queen she was.

The phone rang, and Brax cursed out loud when he saw the name. He almost sent his wife to voicemail, but what if there was an issue? He just wanted the whole damn thing over and done with. And after that, he never wanted to see or hear from the bitch again.

"What?"

"Why can't we do this in New York? Why do I have to fly to LA?"

For fuck's sake.

"The divorce case is being heard in California, remember? Judge Polk is squeezing us in at the end of the day on Tuesday as a favour." The judge was a member of Nyx, and he'd expressed his sympathy over the upcoming proceedings. "Even your fucking lawyer is in LA. If we start over in New York, it'll take months, and I'm not waiting months."

"It's because of her, isn't it?"

"You'll have to be more specific."

"Meena."

Why bother to deny it? "Meera. Her name is Meera."

"I knew from the start she was different." Brax wasn't a violent man, not with women anyway, but he still longed to slap the smugness out of Carissa's voice. "You never looked at me the way you look at her."

There was a good reason for that. "No, I didn't."

"Put me out of my misery—where did you hook up with

her? We never did catch you in the act. Go on, you can tell me now the settlement's agreed."

"I didn't hook up with her anywhere. She won't sleep with me while I'm still married."

Carissa's cackle set Brax's teeth on edge. "How delightfully old-fashioned. Ah, well. Her loss is my gain. I'll fly out tomorrow."

"It's the least you can do."

"I'll need a car to meet me at the airport."

"Arrange your own damn car."

For one last time, Brax allowed himself the satisfaction of throwing the phone at the wall. Forty-eight hours, and this would all be over.

Or so he thought.

"Late? What do you mean, you're going to be late?"

"There's a problem with the plane," Carissa whined.

"What kind of a problem?"

"How should I know? A technical problem. They need to fix it before we can fly."

A pity. If Carissa fell out of the sky, it sure would make life easier. Brax gave a sigh. No, he couldn't expect several hundred other people to sacrifice themselves at the altar of his poor judgment.

"So take a different plane."

"You think I haven't tried that? There's an issue with the booking system."

"A different airline?"

"The glitch is universal. The whole damn airport is in chaos."

"Go to a different airport, take a private flight; I don't care. Just make sure you get here before the hearing."

"How do I book a private flight? Sophie's on vacation."

Brax had reached the end of his tether with this woman. Every day, every hour, every minute, she became more unbearable.

"Work it out for yourself."

He was debating the wisdom of one more glass of whisky when his desk phone rang. Now what?

"I thought I said to hold all calls?" Shit. He shouldn't take his bad mood out on Meera. "I mean, please hold all my calls today."

"Sorry, Brax, it's Lyndsey from the front desk. Meera's father is on line one."

"Why are you telling me this? Put him through to Meera."

"She isn't answering her phone, and he's asking to speak with her boss."

Brax crossed his office in long strides and pulled open the adjoining door. Sure enough, Meera wasn't at her desk. She must have gone for lunch. At least she hadn't heard his verbal altercation with Carissa, but what the hell was he meant to say to her father? And why was he calling? She'd always given the impression that they didn't get along.

But he couldn't just ignore the man. He needed to make a good impression. Thank fuck he hadn't swallowed that extra finger of Scotch.

"Put him through." A pause. A *beep*. "Braxton Vale speaking."

"This is Bill Adams. I understand you know my daughter?"

Not as well as Brax would like. "Indeed. She works here as my assistant."

"See, we haven't been able to get ahold of Meera for a few days. She's normally real good about calling."

"It's possible that she might have had other things on her mind. We've had a busy few weeks, work-wise."

"So she's okay? Can I speak with her?"

"She's perfectly okay. She brought me coffee half an hour ago, but she's not at her desk right now. I think she stepped out to get lunch."

"Could you ask her to call us? Her momma worries."

"I'll certainly do that."

Instead of hanging up, Bill Adams carried on talking. "She's doing okay there? In her job?"

"She's the best assistant I've ever had. Goal-driven and organised."

"Good, good. Between you and me, we were worried about her while she was at college. She found it hard to settle, and then she wanted to go travelling around Europe. Europe! With all this great country has to offer, who needs to go to *Europe*?"

"Learning about a different culture can be a valuable experience."

"She already backpacked around South America after high school. Spent a whole year picking macadamia nuts and teaching kids to speak English." Bill Adams chuckled. "I'm just glad things are working out."

"I'll remind her to call you."

"Thank you, sir. I appreciate it."

Not quite what Brax had expected from Meera's father, but Bill Adams seemed a nice enough fellow. He wrote a note to himself. *Meera call father.* Maybe he'd have that extra drink after all? Meeting the parents was something to celebrate, even if it was only a brief chat over the phone. Had he come across okay? Not too garbled? He'd gotten off on the wrong foot with Madeleine Dunn from the start, not that there was a right foot with that woman. Carissa's mother was a bitch, genetics at work. For the first five years of his marriage, he'd received a Christmas card addressed to Braydon. Then the cards had stopped. Had she ever known his name, or was she on some permanent passive-aggressive power trip? Grey had a minor in psychology—maybe Brax should ask him?

He checked the internet and found that Carissa hadn't been lying about the delays at Newark. Whatever was going on with the system, there were issues at JFK as well. He fired off a message to his lawyer, informing him of the delay and telling him not to bother coming in early. An email arrived from the real estate agent who was assisting with the property search—had Brax arrived at a decision yet? A yawn came as he considered his options. Was a week without sleep finally catching up with him? The warehouse was a definite no due to zoning issues, and Justin didn't like the smaller property either, the one Brax had been most hopeful about. The old mansion… That was a possibility, but also a money pit. He wasn't certain he'd have the funds after the divorce to do it justice. Plus it was a little way out of the city, more secluded but less convenient. Although it did have the benefit of space. Forested land, overgrown gardens, an old horse barn. It was the type of place he'd snap up as an addition to his portfolio, but not the centrepiece.

Keep looking, he wrote back.

CHAPTER 27
BRAX

The ringing phone woke him.

Why didn't Meera answer it?

Right, because it was his personal phone.

And the room was also dark.

What the fuck? How long had he been asleep? What time was it? He'd made it to the couch in his office, and someone had put a blanket over him—probably Meera before she went home. He squinted at the phone, his vision blurred because he'd forgotten to remove his contacts. Six a.m., and Alexa was calling. Damn, it was too early for another lecture. He let the brat go to voicemail, switched to his glasses, and then saw that Carissa had sent a text ten minutes ago. She was on a plane, finally. This time tomorrow, he'd be a free man. A poor man, but a free one.

Another text to his lawyer, and he closed his eyes again. Should he sell the apartment in San Francisco? If he did, he'd be able to buy a place in LA. But if Phoenix progressed as he hoped, he'd open at a second location in San Francisco in a year or two, and then he'd need a place to stay. Maybe he could rent the apartment out for a while? Or stay there with Meera for a month to decompress first? No, he wanted to take

Meera to Paris. There'd be no stay at the Ritz, but two weeks in a nice hotel was doable. Somewhere near the Montmartre. The Montmartre was Brax's favourite part of the city, an eclectic mix of old and new, of gaudy and traditional. The Sacré-Cœur and the Moulin Rouge. The vineyard in Rue Saint-Vincent and the art of the Belle Époque. The cobbled streets. The view from the top of the hill. The *funiculaire* taking visitors down to the red-light district of Pigalle.

How his life had changed in just a few short months. Things that had once seemed so important, suddenly they weren't so vital anymore. Two years had passed since he visited France, longer still since he took a trip with no agenda, no people to see or places to be. When had he last done something impulsive? Something totally unplanned? Probably…nine years ago, not long before Ruby's murder. He'd gone to pick up a burrito with Jerry, found the restaurant had been closed due to a health violation, and ended up on the summit of a volcano in Uruapan. Her idea, not his, but he'd gone along with it. He'd also twisted an ankle on the descent, and they never did get the damn burritos.

Upon reflection, those days in Blackstone House had been the best of his life. True, he'd never had any money, but he did have a hell of a lot of friends. And fun, even with Jerry. She'd kept herself to herself most of the time, and she'd had an unfortunate tendency to act like a cold-hearted bitch, but beneath the icy surface lurked a wild streak.

Whatever happened with Meera, he vowed not to spend quite so much time working in the future. When he was old and grey, he wanted to remember the adventures, not the inside of his office.

A knock at the door woke him, soft but insistent. Was it time yet? Had Carissa arrived? A glance at his watch told him that was impossible—at eight a.m., she'd still be in the skies above flyover country.

"Mr. Vale?" Meera opened the door a crack. "Are you awake?"

"Why are you here so early?"

"I...I'm worried about you. Did you stay here all night?"

"Yes, but at least I slept."

"Do you want coffee yet? Something to eat?" She eyed the empty Scotch bottle on his desk. "Tylenol?"

"Just coffee."

"There's somebody waiting in reception to see you. I told her that you were unavailable, but she's not taking 'no' for an answer."

"Who is it? I blocked out my schedule today."

"She introduced herself as Alexa, but she wouldn't give a surname."

Now Brax sat up. Alexa? No, Alexa didn't do face-to-face meetings. Alexa hid herself away in dark corners, both on the internet and in the real world.

"What does she look like?"

"Petite, blonde, young. Very young. There are two men with her, but she wouldn't tell me who they were either."

Fuck, it really was Alexa?

"She's actually the same age as you."

"Are you sure? No, I don't think so. She looks about sixteen."

And when she'd claimed to be sixteen, she'd looked twelve.

"Send her through."

"And the men?"

"Them too."

"Should I make coffee for everyone?"

"Why not? Cream and one sugar for Alexa. I don't know about the others."

Why would Alexa come to the office? There could only be one reason—she'd been meddling again. Alexa was fond of breaking rules and societal norms. Call it a hobby. Sometimes she interfered for the better, and sometimes she interfered for the worse. Such as the time she hacked a pizza delivery app soon after she moved into Blackstone House and sent food all over the neighbourhood. If she liked you, you got a supreme with extra cheese. If she didn't like you, you got a margherita with triple jalapeños. What was the reason for this carb overload? The owner of the pizza place had hit a dog with his car outside Blackstone House. Deliberately, according to Ruby, who'd witnessed the incident. Alexa was terrified of dogs, but she liked assholes even less.

"Uh, Mr. Vale? Do you think I could take a slightly longer lunch break today? I can make up the time this evening. I just have a personal errand to run, and—"

"Take the rest of the day off."

"That really isn't necessary."

"Take the day off, and don't be late tomorrow morning."

"If you're sure…"

"I'm sure. Bring Alexa in."

Two minutes later, there she was. A pit bull in a chihuahua's body, followed by Chase and a man who had to be either a lawyer or an accountant. He had a briefcase and a sharp, pedantic look about him. Curiosity got the better of Brax, and he scanned Alexa from top to toe, taking in the sun-bleached blonde hair piled on top of her head, the golden tan, the designer sportswear, and the imperious attitude.

"You look well," he said.

She snorted. "You look like shit. I realise money doesn't buy happiness, but apparently it doesn't buy razors either."

"Women find a two-day beard attractive, or so I've been told."

"How about the eyebags? You need to use some of that bee-venom gloop Carissa spends three hundred bucks on."

Chase set the three laptops he was carrying in a neat line on Brax's desk, then pulled up a chair, presumably for Alexa. Damn, his brain hurt. Meera hadn't even brought the coffee yet.

"Alexa, what are you doing here?"

"Saving your stupid ass from your dumb impatience. I need coffee."

"Coffee's on its way, and that isn't a proper answer. Who is this gentleman?" Brax waved a hand at the lawyer-slash-accountant.

"Don. Where's your printer?"

"Next door, in Meera's office."

"Aw, you have adjoining rooms? That's so cute."

Alexa had two of the three laptops out now, bulky things built for power rather than aesthetics. Don slid his own computer out of the briefcase and looked around.

"We'll need more chairs," he said.

Meera picked that moment to walk in with a tray, and she stared at the desk, no doubt wondering where the hell she was meant to put the drinks. Brax shoved his own laptop into a drawer, cursing Alexa under his breath. Didn't she realise he had enough on his plate today without a cosy reunion?

"Can you find more chairs?" Don asked Meera.

"How many chairs?"

"Three."

"Uh, okay." She looked to Brax, questioning, but all he could do was shrug.

"Is there any popcorn?" Alexa wanted to know. "Today's a popcorn day. And bring water for Brax and his hangover."

"We have cookies. Or I could go out and—"

For crying out loud. "The cookies are fine."

"Are they the good kind with chocolate on them?" Alexa asked.

Meera gave a shaky smile. "There are amaretti, chocolate chip, and shortbread. Oh, and I picked up some macarons from the patisserie yesterday."

Alexa pointed at her. "She's a keeper."

Tell Brax something he didn't already know.

Ten minutes later, they had chairs and cookies, and his desk looked like the love child of corporate America and a stick of dynamite. Meera had run for her life, and Chase was lying on the couch, reading a paperback.

"Alexa, what the fuck is going on?"

"Shush. I don't have time for questions, not when I had to waste two hours flying here because *you* couldn't answer your damn phone. Should we put this on the big screen? Yes, I think we should put this on the big screen."

Code scrolled across her laptop, and she hijacked his TV.

"Don, I realise this might be an awkward question, but who are you and what are you doing in my office?"

"I'm Ms. Stone's lawyer, and I'm drafting your divorce settlement agreement."

"Well, stop. My lawyer already did that."

"Don, keep typing." Alexa clicked one of her three mice. "Brax, sit down. We're just getting to the good part."

Dare he even ask? "Which is?"

"Carissa's downfall in glorious technicolour. Talk about time pressure. We had to fuck up an entire airport to buy a few extra hours. Okay, I haven't had time to edit this properly, so we'll have to fast-forward through the boring bits."

The screen was split into four, but the lower left quadrant was black. They were looking at a packed bar with a variety of clientele—young and old, every creed and colour—many of whom were guarding wheeled cases and backpacks. One camera focused on the counter, and the other two gave a wider view.

"Is this the airport?"

185

"Newark, yes. Good to know you still have at least one functioning brain cell left."

Brax stiffened as Carissa walked into shot, an Hermès purse slung over one shoulder as she talked on the phone. She looked around for somewhere to sit, then slid onto a stool vacated by a man wearing a Hawaiian shirt. The lower right quadrant showed her in close-up. Whoever was filming, they were sitting right next to her. And talking. Carissa chatted to her companion, growing more animated as time passed, smiling more and more often as she checked her watch and ordered the bartender around. Brax thought he spotted subtle signs of flirting—hair twirling around a finger, the way she checked her reflection in the mirror behind the bar, a change in posture that accentuated her breasts.

But her companion…was female.

Was he mistaken?

"Okay, this is just blah-blah-blah social engineering…" Alexa skipped the footage along, day turned to dusk, and the bar emptied out. Carissa appeared to have drunk most of a bottle of champagne by herself. Starting the celebrations early? "Ah, here we go."

Carissa and her new friend speed-walked through the airport, talking, gesturing. Carissa was definitely drunk. At one point, the other woman, an athletic redhead dressed in a skirt suit and carrying a purse not too dissimilar from Carissa's, had to steady her as she almost fell out of her shoes. What had they done? Bonded over a shared love of designer leather?

The pair headed for an airport hotel, and Alexa added a voiceover.

"Oh dear. There's only one room left. Or so the booking system thinks. Do you realise how much sleep I haven't had this week?" She drained the last of her coffee, and Brax pushed his mug toward her. "I gave them a nice view of the parking lot."

The top half of the screen darkened, and the fourth quadrant flickered to life, showing the inside of a hotel room. Utilitarian furniture, uninspiring art on the walls, and a king-sized bed with a pattern designed to hide stains.

Holy fuck. Brax leaned forward in his seat, waiting for Carissa to protest as the redhead pushed her onto the bed. But instead, his wife pulled the virtual stranger down after her and locked lips. Carissa was drunk, but not so drunk that she didn't know what she was doing. Not so drunk that she couldn't unbutton the redhead's shirt with a reasonable degree of coordination.

"Do you want to see all the gross bits? Don already summarised them for court."

Court? It barely registered. What the hell was Carissa doing? They'd been married for eight years, dated for over a year before that, and Carissa had never shown the slightest interest in women. Had she? Before Brax, she'd been dating a frat boy, some economics major whose daddy owned a house in the Hamptons.

"Let it play."

Carissa was really into this. It was clear that she knew her way around the female body, and not just her own. Although she was still content to lie back and let someone else do the hard work. The redhead was down to black lace panties and thigh-high stockings now, her head buried between Carissa's legs. Brax took a sip of water to moisten his dry mouth, wishing it were Scotch. Who the hell was she? The woman deserved a medal because Carissa was bitter to the core. Had Alexa paid her to—

A tattoo came into focus, small, but the camera was remarkably high resolution. Brax spluttered water as he realised. He knew that ass. He'd been intimately acquainted with *that ass*.

He'd also picked out the tattoo—a heart with horns and a demon tail. That had been another impulsive idea of Jerry's.

Hey, let's get tattoos. Bet ya can't take the pain, Georgetown boy.
She'd gotten the heart, and he'd ended up with the Chinese
word for "asshole." Jerry swore the tattoo artist had said it
meant "strong," but he'd never been entirely certain that she
was telling the truth.

"Is that *Jerry*?"

"That's the view you recognise her from?"

"She's changed her hair." Copper curls had replaced a
dark-brown ponytail. Was it a wig? "And I didn't realise she
was into women."

Was every lady in his life bisexual, and he'd just been too
blind to see it?

"She isn't, but she doesn't mind taking one for the team if
the need arises."

"But...but..." For once in his life, Brax was speechless. "I
mean, how did she get involved? Jerry disappeared after we
left Blackstone."

"She might have disappeared from your life, but she never
disappeared from mine."

So many secrets...

"What did you do, call her up and ask her to honeytrap
my wife?"

"Pretty much, yeah. She hates Carissa too."

"I didn't realise she'd ever met Carissa."

"She hadn't, but Carissa finished her shampoo once and
failed to replace it. *So* inconsiderate. Anyhow, enough chat
about the past. Let's worry about the future. There's nothing
in your prenup that says the adultery has to be with the
opposite sex. Don checked."

How had they even gotten a copy of the prenup? Brax
opened his mouth to ask, then closed it again. He kept a
scanned copy on his laptop. Alexa rooted through his files at
will.

"That's correct," Don confirmed. "There are no restrictions
on species, gender, or sexual orientation."

"Your court appearance is at four, and Don's started revising the settlement to represent the fact that you spent eight years making all the money and she's just been spending it. But you'll probably want to get your lawyer on board as well. He's more familiar with the details."

"How did you know?"

"About the court appearance? It's in your calendar."

As a private appointment, but that made no difference to Alexa.

"No, that Carissa would go for Jerry."

"Oh, that was thanks to Ruby. She mentioned to Grey that Carissa hooked up with a friend of hers, remember? You told me two months ago."

"How did that help? It happened before we got married."

"Because I asked Grey for more info, and he said it was a bartender named Tony."

"And?"

"Ruby's bartender friend was Toni with an I, not Tony with a Y. Antonia. A woman. So that piece of info set the ball rolling. Did you know Carissa sleeps with her assistants? Every single one of them is either bi or lesbian."

Chase moved his legs in a hurry as Brax slumped onto the couch. His head was pounding now.

"No, I didn't know."

"We started going after the ones who've quit, but they're under heavy NDAs. Hea-veeee. I'm talking black holes. Ari's been chasing them all over the East Coast, but only one would talk, and that was off the record. Carissa's been rubbing your nose in it for years, dude. While you've been losing your mind through abstinence, she's been having nooners before she goes to the spa. But her current squeeze is on vacation, so we figured she'd be gagging for it. A splash of alcohol, a few suggestive words, and voilà! She has a thing for redheads. Did you spot that seven out of her nine assistants have had red hair?"

"I never noticed."

Should he have done? Carissa had never gone out of her way to introduce Brax to her staff, but the information had probably been in the investigative reports. Now he was kicking himself.

"That was actually Ari's observation. Anyhow, it's done. Now you can negotiate a new settlement and drop-kick the bitch out of your life. I need more coffee. Can someone get me more coffee?"

Chase jumped to his feet. "On it."

Brax needed to call his lawyer and get him here pronto. Alexa…she'd just changed everything. And so had Meera. By resisting temptation that night in Virginia, she'd allowed him to keep the upper hand, and now he'd win the war. Brax rose too, and this time, he kissed Alexa on the head.

"Yeuch," she said.

"Thank you."

"Somebody had to keep you from making the biggest mistake of your life."

"I mean it. And I'm also sorry for what I said about Nolan."

"Does *he* know?"

"That you had a crush on him? I don't think so."

"Good. Don't tell him. He always thought of me as a little sister anyway."

"Your secret is safe with me."

"Where are the macarons?"

"Right here. Do you want lunch before you go back to… wherever it is you came from?"

"Lunch and dinner."

"Dinner?"

"You think I'd miss this meeting? Seeing Carissa apoplectic will be the highlight of my month. How long do you think this video should be? Should I tease her with an intro, or get straight to the fun parts?"

"Use an intro." Brax wanted to prolong her suffering the way she'd done to him. "I need to thank Jerry. Where could I send a gift? Is jewellery appropriate? A car?"

"The only jewellery she wears is a HOG's tooth necklace, and she's still driving the shitty old Porsche her dad left her."

"That thing was due for car heaven a decade ago."

"She had it professionally restored, but it breaks down most months. Just get her a bottle of mouthwash."

"Mouthwash? Why would I—" Brax glanced at Alexa's screen, frozen on a scene of Jerry going down on Carissa. Yes, mouthwash would probably appeal to Jerry's deranged sense of humour. "I'll head to the drugstore right now."

The meeting with Carissa and her lawyer was one for the memory books. She turned beet red and began spluttering, accusing them of dirty tricks, but she couldn't change the one basic fact: that she'd slept with somebody else while she was still married to Brax.

He made her a new offer—five million bucks if she signed on the dotted line before the hearing in the afternoon. Otherwise she could try fighting him, waste the money on legal fees, and he'd win in court. Her lawyer advised her to take the deal. She said she would if she could keep the apartment in New York. Brax didn't want the place anyway— it was filled with too many reminders of the woman he longed to forget. So he agreed.

It was done.

Alexa had watched the meeting via the camera in Brax's office, not in person, but she was waiting in the hallway when Carissa exited.

"Did you enjoy the video?" she asked.

It took a moment, but finally recognition dawned. "You're that child from Blackstone House."

"Yup. The child who grew up and became a movie director."

Brax could practically hear the cogs turning in Carissa's head. He'd told her more than once that Alexa was wise beyond her years.

"You? *You* did this?"

"Do you remember nine years ago when you stole my last three Ladurée macarons out of the refrigerator and ate them?"

"What are you talking about?"

"I thought not. Anyhow, I told you it was rude and you should apologise, and you told me to get over myself, and I told you that you'd regret it someday, and you told me to grow up." Ah, now it was coming back. "Well, now it's 'someday.'"

Carissa's voice was a mix of incredulity and fury. "You cost me over four hundred million dollars because of three macarons?"

"And also because you're a shitty person. Bet you wish you'd apologised now."

Carissa went for Alexa's throat, but Chase got between them. The wails were deafening as the lawyers pulled them apart, but not before Alexa got a vicious elbow in Carissa's side. Brax found himself smiling. Yes, this was the highlight of his month too.

He waited until Carissa had disappeared into the elevator before he gave Alexa a side hug.

"Good thing she didn't take your white truffle shavings."

"If she had, that video would be on a billboard in Times Square."

"I'm sorry I ever brought her into your life."

"Don't worry. I fixed the problem soon afterward."

"What do you mean?"

"Me and Grey used to collect all the spiders and put them

in your room because we realised she hated them. Voilà: no more Carissa."

"I love you. In a purely platonic way, of course." Alexa wrinkled her nose, but Brax knew that secretly, she was pleased. "I'm glad you came here, sweetheart. It was good to see you again. Don't be a stranger."

"Whatever." She headed for the stairs, Chase following with the laptops and a gift bag full of mouthwash, and Brax wasn't sure he'd ever see her again. "I need to get back to the Batcave." She flashed one last smile before she disappeared into the night. "Carissa's mole here is Selena Bateman. She works in the finance department."

CHAPTER 28
THE ASSISTANT

"Come on, Meera. Answer the damn phone!" I begged, but it was still turned off. I left one final message. "If you don't get back to me by this time tomorrow—it's, uh, nine a.m. in LA—then I'm coming to find you. Please call me. *Please*."

I sent an email saying the same.

Where the hell was she?

When I'd visited the Portuguese consulate on Monday, they said they couldn't help. That they were there to assist Portuguese citizens abroad, and if an American citizen had gone missing in Portugal, then I should call the US embassy in Lisbon. I'd already tried that. They said I'd need to file a missing persons report with the Portuguese police, and we all know how that went, don't we? Anyhow, I'd become, well, my high school English teacher would have described it as "overwrought," and when I couldn't keep my tears in, the consul's assistant had promised to make some calls.

Yesterday, I'd visited the consulate again to hear the results. The local police had found the hostel where Meera was staying, and the manager said she'd gone to the beach with a guy. Another tourist, he thought. Blond, skinny, spoke with a French accent or maybe Belgian. She'd asked the manager to store her bicycle and some of her belongings for a week until she got back.

Wasn't that good news? The consul's assistant thought it was good news.

But I wasn't so sure.

The story sounded plausible in theory, but why hadn't Meera told me of her plans? And why wasn't she answering the phone? Perhaps the device had been stolen, the consul's assistant suggested. Or she'd lost it. Or dropped it. Or forgotten the charger. There were plenty of explanations, but none of them felt right. Meera would have found a way to contact me. Borrowed a phone, found an internet café, sent a damn postcard.

And then there was the room at Pedro's brother's house. She'd been so excited to find a new place, ready to move on with the next phase of her life sans Alfie. Her move-in date had been yesterday. Would she really have sacrificed her work at the eco-project for what she herself had called a rebound fling?

I couldn't see it.

If the hostel manager was correct, Meera would return to Fundão sometime tonight. She'd meet her friends, talk to the staff at the hostel, and realise I was searching for her. Tomorrow morning, that was the deadline. If I didn't hear from her, I'd pawn my jewellery, the beautiful gifts from Mr. Vale, and fly to Portugal.

Once again, I considered calling Meera's parents, but if I was overreacting, if she was just distracted by a hot French (or maybe Belgian) guy and having a great time, I'd ruin her life for nothing. And my own. No, I had to look for her in person. The more notice my brothers had of my intentions, the more likely they were to find me, but if I booked a ticket and drove straight to the airport, do not pass go, do not collect two hundred dollars, I figured I'd be able to get out of the country without being caught. Getting back in would be a whole other challenge, but I'd cross that bridge when I came to it. Celeste said I could stay with her in Paris for a while until the heat had died down.

I still had no idea what to tell Mr. Vale. Leaving any job with no notice was horribly unprofessional, but leaving one where I was not-so-secretly in love with my boss would be a hundred times harder. For a moment, I considered telling him the truth. The whole story. That I was Indali, and Meera was Meera, and my father was a high-handed control freak. But I couldn't bear to see the look on Mr. Vale's face when he realised I'd been lying to him for all these months. Better to slip quietly out of his life.

For what was likely to be my final day at Dunnvale Holdings, I made an effort to dress nicely. A pencil skirt and silk shirt, the pumps Mr. Vale had bought for me at the airport, my lovely earrings and necklace. I should have known when Meera and I started this charade that something would go wrong. That it would all end in tears.

Although when I arrived at Nyx, the tears weren't mine; they were Selena's. She rushed past me carrying a cardboard box full of stuff, her expression tight.

"Selena, what's wrong? What happened?"

She didn't answer, just walked out the door and kept on going.

"What happened?" I asked Lyndsey when I reached the third-floor reception area.

"I have no freaking idea, but if you find out, tell me."

Around the corner, I saw Charlotte by the water cooler, filling a glass jug that already contained slices of lemon, cucumber, and strawberry.

"What's with all the fruit?" I asked.

"*Cosmo* says it'll help me to lose weight."

"You don't need to lose weight."

"You think? I could barely fit into my thong on Saturday. I've joined a gym too—wanna come?"

"Uh, I don't think I'll have the time." The clock was ticking, loud and clear. "What happened to Selena?"

Charlotte lowered her voice to a whisper. "Mr. Vale fired her."

He'd done *what*? "Why? Why would he do that?"

"I have no clue; she wouldn't say. She just threw all her stuff into a box and left. But if you find out the reason, let me know."

"Uh, sure."

I headed into my office. Mr. Vale had been in such a weird mood recently, but firing Selena was extreme. She was good at her job, he'd always said so, and such a fun person to be around.

There was a bound document on my desk. No note. For crying out loud—was I meant to mail it, photocopy it, or shred it? Why couldn't he just communicate? I scanned the first page—it was some kind of legal thing.

This divorce agreement ("this Agreement") is made and entered into as of the Effective Date by and between Braxton Louis Vale ("the Petitioner") and Carissa Madeleine Dunn ("the Respondent")...

Frantically, I flipped through to the end. Four signatures, all dated yesterday. Mr. Vale, Carissa, and two witnesses. Oh, hell, he'd done it. He'd really done it.

He'd gotten divorced, which meant he'd lost everything.

Was that why he'd let Selena go? Was she just the start? Had Carissa decided to close Nyx? It wasn't as if she had a clue how to run the club herself, and the building would be worth millions as real estate.

Gingerly, I pushed open the door to Mr. Vale's office, half

expecting him to be passed out drunk. But he wasn't. He was sitting at his empty desk, clean-shaven, no tie, his top shirt button undone.

Waiting.

But for what?

"You...you really did it?"

"I really did it."

"You gave up everything? This place?"

"Almost. I would have, but luckily it didn't come to that. Some old friends stepped in to help, and Carissa made a rare mistake."

"So Nyx is still yours?"

"Yes, and it always will be. Come and sit down, Meera."

I headed for the visitor chair in front of his desk, the place I usually sat, but he shook his head.

"Not there." He tapped the desk in front of him. "Here."

"You want me to sit on your desk?"

"I do."

He had the old gleam back in his eye, the cocky confidence, the glint that said "I'm going to ruin you and you're going to enjoy it."

I sat, eyeing him warily as goosebumps popped out on my arms.

"Good girl."

He ran his hands down my legs, then put my feet on the arms of his chair, my legs spread, the heels of my pumps digging into the soft leather, my panties exposed. The goosebumps turned into a shiver. I'd never felt quite so vulnerable.

Or quite so turned on.

Mr. Vale's divorce was finalised, and there was nothing between us now. Nothing to keep us apart. Well, nothing except the fact that I'd probably have to leave the country in the morning, anyway. My guilt complex was at war with itself. Deep down, I knew that he'd pushed the divorce through because of me, because of the heat that simmered between us every time we were close. But I didn't want to lead him on, to give him hope that we could have a future together and then fail to deliver.

He deserved more.

But then there was the selfish part of me—she wanted her say too. If my family tracked me down, I'd be forced to marry Karam, to submit to a man I hated. I'd have to give up everything for him. But he wasn't having my virginity. No, that gift would go to a man I loved.

So when Mr. Vale rose out of his chair and kissed me, his breath rough, his gaze heated, I kissed him right back.

I'd always worried that my lack of experience would stall me, that I'd make some embarrassing error, but now I realised my fears had been unfounded. Mr. Vale led, and I followed. He was in control. And the way he looked at me… I felt beautiful. Sexy. When Karam looked at me, I felt like a specimen under a microscope. As if he was assessing my many flaws.

Strong arms wrapped around me, a shield against all that was wrong in my world. I gave in to the moment, to the man, tipping my head back to allow Mr. Vale easier access as he ran the tip of his tongue along my jawline. Time slowed; my heart raced. His kisses were a drug, and I'd never get enough.

"My Meera," he murmured.

Yes, I was his. Wherever I was, whoever I was with, my heart would always belong to Braxton Vale.

"Are you expecting me to do any work today?" I asked, just to check. I was fairly sure I knew the answer already, but I wanted to be certain.

"Work is off the agenda. Your job today is to moan my name every time you come." Oh my. "And I don't mean 'Mr. Vale.'"

"Then why do you keep making me call you that?"

"I knew from the moment I met you that you'd change my life, and I thought it would keep some professional distance between us."

"Did it work?"

"What do you think? Every time you said it, my cock twitched, and because I'm a sick motherfucker, I decided I liked that."

"Brax…" I tried it out for size.

"Better. Fuck, I need to taste you."

I thought he'd kiss me again, but instead, he inched my skirt up, higher, higher, before burying his head between my legs. He feathered soft kisses up my inner thighs, then traced the delicate seam between my leg and my torso with his tongue. I squirmed, but he pushed me down on that enormous desk of his, hooking my legs over his shoulders as he did whatever he pleased.

"Do you have any hard limits, Meera?"

"W-what? I don't understand."

"Things you definitely don't want me to do?"

I definitely didn't want him to push a chopstick into my urethra—I'd seen the aftermath of that and it wasn't pretty—but I was quite sure Brax wouldn't be that stupid, so I just shook my head.

Then gasped as he pushed my panties aside and went to work with his tongue. That *magic* tongue. He circled my clitoris, licking and sucking and teasing, showing me everything I'd missed out on thanks to my father's constant meddling.

But…but at that moment, I was glad he'd interfered. Glad he'd paid off all the men who'd come before. Because there was no one I'd rather be doing this with than Braxton lizard-tongue Vale.

"You taste even sweeter than I thought," he murmured, pausing for a moment to study me.

"Don't you dare stop."

His familiar smirk made an appearance.

"Looks as if I'm not the only one who can be bossy."

"I learned from the master, okay?"

He chuckled against me, which did nothing for my self-control, and I tunnelled my hands through his hair as an orgasm tore through me like wildfire, igniting every nerve ending. I remembered his instruction as I arched off the desk, but his name had been on my lips anyway.

"Brax..."

I was still trembling when he met my gaze, his chin glistening with my juices, looking so damn pleased with himself. As he had every right to be.

"You have no idea how many times I've fantasised about doing this." He sighed and tore my panties right off. "And that." Great, now I'd be going home sans underwear. "You're everything I imagined."

And he was more than I'd ever dreamed of. I sat up to kiss those delicious lips again, tasting myself as well as him. As we paused for breath, I glanced down and saw the outline of his cock straining at his pants, and I was unprepared for the heat that rushed through me. Heat followed by a wave of apprehension.

"Are you going to fuck me here?" I whispered.

Another question rode hot on its heels. What if I wasn't good enough?

"Not here. Tempting though it is with you draped over my desk like that, your first time is going to be in a bed, Meera."

"So you're going to fuck me upstairs?"

"No, I'm going to make love to you upstairs. There's plenty of time for fucking later."

But there wasn't. If Meera hadn't called me back by morning, this would be over. Because I'd have to go and find her.

Brax lowered me again, then slowly unbuttoned my shirt and spread it out on the desk like butterfly wings under my sweat-soaked back. Sex was a musky, damp affair, and I discovered I loved every moment of it. And I loved the man with me. He pulled down my bra cups so my breasts bulged over the top and pinched my nipples into hard peaks. Brax wasn't rough, but he wasn't exactly gentle either. A hint of pain...was more pleasurable than I'd ever thought it could be. No, that wasn't a limit. Hard was followed by soft, his tongue again, and I felt the first stirrings of another orgasm. I was a dripping mess, but Brax didn't seem to care.

"Come for me one more time, and then we'll move this to the bedroom."

"Make me."

He flashed me a filthy grin. "Challenge accepted."

This time, he slid a finger inside me, just one, and stroked a spot I didn't even know existed. I detonated underneath him, and this time I didn't moan his name. I screamed it.

"Shit! The finance department must have heard that."

"Do you care?"

"Yes? They'll realise what we're doing in here."

"Does that matter?"

"Well—"

"Do you think you're going to be my dirty little secret? Because that's not how this is going to work. I want everyone to know you're mine and nobody else's."

"Uh..."

"Just in case you haven't realised, this isn't some sordid little affair with my secretary. I'm in love with you, Meera."

Indi. My name is Indi.

"I...I don't know what to say."

"You'll say it when you're ready." There was that confidence again. "Can you walk upstairs, or do I have to carry you?"

"I can walk."

Barely.

In the elevator, I watched us in the mirrored wall, my shirt buttoned wonkily, my too-long bangs flopping over my eyes as my head rested on Brax's shoulder.

"What are you thinking?" he whispered.

"I'm thinking that my life is a mess, but there's nothing I'd change about being here today with you."

That was the honest truth.

Brax's bed was a huge metal four-poster, the head and foot a series of interlocking curves and rectangles that matched the Art Deco style of the building. The sheets were dark red, and in my culture, red was associated with Durga, goddess of strength and protection, a fierce warrior who embodied courage I could only dream of.

"Carissa has never slept in this bed," he told me. "I remodelled last year."

"Keep her name out of our bedroom." I clapped a hand over my mouth. "Sorry, I'm so sorry. I didn't mean to—"

He took my hand in his and kissed my palm. "She's gone."

And so was my shirt. Brax yanked it open this time, and buttons scattered everywhere. Dammit! My skirt pooled at my feet and I stood there almost naked, a deer in headlights because I knew what was coming next. I wasn't scared, but I was definitely nervous.

And Brax was definitely wearing too many clothes.

"You still have your shoes on," I muttered. "And everything else."

"Then take it all off."

My hands trembled as I unbuttoned his shirt and got my first proper look at Braxton Vale. A smooth chest, hard and defined but not too muscular. Just perfect. Tentatively, I ran my fingertips over his skin, so aware of him watching me.

"Am I doing this right?" I whispered.

"There's no right or wrong, only what feels good and what doesn't. Exploring each other's bodies is natural."

I walked around him, tracing the contours of his back, admiring the view, pausing to press my lips to each shoulder blade. The man was gorgeous. Of course, he was well aware of that.

"Can I?" I asked as I reached for his belt buckle.

"Be my guest."

He was hard already, his cock forming a tent in briefs I was all too familiar with, seeing as I'd bought them three weeks ago. What I wasn't familiar with was the deep V on either side of his torso, disappearing into the waistband. He really did spend a lot of time in the gym, didn't he? Not that I was complaining.

The other surprise? The tattoo peeking out above his right butt cheek. I inched the waistband of the briefs down and found not only a taut ass but also two Chinese symbols, each a couple of inches high. Wow. I'd never pictured him as a tattoo guy.

"What does this mean?"

"Asshole."

"I'm sorry?"

"It was a joke, by either the tattoo artist or the woman I was with at the time. Probably the woman."

"A girlfriend got 'asshole' tattooed on your butt? What did you do to upset her?"

"I believe the correct term is 'tramp stamp,' and she was just a friend. Okay, a friend with occasional benefits, but definitely not a girlfriend. And she had a twisted sense of humour. I considered getting the ink removed, but I figured it's a part of who I am."

"At least it doesn't say 'egg fried rice.'"

Brax laughed. "True."

I crouched to untie his shoes, and he stepped out of the pants.

We were both down to our underwear now—well, just a bra for me since he'd already ripped off my panties—and I'd always thought I'd feel uncomfortable under such scrutiny. Brax's eyes were hungry, but my skin prickled with desire, not worry.

He fiddled with the clasp of my bra for a moment, then gave up and tore that off too, leaving me in the high-heeled pumps and nothing else. I started to remove one, but he shook his head.

"No, leave them on. I want to feel those heels digging into my ass later."

"To share the pain?" I asked without thinking.

Meera said her first time felt as if she were being split in half. Since it had taken place in the back seat of a car, she'd also bruised her elbow and cricked her neck. Thanks to my medical training, I understood the pain would depend to a degree on the amount of hymenal tissue I had, but I was under no illusion that it wouldn't hurt.

Brax tilted my chin so I couldn't avoid his gaze. "I can't promise it'll be painless, but I'll do my utmost to make it pleasurable. You're trusting me with something precious, and I'm not going to abuse that trust."

Of that, I was certain. "There's nobody I'd rather be doing this with."

"Good."

"So, can we just…you know, get it over with?"

"No. No, I think we'll take our time."

He wasn't kidding.

The morning drifted by on a cloud of pleasure. Brax gifted me with three more orgasms, all from his fingers and tongue, and I got my first taste of his impressive dick. I'd been way, way off the mark with my comment the first day we met—the Porsche sure wasn't a penis extension. I braced for him to ejaculate in my mouth, but instead, he pulled out and shot ropes of cum over my breasts, then massaged it into my skin as I watched. Holy hotness. I lost my vocabulary entirely—all I could moan was his name.

And still we didn't have sex. No, he left me boneless in his giant bed while he went downstairs to collect lunch, then fed me delicious morsels of gourmet food while we both sat naked among the pillows. He poured champagne into my navel and drank it. He drizzled warm caramel over my stomach and licked it off. He circled ice cubes around my nipples and kissed the goosebumps.

He told me he loved me, but I couldn't say it back.

Not until tomorrow.

Not until I knew where fate would take me.

Darkness descended, and I fell into a sleepy haze. Only then did he finally, finally roll on a condom.

"Tell me if you want me to stop," he murmured. "I don't want to hurt you."

I can't lie and say it didn't hurt at all, but the pain as he stretched me was strangely exquisite. Flames flared in my belly, filling my veins with molten lust. He went slowly, so slowly, and once he'd filled me, he peppered me with kisses on my lips, my shoulders, my breasts, giving me time to adjust.

"This is a first for me too," he murmured as he began to slide in and out of me in smooth strokes. "The first time a woman's been mine from the very beginning. I don't think I'll last long."

"Take whatever you need."

"I only need you."

My heart swelled and ached at the same time. As Brax moved faster, I grew a little sore, but I didn't say a word because every soft kiss, every gentle caress, made the pain fade into the background. And I wanted to give him this. I wanted to give him everything. He came with a long groan and gathered me up in his arms, worshipping me with sweet words interspersed with the occasional mention of filth. This was a day I'd remember forever, for all the right reasons.

I loved Brax Vale with every piece of my heart and soul.

That was my last thought before I fell into an exhausted sleep. I didn't dream. How could I when my dream was real and wrapped around me?

CHAPTER 29
BRAX

For a moment, Brax thought he'd dreamed the whole thing.

When he woke, the other side of his bed was empty, the apartment silent. But no, the room smelled of sex, and the remains of a lacy bra lay on the floor beside the nightstand. So where was Meera? He rolled out of bed, relishing the glorious ache that only came from a twelve-hour sex session, and checked the bathroom, the dressing room, and the kitchen, but there was no sign of her. Had she, for some unholy reason, thought she should go to work today? Without her underwear?

He called his own extension, but she didn't pick up. Her cell phone went straight to voicemail, and a hint of worry crept into Brax's thoughts. Then he found the note.

She'd left it propped against a vase in the hall, a hastily penned paragraph written on the back of a been-and-gone benefit invite that he hadn't gotten around to recycling yet.

Brax,

I never wanted to have to write this letter.
Firstly, I want you to know that I love you. Every
piece of you, exactly as you are. Secondly, there are
some things I never told you about me. I wish we
could be together, but with the hand life dealt me,
it's an impossible dream. Just know that in my heart,
I'll always be yours.
　　　Meera

What the hell?

She was dumping him? And this was how she chose to do it? After the best night of his life, she wrote him a fucking note? She loved him, but she couldn't be with him? What was this bullshit?

Her clothes were gone, and her shoes were gone. She'd run out of his apartment and headed…where? Home? What hadn't she told him? Why did that stop them from being together? Did she have a secret boyfriend squirrelled away? No. No, she might have been able to fake the sweet inexperience, but she couldn't fake a hymen. Could she? There were medical procedures these days, and— *No.* She hadn't been faking.

Something a little like panic made Brax's chest tighten. He'd just freed himself from Carissa, and now his life had fallen apart again. Carissa. Suddenly, he knew. He knew Meera's secret. The timing gave it away. She *had* been on Carissa's payroll, a beguiling sorceress sent to tempt him. But instead of completing the mission, she'd saved him from his raging lust. That night in the limo, she'd had him. If she'd come back to his apartment, he'd have slept with her, and she could have collected whatever bonus Carissa had promised.

But she didn't.

She'd betrayed her real boss instead of him.

Was that why she'd run? Because Carissa had threatened to reveal all in revenge? Fuck, it was his fault—he'd been the one to tell Carissa the truth, that Meera had refused to sleep with him.

It hurt, knowing that Meera had come into his life under false pretences, but their feelings were real; he was certain of that. He loved her, and in the note, she said she loved him. They could still make this work. If she'd just talk to him instead of running, they could make it work.

He needed to find her.

In his dressing room, he threw on the first clothes to hand —jeans, a T-shirt, tennis shoes without socks. Where had he left the car key? Think, dammit, *think*. Traffic was awful, as usual, but she'd have gotten stuck in it too. Brax knew where her apartment was. He'd even driven past it a couple of times, trying to work up the courage to tell her how he felt. He'd also strongly considered renting her a better place and telling her it was a perk of the job, because her neighbourhood was rough, but that would have meant tossing gasoline on the divorce bonfire.

On the way, he tried calling her again, but she still didn't pick up. And she complained that *his* communication skills were poor? Sheesh. Finally, he made it to her street, but there was nowhere to park. A cab had taken the last spot outside her building. Would it leave soon? The driver was still inside.

Then he saw her.

Meera was hefting a suitcase down the front steps, her hair blowing in the wind as she headed for the cab. No way. She wasn't getting into it. Brax wasn't going to chase her all over LA. He abandoned the Porsche in the street, ignoring the cacophony of horns and the angry shouts of other drivers as he ran toward her.

"Meera, stop!"

She froze, and when he got closer, he saw the dirty tracks on her cheeks. She'd been crying.

"Just wait."

"I...I can't."

"We need to talk about this."

She shook her head, and another tear fell. "I have to get to the airport."

The airport? Where was she flying to? "You're just leaving? You said you loved me—doesn't that count for anything?"

"I wish it could, but...but it's complicated."

"I know you're working for Carissa."

Instead of that being the "gotcha" Brax had hoped for, Meera merely looked puzzled.

"Carissa? What?"

"She sent you to seduce me, but it's okay. I forgive you."

"No... No, she didn't."

Meera wasn't lying, not about that anyway. So what was the big secret? What didn't she want to tell him? As if the morning weren't bad enough already, people on the street began yelling.

"Move your fucking car, asshole."

"You're blocking the damn road."

A woman took Brax's side. "Shaddup, this is like a movie. Are you filming a movie?"

"Meera, please, just tell me what's going on."

"I have to catch my flight."

He took a deep breath. "Then I'll drive you to LAX myself."

"I—"

"What's the problem? You said you need to go to the airport? I'll take you to the airport." Thank fuck Brax had picked up his wallet before he left. He extracted a hundred-dollar bill and held it out to the cab driver. "Your services are no longer required."

The guy snatched the cash out of his hand, no doubt relieved to be free of the traffic jam and the drama. Now Meera didn't have a choice. She'd have to ride with Brax or risk being late. Just in case she needed any further help in making up her mind, he hefted the suitcase into the Porsche's trunk, slammed the lid, and opened the passenger door. Meera climbed inside. Stiffly, but she got in. Several stuck drivers cheered, but Brax had little to be happy about. He pulled away slowly, in no hurry whatsoever. Yes, he'd drive her to the airport as promised, but he'd take his sweet time doing it.

"So, why did you run out on me?"

"I...I don't know where to start."

"How about at the beginning?"

"At the beginning..." she echoed. "At the beginning, I..." She paused and took a long breath. Let it out. "I was born Indali Azarin Vadera in Springfield, Massachusetts."

"Indali? That was your name? When did you change it to Meera?"

"I didn't. I'm still Indi."

Indi? But that made no sense. He'd been calling her Meera for months. In the office, in his daydreams, in bed.

"Then why are you calling yourself Meera?"

"My best friend is Meera. I sort of...borrowed her identity. We look almost the same."

"Why?"

"You said to start at the beginning." Another pause. "My family still lives in Springfield. My father's side is wealthy. Not your league of wealthy, but very comfortable financially. My life, though, it wasn't comfortable. My first mistake was being born female. My second mistake was having an independent streak." She closed her eyes for a moment, steeling herself. "My father, he's very traditional. A woman's place is in the home, cooking and cleaning and raising the children, that kind of traditional. My late grandfather was more progressive, and it was thanks to him that I was allowed to go to college, but in my father's eyes, I was only whiling away time until he found a suitable man for me to marry."

Fuck.

"Tell me you're not married?"

"No, I'm not. That's why I left. Because I didn't want to marry the man he chose. I wanted my own life, a career that fulfilled me, a husband I married for love rather than out of obligation. I couldn't have any of that in Massachusetts."

"That still doesn't explain how you ended up on my payroll as Meera."

"Meera was my roommate in college. We shared an apartment for four years, but she had her own family problems. Her folks are quite pushy. It didn't help that she signed up to study engineering and then switched to environmental science without telling them, or that she wasted a year partying. But she knuckled down from year three, after her father threatened to cut off her allowance."

"So she's the environmentalist? What did you study?"

"Oh, I went to medical school. I was meant to start my residency at Johns Hopkins last summer, but I had to quit before I got there."

Oh, I went to medical school. She was a doctor; she just threw that out so nonchalantly. Guess that explained the Heimlich manoeuvre. His Meera was smarter than he'd ever suspected. No, not Meera. Indi. And was she even his anymore?

"Because your father made you quit? But you're an adult."

"He has ways of forcing people to do things. And I may be an adult, but in his eyes, women are property. Unmarried, I belong to him. When I've got a ring on my finger, I'll pass into the ownership of my husband."

"That's archaic."

"Yes, but it's also how things are. My brothers are the same. Raj married four years ago, and he already has three kids, all girls. You can't imagine how annoyed he is about that. His poor wife—she just has to keep going until she gives him a boy."

At least Indi was talking now. Brax hated every word she was saying, but he still wanted to hear it.

"What if the boy never comes?"

"Honestly, I don't know. Maybe he'll get a new wife?"

"He didn't marry for love, then."

"No, his wife came from a good family in Mumbai. It was a strategic match. She's everything I'm not—homey, subservient, family-oriented. Oh, and she can cook. I can't cook, not at all, which is weird because my mom's an excellent chef, but... Never mind."

"You don't want children?"

"Maybe? Someday? I just hoped to establish myself in a career first, and... Why are we even talking about this?"

"Too early for the 'kids' discussion?"

"Don't you understand? I can't stay with you, no matter how much I might want to. I don't have Meera's passport, only her driver's licence, so I had to book the plane ticket in my own name. My little brother's a cop, and he'll have me on some kind of a watchlist, I know he will. Then they'll catch up with me and drag me home to marry Karam, who's a self-centred asshole, by the way. He wants me to have breast augmentation surgery before the wedding so the photos will look better."

"There's nothing wrong with your breasts."

"You don't think they're too small?"

"Any more than a mouthful is a waste." Interesting though this discussion was, it still didn't answer the airport question, and they were on a deadline. Brax had less than half an hour to persuade her to stay. "Where are you flying to, Indi?"

"To find Meera. She's disappeared. I kept telling myself it would be all right, that she'd just met a guy and lost track of time, but it's been over a week, and she hasn't been in contact once. Her phone's turned off, and her social media accounts are dead. She always posts every single day. It's part of our cover story."

"Your cover story? For hiding from your, what? Your fiancé? Did it get that far?"

"We had a huge engagement party. It was excruciating. But Meera needed a cover story too—her family isn't as bad as mine, but they didn't like her boyfriend, and the two of them wanted to spend a year backpacking around Europe, working on environmental projects. Her family, especially her grandfather, wanted her to—and I quote—stop messing around with trees and get a respectable job. He threatened to leave his house to a cat sanctuary otherwise, and while cats are very lovely, I'm sure, do you know how hard it is to buy a house these days if you don't have family money?"

Now Brax was starting to piece things together. "So Meera and the boyfriend went to Europe to hug trees, and you fulfilled her familial obligation?"

"To plant trees, and they were engaged, but yes."

"So working for me counts as a respectable job? I take it you didn't tell her about the sex club?"

"Uh, I might have mentioned it. Please don't be mad at me."

She turned to look at him, and when she bit her lip, how could he be angry?

"Did you give her any details?"

"No, I just said it was super fancy." A shy smile. "She kept asking when I was going to head down there and find myself a hot man, but it turned out he was sitting in the next office."

Brax reached across the centre console to squeeze Indi's hand, and when she didn't snatch it away, he had to take that as a good sign.

"Then I'm not mad. Why do you need to go and look for her? Where's the fiancé?"

"Lisbon, I think. Three weeks ago, he dumped her for a girl he'd just met and left town."

"And people think *I'm* an asshole?"

"If the tattoo fits… Sorry, I'm so sorry."

"Stop apologising."

"Sorry. Uh, crap. Anyhow, nobody but me thinks there's anything wrong. Her parents might be getting worried that she hasn't checked in, but obviously I can't call them, and they think she's in LA in any case."

Ah, fuck. "Her father called me on Tuesday. You were at lunch, and with everything that happened, I forgot to tell you. I said you—she—was fine."

"See? That's exactly my point—nobody's looking for her." Indi blew out a breath, but at least she didn't seem upset by the misunderstanding. "The police said she went to the beach with a French guy, and she's probably having a great time and simply forgot to call, but they don't know Meera. Something's happened."

"And so what's your plan? You're just going to go over there and start asking questions?"

"Well, yes?"

Brax felt like hitting his head on the steering wheel. In many ways, Indi was so incredibly smart, but she could also be painfully naive. He couldn't yet be sure whether her fears were grounded or not, but he did know one thing—the two of them were in this together.

"If some harm has befallen Meera, and you poke around and stir up a hornets' nest with your questions, how do you know that whatever happened to her won't also happen to you?"

The long silence told Brax she hadn't considered that possibility.

"I guess I don't," she said finally. "But that's a chance I'll have to take, isn't it? I can't sit in LA and do nothing."

Add "brave" to her list of attributes. And "foolish." Perhaps "pigheaded" too.

"Do you even speak Portuguese?"

"No, but I have three different translation apps."

"And does anyone know where you're going?"

"My friend Celeste. She lives in Paris, and I'm going to check in with her every day."

Brax sighed, and when the light turned green, he made an illegal U-turn, ignoring the furious honks that followed. Indi didn't much like that move either.

"What are you doing? Where are you going?"

"We're going home."

"No! You promised you'd take me to the airport." She unclipped her seat belt. What was she planning to do? Jump out of a moving vehicle? "I'm going to miss my flight."

"Yes, you absolutely are."

"You know what? That tattoo on your ass is one hundred percent correct. It should be on your forehead."

"It would be an interesting talking point at parties, don't you think?"

A grocery store came up on the right, and Brax pulled into the parking lot, keeping a wary eye on Mee— Indi in case she tried to make a run for it. He was still trying to get used to the new name.

"How confident are you that your family will try something stupid?"

"Confident enough that I moved three thousand miles away and assumed a new identity."

Okay, in hindsight, that had been a stupid question. Brax opened his wallet and slid out a credit card.

"When did you book the flight?"

"Right before I left my apartment."

She hadn't tried to escape, but her voice had turned sullen. Sulky. The pout was actually quite cute.

"Book another flight—now, this second. Not to Portugal. To South America, maybe. Or the Caribbean. And in two hours, book another flight. The same two hours after that. Rinse and repeat."

"Why? I don't want to go to South America."

"Because if your family has six different places to look for you, they're less likely to find you in Portugal."

"But I can't get to Portugal now. Thanks to you, I won't make boarding. And I can't afford to pay you back for six plane tickets either."

"I'll treat that second part of your comment with the contempt it deserves. And we're going to fly to Portugal from a different airport where the staff understand the meaning of discretion."

"*We're* going to fly?"

There was that naivety again. She really thought he'd let her do this alone? Brax tucked a stray lock of hair behind Indi's ear, pleased when she leaned into his touch.

"You can run from me, my sweet, but I'll always find you. Shit, that sounded creepier than I intended. Of course I'm coming."

"You'd help me? Even after all the lies?"

"On one condition?"

"Which is? It doesn't involve chopsticks, does it?"

"You don't like Chinese food?"

"Never mind. What's the condition?"

"No more lies. You tell me the absolute truth from now on, and I *will* have you thoroughly background-checked to make sure."

"But...but why? Not the background check—I understand why you'd want that done—but why help me at all?"

"Because underneath the lies, you're still the same person I fell in love with, more or less. The sexy-as-hell ingénue. The girl who follows her heart, even when it's not an easy path to take. The woman who'd risk everything for a friend. And you fell for the man who understands what it's like to be trapped in a loveless marriage. The man who missed an opportunity to save a friend and wishes he could turn back the clock. The man who changed his name to escape his past, albeit slightly more legally than you did."

"You changed your name? Why?"

"We can discuss that later, when we're in the air. It's nothing that you need to worry about, I promise. But right now, we need to get home, make new travel arrangements, start some preliminary enquiries, and find a suitable place to stay because you didn't book accommodation, did you?"

"I thought I'd just get a bed in the same hostel as Meera."

Brax hadn't spent the last decade of his life working his ass off in order to stay in a hostel.

"Find somewhere else. A good hotel or a villa. Book it in my name so it doesn't link back to you."

"But—"

"If the words on the tip of your tongue include any complaint about affordability or a suggestion of paying me back, don't waste your time."

Indi closed her mouth again.

"Where's your necklace?" Brax asked.

"I pawned it to pay for my flight," she said in a small voice.

"Ask Charlotte to pick it up. And put your seat belt back on. Actually, no. Kiss me, and then put your seat belt back on."

"Are you always this bossy?"

"Only when the woman I've waited my whole life to meet does something monumentally stupid, like trying to play detective in a foreign country on her own." Brax smiled because now he knew he had her back. "And also in the bedroom."

Indi shifted to her knees and leaned over the console to kiss him deeply, her arms wrapped around his neck and her fingers tunnelled into his hair. He had her, and he was damn well keeping her.

"I like you bossy in the bedroom," she mumbled.

Yes, this woman was definitely his.

CHAPTER 30
BRAX

"You need a favour? Didn't I do you enough favours this week already? Jerry says thanks for the mouthwash, by the way."

"There have been some interesting developments," Brax told Alexa. She was back to her regular form now—a cartoon avatar in an app.

"Like what?"

"I fell in love with one woman, and she turned out to be someone else."

"You'll have to elaborate."

So he did. He detailed the events of the past twenty-four hours, from informing Indi of his divorce yesterday and waking in the morning and finding her missing, to her confession in the car, skipping the dirty parts because Alexa didn't need to know about those.

"So I need an enhanced background check on Indali Vadera, plus anything you can find on the real Meera Adams. Indi's concerned about her safety."

"I don't know how I missed this," Alexa grumbled, sounding thoroughly pissed off. She didn't often get things wrong, and on the rare occasions she did make a mistake, she tended to beat herself up about it. "I checked the DMV, her Harvard transcripts, her— Oh, whoa. They're basically twins." A picture flashed up on the screen. "See?"

At first, he thought Indi was on the right, but then he realised his error—that was Meera, and Indi had changed her hairstyle to match her friend's. If you looked closely, you could see the subtle differences. Meera's skin was a smidgen lighter, her eyes a slightly darker shade of brown. Was her nose wider, or did the camera angle just make it look that way? Or the lighting? It was like seeing double, except Meera wore a carefree smile and Indi was oh-so serious.

"They're practically identical."

"You're sure they're not related?"

"Apparently not. Can you take a look at Indi's history? Her father's name is Arjun Vadera, and her brothers are Rajan and Vimal." In line with their "no more secrets" policy, Indi had given him the details on the drive back to Nyx. "The ex-fiancé is Karam Joshi. Where did you find the picture?"

"Indali Vadera's Facebook page. She hasn't used it in over a year. Before that, she posted about life at Harvard, medical stuff, more pictures of her and Meera. Eeuw, some guy got a chopstick stuck in his bladder."

"How the fuck would he do that?"

"How the hell should I know? I'll dig deeper, okay? Into Indi's background, not the chopstick thing. That's gross."

"And Meera Adams?" Brax recited her last known address. "She's been out of touch for a while. Indi says she can be impulsive, but she's also reliable when it comes to calling."

"I'll see what I can do. Anything else?"

Alexa's tone was sarcastic, but Brax ignored that.

"Since you travel a lot and seem to move in some interesting circles these days, do you know of any Portuguese-speaking guns for hire? I'm speaking metaphorically. I need people with investigative experience who'll do whatever it takes to find a missing woman. Dawson's already agreed to come."

His old roommate had joined the U.S. Navy after they left Blackstone House, and he'd made it all the way to the SEALs before he got dishonourably discharged for punching a senator. The general consensus was that the senator deserved everything he'd gotten, but the powers that be had decided to make an example of Dawson.

"Ask Ari too. She works part-time for that weird dude in Vegas, but her days are flexible, and she's smart."

"I'll try her."

"Hand on heart, do you honestly think bad shit happened to the real Meera?"

"I don't want to worry Indi more, but from what she's told me, there's a definite possibility that her friend has come to some harm."

"Let me check around and see who else is available. Have you found a plane, or do you need one of those too?"

"I need one of those too. Do you have a contact?"

"Give me a few hours, and keep an eye on your phone."

By dawn, Alexa had pulled yet another miracle out of the bag. Brax owed a whole lot of favours to people he'd never even met, but he'd worry about that later, and he'd gladly pay up. Dawson had arrived from Canada, and Ari had driven through the night from Santa Cruz.

Instead of leaving from LAX, they'd be flying out of San Bernardino International, a former military base that catered mainly to cargo operations, private aviation, and the United States Forest Service. Alexa had promised a plane would be waiting, plus a guy who knew how to ask questions in Portuguese and could spare a week to help, but no more.

Project AVA would be swimming in money after this.

And Brax had his girl back, but Indi was different. Not in a bad way, just different. Relieved that her secret was out but scared in case her friend had come to harm. Was Brax upset about the lies? He couldn't pretend to be happy that she hadn't trusted him sooner, but he understood her reasons. Information was trickling in from Alexa now, bits and pieces of Indi's former life.

The shocker came just after six a.m.

"Did she mention the arrest warrant?" Alexa asked.

Brax had headed to the kitchen to grab some food for the trip—who knew what Alexa's plane would come with?—and he nearly dropped his mug of coffee.

"What arrest warrant?"

"Indali Vadera is wanted for theft."

"Theft? What did she steal?"

"*Allegedly* steal. A thirty-thousand-dollar Rolex belonging to her father. You want a copy of the report? It says she snatched the watch out of his safe."

Brax closed his eyes and took a deep breath. Indi had promised no lies. A lie by omission went against the spirit of the agreement. He glanced toward the doorway that led to the bedrooms. She'd tossed and turned for the short time they'd spent in bed together, then drifted off just before they were due to wake up.

"Email me the report."

He headed for his private office beside the gym. Actually, "gym" was too grand a word for it—the room contained a treadmill, a stationary bike, and a rowing machine, plus a set of free weights. If he wanted a more comprehensive workout, he went down to the first floor and used the club facilities.

The report pinged up on his laptop screen, and he scanned the details.

"That motherfucker," he muttered.

"You'll have to be more specific."

"Look at the name of the officer who signed the report."

"Damn. Her own brother?"

"She said he'd be watching for her to reappear." And an arrest warrant would ensure that if she was pulled over for something as innocuous as a traffic violation, he'd be notified. "It's dated at the end of June last year. According to Indi's résumé, she was already in California by that point. I can't see her returning home to Springfield to steal a watch and then flying back here again."

"People lie on their résumés all the time."

"So I'll have to check it out."

"Do you need to delay the trip to Portugal?"

Another glance toward the bedroom. "No. But we'll have to be careful—do they check for arrest warrants at the airport?"

"Yes and no. TSA won't check if she's flying domestically, but CBP has access to the FBI's NCIC database, so they might pick it up."

"Stealing a watch isn't a federal crime, is it?"

"No, the Feds just run the database. Some agencies enter every outstanding warrant in it, even for traffic fines, while others don't bother. I could delete the entry for Indali, but if the brother's monitoring things closely, he might notice, and that's an inconvenience we don't need."

"So are you saying she shouldn't travel abroad?"

"No, I'm saying that by the time you're done with this whole shebang, you'll owe so many favours that you'll wish you were still married to Carissa. Are you sure this woman is worth it?"

"Yes."

"Then I'll find a workaround."

But Brax had sounded more confident than he felt. An arrest warrant? His business was mostly legal, but he definitely didn't need scrutiny from the authorities, no matter how many high-ranking officials might visit The Dark.

225

He padded back to the bedroom.

"Indi?"

Nothing.

"Indi, wake up."

He nudged her shoulder, and she knifed into a sitting position.

"What…where…?"

"Tell me about the arrest warrant."

Brax figured that if he caught her off guard and half-asleep, she wouldn't have time to think up a story. That way, he'd get the truth.

"Arrest warrant? Huh? Who got arrested?"

"Nobody yet. There's a warrant out for your arrest."

Her face was a picture of absolute horror. "I… Why?" Then she gasped. "That man is such a jerk!"

"What man?"

"My ex-landlord. I signed a lease for a year, but there were roaches. There were roaches *everywhere*. The bathroom, the closet, under the bed. I poured cereal one morning, and a roach fell into the bowl, and that was the final straw. He threatened to report me—well, Meera—for breaking the lease, but I didn't think he'd actually do it. Will it go on her record? How can I fix it?"

She spoke the truth. Nobody could fake that level of disgust.

"What were you doing last June? Where were you?"

"Uh, here in LA, mostly. I left Massachusetts on the…uh, on the third."

"Were you working in June?"

"From the…the ninth, yes. No, the tenth. The interview was on the ninth, and they said I could start right away."

"Where?"

"Silver's Gym. It's in the Warehouse District. Why? Why does that matter?"

"What days did you work?"

"Wednesday through Sunday."

"Can you prove that?"

"Maybe? I can't remember exactly what my contract said. There was a shift schedule on the wall in the break room. Possibly my boss would recall? Probably not, though."

"Why did you leave?"

Indi grimaced. "I was a little too forthright with my views on steroid abuse. I was only trying to help—I mean, what man wants shrunken testicles, erectile dysfunction, and an increased risk of prostate cancer? But anabolic steroids can also cause mood swings and aggressive behaviour, and it turned out they didn't want my advice."

"Did they hurt you?"

"Oh, no. My boss just yelled a bit and told me I wasn't a good fit for the role. But why all these questions?"

"Your father filed a police report saying you stole a watch from his safe."

"From his safe? How would I do that? I don't even know the combination—he changes it every month, and it's not as if he'd trust me with the details." Indi's voice got higher in pitch as the news sank in and she began to panic. "And why would I take a watch? I already have a watch."

"So you could sell it, probably."

"If I was that desperate for money, I'd have taken the cash he keeps in his desk drawer. There's a false bottom he thinks I don't know about. And I didn't even go back to freaking Springfield before I left Massachusetts. I just sold all the stuff I didn't need and got on a bus in Boston." She buried her head in her hands. "Every time I think this can't get any worse, it does. Is someone coming to arrest me? Should I get a lawyer?"

Brax believed her.

"Not right now. At some point, we'll have to deal with this, but we have more important things to worry about today." Brax glanced at his own watch. "We have to leave in thirty minutes."

"What if I get arrested at the airport? What if—"

"You won't be." Alexa had said she'd find a workaround, and although she was a pain in the ass who paid lip service to the law most of the time, Brax trusted her. "I promise you won't be."

CHAPTER 31
THE ASSISTANT

He'd really done it. Brax had really arranged a private jet. The gleaming white bird was parked on the tarmac outside the executive terminal, so near and yet so far. Would we make it on board? Because there was a man in a uniform waiting ahead of us, and the police thought I was a freaking criminal. I'd always assumed that Vimal would abuse the privileges of his job to find me, but I hadn't dreamed he'd actually try to have me arrested.

"Let me do the talking," Brax said under his breath. "You're the trophy girlfriend of a wealthy businessman—act entitled."

I'd always tried not to do that. And would it be enough, anyway? I had "guilty" written all over my face, and I hadn't even done anything. Well, except for walking into Brax's life and turning it upside down. He'd just gotten free from one troublesome woman, only to get tangled up with another one.

"Good morning, sir. Ma'am." The man nodded to both of us. His uniform said he held some kind of authority, but he wasn't a cop.

"Morning." Brax had our passports in his hand, but he didn't offer them.

"Do you need a ride to your plane?"

A ride? Why would we need a ride? The plane was right there, and a porter was taking care of our bags.

"That won't be necessary."

Uniform Guy opened the door for us.

"The other members of your party are already on board. Have a good flight, sir. Mind the step, ma'am."

That was it? No rifling through my suitcase? No removal of shoes? No awkward pat-down? This was my dream life, apart from my best friend being missing, obviously.

Brax gripped my hand as we walked to the plane, and I thought the gesture was part of the act, that he'd drop it as soon as Uniform Guy was out of sight, but no, he didn't let go until we reached the bottom of the stairs. My father used to march onto planes while my mom struggled with the bags, but with one of those weirdly intimate touches to my lower back, Brax signalled that I should go first.

"You *are* a gentleman."

He'd claimed that a while ago, and at the time, I hadn't believed him. But now I knew he spoke the truth.

"No, my queen. I just want to admire your ass."

Now he was lying. Brax might have a dirty mind, but chivalry was ingrained in his DNA. Still, I put a little wiggle on as I climbed up the steps, then stopped short at the top when I realised the pilot was watching me.

"Welcome aboard, ma'am. I'm Brett, and I'll be your pilot for this trip."

"Nice to meet you, Brett." I didn't have to act entitled anymore, right? That was just for the security guy? "This plane is much bigger than I thought it would be."

"We need the range," a voice said from my right. "We'll be flying almost six thousand miles today."

I turned to find an older man lounging against the wall, early forties at a guess, although the weathered face combined with an obviously toned body made it hard to tell. A lecture about sunblock was on the tip of my tongue, but I held back. In any case, the creases only made him look more appealing, handsome in a James Bond, battles-hard-fought kind of way. But his fashion sense didn't come close to 007's. This guy wore a Hawaiian shirt, cargo shorts, and sandals. At least he'd forgone the socks.

He gave me a lazy salute. "Priest. Co-pilot."

"Mr. Priest?"

"No, just Priest."

Okay, there were some definite downsides to flying private. This guy looked as if he'd be more at home on a surfboard than in a cockpit. Which, coincidentally, was what I tripped over when we walked farther through the plane. The surfboard had been abandoned in the aisle, propped against a seat.

"Sorry about that, sweetheart. I'll stow it properly once we have your luggage on board."

I'd almost landed in a woman's lap, but thanks to the quick reflexes of the man sitting opposite her, who grabbed my arm, I stayed more or less on my feet.

"You must be Indi? I'm Dawson."

It was strange hearing people use my real name again. "Thank you for coming."

He was an old friend of Brax's; I knew that much. He was also big. Tall, broad, muscular, and definitely more polished than Priest. Dawson's chocolate-brown hair was close-cropped, and he'd remembered to shave.

"And I'm Ari."

This was the private investigator? Brax had mentioned she was a woman, but I was surprised to find that she wasn't much older than me.

"I'm so grateful to you for giving up your time to help."

"Brax can be very persuasive."

"Oh, I know."

He'd persuaded me right out of my panties, and I'd enjoyed every second.

Priest ambled past with the surfboard, Brett returned to announce our bags were on board, and a minute later, the plane's engines roared into life. The front cabin seated ten, and I buckled myself into a seat beside Brax for the take-off.

Brett's voice came through the speaker. "Weather's looking good, folks. We should be on the ground in Nevada in just over an hour."

Nevada? But Meera was in Portugal.

This was clearly news to Brax as well. "Why are we going to Nevada?"

"Need to pick up the rest of the team," Priest told us. "And the rest of the luggage." He headed toward the cockpit. "There's a bedroom at the rear if you two lovebirds want to join the mile-high club."

My cheeks burned as he disappeared. Although... The mile-high club? With Brax? That would be something to never tell our grandchildren.

"What does he mean?" Brax asked Dawson. "What 'rest of the team'?"

"Beats me. This is Alexa's circus. We're just the clowns."

Alexa?

"Does he mean that blonde girl? The one who came to your office?" I asked Brax.

Dawson's turn to do a double take. "Alexa came to your office?"

"It's a long story, but yes. She showed up on Tuesday morning with a tape of Jerry doing unmentionable things with my ex-wife. *Ex-wife*. You have no idea how much pleasure it gives me to say those words."

"*Jerry?* How did Jerry get involved?"

Ari's eyes widened. "Do you mean Jerry Knight? From Blackstone House? I thought she disappeared?"

"Well, apparently, she and Alexa have been besties for the

past decade, and Alexa just forgot to tell us. They cooked up the scheme between them. And that guy"—Brax pointed toward the cockpit—"was involved as well. I recognise him from the tape."

"The dude in the Hawaiian shirt?"

"Yes. Do you have any idea who he is?"

Dawson shook his head. "Never met him before, but he's an operator. I see it in the way he moves. Former Delta, I think."

"What makes you say that?"

"When we met, he smacked me on the back and said I must be the pussy from Six."

I was lost. Completely lost. "I don't understand any of this. Who's Jerry? What's Blackstone House? And six?"

"She doesn't know about Blackstone?" Ari asked.

I shook my head no.

"Well, buckle up. This story's a doozy."

I pointed to my seat belt. "I'm already buckled up, so can somebody please tell me what's going on?"

Brax sighed. "It should be me." The plane began to move slowly along the tarmac. Normally, I enjoyed the take-off, the exhilaration as a plane soared into the air, but today, I was too tense to breathe. "Blackstone House is our former home. Mine, Dawson's, and Alexa's. Eleven years ago, in the summer before my third year at Georgetown, the apartment I was living in got condemned, and I needed to find a new place to live. I saw an ad online—rooms available, rent discounted in return for help with maintenance."

"Maintenance, my ass," Dawson cut in. "The place was falling down."

"It needed a full renovation. But at fifty bucks a week near DC, the offer was too good to pass up. Blackstone House was a huge old place—nine bedrooms, six bathrooms, and a full basement."

"Three acres of land, a derelict garage out the back. Remember the grill in the yard?"

"How could I forget? There was no kitchen to start with," Brax told me. "After we dealt with the structural issues, that was the first project we tackled. And although it was hard work, it was fun. We all got along well."

"After Joey left, anyway. He was an asshole."

"Yes, Grey was a definite improvement. Anyhow, there were nine of us to start off with—me, Dawson, Zach, Grey, Justin, Nolan, Levi, Jerry, and Ruby. Alexa came along later."

It was fascinating to hear about Brax's past. Although he wasn't necessarily secretive, he didn't tend to volunteer personal information. And he'd built a life from almost nothing, hadn't he? That gave me hope.

"Levi owned the place," Brax continued. "He won it in a poker game. An odd man, but I didn't think he was a bad one, not at first, anyway. Sometimes he used to stay with us, but other times he went home."

"His parents lived in Maryland," Dawson said. "Just across the state line. And his mom made Carissa look like a saint."

"Levi was firmly under her thumb. She called him every half hour, checking up. *Did you remember to brush your teeth? Have you taken your pills? It's cold outside, you should wear a sweater.* It never stopped."

"And if he didn't report in when he should, she used to drive over."

"Maybe that's why he snapped?" Ari suggested. "The pressure could've gotten to him."

He snapped? I began to get an uncomfortable feeling about this.

"He was twenty-one years old," Brax said. "He could have cut her off the way I did with my father." Another sigh. "But he didn't. And then one night, he murdered Ruby."

I gasped, searching desperately for a sign that Brax was joking. But he was dead serious.

"He...he killed her?"

I was pinned in my seat as we accelerated for take-off, and Brax paused for a moment before he answered.

"The official cause was death by asphyxiation, but he also stabbed her."

"And raped her," Ari added, shuddering.

"He claimed it was consensual, but the autopsy said there was bruising. I still feel sick just from thinking about it."

"Zach said the press went crazy after that. They camped outside the house for weeks."

Ari knew Zach? Were they friends? I eyed up the diamond on her finger—could they be involved with each other? Engaged?

Brax nodded. "It was a slow month for news on Capitol Hill, so the reporters moved south. And Levi Sykes's parents were rich. His father ran a consulting firm, and he had connections. They couldn't believe their son was guilty, so naturally, they tried to pin the crime on one of us."

"All of us, at one point," Dawson said. "They said it was a satanic ritual gone wrong, and we were covering for each other. I mean, I got why they were upset, and in the beginning, none of us thought Levi was capable either, but the only other person who could have done it was Justin. Nobody else but Jerry was alone in the house at any point that evening, plus there was DNA evidence."

Brax shook his head. "It wasn't Justin. No way. Would he really have paused in the middle of carving a pentagram on Ruby's chest to call his fiancée?"

Ruby had been mutilated? Now I felt sick as well, and I didn't even know her. I'd seen the results of knife wounds in the ER, and they were always messy. And painful.

"Didn't anyone hear her scream?"

"The carving happened post-mortem."

Was that better or worse? Better, I decided. At least she hadn't suffered quite as much as she might have done.

"I'm so sorry that happened to her. And that you lost a friend."

"Two friends. I considered Levi a friend too."

It just went to show that no matter how well you thought you knew a person, they could still surprise you. Look at Meera and Alfie—they were together for years, and he'd still hurt her badly.

"I'm sorry."

"It was after Ruby's death that I changed my name. Not only because of the bad press, but out of solidarity with my mom after my parents' divorce. Vale is her maiden name."

Which was why Brax understood my identity switch. Our situations weren't the same, not at all, and we were very different people, but we had these thin threads in common. And love. So much love. This man was it for me.

We'd reached cruising height now, and the plane levelled out. Priest emerged from the cockpit to get himself a drink and say a few words to Ari. His presence made me twitchy. Although he wasn't looking in our direction, I knew he saw everything. Heard everything. I took Brax's hand, and he brought mine to his lips.

"Get some rest, Indi. It's going to be a challenging week."

CHAPTER 32
BRAX

Another delay.

The plane touched down in Nevada, not at Harry Reid International as Brax had assumed it would, but at what looked like a military airfield. The other planes were green, the vehicles were green or desert camouflage, and the hangars were beige.

"Where are we?" he asked as their plane taxied across the vast expanse of tarmac.

Priest reappeared from the cockpit. He didn't quite have to duck in the cabin the way Dawson did, but it was a close thing.

"I could tell you, but then I'd have to kill you. Just sit tight."

A convoy of jeeps appeared, three of them, and the third had more surfboards sticking out of the back.

"Any ideas?" he whispered to Dawson.

"I think we're at Creech Air Force Base."

The vehicles parked in a semicircle around the door, and Chase climbed out of the nearest, carrying a leather messenger bag. What the hell? Obviously Alexa was involved with this, but why was Chase on a military base?

237

A stunning redhead exited the second vehicle, followed by… It took Brax a second, but holy fuck. *Jerry?* It helped that he'd seen her recently, if only on film. She moved with catlike grace, the sun highlighting muscles in her back that hadn't been quite so evident in Alexa's home movie. She'd dressed for…what exactly? Today, she wore tailored shorts in a mushroom colour, a black tank top, and combat boots.

"Do you see who I see?"

Dawson's reaction was the same. "Holy fuck."

Jerry said something to the redhead, and they began unloading bags from the second jeep. Several men in fatigues rushed to help them as Priest strolled to the back of the plane once more.

"Who is it?" Ari asked.

"Jerry."

She pressed her nose to the window. "Which one?"

"The brunette."

Jerry had worn her hair long during the Blackstone days, but today's graduated bob suited her. When she pushed her aviators on top of her head and began climbing the steps, Brax rose to greet her. He owed her a debt of gratitude that he had no idea how to repay.

"Long time, no see."

He leaned in to kiss her on the cheek, and she flashed a grin as she smacked his ass. Well, just above it.

"We're even for the tattoo now, yes?"

"Are you finally admitting that you knew what it said?"

"I admit nothing."

"You haven't changed a bit."

"Oh, you think?"

Brax glanced out of the window, where men were still loading bags onto the plane down below.

"I suppose you did travel much lighter in the old days."

Jerry gave a one-shouldered shrug. "Right now, we have no idea whether this is going to be a vacation, a training exercise, or a diplomatic incident, so we need to prepare for all eventualities." She nodded. "Dawson."

He stood behind Brax, slightly bent. "Jerry. I don't know whether to hug you or salute you."

"Either works."

"You're military?" Brax asked.

For a moment, he thought Jerry wasn't going to answer. She always had been cagey. But after a moment's consideration, she shrugged again.

"Officially, I'm Sergeant Knight, retired."

"Sergeant?" Dawson sounded sceptical. "On an air force base?"

"Shh, don't tell them. Congrats on breaking Senator Presley's nose. There isn't a person among us who hasn't been tempted to do that."

"It cost me my career."

"Yes, that was unfortunate. And I was this far"—she held up a thumb and forefinger a fraction of an inch apart—"from coming to see you, but then you met Violet. If you ever need a job, let me know."

"What are you doing now?"

"I could tell you, but then I'd have to kill you."

"That's what the other fellow said."

"Who, Priest? Trust me, no one would ever find the body." She turned toward the rear. "How long until we leave?"

"Five minutes," someone yelled back.

"You must be Indali." Jerry stepped forward to study her. "Congratulations on hooking up with this jackass."

"Thank you, I think."

"Which leaves Ari? Zach's a good guy, which means I have to do the 'overprotective friend' speech. Don't hurt him or I'll fuck you up, yada yada yada. Tell me there are snacks on this bird?"

Ari just stared at her. Jerry was definitely an acquired taste; Brax would be the first to admit that. They'd gotten along as roommates, liked each other well enough as friends, and slept together occasionally during the brief periods when he wasn't dating anyone. He'd never worried about her getting attached. Jerry didn't do relationships, and although she was technically proficient in bed, she'd always kept an emotional barrier in place. Whether that was accidental or deliberate, Brax couldn't be sure. Once, after a little too much to drink, she'd confessed that she had sex because it was the only time she felt a human connection, however fleeting. But he also knew that deep down, no matter how much she might try to deny it, she had a heart.

Because she was here, wasn't she?

The redhead appeared in the cabin with Chase, and up close, she looked even better. She could make a fortune in The Dark, not just because of her looks, but due to her aura. It said "Don't fuck with me." Give her a whip, put her in leather, and she'd make a first-class dominatrix.

He offered a hand. "Brax Vale."

"You can call me Tulsa."

"You're coming with us?"

"No, I'm just here to oversee the security screening."

Now what was Alexa playing at? "Security screening?"

"Oh, chillax, I'm joking. Echo told me about your girlfriend's little problem."

"Echo? Who's Echo?"

Chase reached forward and presented Brax with a passport. "She means Alexa. This is for Indi."

"Why is she called Echo?"

"Nobody uses real names around here."

Brax thumbed through the passport's pages. If this was a forgery, it was a damn good one. He reached the detail page and swallowed hard when he saw the name. *Indali Vale.* He stared harder, but there it was in print. *For fuck's sake, Alexa.* This was her workaround? Didn't she realise that Indi was trying to avoid marriage altogether, not be flung headlong into a fake one? And as for his own feelings... He found he didn't hate the idea as much as he should have.

"I spent a year in Brazil when I was younger, so I'm here to help with translation where necessary," Chase said. "If Meera's okay, I'll just soak up the culture. Alexa's slammed with work, so she'll cope on her own for a week or two as long as people bring her food."

"And my daddy's second wife was Portuguese, so I'm on translation duty too," Tulsa added. "Are there any snacks around here? We skipped breakfast."

"Snacks are in the galley," Priest told them as he headed back to the cockpit. "It's self-service. Jezebel, make yourself useful and close the door."

Jezebel? Who was Jezebel?

Jerry, apparently. Brax raised an eyebrow as she walked past.

"It's just a name. I have twenty of those."

"Is Priest your boss?"

Tulsa answered for her. "He likes to think he is."

Figured. Somehow, Brax couldn't imagine either of those women taking shit from anyone.

"Brax, did you sleep with Jerry?"

Indi spoke in a whisper, but it might as well have been a shout. Since nobody else was using the bedroom, he'd led her back there to try and get some sleep, but it seemed that her mind was working overtime.

Lying wasn't an option, though.

"It was a long time ago."

"I'm not like her."

"And I'm very glad about that." He paused for a moment,

but she didn't speak. "Does it upset you that I have a history with Jerry?"

"Not really. As you said, it's in the past. I guess… I guess I just worry that I'm not good enough. She's obviously successful at whatever she does, so confident too, and I'm only a mediocre PA."

Was that really how Indi saw herself?

"You couldn't be mediocre if you tried. And much as I'd love to keep you as my PA, your place is in a hospital. As soon as we get the situation with your father resolved, anyway."

"You'd let me go back to medicine?"

Let her? For crying out loud. Indali must have grown up in a spectacularly unhealthy environment.

"I prefer the term 'support you.' And yes, of course I will."

Several doctors were members of Nyx. He'd speak with them, see if they knew of any vacancies at LA hospitals. He had no doubt Indi would impress an interview panel, but it wouldn't hurt to get her foot in the door.

"I'm glad you spilled my coffee that day."

"So am I."

She lapsed into silence, and her breathing grew slow and rhythmical. Good. They both needed to rest before they reached Europe. When they landed, it would be nearly midnight, LA time, and early morning in Portugal.

But she wasn't asleep.

"Brax?"

"Yes?"

"That thing Priest said about the mile-high club… Are you a member?"

You'd think he was, but no. By the time he could afford to fly, he was married to Carissa, and she'd refused to squash into a tiny lavatory with him. And in later years, when he could afford to charter a jet, she'd refused to sleep with him at all. Not even a hate fuck.

"No, I'm not."

"Do you want to be?"

"With you? Hell yes."

"I can't stop thinking about what we did on Wednesday. I always dreaded my first time because I thought it would be awkward, and painful, and embarrassing, but...but it blew my mind."

"Good."

Brax swept her hair to one side, giving himself access to the delicate skin of her neck. As an erogenous zone, the neck was vastly underrated, the earlobes too. Indi let out a pleasing moan as he feathered kisses along her jaw.

"But..."

He hated buts. Butts were great, buts not so good.

"But what?"

"I feel...guilty? Meera's missing, and I'm here with you."

"And you feel bad about enjoying yourself?"

"Exactly."

"We can't get to Portugal any faster. You have two choices at the moment: sleep or come. Pick your poison."

She was seriously considering it, wasn't she? In truth, he hadn't thought Indi would be the adventurous type, and he was fine with that, but if she had a daring streak tucked away at the back of that sharp mind, she'd literally be his dream woman.

"What about the other people on the plane?" she asked. "What if they hear us?"

"They probably assume we've been at it for hours already. And I can assure you that not a single one of them will care."

"Do you have a condom?"

Thank fuck he'd put a handful in his wallet. He had more condoms than cash. And there was another box in his suitcase.

"Yes. Are you sore from Wednesday?"

She shook her head, and when she bit that lip, he was gone.

"Roll onto your other side."

"I won't be about to see you."

"No, but you'll be able to feel me. Trust me, my queen, I know exactly what I'm doing."

She obeyed.

Indi had worn a dress on the plane, one of the dozen outfits that Brax had asked Teresa to pick up for her yesterday. Now he inched the maroon silk up her thighs and slipped a finger under her panties. Soaked already? She must have been considering the mile-high idea for a while. He owed Priest a bottle of Scotch for putting the idea into her mind, the good stuff.

Brax stroked her clit, and fuck, she was so wonderfully responsive. Her ass pressed against his rapidly hardening cock, and he knew this wouldn't take long. Impromptu, slightly risky sex—he'd last about two minutes himself. But with the mile-high club, he'd always believed it was about the destination rather than the journey.

He trailed a finger through her slick folds, then circled the tiny bud of nerves that gave a woman so much pleasure. Indi squirmed in his arms, and he loved that she didn't hold back. She was almost there. So damn close. He shifted his other hand to muffle her cry if it came, and it did, half a minute later as she stiffened and then relaxed in his arms.

She was slick with sweat, a wet, sensuous heat that he basked in. Some people thought sex was messy, but that was a lie. Love was messy. Sex was beautiful.

Brax rolled on a condom and slid Indi's panties to one side. Leaving them on only added to the thrill. Slowly, so slowly, he took her from behind, and she was so deliciously tight. He was her first, and he intended to be her last as well. Brax didn't share. Okay, perhaps he had in the past with Zach, but not Indi. She was his, and his alone.

He could hear voices in the main cabin as he thrust, maybe Jerry and Tulsa. A cough. The *clink* of a glass.

"There," Indi choked out. "Right there. Oh…"

He gave her what she asked for. Would she come again? He was up for the challenge in every possible way. He kissed her neck, her back, her shoulders, and she rewarded him with soft whimpers that brought out his inner caveman.

His.

She was his.

Then she clenched around him, gasping his name into his hand, and he followed her over the edge, his cock pulsing as he spilled into her.

This woman was his, and he was never letting her go.

CHAPTER 33
THE ASSISTANT

Everyone knew what we'd done on the plane; I was certain of it. My legs had been as bendy as an IV tube when Brax helped me down the steps in Porto, the nearest airport to Fundão with a runway long enough to accommodate the jet. Apparently it could land closer, but it couldn't take off again.

But nobody said anything as a customs official gave our baggage a cursory glance, wished us a pleasant vacation, and headed back to the terminal. Four vehicles were waiting for us, sleek SUVs, two black, two white. There was a brief delay as we strapped surfboards to the roofs, but soon we set off on the three-hour journey to Fundão.

And I was terrified. Terrified by what we might find, or that we'd find nothing at all.

I checked my phone again, praying for a message from Meera, wishing I could call the whole search off, apologise profusely to these people who'd dropped everything to help me, and slink off home. Wherever home was.

"Are you ready?" Brax asked.

"No."

While we'd been joining the mile-high club—Meera was

going to choke when I told her about that—the others had been plotting. We'd spent the last hour of the flight together in the main cabin discussing their plan. They wanted me to make the initial approaches to Meera's colleagues at Quinta do Lago, to Pedro's brother, and to the owner of the hostel where she'd been staying. Those were all people who'd spent time with her recently, and hopefully, one of them would be able to provide further details of the French-slash-Belgian guy she'd been hanging out with.

The hope was that the witnesses might be more open with a female friend than with a cop or, say, Dawson or Priest. Brax and Ari would come with me for moral support, and Tulsa would translate when necessary.

Meanwhile, Jerry and Chase would visit the police to see what they had to say, while Dawson and Priest were heading to Lisbon to search for Alfie. Alexa had been sending through leads as she found them, and the team had a good idea where he was.

"Just ask the same questions you would have asked if you'd come alone, and let Ari chip in if necessary. It'll be over before you know it." Brax was driving, but he glanced across at me. "Alexa sent me your college transcript and a bunch of notes from your professors. There were several mentions of you staying calm under pressure."

I didn't even want to know how she'd gotten ahold of that information.

"But that was in a medical setting where I knew what I was doing."

"You're a *very* fast learner." The satnav told us our destination was approaching. "Is that the place? Up there on the right?"

"I think so?"

Alexa had told Brax that we'd be staying in "some old farmhouse," but this was gorgeous. Low white buildings with thick tiled roofs set around a stone courtyard, and plenty of neatly pruned trees for shade.

"There's a pool around the back," Chase said as he appeared from one of the doors. He and Ari had arrived before us, Jerry and Tulsa too. "And the property also comes with a haunted wine cellar and a roof terrace. At least I should go home with a tan."

Haunted? "There's a ghost?"

"I doubt it, but the locals seem to think so."

"Who paid for this?" Brax asked. "I'll need to reimburse them."

"You paid for it. Alexa used your credit card."

"How did she— Never mind. What about the plane?"

"Priest borrowed it from a friend. No payment required, but a donation to the Blackwood Foundation would be appreciated."

"Consider it done."

Chase checked his watch. "We should get started."

Quinta do Lago was pretty in a rustic kind of way. A stark contrast to our rental house—rough and homey versus modern and minimalistic. Pedro was a friendly Portuguese guy in his mid-thirties, smiling and enthusiastic as he talked to a group about the ecological project he was heading. Hair hung down his back in locs, and his tan said he spent a lot of time outdoors. Best of all, he spoke good English.

"You're here to look for Meera?" he asked once he'd finished with the group. "You're Indi? She spoke of you often."

"I'm worried about her. She hasn't answered my calls for nearly two weeks."

"And you came all the way from America?"

"Wouldn't you get on a plane if your best friend was missing?"

He considered the question for a moment. "I would do that. And of course I'm worried about her too, but I'm not certain how much help I can be. She didn't tell anyone here of her plans."

"The police said she went to the beach for a week with a man, a blond man, possibly French or Belgian. Do you know who that might be?"

"No. No, I don't, but I suppose it's possible she went to the beach on impulse. Meera changed in the weeks before she left. Became, uh, how do you say this? Wild?"

"After Alfie met that other woman?"

Pedro's face clouded over. "Yes. That, we weren't expecting at all. One day, he and Meera were planning their future together, and the next…" He shook his head. "*Ele é um idiota.*"

"He's an asshole," Tulsa helpfully translated.

Tell us something we didn't already know.

"Can you talk us through those weeks?"

"Alfie was becoming disillusioned with the project, that was clear, but Meera's enthusiasm never decreased, even with the bad weather we had. We spoke about building a *casa do jardim*—a space for her to host yoga retreats in the summer—and then she left."

So she'd definitely been planning to stay here, but had she rethought her plans after Alfie ditched her? I could see her changing her mind about spending the entire trip at Quinta do Lago, even having a wild few weeks as she decided on a new direction, but I couldn't see her changing her whole character overnight. Meera hated to disappoint people. That had been the reason for our elaborate identity switch in the first place. No, she wouldn't have walked out on Pedro like that, not without saying a word.

"You don't suspect anything bad could have happened?"

"In Fundão? It's a very safe city."

Clearly not that freaking safe if Meera had vanished.

"The last man she was seen with was a tourist. Maybe he took her somewhere other than the beach?"

"I suppose that's possible."

Why wasn't Pedro being more helpful? Was he worried the town's reputation would suffer? Did he just want to avoid getting tangled up in the mystery? Or could he have been involved? Meera had liked him, but I wasn't sure I did. If she had one fault, it was that she'd always been too trusting. Should I press for more information? I didn't want to alienate Pedro, but at the same time, he hadn't told us much.

Thankfully, Ari took over. "Wasn't Meera meant to move into your brother's place?"

"Yes, and she even paid a deposit for the room. Then she didn't show up."

She'd paid a deposit when she didn't have much money. If she'd been planning to leave permanently, she'd have kept the cash, wouldn't she?

"Did you speak to the police about her disappearance?"

"Are you another friend of hers?"

"I'm a friend of Indi's."

Pedro sighed. "Then maybe you don't know how Meera was. I don't want to speak badly about her, but the past few weeks were…difficult. She kept showing up late, and some days, she was drunk."

"Drunk? How did she get to work?"

"Either she rode with Polina, or she came by bicycle. Dieter nearly hit her one morning. She was weaving all over the road. And two days before she left, she got into a fight with Benji. Everyone heard the shouting."

A fight? This was new. Brax slipped an arm around my waist for support—he must have realised how fragile I was feeling right now.

"What was the fight about?" Ari asked.

"I don't know all the details, but Benji was a friend of Alfie's. I think he was defending Alfie's decision to leave."

"Does Benji work here?"

"Yes, he was digging swales with Alfie and Meera."

"Can we speak with him?"

"He drove into the city to pick up supplies, but he should be back soon."

"While we wait, can we meet the rest of the staff? Meera might have mentioned her new friend to somebody."

A pause. "You really think something bad could have happened to her?"

"Yes, we do."

Pedro swallowed, looking slightly more nervous than when we'd arrived.

"Let me introduce you to everyone. But first, I'll call Benji to see how long he'll be."

"I just said if that's how she behaved, I wasn't surprised that Alfie had left, that was all."

Benji was British, a slim guy with a short ponytail sticking out from beneath a "Drop Seeds, Not Bombs" ball cap. Strands of brown hair kept escaping, and he had a habit of tucking them behind his ear as we talked under a grey sky beside an old barn. Dirt streaked his jacket, and his boots were caked in mud.

"That was all?" I asked. "You didn't think your words might upset her?"

Ari elbowed me in the side at the same time as Brax squeezed my hand.

"What Indi means is that Meera was already devastated about the breakup," Ari said. "What triggered the conversation?"

"She was hungover again, ranting about everything. I just wanted to work, you know? And she wouldn't shut up."

"You were friends with Alfie?"

"We got along."

"Were you surprised when he left for Lisbon?"

"Yes and no. I mean, it was obvious he was sick of spending time here. Meera was the ecologist, not him. I figured he'd find work in Fundão while she carried on, but then he met Beatriz, and man, she was hot. They just hit it off."

"You know Beatriz?"

"Sure, she was a waitress at Café Lusitano. We all go there for coffee."

"Meera too?"

"Yeah, the two of them were friends before the Alfie thing. Well, sort of. Beatriz used to talk shit about her behind her back."

"What kind of shit?"

"She made fun of her for working here. Said she cared more for bats than she does for people."

I couldn't keep my mouth closed. "That's just not true. She cared—"

"She cared about both," Ari said firmly. "Do you really have bats?"

"There are horseshoe bats in the barn." Benji gestured toward the building beside us. "Bats are cool—did you know they use them in the libraries here for conservation?"

"How does that work?"

"The bats eat the bugs that would eat the manuscripts. That's one reason we like having them here—they take care of the insect pests and allow us to reduce our pesticide use. Plus they help with pollination, and their guano makes a good fertiliser."

"Maybe Meera had the right idea?"

"Yeah, probably." Benji sighed. "This is a mess. Alfie was

an arsehole for pissing off to Lisbon, and Meera went crazy after he left. Hanging out in the bar every night, drinking too much, bitching constantly."

This was the same story we'd heard from five other people while we were waiting for Benji to return. That Alfie had behaved like a prick, and there was plenty of sympathy for Meera until she started acting out. The women still felt sorry for her, but the men had labelled her as "difficult" and "slutty." More like traumatised—her life had been turned upside down, and she'd been desperately trying to reclaim her confidence.

"Do you have any idea which bar she went to?"

"Kredo, mainly. Sometimes Mercado. Definitely not Mythos, not anymore, because that's where Alfie used to work."

"Did she mention spending time with a French or Belgian guy? All we know at the moment is that he had blond hair."

"Nah, the times I saw her out, she was with a Portuguese guy."

"The same guy? How many times?"

"Twice? Maybe three times?"

"Do you know who he was?"

Benji shook his head. "Not his name, but he always said hello. Try asking Katie. Meera and her always gossiped while they were working."

"Is she here today?"

"She was in the herb garden earlier."

CHAPTER 34
THE ASSISTANT

"If there was a French guy or a Belgian guy, she must have met him literally that night. Here, try this dill." Katie held out a tufty bunch as we sheltered from a rain shower in a giant polytunnel. "Last year, I planted it right in the ground and slugs ate it all, but this year, I planted it in plug trays and it turned out amazing."

Katie was a fellow American, and this was her third trip to Quinta do Lago. She'd spend a few months working on the land, then return to the US to visit with family and take seasonal work—last year, she'd found a job as one of Santa's elves from September through December. Yes, September. Christmas started early these days, and the mall she worked in wasn't about to miss out on a commercial opportunity. One summer, she'd been arranging Halloween displays.

I sniffed the dill cautiously. "Very good."

"Try it with pierogi. Dorota's visiting from Poland this month, and she makes amazing pierogi. That's one thing I love about being here—the food's always better than we get back home. Everything's so fresh."

"Did Meera mention a new boyfriend of any nationality?"

"There was a guy called Javier—I think he was Spanish,

and also Afonso. He was local. But I wouldn't call them boyfriends, more like one-night stands." Oh, Meera. "She preferred dark-haired guys." Which figured. Alfie was blond. "And the day she disappeared, she told me she was going out salsa dancing. She didn't mention hooking up, although I guess it's possible she did that too."

"What do you think happened?" Ari asked. "You were probably as close to her as anyone in those last few weeks."

"Honestly? I'm worried. The guys say she just went off with a new boyfriend, and I suppose…I suppose at first, I wanted to believe that. But then she missed a yoga class without telling any of her students, and she loved teaching yoga."

Ari squeezed her hand. "We're going to find her."

"Is there anything I can do to help?"

"Do you know which bar she went to?"

"I just assumed it was Mercado. They have salsa dancing on Wednesdays. It's always popular, and there's an instructor to help people. Meera likes him, but he's Brazilian, not French."

At that moment, I swore if I ever broke up with Brax, I'd find solace in pints of ice cream and romcoms, not in the arms of another man. This was a nightmare. But Brax was right here with me, going above and beyond, and I knew he was the only man I'd ever want. One in a billion. The money didn't matter; it was the person inside I loved. His strength, his kindness, his ability to give me hope.

As we walked away, I leaned in to kiss his cheek.

"What was that for?"

"For being you."

The hostel was a depressing building on the outskirts of Fundão. Meera had picked it because it was cheap and within cycling distance of Quinta do Lago, not for its facilities, which would have received half a star at most. The manager, Silvio, wasn't happy about our presence, and he didn't speak much English, but he did look as if he'd seen a ghost when I walked in. Cue rapid-fire Portuguese, which I understood none of.

"He thought you were Meera," Tulsa explained. "Which was a surprise to him, especially after the police visit."

"Can you ask him what he knows?"

"I already told everything to the police," he told us via Tulsa. "I can't help you."

"The police aren't looking for Meera; we are. You were the last person to see her—could you just tell us about the man she was with?"

"There's not much to tell. I only spoke with him for a minute while he waited for her. Right here." Silvio waved around the lobby we were standing in as Tulsa translated. This was no hotel. A rickety desk stood in one corner, and there were half a dozen plastic seats near a rack that held flyers for local attractions. "They were going to the beach."

"Which beach?"

"They didn't say."

"Who told you they were going to the beach?" Ari asked. "Did he say it, or did she?"

Silvio pondered for a moment. "He did."

"Where's the nearest beach? Near Leiria or Coimbra?"

A shrug. "It's possible," Tulsa translated. "But there are many river beaches in Castelo Branco, so they could have gone to one of those."

"Did either of them give a timescale for their return?"

We already had that information from the police, didn't we? Why was Ari asking the same question?

"A week, he said." Another shrug. "But maybe more, maybe less. The beaches here are very beautiful."

"How were they planning to get to the beach?" Ari asked. "Meera didn't have a car."

"Probably he had a car."

"Probably? You didn't see a vehicle?"

"I didn't look. Why would I? A guest going to the beach with a friend is nothing unusual. Or maybe they took the bus? There's a stop on the next street."

I didn't much like this guy. Meera's colleagues at Quinta do Lago had been helpful, possibly feeling guilty that they hadn't raised the alarm, but the manager of the hostel treated us as though we were nuisances.

"I understand Meera left some of her stuff here? And her bicycle?"

"That's right."

"Is it normal for people to do that?"

"It happens enough that we have a storage room. Tourists want to make side trips, and they don't want to pay for a bed they're not using while they're gone."

"Could we take a look?"

He shook his head. "What if you steal something? I don't want to get into trouble."

"A woman is missing."

"If the police want to look, then they can do that. But I'm not giving people off the street access to private belongings."

"Tell us more about the man you saw—how old was he?"

"Her age."

"Tall? Short?"

"Average."

"What about his hair? Was it dark blond? Light blond? Long? Short? Did he have a beard?"

"Short, I guess, but not shaved. Dark blond—not quite brown—and yes, he had a beard."

"Any jewellery?"

"I wasn't paying attention."

A couple walked in, young, both wearing backpacks, and

the manager turned away, dismissing us with a hand. The message was clear: conversation over. His tone turned servile as he greeted the newcomers in Portuguese.

"Let's go," Ari said. "We can come back later if we need to."

Back at the house, the disappointment continued. Jerry and Chase had arrived from the police station, and the cops had been as helpful as Silvio. Jerry was sitting on the kitchen counter when we arrived, her feet dangling as she carved slices off an apple with a nasty-looking penknife. Through the window beyond, I could see Chase lying beside the pool in a pair of Speedos. Meera would have rated him a ten for sure.

"The cops don't wanna know," Jerry told us. "They said she isn't the first backpacker to leave the area without announcing her plans, and she won't be the last. Most of them show up in a few weeks, and if the department expended resources looking for these people, they'd never solve any actual crimes. Alexa looked up their solve rate. It's a fuckin' joke."

Her words sent a chill through me.

"Most of them. *Most* of them show up in a few weeks. What happens to the ones who don't?"

"Fifty bucks says the reports sit in the bottom of a file cabinet somewhere, gathering dust. Do we have any potato chips?"

"Potato chips? Who cares about potato chips?"

"An army marches on its stomach."

But we weren't an army. We were a small group of people searching for a needle in a Portuguese haystack. Meera had been missing for ten days already, and we were running out of time.

Mercado was a riot of colour, cocktails, and crowds. Music thumped from hidden speakers, so loud that I could barely hear Brax speaking next to me as we dodged our way across the room. He pointed toward the bar, and I got the message—we needed to talk with the bartenders. Ari had stayed outside with Tulsa to tackle the door staff. Chase and Jerry were dancing. I had no right to complain because they'd taken time off work and travelled halfway across the world to assist, but I couldn't help wishing they'd take Meera's disappearance a tiny bit more seriously. And maybe I was a tiny bit jealous of their dancing ability as well. I had two left feet, and if I spent longer than five minutes on a dance floor, someone would end up with a broken toe.

"Hey, Meera!" The nearest of the three bartenders greeted me with a grin. It was slightly quieter here, but we still had to shout. At least he spoke English. Was his accent Australian?

"I'm not Meera, but we're looking for her."

He leaned closer, squinting. "Damn, you two could be twins. Try Quinta do Lago—she works there most days."

"No, she's gone missing. She hasn't been at work."

"Can we speak in private?" Brax asked.

"No way, mate. It's packed in here."

Brax held out a hundred-euro bill, and the man's eyes lit up. He called to his colleagues, "Back in five," and beckoned us through a door at the side of the bar.

"Is this about Meera?" he asked when the door closed behind us. "I haven't seen her this week."

We were in a storeroom piled high with boxes. A table and chairs sat against one wall, and a sink in the corner held dirty plates. Brax did the talking, and I was grateful. Tiredness was beginning to catch up with me.

"How about last week?" he asked.

"Yeah, maybe?"

"Think hard."

"She came on Wednesday for the salsa club, I'm ninety

percent sure. She was dancing with Miguel, and then Miguel's girlfriend showed up, and there was a fight. Not, like, a physical fight, but words, you know?"

"Was the argument serious?"

"I doubt it. The girls had both been drinking, and I bet they forgot about it by the morning."

"What does Miguel look like?"

"Dark hair, ponytail, kind of skinny. Always wears a bandana around his neck like a cowboy."

Not the man we were looking for, then.

"After the fight, what did Meera do?"

"Carried on dancing, probably."

"Did you see her with any other men? We're particularly interested in a blond man with a French accent who might have been present that night."

"I don't remember anyone like that, but you should talk to Lucia. She's got a thing for French guys, and she was working behind the bar as well."

"Is she here?"

"Nah, she went to see friends in Lagos this week. She'll be back on Tuesday. Or maybe Wednesday. She's scheduled to work Thursday." The guy thumbed through papers pinned to a corkboard. "Yeah, Thursday."

"Do you have a number for her?"

"You really think something happened to Meera?"

"Yes," I said. "It's as if she dropped off the face of the earth last week."

"Then I guess Lucia wouldn't mind if I gave you her contact info."

"Can you also ask your colleagues if they've seen Meera recently?"

"Sure, I'll do that."

Brax and I headed outside and called Lucia right away, but she didn't pick up. He left a message. What was it with people not answering the phone this week? Ari and Tulsa were finished with the door staff, and Ari's face told the story. They'd found nothing.

"Poof. Vanished," she said. "They remember Meera arriving on Wednesday, but nobody saw her leave. There were some issues with a guy and a peanut allergy at around ten p.m., though, and everyone was preoccupied, so she could have slipped out unnoticed. And they said she always used to walk home, so there's no point in speaking with cab firms."

This was hopeless. Even with a team of six, plus two more people in Lisbon, we were getting nowhere. What had I possibly thought I'd achieve alone? Brax must have sensed my despair because he kissed my hair and held me a little tighter.

"We'll find her," he promised, and I so wanted to believe him.

"But how? Nobody knows anything."

"Somebody does. We just haven't spoken to the right person yet."

CHAPTER 35
BRAX

Brax watched from the corner of his eye as Jerry danced with a blond guy. Her body language said she was into him, but her eyes told a different story. She was bored, and he was too drunk or too dumb to notice. A minute later, she peeled away and headed in Brax's direction.

"It's not him. He's German, and he only arrived in Fundão last Friday. Chase found three girls who know Meera, but none of them have seen her since last Wednesday."

He materialised at her elbow. "They're all going to ask their friends about Meera."

"Good thing you brought a burner phone. They'll call you whether they have any info or not."

"I'm good at letting women down gently."

The longer Brax spent with Chase, the more convinced he became that the man was gay. But Chase kept his personal life just that: personal. Still, he knew how to charm the ladies, and that was the only thing that mattered tonight.

Tonight. It was edging closer to tomorrow. Midnight was rapidly approaching, and they still had no concrete information. With the bar's patrons taking advantage of the discounted cocktails—two for one on the house special—the window for gathering any meaningful information was closing fast.

"Do we want to persevere here?" he asked. "Or should we get some rest and start fresh tomorrow?"

Indi in particular was flagging. She'd barely slept on the plane, and jet lag was catching up with her.

"We should carry on," she said. "Every minute could make a difference."

But Ari shook her head. "I don't think we're going to learn anything more in the bar, not tonight anyway. Maybe on Wednesday when the salsa crowd is here again."

"But that's four days away."

"We won't be sitting around in the meantime."

"But—"

"No point in flogging a dead horse," Jerry said. "We can pick up a pizza on the way back."

Brax laughed. "This isn't Vegas or LA, my darling. You're not going to get a pizza at midnight in Fundão."

In Blackstone House, Alexa and Jerry had been the foodies. Alexa focused on quality, while Jerry valued quantity. He'd half expected her to be the size of a horse by now, but she seemed to offset her calorie intake with exercise.

"Somewhere will be open. I'll ask that guy."

"What guy?"

She nodded toward a dark doorway opposite. "Him. He's a local."

Brax hadn't even noticed the man. He appeared to be homeless, wrapped in darkness and a dirty sleeping bag. When they got closer, Brax spotted a small dog nestled among the folds.

"Hey, is there anywhere to get food around here?" Jerry asked, offering twenty euros. "A pizza?"

The guy blinked a couple of times, as if he thought he might be imagining the money. Then he snatched it before it could disappear. Tulsa spoke, presumably translating Jerry's question.

"*Sim, sim, uma loja de frango.*" He pointed up the street. "*A loja é ali, virando a esquina.*"

"A chicken place around the corner?" Tulsa asked Jerry.

"Sounds good to me."

Ari crouched down, and the dog crept out to sniff her. "Can you ask if this is his usual spot?"

Tulsa obliged.

"Yes, he's here every night."

"Did he see Meera?"

Brax expected the answer to be a shrug or a shake of the head, but after some back and forth and gesturing at Indi, what they got was enthusiastic nodding.

"*Sim, ela sempre para para acariciar Fofa.*"

"He says a woman who looks like Indi but with longer hair always stops to pet the dog. He doesn't know her name, but it sounds like Meera."

"*E ela me dá dinheiro para comida de cachorro.*"

"And she gives him money for dog food."

The excitement in Ari's voice was palpable. "Has he seen her recently?"

"*Eu não tenho nada a fazer além de assistir.*"

"He says he has nothing to do but watch." More discussion followed. "The last time he saw her was after the salsa night. Not this week, but the week before. She gave him the change in her pocket, promised to bring him another blanket because it was cold, and then she walked off in the direction of the hostel."

"Alone?"

"Totally alone."

Well, shit. So she hadn't picked up a man in the bar. Where had she met him? Brax fished another hundred out of his wallet and handed it to the man.

"Tell him to buy a blanket."

Tulsa did so, and added an extra hundred of her own.

"It's for the dog food," she explained. "We have dogs. They're pains in everyone's ass, but kinda cute."

It felt as if they'd gotten somewhere today, but despite that, they were still a long way from locating Meera. They found the piri-piri chicken place, and Jerry ordered enough food to feed a small army, although Indi said she couldn't stomach a thing. If she didn't eat tonight, Brax would get up early and make her breakfast. She needed to keep her strength.

He turned to gaze at her, sitting close in the back seat of the SUV as Chase drove. Having someone to care about again was strange, but a good strange.

"What?" she whispered. "Do I have something on my face?"

"You're beautiful, that's all."

"I'm lucky."

They reconvened in the farmhouse kitchen with buckets of chicken and fries and rice and salad. Jerry had managed to find donuts as well. There might have been plenty of food, but they were out of leads and low on hope.

Priest had called just after they arrived back at the house —he and Dawson had located Alfie, who was of no use whatsoever. Remorseful, yes, ready to drive back and join the search for Meera, yes, but helpful in any way? No. Then Beatriz had walked in and heard him confess that he'd made a terrible mistake by leaving Meera, and she'd begun beating him over the head with a chouriço, which was apparently a kind of spicy sausage not too dissimilar from Spanish chorizo. Priest and Dawson had ended up separating them, then playing referee while Alfie hurriedly packed a suitcase. Nobody knew where he planned to stay. Nobody cared.

Ari dipped a fry in spicy sauce. "It all comes back to one place, doesn't it? The hostel. Only one person saw Meera with the blond French guy."

"You think the manager was involved in Meera's disappearance?" Brax asked.

"I think he's being cagey about something. In my experience, guilty people act one of two ways—either they fall over themselves to be helpful, or they obstruct. He did the latter. I mean, he wouldn't even let us look at her belongings."

"If he hurt her…" Indi started.

"That's only one possible scenario. Another is that the blond guy was a guest at the hostel, and Silvio doesn't want the bad publicity."

"So what can we do?"

"We can talk to him again. And if he still isn't forthcoming with information, we'll talk to the other residents. Someone will know who this man is."

"If he exists at all," Brax said.

"That's another scenario. Or Silvio could have given us a false description to throw us off the scent."

"Maybe the culprit is a friend of his?" Chase suggested. "Another local?"

"That's a fifth option."

Indi was already on her feet. "We have to go and speak with him. Make him tell us the truth this time."

"Easy, tiger." Jerry picked out a donut. "If you turf him out of bed in the middle of the night, he won't speak to you at all. Go tomorrow after breakfast, once you've had some sleep. You'll get a better reception then."

"Sleep? How can I sleep?"

"You want a tranquilliser?"

Jerry took sleeping pills now? She'd suffered from

insomnia in Blackstone House, but she'd always refused pharmaceutical help.

"No."

"Suit yourself." Jerry hopped off the stool, donut in hand. "Some of us need to rest. See you in the morning."

CHAPTER 36
THE ASSISTANT

S leep?

Sleep was impossible, for me anyway. Brax had drifted off almost immediately, his arms wrapped around me, but I just couldn't stay still. Did I have restless legs syndrome? My feet felt as if there were ants scuttling under my skin.

When Brax rolled over, one arm flung out to the side, I took advantage of my new-found freedom to go breathe some fresh air on the balcony. Well, it was more of a terrace, but on the second floor. A walkway ran underneath, and just in case anyone got the urge to do laundry, there was a drying rack with—

I froze.

Someone was out there.

I heard the quiet *crunch* of footsteps on gravel, the murmur of voices.

My mouth began to open, ready to scream, but then I realised the voices were female.

Who was in the yard?

I leaned over the stone balustrade, squinting into the darkness as Jerry and Tulsa walked past. Jerry paused, nose in the air like an animal sensing danger. Then she looked up.

Busted.

"What are you two doing?" I asked.

"Go back to bed, Indi."

"I can't sleep. Are you going out somewhere?"

"Next time, just put the tranq in her damn drink," Tulsa told her.

Jerry muttered something that sounded suspiciously like "Lesson learned."

"Hey, that's not very nice."

I couldn't see Tulsa's eyes in the dark, but I just knew she was rolling them.

"Oh, honey, we don't get paid to be nice."

"We can't sleep either," Jerry said. "And it's a beautiful night. There's not much light pollution around here, so we thought we'd drive a few miles out of town and take a look at the stars. It's very relaxing. Want to come?"

With them? While Brax might have trusted these two women, I wasn't totally sure I did. Jerry in particular had a darkness about her. She said the right things and did the right things, but her smiles never reached her eyes. Plus she drove too fast.

"Riding in a car won't help me."

"Chase put a bottle of wine in the refrigerator—why don't you get yourself a glass?"

Alcohol wasn't the solution either, but I nodded. "Enjoy your drive."

Downstairs, I tried to read one of the novels I found on a shelf in the living room, but after staring at the same page for five full minutes, I admitted defeat and headed for the kitchen. One glass of wine might take the edge off. Just one.

Two glasses later, I crawled back into Brax's arms, and this time, I managed a fitful doze. What would the morning bring?

The answer? Not much.

I visited the hostel with Ari and Tulsa again, but this time we traded Brax for Jerry while Brax stayed behind to check in with the staff at Nyx. He usually called each location at the end of the evening, just to make sure everything was running smoothly. He'd offered to come with us instead, and although I would have liked his support, we had enough people for the task, and I couldn't monopolise every minute of his time.

Silvio denied that the French-slash-Belgian was one of his guests and claimed he'd never seen the man before that day. Which made me even more certain that he wasn't being truthful because where else would Meera have met him? Was Silvio lying about the suspect's description or about his entire existence? He answered Ari's questions grudgingly, but when Jerry leaned over the desk in the corner and began thumbing through paperwork, he lost his cool entirely and yelled at us to get out.

"Why did you do that?" I asked when we stepped into the sunshine. Yes, I was a little peeved. "Now he won't help us at all."

"Because I wanted to see how he'd respond."

"He wasn't helping anyway," Ari said.

"But he was our best lead. Our only lead. What can we do without him?"

"Eat lunch?" Jerry nodded along the street. "The café over there got a great write-up in the guidebook. The sandwiches are to die for."

Don't snap, Indi. Just breathe. "Do you ever think of anything but your stomach?"

"Rarely, but it's been known to happen."

Tulsa checked her watch. "Lunch? More like brunch. I

want to try the pastel de nata—you know, those little tarts with the custard?"

"What about Meera? Don't you think she's more important than dessert?"

"Relax, sweetie. Have a donut. It might help your mood."

I looked to Ari, hoping she'd be the voice of reason, but she'd been corrupted.

"We did skip breakfast."

"So?"

"And we should talk, come up with a plan."

"But—"

"We need to do this properly. We'll be able to see people coming and going from the hostel while we eat, and I'm going to look through social media check-ins for people who stayed there at the same time as Meera did." Ari touched my arm in a kind gesture of support. "Plus you should eat. You've barely touched a mouthful this whole trip, and you already look thinner."

"I just hate wasting time. Hate the thought of sitting in a café while Meera…while Meera…" A sob welled up in my throat. "If she's still alive"—I dreaded to think of the alternative, but the realist in me understood it was a possibility—"she could be hurt."

"We'll find her faster by making a plan than by running around like headless chickens and antagonising the main suspect further."

"Hey, what did you think of the chicken last night?" Jerry asked Tulsa.

"Overcooked and kinda bland."

"Same. There's a place on the other side of the city that's meant to be better."

I put my head in my hands and wished Brax were here. These two gave a whole new meaning to the word "impossible."

271

"We have movement," Jerry said as she sipped a cappuccino.

The café was a tourist place with the prices to match. At one time, I'd never noticed the cost of things, but the move to LA had changed me. Now I shopped by special offer rather than brand, and I winced at the *preço* column on the café's menu.

Jerry had already eaten a sandwich the size of my head and washed it down with a pint of cola. Now, it seemed, she was going for caffeine overload. This was her third coffee. And me? I'd picked at a salad.

"What movement? Where?"

I started to turn, but Tulsa grabbed my head and held it still in a vise-like grip.

"Don't look."

"What's happening?"

"Silvio's loading a trash bag into his trunk."

"I fucking knew it," Jerry muttered.

"What's in the bag?" I asked.

Tulsa shrugged. "At a guess? A bunch of Meera's things. Her diary, her weekend bag, her toiletries, most of her underwear, some shoes, her bathing suit, a towel, her phone charger, her purse… All the stuff she'd have taken if she went to the beach for a week."

My chest seized. "And you don't think she did go?"

"Not even a little bit."

"Then…then what?" I could hardly breathe. "What happened?"

"Finish your salad—we'll be back."

She and Jerry rose in unison, and they were halfway to the street before I unfroze. I tried to follow, but Ari grabbed my arm.

"Let them go. They know what they're doing."

"Do they? They don't seem very professional."

"What were you expecting?"

"What do you mean? I realise they're doing this for free, but maybe some communication would be nice? And less eating? Have you ever worked with these people before? Are they even competent?"

"I don't know them personally, but I know Alexa, and Alexa wouldn't send anyone that she didn't think could do the job."

"Are you sure? They told me off for not getting enough rest, and then they went stargazing in the middle of the night."

"Stargazing?"

"Apparently, there's not much light pollution. Jerry said it was relaxing."

"Does Jerry strike you as a person who knows how to relax?"

"I guess she doesn't."

"Right. And if they were out last night, that actually explains something I was puzzling over."

"What's that?"

Ari took a sip of coffee. Mine was probably cold by now.

"When Tulsa ran through a list of things that could be in that trash bag, what was missing?"

"I don't freaking know! I'm not an investigator. I'm just a doctor-slash-PA who's terrified her best friend is dead."

There, I'd said it. The four-letter word that had cost me sleep every night for the past ten days. What if Meera was gone? What if we never found a trace of her?

"Shh, keep your voice down in public." Ari lowered hers to barely a whisper. "The phone. Tulsa mentioned a phone charger, but not a phone."

"An oversight?"

"Does Tulsa seem like the type to make an oversight?"

I echoed my previous words. "I guess she doesn't."

"Then the omission of the phone was deliberate. I bet you five bucks she has it."

"How the hell could she have Meera's phone?" My voice had risen again. "Sorry."

"Because when Jerry said 'stargazing,' she meant 'breaking and entering.' No way would she have started poking around at the hostel earlier if she thought there was a chance of evidence being destroyed. They already have what they need. She just wanted to provoke a reaction, and we got one."

Wow.

"Do you have any other questions?" Ari continued. "I'm sorry if I haven't talked things through with you enough—my mind's going at a hundred miles an hour on a case like this, and I don't tend to take time away from the nitty-gritty to provide a full report if that hasn't been requested."

"I have a hundred questions, but I suppose the most important one is why are we still sitting here?"

"Because there are times when you push, and times when you hold back to see what unfolds. Things are unfolding. Silvio is spooked, and when people are nervous, they make mistakes. Let's see what Jerry and Tulsa find. Plus Alexa's a cyber guru, and she'll be taking a look at that phone as soon as it reaches her."

"I just feel so…so helpless."

"I feel better knowing that Alexa's involved. Her methods are unorthodox, but she gets results."

"I wish they'd tell us what they're doing."

"There's a part of me that does too. But a bigger part would rather stay in the dark. When Alexa dodges questions, it's usually because I won't like the answers, and I suspect Jerry and Tulsa are cut from the same cloth."

"Jerry scares me a bit."

"Me too. But at least she's on our side."

CHAPTER 37
BRAX

"What the fuck?" Brax asked.

Jerry paused halfway across the kitchen. "Relax. Go back to bed."

"Relax? How the hell can I relax? You're carrying a body." A man, judging by the shape, and reasonably slender. The bag over his head hid his identity. "Is he dead?"

"No, just sleepy. And technically, I'm only carrying half of him."

Because Tulsa had the feet. But that didn't make the situation any better.

"Explain."

Brax had known they were up to something. When he'd spoken with Alexa earlier, she'd been even more evasive than usual, although Jerry's caginess was nothing new. But this... Brax had been known to skirt the law on occasion, but he'd never kidnapped anybody.

"Since the cops seem hesitant to ask Silvio questions, we figured we'd try the DIY approach."

"Have you lost your damn mind? My girlfriend is upstairs, waiting for me to bring her a drink, and there's an unconscious murder suspect in the kitchen. What are you going to do after you've questioned him? Give him Tylenol and let him go back home?"

Jerry considered the question for a moment. "Probably not. It depends on how involved he was in Meera's disappearance."

"Right now, we don't know for sure that he was involved at all."

"Yeah, we do. You never used to be this uptight, Brax."

"And you never used to be a raging psychopath."

Tulsa blew out a breath. "Ouch. Ex-lovers' tiff."

"Wrong. I'm the same person I always was," Jerry said. "You were just too busy fucking me to notice."

"That's—"

Jerry held up a hand, dropping one side of Silvio in the process. His head hit the terracotta tiles with a *crack* that made Brax wince.

"I'm not done. You asked for help, and we're here providing that help. The brief was to find Meera Adams as quickly as possible, and that's what we're doing. But if you prefer, we can go surfing, and you can ask the police nicely if they'd mind interrogating this piece of shit. Up to you, dude. I get results. I don't play by some arbitrary set of rules."

Whatever Jerry said, this wasn't the woman Brax had known a decade ago. She was tougher, more confident, and that confidence had turned her into a brick wall. Hard and unforgiving. Kind of like Alexa, but with added duct tape and no agoraphobia.

"What are you planning to do? Torture him?"

"Do I detect a hint of disapproval? That's rich coming from the man with a troupe of dominatrices in his basement. Is that the right plural? Or is it dominatrixes?"

"You can use either. And everything that happens in The Dark is consensual."

"With each minute you delay, we're potentially a step further from finding Meera. You really want to let this asshole sit in a police cell saying, 'No comment, no comment, no comment,' while the other motherfuckers burrow deeper underground?"

Wait a second...

"What motherfuckers? You don't think Silvio was working alone?"

"No, I don't. Because after we riled him up this morning, he fired off a message to a burner email address saying *Be careful, people are asking about the last girl*. Then he deleted it from the 'sent' folder."

"How do you—" Brax answered his own question. "Alexa."

"We installed spyware on his computer last night."

"Last night?"

"We also took a look in the storage room. Meera's wasn't the only suitcase in there. There are seven others, and five of them belong to women. Of those five women, three have since been reported missing."

Four missing women.

Four families missing daughters, sisters, grandchildren, and a police force doing nothing at all. If the cops could be persuaded to get off their asses, did they have the chops for an investigation like this one? Brax was no legal expert, but judging by their performance so far, he'd have been surprised if they even managed to obtain a warrant to search the hostel, whereas Jerry and Tulsa had gone in the night they arrived in the city.

Could Meera be alive? Although he hadn't mentioned his fears to Indi, he secretly suspected they'd be hunting for a body. Over a week with no communication whatsoever? A woman who'd left a job she loved and shunned her best friend?

And Jerry was right about one thing: Brax *had* changed. After seeing what Levi had done to Ruby, he'd realised that some of his fellow men were wolves in sheep's clothing. He'd always wished that he could turn back the clock and do something, anything, to prevent what happened.

Now was his chance. Not with Ruby, but with another woman who'd fallen prey to the worst side of human nature.

"Do you really think you can get information from this piece of shit?"

"Sure," Jerry said. "With the right incentive, every man will talk."

"Where are those tranquillisers? Indi's a light sleeper, and I do *not* want her waking in the middle of this. Do the others know what you're doing?"

"Priest and Chase, yes, of course. Dawson, maybe. Priest filled him in on some of the details. Ari, not exactly, but she's smart. She has an idea, but Alexa reckons she'll keep out of the way." Jerry picked up Silvio's spare arm. "Can you get the door to the cellar? And we'll also need the cigar cutter in the top drawer beside the stove."

"I'm assuming you haven't taken up smoking?"

Now Jerry grinned, and the effect was somewhat chilling.

"Welcome to the dark side, Brax."

Either Jerry was into bondage, or she'd had experience with this type of interrogation. She trussed Silvio up like a rope bottom and attached him securely to a wine rack, all before he regained consciousness. Lastly, she removed his footwear and stuffed a sock in his mouth. A poor substitute for a ball gag, but needs must.

Brax watched from the shadows as the man's eyes flickered open, saw the confusion that turned to fear when Tulsa stepped forward. The women were both wearing ski masks now, and Jerry had made Brax tie a scarf around his face, hiding everything but his eyes. Was this an indication that they intended to release the man at some point? Or merely standard operating procedure?

Tulsa did the talking, and although Brax didn't understand Portuguese, he recognised the man's tone. Belligerent.

"His attitude changed when he realised she was a woman," Jerry whispered. "Did you see?"

"Yes."

Silvio thought she wouldn't follow through on whatever threats she was making, that somehow, he still had the upper hand because of his dick.

That soon changed when she lopped off a little toe with the cigar cutter. Brax's stomach lurched, and Silvio screamed into his makeshift gag while Tulsa studied her handiwork. Blood trickled across the floor, or rather across the plastic sheeting. This kidnapping had been well planned, Brax had to concede. At least nobody needed to get out a mop.

"Removing digits with a cigar cutter is an art," Jerry whispered. "The movies make it look so easy, but if you don't position the blade right, it gets stuck in the bone."

"I assume you've had practice?"

A shrug. Brax took that as an affirmative.

Now Silvio was sobbing, tears mingling with blood, words spilling from his lips like water from a faucet. A confession? Since Tulsa didn't seem ready to chop off any more toes, Brax was inclined to think so.

"He has two daughters," Jerry said, keeping her voice low. "He doesn't want them to grow up without a father."

"You speak Portuguese?"

"Nowhere near fluently, but enough to get by." Her expression darkened as she listened. "Silvio is a middleman. He sold Meera."

"*Sold* her?"

"Shhh. Keep your voice down. If he spotted a girl that fit certain criteria, he informed the buyer, and they picked her up. They paid him for the information." A pause. "Ten thousand euros."

Ten thousand euros? Hell, Nyx sold bottles of wine that cost more. That a man should broker any woman was vile, but for so little? That added another layer of obscenity.

"He's at pains to point out that he never sold a woman if she was a mother."

Did he expect thanks for that? Silvio's voice rose as Tulsa crouched in front of him.

"*Não, não, não!*"

"*Me diga!*"

More rapid-fire Portuguese was followed by a calmer discussion, and finally, Tulsa nodded. Did they have what they needed?

"She said she's going to check out his story, and if he lied, she'll be back and he'll regret it."

"So we're just leaving him here in the cellar?"

"What else are we meant to do with him? Offer him a spare bedroom? We have to work with the facilities available, and sadly, there's no holding cell."

"If we need more information, we could try wineboarding him," Tulsa suggested.

"Wineboarding?"

"Waterboarding is so passé." She nodded toward the stairs. "Let's talk up there."

This time, Alexa joined in the conversation, making a rare appearance on screen in person rather than substituting her cartoon avatar. She looked tired. Hardly surprising if she was working Meera's disappearance as an extra job on the side. Not to mention the fact that the Portugal team had stolen her assistant and, therefore, her bringer of caffeine.

"Meera's phone is on its way to me," she said. "Priest put it on a plane earlier, but in light of the new information, I doubt we'll find anything useful on there."

Now that they knew Meera had been snatched, tactics would have to change. Dawson could stop tracking down friends from the list of names Alfie had provided. Quinta do Lago was a dead end. Silvio and his partner in crime were the focus.

The coffee pot was full, and they were ready for a long night.

Tulsa took over. "Silvio tried to downplay his involvement. If he identified a suitable candidate—a foreign woman no older than twenty-five, pretty and with no travelling companions, somebody no one would miss—he'd email his contact with a name and picture. If he received confirmation that his suggestion was acceptable, he'd drug the woman, and a courier would pick her up at the appointed time."

"What was in it for him?"

"Ten thousand euros in cash, delivered by the courier."

"Who's the contact? How the hell did he get involved in this?"

"The hostel hasn't been profitable for years. Silvio's the owner of the place as well as the manager. Not so many people want to visit the interior anymore, and those that do come prefer to stay in Airbnbs. Fundão's population has been decreasing, which has depressed the property market, so when folks leave, they rent out their homes instead of selling them. Anyhow, Silvio borrowed money, got into dire financial straits, blah blah blah, and rather than going bankrupt, he started a sideline selling access to young women."

Holy hell. How were they meant to explain this to Indi?

"Selling young women to who?" Alexa asked.

"He claims he doesn't know."

"Bullshit," Brax blurted. "You don't just stumble into a

criminal enterprise. What did they do, advertise on Craigslist?"

"No, an old high-school friend recruited him. They met by chance in a bar in Porto four years ago, and Silvio confessed his troubles over bad music and cheap liquor. The friend said he had a solution—all Silvio had to do was identify women suitable for a new 'business opportunity.'"

"That's what they called it? A business opportunity? What happens to the women? Where do they go?"

"Where do they go? He doesn't know. But in the initial phone call, he was told that rich foreign men like to marry pretty English-speaking girls."

"So he's sourcing mail-order brides?"

"Sure seems that way."

"And the man has daughters himself? He's a monster."

"He said the only women he recommended—that was the word he used, 'recommended'—were unhappy. Lonely, struggling financially, disappointed with the world in general. He believed that the new life would be better than the old one."

"That's bullshit."

"Clearly, but I think he's genuinely convinced himself of that. Whatever helps him to sleep at night, I guess."

"He doesn't deserve to sleep at night."

Jerry took a sip of black coffee. "Fun fact: sleep deprivation as a form of torture is outlawed by the Geneva Conventions, and yet here we are, existing on artificial stimulants."

"Caffeine is natural," Alexa pointed out. "It grows in plants."

"It's also dangerous in high enough quantities. Although overdosing is a challenge—you have to compensate for the bitterness."

Jerry wasn't talking about an accidental overdose, was she? The revelation made Brax shudder. All these years, he'd assumed that Alexa was the renegade of Blackstone House, but Jerry had been hiding a much darker side than he'd ever suspected. A part of him was appalled—there was a man tied up in the cellar, for crying out loud. But the bigger part was relieved. Relieved that Jerry was on their side and competent when it came to unorthodox operations. Meera's life could depend on it.

"Can we stay on track here?" he asked. "Who's selling these so-called brides? Where's Meera?"

"Silvio doesn't know," Tulsa said. "He wasn't involved in that side of the operation, or so he claims, and on balance, I believe him. But that old high-school buddy mentioned the name of a place once. *Estrada do âmbar*—it translates as 'amber road.' Silvio got curious and looked it up, but the only reference he found was for an ancient trading route that ran from the Baltic Sea to the Mediterranean. If Meera's located somewhere along it, we'll have a hell of a job to find her."

The Baltic to the Med? That had to cover thousands of miles.

"If this school friend has additional information, why aren't we talking with him?"

"Because last year, the guy jumped off the roof of his apartment building, bounced off the hood of a police car, and got run over by a semi-truck. His death made the news. Obviously, we'll confirm the details. And by 'we,' I mean Echo."

Alexa spoke up. "He might have been useful, but I already know what Amber Road is. It's an online marketplace. The dark web's equivalent of eBay. The guy who runs it is called Ivan the Magnificent—Mag for short—and he has a reputation for being trustworthy, or as trustworthy as a man gets in that space. Most of those types of marketplaces are set up for exit scams, but Amber Road has been running for almost four years."

"Exit scams?" Jerry asked.

"Payments are held in escrow until the buyer confirms receipt of the goods, and only then are the funds released to the seller. Amber Road deals mainly in crypto. In an exit scam, the site owner waits until there's a fuck-ton of money on hand, then closes the marketplace and steals it all."

While Jerry was concerned with the logistics, Alexa's words were sinking in. Just when Brax thought this nightmare couldn't get any worse, it did.

"Do I have this right? Meera's abductors are planning to sell her on the internet?"

Jerry shrugged. "Sounds plausible."

"How can you be so casual about this?"

"What do you want me to do? Gasp? Cry? Wring my hands and panic?"

"You could try sounding a little more horrified."

"The world sucks. What's new? We should get some sleep."

"Sleep?"

"It's that thing where you close your eyes and snore."

"I don't snore."

"Sure, snookums, you keep telling yourself that." Jerry rose and patted him on the shoulder. "Sweet dreams."

"Wait, wait! What about Meera?"

"I don't have a fucking clue how Amber Road works. Do you?" Jerry already knew the answer. "So we'll let Echo work while we rest."

"Divide and conquer," Alexa said. "I need coffee. Where the hell is Marcel?"

"Who's Marcel?"

Jerry ignored the question. "Just go to bed, Brax."

"How do you expect me to sleep?"

"I still have plenty of tranquillisers."

"Thanks, but I'll pass."

CHAPTER 38
THE ASSISTANT

I blinked in the light flooding through the window, trying to get my bearings. My eyelids were heavy, my head filled with sludge. Where was I? What day was it? Beside me, Brax was still asleep, one arm draped loosely over my stomach as he breathed softly.

How easy it had become to spend time with this man.

I'd always told Meera that I dreaded the thought of sharing a bed, of sharing my life with— Holy hell! I knifed up. Meera!

Brax's hand fell to the side, but he didn't wake. I leaned down to kiss him on the cheek.

"Sleep for a few minutes longer. I'll make us coffee."

It was the least I could do. After all, he'd fetched me a glass of milk in the early hours. Why did I feel so giddy? Were the events of the past two weeks catching up with me? I had to grip the bannister as I walked down the stairs, and of course Jerry and Tulsa looked wide awake when I got to the kitchen.

"You think we should put in a bid?" Tulsa asked.

"There are nearly four days left. Why show our hand now?"

"How high is the auction likely to go? What we need is a 'Buy it now' price."

These two were unbe-freaking-lievable. "Are you *shopping*? My friend's been *abducted*. Can't you take anything seriously?"

Jerry peered at me over a mug of coffee. "We're shopping for your friend."

"She doesn't need a dress or a pair of shoes. She needs to be rescued."

If she was still alive. I *had* to believe she was still alive. The alternative was too horrible to contemplate.

"No, you don't get it. We're trying to buy Meera."

"What? What are you talking about?" It was too early in the morning for this. "I need caffeine."

"There's coffee in the pot. Chase got the good stuff."

But was it made with Hawaiian Kona beans and served at 140 degrees exactly? Someone had left mugs lined up on the counter, so I nudged two closer to the machine and poured.

"What do you mean, trying to buy Meera?"

"She's up for auction. The top bid is only fifty thousand bucks, but it'll probably increase."

"Oh, it definitely will." Alexa's voice came through the speaker. "The last girl went for two hundred and seven thousand, and she wasn't as pretty, in my opinion."

"I...I...I don't understand."

Jerry turned the laptop around to face me, and I peered at the screen. And saw Meera. Meera, looking thinner than I'd ever known her. She was wearing heavy make-up and a green sequined cocktail dress, but no amount of gloss could hide her misery.

And that was only the start of the horror. A countdown ticked beside the picture, showing three days and nineteen hours. Did I want to place a bid? The mug slid out of my hand and smashed on the tiled floor, coffee splashing everywhere.

Jerry took another sip of her drink. "Good news that she's still alive, huh?"

"Good news? *Good news?* A vile brute is trying to sell her like a piece of meat. Wait, is this a sick joke?"

I mean, it had to be, right? This was the twenty-first century. Slavery was illegal. A woman couldn't just be auctioned off on the internet. My chest seized, and I fought to control my ragged breathing. This couldn't be real. This couldn't be *happening*.

"Relax, Brax will pay whatever's necessary to get her back."

"Good thing Carissa's out of the picture," Tulsa added as Chase silently appeared and began mopping up coffee. "Could have been awkward if she'd taken him to the cleaners."

I was still dreaming. I had to be. My friend wasn't being sold on hell's version of eBay, and these two lunatics weren't calmly discussing that fact over coffee. No, it was impossible.

"What happened?" Brax asked from behind me. "What's going on?"

"I don't even know anymore."

"We found Meera," Jerry told him. "Well, kind of. Apparently, she's fun, feisty, and available for delivery worldwide."

If looks could kill... Brax glared at Jerry with the fire of a thousand suns, but she didn't wither. Meanwhile, I felt quite sick.

"We're not meant to be discussing this," he said through gritted teeth.

"What, you think it would be better not to tell her? Indi's stronger than you think."

Was that meant to be a compliment? I tried to hide the fact that my knees were trembling.

"Did you know about this?" I asked him. "About this...

this…"—there weren't adequate words to describe what had happened to Meera—"this horror?"

"No. Not any of the details. I was aware that we were following up a lead related to the dark web, that was all." He leaned past me to look at the screen. "It's an auction?"

"Yup."

"Alexa, bid whatever you have to in order to get Meera back."

"See?" Jerry mouthed at me.

But although my heart swelled at Brax's generosity, his offer did nothing to calm my nerves.

"What if it turns into a frenzy? What if someone outbids you at the last minute? And the end of the auction is three days away—anything could happen to her in that time."

Alexa clicked on the seller's profile. His name was Casa Nova. That meant "new house" in Spanish, didn't it? Or was it a play on the name Casanova? There were no personal details, just a close-up of a collar and tie for a profile picture, and a proclamation that he was the world's best supplier of hot women, all tastes catered to, message with requests.

"Casa Nova has good feedback," she said. "Mostly five stars. Oh, this asshole docked a point because the woman's breasts weren't as big as they looked in the pictures."

That was when the true extent of the situation hit me. *Meera wasn't the only girl this had happened to.*

"How many?" To my own ears, my voice sounded hollow. "How many others are on that site?"

"Right now?" *Click, click, click.* "Six more."

Mostly five stars. The seller had 293 ratings. Did each one of those represent a woman who'd been sold? A life that had been stolen? Who held an auction for a freaking *person*?

"Why haven't the police stopped this?"

Alexa's avatar shrugged. "Either they can't find Casa Nova, or they don't know it's happening."

"How can they not know? It's right there on the internet."

"That's the beauty of Amber Road—it's invite only. Buyers have to be sponsored by an existing user."

"So how did you get access?"

"I know people, and sometimes I buy stuff there."

"*You* buy stuff?" I turned away, incredulous, and at least Brax seemed as shocked as I felt.

"Databases and access codes, not bloody people," she said. "Brax, don't look at me like that."

"Like what?" Brax asked, scrubbing a hand through his hair.

"All judgey and holier-than-thou. It's not as if you haven't benefitted from my purchases in the past."

"What about the other women?" I fought the tears that threatened to fall as I glanced at the screen again. "If we manage to buy Meera back, what happens to them?"

Silence.

"Well?"

Finally, Brax spoke. "Once we have Meera, we can go to the police. With her statement and any additional information she can provide, they'll have to investigate the matter."

"And meanwhile, those other girls could end up anywhere."

"Indi, I hate the state of affairs as much as you do, but we don't have any other leads. Meera could be anywhere. At least this way, we'll be able to save her."

The clock was ticking; he didn't need to tell me that. But I hated the idea that six other women would suffer a worse fate than Meera's. Alexa brought them up on screen. *Greta, Rebecca, Karine, Nicola, Elin, Annalise.* But those names weren't real. Meera had been called Juliet.

"Save her by giving them what they want? Money? So they can carry on taking even more women and selling them off like cattle?"

"We won't give up. We'll keep pushing the police, and I can hire a team of investigators."

Which might provide a long-term solution, but these women, the ones here in front of me, would go through untold anguish first. Karine, with her teary smile. Elin, a petite girl who couldn't have been more than twenty. Annalise, with the bruise peeking out from under the bra she'd been photographed in.

"There must be another way."

"If there was—"

"There is." Jerry glanced at Tulsa, and an unspoken message passed between them. Tulsa nodded. "But Brax won't like it."

"What is it? I'll do anything."

I was a doctor, whether I practised medicine or not. My job was to help people. To save them.

"We have a way of contacting these people. An email address. It's possible that we might be able to send them a girl via the same route Meera took."

"You mean we let them abduct yet another innocent victim? Have you lost your mind?"

For the briefest second, Jerry's eyes widened, while Tulsa and Alexa both burst out laughing.

"Even I'm not that fucking crazy." Jerry shook her head. "No, I was talking about you."

"W-w-what?"

Brax took hold of my hand and squeezed it in a death grip. "You *are* that fucking crazy. Indi's not going anywhere. I'll pay every cent I have before you use her as bait."

"Told you he wouldn't like the idea."

I couldn't blame him. I didn't like it either.

"Think of an alternative," Brax said.

"Then we're back to plan A. I'd go myself, but there's no way I'd pass for twenty-five, and neither would Tulsa. Plus there's the bullet hole in my thigh."

"What bullet hole?" Brax asked.

"Why do you think I kept a pair of stockings on in that video?"

"What video?" I asked.

Brax shook his head. "It doesn't matter, and it's also irrelevant. Nobody else is going to get kidnapped."

But Alexa begged to differ. "Statistically speaking, that's not true. Each auction lasts two weeks, and there are seven women on offer at this moment. So they grab one every two days. Which means—"

I knew exactly what it meant. "What if you lost me? What if they gave you the slip and I ended up on this website too?"

Brax's grip tightened, and now it hurt. I tugged my hand away, and he released me in an instant.

"Sorry, my darling." He stroked a thumb over my knuckles. "Nobody will lose you because you're not going anywhere."

I curled an arm around his waist instead. I loved this man, and I didn't want to fight with him, but at the same time, I couldn't sit in this luxurious house and let other women go through hell. So I looked to Jerry. She seemed to be in charge here.

"Tell me."

"We'd use a surveillance team and a tracking device."

"How long do you think the police would take to arrive?"

Tulsa let fly with a peal of laughter. "Oh, honey, we want to rescue you, not create a hostage situation. We'll pick the two of you up ourselves."

"But what if these people are dangerous? I mean, they're kidnapping innocent women."

"We'll be careful, Scout's honour."

"Were you actually a Girl Scout?"

"Okay, you got me there. Pinky promise?"

This was *crazy*. Was I actually considering getting kidnapped on purpose with only the two slackers on hand to rescue me? Jerry hadn't lost her mind; I had. But those other girls… How could I sleep at night if I left them there?

Brax must have read my thoughts. "I understand how difficult it is to watch this unfold, but putting yourself in danger isn't the answer."

Chase surprised me by speaking up. The coffee was gone, and he was sweeping the last of the china shards into a dustpan.

"Jez and Tulsa can do this. Brax, think about it. Think about what happened earlier in the week. You know they can pull it off."

"I don't know a damn thing," he snapped.

Panic began welling up inside me, not just the prickle of fear I'd felt when I thought I was being followed to my apartment, but full-on, out-of-control terror. There could be no good outcome to this.

"I need air."

Brax took a step toward the door. "We'll head outside."

"Please, just give me a minute alone to gather my thoughts. I can't… I just can't…"

How had Meera's European vacation gone so badly wrong?

CHAPTER 39
BRAX

The moment the back door closed behind Indi, Brax turned to his former housemate.

"What the hell are you doing?"

"Trying to help?"

"By filling Indi's head with potentially fatal ideas?"

He'd only just met the woman he wanted to spend the foreseeable future with; he wasn't about to lose her.

"They're not going to kill the merchandise." Jerry waved a hand at the laptop screen. "Case in point. A woman's worth hundreds of thousands of bucks. All they have to do is keep her alive for a couple of weeks, and then they can buy a new Ferrari or whatever."

"What if you lose her? People can give surveillance the slip. And if they search her, they'll find a tracking device."

"No, they won't. Not if it's inside her."

"Tell me you're joking?"

"I can't. Really, I've told you too much already. But I can promise you that this operation is well within our capabilities."

"Jerry, what have you been doing for the past nine years?"

"I…" She took a sip of coffee. A stalling tactic, no doubt. "I started out looking for my father, and then I got sidetracked."

Her father? Brax had vague memories of her mentioning the man, but as far as he recalled, the two had never met. Jerry had been the result of a fling between Britta Knight and a man named Jeremy Pope, who'd vanished from Jerry's life before she was even born. But not completely. Firstly, Jeremy had made enough of an impression that Britta named her daughter after him. And secondly, for the next eighteen years, she'd received two thousand bucks a month by direct deposit and an extra thousand on Jerry's birthday. Jeremy hadn't abandoned his offspring, but not once had he ever gotten in touch. And then, on Jerry's eighteenth birthday, a car had appeared in the driveway, a vintage Porsche that she'd spent half of her Blackstone House days tinkering with in an effort to get it to run smoothly. It never had.

But Jerry had set out to look for her father?

"Did you find him?"

"If he's alive, he doesn't want to be found."

"So you gave up looking and joined the U.S. Army instead?"

A shrug. "It seemed like a good idea at the time."

"Then what? What did you do after that?"

"Then…I took a job solving problems. And I can tell you that we're not going to get a better opportunity to solve this one than we have with Meera right now. Thanks to Silvio, there's an open line of communication, and the team is already here."

"But what would the end-game be? Are you planning to chain Meera's captor in a cellar and cut off his toes?"

"No, but if he quietly disappeared, the world would be a better place."

That truth was undeniable, but the idea of Jerry disappearing him… Fuck.

Tulsa smiled brightly. "We can make it look like an accident."

Zach had always said that if anyone in Blackstone House was capable of taking a life in cold blood, it was Jerry, but the cops had quickly ruled her out of having any involvement in Ruby's death. What were the chances of two killers living in one house? Brax shuddered, suddenly chilled to the bone even though the temperature in the kitchen remained steady. Maybe Carissa had been right when she said the place was creepy?

"You're overthinking," Jerry said.

"Of course I'm overthinking!"

"You have questions?"

"What happened to Ruby?" Brax blurted before he could stop himself.

"Ruby? How did we get onto the subject of Ruby?"

"Because she's dead. And now you're talking about killing people."

Too late, it occurred to Brax that if Jerry was capable of murder, then challenging her was probably a bad idea. But Jerry just shook her head.

"A logical question, but I had nothing to do with Ruby's death. And truthfully, it's always bugged me that I didn't see it coming. That whole pentagram thing? Strangulation? Levi must have been high."

When Brax didn't speak, Jerry sighed.

"I know you don't trust me, and in your situation, I wouldn't trust me either. But if I'd had to kill Ruby—and fuck knows why I'd have done that because I liked her—then I wouldn't have done it at home. That was just dumb, and I'm not stupid, Brax."

No, she wasn't.

"You think it was drugs? That's why he did it?"

Like Grey, Jerry had distanced herself after the murder. While the rest of them—except for Alexa, who'd been in foster prison, as she called it—had discussed the case a number of times, Brax had never heard Jerry's thoughts on the matter.

"All those pills he popped? He probably got a bad one. What good does rehashing the past do? We can't bring Ruby back, but Meera's still alive. We should focus on her."

Another hard truth.

For years, Brax had dreamed of escaping from his old world, but thanks to Carissa's antics, he found himself at the intersection of two new ones: Alexa and Jerry's lawless enclave and Indi's tangled wonderland. The difference between them? Until now, Indi had been a mere passenger on this ride, while Jerry drove like a maniac.

Past and present had collided, but how would the future look? If Indi stayed passive and six women disappeared, the guilt would haunt her forever, and Brax had seen what guilt could do to a woman. Dawson's sister hadn't been able to live with her mistake. He'd helped Dawson to arrange the funeral.

"How certain are you that you can get the women back?" he asked Jerry.

"Indi? Ninety-nine percent. I'm not going to lie and tell you a hundred because there'll always be risk involved. Meera? The same. If the op runs into a problem, we'll back off until you can buy her. The other women? If they're being held at the same location, mid-nineties. If they're somewhere else? Who the hell knows—it all depends on what information we're able to extract."

Ninety-nine percent. A one percent chance that they'd lose Indi. If Brax were gambling in Vegas, he'd play those odds, no question, but this was the woman he loved. Could he take the risk? The alternatives weren't palatable either—sure, Brax could liberate Meera, hell, he could bid for all the girls, but then where would it end? The seller would only get richer, and no woman under the age of twenty-five would be safe.

Could Jerry pull this off? A month ago, he'd have laughed

at the idea, but then he'd seen what she'd done with Carissa… He didn't trust Jerry, not even a little, but he had to concede that she seemed competent.

"If this happens, the seller has to go to jail, not disappear. He should face justice. If those reviews on Amber Road are accurate, hundreds of other women have been taken. They need to be found, or at the very least, their families need closure."

Jerry glanced toward Tulsa. "We can take the people at the house alive. Does that mean you're on board with this plan?"

Meera, Greta, Rebecca, Karine, Nicola, Elin, Annalise.

"The police haven't exactly covered themselves in glory so far, have they?"

"Is that a yes?"

"I need to speak with Indi. The final decision is hers. But if she wants to go ahead, I won't stand in her way."

CHAPTER 40
THE ASSISTANT

This was either the smartest thing or the stupidest thing I'd ever done.

Before we left for the hostel, before Brax kissed me for what might have been the final time, he'd told me that it wasn't too late to back out. But it was. The preparations had been made. Jerry had glossed over the details, but I knew Alexa had pretended to be Silvio and sent an email to the kidnappers, telling them that Meera's sister had arrived in town and kept asking difficult questions. Perhaps, Alexa-slash-Silvio suggested, the easiest way to avoid an American woman stirring up trouble would be to pick me up too. The kidnappers had taken the bait. The fact that Brax had pushed the bidding on Meera up to a hundred and fifty thousand bucks had probably helped.

As for Silvio, he was being oddly cooperative this evening. Had Brax paid him to help? I felt sick at the thought, but I didn't dare to ask, and I also wasn't certain I wanted to know. Apparently, he usually gave his victims a drink containing a sedative, but since I was a special case, I sipped regular wine while Silvio hobbled to the door to let his accomplice in. I had no idea what he'd done to his foot, but I hoped it hurt.

I'd been seated in Silvio's office—standard procedure, he said. After the two men had spoken for a few minutes in Portuguese, they each took one of my arms and led me toward the door. That was when my heart began hammering. *This is really happening.* Since I was pretending to be drugged, all I could do was stumble and mumble as they half carried me to a waiting SUV. Before the accomplice bundled me inside, he patted me down and gave my phone and watch to Silvio. The phone was a decoy, a cheap smartphone registered to Indira Adams, just in case anyone happened to check. Alexa paid attention to detail. I made a weak protest as the man cuffed my hands behind me in the back seat, all the time knowing how scared Meera must have been when this happened to her. That's not to say I wasn't fearful—what if the rest of the team lost me? My biceps still ached from the tiny tracking device Jerry had inserted into my left arm using a touch of local anaesthetic and an oversized hollow needle. It was powered by kinetic energy, she'd told me. The battery would last for a day, and after that, I'd have to recharge it by moving.

Now I was travelling toward a destination unknown, and I'd never felt so alone in my life, not even when I moved to Los Angeles. I had to trust someone was following, but I couldn't see them. There were no headlights glinting in the mirrors, no cars close behind us when we turned.

What if I ended up on that auction site?

What if I was sold to a stranger to serve at his pleasure?

Marriage to Karam seemed an attractive option in comparison. Sure, he was an asshole, but I couldn't see him purchasing a human from the internet.

How long did the journey take? Two hours? Three? Without a watch, I lost track of time. The driver turned on the radio and fiddled until he found a rock station as we wound through country roads and then joined the freeway. Carefully, I tested my hands. Not only were they cuffed together, but they were also attached to a loop of cable that stuck out from the gap at the back of the seat. I couldn't escape from the vehicle, even if I wanted to.

Which was probably why the driver felt happy leaving me there while he filled up with fuel at a quiet gas station in the middle of nowhere. That told me he'd been doing the job for a while. He'd grown complacent. Learned not to expect trouble. His actions gave me a small measure of comfort, but that was nothing compared to the relief I felt when a dark-coloured sedan pulled up at the pump beside us and Tulsa climbed out. She was wearing a blonde wig and a shapeless sweater, but I recognised her cowboy boots. She'd had them propped up on the kitchen table this morning, casual as she planned my visit to the underworld. They hadn't lost me. She didn't look in my direction, just pumped gas and strolled into the attached convenience store to pay, but *she was there.*

All I had to do was stay calm and wait for rescue.

The sky was beginning to lighten when we bumped down a rutted track to a farmhouse not too dissimilar from the one we'd rented near Fundão. Rustic in style but modern, well cared for. The driver continued past that building and around to the rear, where he stopped the SUV outside a barn and honked the horn. A huge door at the front slid silently to the side, and we drove into the cavernous interior.

"What is this place?" I mumbled, not expecting an answer. The man hadn't spoken to me the whole way.

"Is somewhere for you to stay."

"Like…like a hostel?"

He just laughed and climbed out of the car. The door slammed, and I studied my surroundings without being too obvious about it. The barn had been used to keep horses at some point. Stables lined both sides of a wide central aisle, square boxes with wooden walls at the bottom and bars at the top. I'd tried horse riding once, several years ago with Meera. The experience was one I'd rather forget. My horse got spooked by a groundhog, and I'd barely hung on as it galloped across a pasture, whinnying as it went. Eventually, a cowboy had caught up with me and stopped the thing, and I'd walked back to the stables, ignoring Meera's laughter as I cursed four-legged beasts in general and that one in particular.

But there were no horses here.

I jolted as a pale face appeared between the bars of the nearest stable. Not Meera, but I recognised her. She was the girl they'd called Greta, and her eyes were wide with fear. This was where they kept the women? In a barn? The driver was talking with a man sitting on a couch at the far end. A guard? A chaperone? Satan himself?

A long minute passed before the man rose and came to the SUV, peering through the window before he opened the door.

"What's going on? Where am I?"

Did I sound scared enough? Hopefully, because I sure was terrified.

Nobody answered me, but words were exchanged, and I found myself released from the cable and manhandled into the nearest stable.

"Get away from me! What are you doing?"

The guard's slap caught me off guard, and I saw stars as his hand connected. Seemed that actions spoke louder than words around here. Another laugh from the driver.

Then I heard a sound that made my knees go weak with relief.

"Indi?"

Meera's voice wasn't close, but it was unmistakable. She was at the far end of the barn, but she was here, and she was alive.

This was why I'd come.

"Meera?"

"What are you doing here? How did you—"

Another *crack* of flesh on flesh, this time hers. A man spoke in English this time.

"You will be quiet, all of you, or you will suffer the consequences."

His tone carried authority, as did his footsteps when he headed in my direction. Was this the beast who called himself Casa Nova? He was smaller than the guard, an inch shorter with a lighter build. Dark hair, dark eyes, dark soul. A male version of Jerry. His clothes were casual—jeans and a V-neck sweater, expensive-looking—and when his tongue darted out to lick thin lips, he reminded me of a snake.

Silence had fallen, so I had to assume that Meera and the others understood what the consequences would be, and they didn't want to antagonise him. He studied me, a beast sizing up its prey, and when he whirled one finger in a circle, the guard spun me roughly around.

"Yes, you're prettier than your sister."

That seemed to please him, probably because I'd fetch more money. I only hoped Meera hadn't heard his words. They weren't even true. She had a nicer smile, and Karam wouldn't be asking *her* to get a boob job, that was for sure.

"You can't just keep us here. What did you do? Drug me? This is kidnapping."

"Oh, I don't intend to keep you."

"So what *do* you intend to do?"

He ran a finger down my cheek, and when I jerked my head away, he grasped my chin so hard it hurt.

"You'll be sent to a man who can teach you some manners."

"What man? Sent where?"

"You're not in a position to ask questions." He turned to the guard. "Get her changed. I'll see her tonight."

"Tonight? See me for what?"

But he didn't answer. As he walked away, the guard pointed at a dress laid out on a mattress in the corner. There was also a pair of high-heeled pumps, a hairbrush, and what looked like a make-up compact.

"You will wear this," he told me.

"And if I don't?"

He cracked his knuckles. "You will."

Now I had a choice—I could resist or comply. Until I'd gone to college, I'd spent my whole life doing what others told me to do, and although I'd later rebelled, I'd chosen to run rather than fight. And I couldn't afford to fight now. I only had to survive for two or three days—why risk injuring myself?

My skin crawled as I stripped out of my jeans and sweater. The guard watched me, his gaze dripping over me like slime, but he made no move to touch. Did Casa Nova have rules? A warped code of ethics his men had to obey?

The dress was a brand I didn't recognise, elaborately beaded with a plunging neckline. This was for my promo pictures, wasn't it? The ones they'd post on Amber Road for the auction? I hated that Brax would see me this way, but at the same time, I was proud of myself. A year ago, I wouldn't have been strong enough to do this. Living my own life, despite its many challenges, had changed me for the better.

And in a few short days, it would change Casa Nova's wretched existence for the worse.

CHAPTER 41
BRAX

"Hhis name is Cássio Elvyn Arruda Novo," Alexa said. With only Brax, Priest, and Chase in the house, she'd forgone the cartoon avatar once more, and the screen showed her sitting in a bright room with a view of a swimming pool through the French windows behind. "He's thirty-three years old, and property records indicate that he bought the place in Vila Real seven years ago."

Before that, it had been a ruin. Dawson and Ari were playing tourist in a nearby village, gushing over the traditional houses that lined the cobbled streets and meandering around the craft market set up in an old bullfighting arena while they ferreted out whatever information they could find. The locals, they reported, didn't know a whole lot about the *cara rico presunçoso* who lived at the target property, but they didn't seem to like him much.

"You're sure it's the right man?" Brax asked Alexa.

Apparently, Portuguese parents were limited to a government-approved list of forenames, so there were a surprisingly large number of men with the same name. On the plus side, there were no children in Portugal named

304

Klamydia or Vellveeta or Ebolah. Brax had gone to school with a boy named Dijon.

"Ninety percent sure. I found two other Cássio Arruda Novos, but they both live in the south, and one of them is in a care home."

"He's arrogant." Priest was wearing another Hawaiian shirt from his seemingly limitless collection. He'd arrived at their temporary base of operations soon after Brax's group, bringing with him several hard plastic cases whose contents he'd declined to reveal. "Cássio Novo, Casa Nova. He's playing with us. He thinks he's untouchable."

Chase had found them a short-term rental in the area, another former farmhouse. Fortunately, such properties were common, and the isolation made them ideal for the team's purposes. Novo had clearly come to the same conclusion because he'd holed up in a similar home five miles closer to the Spanish border. After Indi's long ride, they'd ended up in northern Portugal. The nearest city was Chaves, but it seemed a million miles away from their location out in the sticks. Chase was busy ensuring the refrigerator was stocked with food and that everyone had enough insect repellent.

"Hey, I think I found a picture of him." Alexa put it on the screen, and Brax found himself staring at a group graduation photo. "Bottom row, third from the left. The age fits. This Novo has a master's degree in software engineering from the University of Porto, but I guess he found an easier way to make money."

Brax had been trying to contain his fury for the past several days, but he was struggling. Every detail that came out stoked his anger. Silvio had turned to people trafficking out of semi-desperation and a reluctance to lose his home, but Cássio Novo had led a privileged life. He'd been blessed with a good education, and yet he'd decided to sell women instead.

"Not for long," Priest said. "He'll be in jail by Friday."

Friday, and today was Tuesday. Which meant that Indi would have to endure three and a half more days of captivity.

"Can't we go in sooner?"

"Not without compromising the chances of success. We need to map out the estate, gain an understanding of the security measures in place, and identify the people present and their routines. Otherwise, we could get an unexpected surprise."

"I have a surprise," Alexa told us. "Novo's father is in prison for killing his mother."

Priest quirked an eyebrow. "This is getting more interesting."

Alexa had found a newspaper article dated ten years ago. The text was in Portuguese, but she'd run it through a translator, and the accompanying picture showed the same face as the graduation photo. Was Brax looking at the man who'd snatched Indi? He scanned the details.

Today, Fabricio Novo was found guilty of the murder of his wife, Margarida Arruda, following a trial that lasted six weeks. The defence was a surprising one—Novo claimed that his wife had driven him to stab her sixteen times through years of mental abuse. In a shocking twist, Novo's son, Cássio, took his father's side, testifying under oath that he'd heard his parents arguing on the night of Margarida's death, despite the fact that forensic evidence strongly suggested she was asleep immediately prior to the attack. During his court appearance, Cássio was reprimanded by the judge after he referred to the prosecutor as "that feminist bitch" and accused her of ruining an innocent man's life. The jury's decision was unanimous.

"Hoo boy," Priest said. "Our suspect has a temper."

Alexa nodded her agreement. "And a hatred of women. A winning combination."

Fuck. Why hadn't Novo rung alarm bells in the past?

"We need to get Indi and Meera out of there," Brax said.

"And we will." Priest checked his watch. "I have two more men arriving in the next half hour, and after I've briefed them, we'll head over to Casa Nova. Jez and Tulsa have eyes on the place. We believe the women are being held in a barn out back."

A barn? They were being kept like animals? As soon as this was over, Brax was taking Indi on a five-star vacation. A luxury hotel suite, gourmet food, and a private spa. Paris, perhaps?

"Who are the two men? I got the impression your whole team was female."

Priest pulled a face and muttered something that sounded suspiciously like "Yeah, what the fuck was I thinking?" Then he shrugged. "I borrowed the men. You'll receive an invoice from Blackwood Security. Don't quibble over the price—I had to call in a favour to get them at short notice."

"They're competent?"

"They come highly recommended."

Since he left Blackstone House, Brax had fought to maintain control over his life. He'd succeeded in business, and with Carissa out of the picture, his personal life was back on track too. Or at least, it had been. Having to take a back seat and let others make the decisions added another layer of discomfort to an already hellish situation. But he knew he didn't have the right skill set for this particular job.

"Then I'll pay whatever's necessary."

CHAPTER 42
THE ASSISTANT

Dinner was served via a revolving bucket built into the wall of the stable. The guard placed a pre-packaged sandwich and a bottle of water into the contraption, and when he closed it, the food appeared on my side. Presumably, that was how they used to feed the horses, which was understandable because who would want to enter an enclosed space with one of those creatures? Dogs were more my thing. I'd always wanted a puppy—a small one—but my parents hated animals, and after I moved out, I'd always been too busy working to care for a pet.

The guard clomped away, and I was left staring at my meagre rations. I felt sick, but I heard Brax's voice in my head, telling me I needed to eat to keep up my strength. And he was right. I wasn't certain how the rescue would work, but if I needed to run anywhere, I couldn't afford to stumble. There was a chill in the air, and I wrapped the blanket around me before I settled onto the mattress in the corner. The only other thing in my makeshift prison was a porta-potty. At least I'd been given a toilet roll. They hadn't taken that final shred of dignity away from me, although some antibacterial wipes would have been nice.

Reluctantly, I took a bite of the cheese sandwich. The bread was dry, but the cheese tasted surprisingly flavoursome.

"Hey."

The whisper came from behind me, soft, almost too soft to hear. The guard was watching a video on his phone at the other end of the barn, his mind elsewhere. A sitcom? I could make out canned laughter, which meant it was safe to speak quietly.

I dropped the remains of the sandwich back into the package and inched the mattress away from the wall. There was a tiny hole in the old wood where a knot had fallen out, and when I squinted through it, I found a green eye staring back at me. I couldn't see much of the girl's face, but I didn't recognise her from Amber Road.

"Hey."

"I'm Elsa. Elsa McKinley Henderson. Please remember my name. Please."

She spoke with an American accent, and her voice was tinged with desperation.

"Elsa McKinley Henderson. I won't forget."

"What's your name?"

Hell, which one should I use? My real name with its bad memories? Or Indali Vale, the name I wished were mine? No, I had to stick with the cover story.

"Indira. Indira Adams."

"Indira Adams," she repeated back. "I need to give you the other names."

"What other names?"

"The other girls. The ones who were here before. We don't know where they go, but nobody's rescued us, so they're not being set free. We pass the names on so there's a record..." Elsa gulped back tears. "In case... In case anyone ever manages to escape."

If only I could tell her that rescue was coming.

"I'll memorise them."

"I think… I think some have been lost. There are so many."

"I won't forget. We'll be okay, I promise."

But what she said next sent my mind into a tailspin.

"How? How will we be okay? He'll come for you soon. I… I didn't know whether to warn you or not, but I wished someone would have told me."

"Who? Who will come for me?"

"The boss. They call him Cass."

"The man who was here earlier?"

"Yes."

He'd said he would see me tonight. "Where will he take me? Do you know?"

And, more importantly, would Jerry's team be able to follow? What if he locked me in a basement? Would they be able to pick up the tracker signal if I was underground?

"To the house. Don't fight him. Just don't fight him because if he snaps, you'll be stuck here like me. Or maybe that's a good thing?" She gave a hiccupping sob that quickly cut off as if she'd covered her mouth. "Nobody knows where they go afterward."

"What happens in the house?" I whispered. I had a bad, bad feeling about this.

"He calls it 'sampling the merchandise.' He sells us; I know that much."

Now I wished I hadn't eaten that mouthful of cheese sandwich. It was about to make a reappearance.

"He raped you?"

"After he'd thrown me against a fireplace. I wish I hadn't tried to stop him—I can't walk properly anymore, and he's been so angry. I'm damaged goods now. He says I'm stuck here until I recover. And if I don't… Please, just remember my name. Elsa McKinley Henderson. I don't… I don't have a family anymore, and nobody's going to look for me."

"They will. People will find us."

"They won't. The names... There are so many names. Don't fight him," she said again. "The others say that if you just lie there, it doesn't last long."

The others? A chill ran through me. Actually, it was more of an icy tsunami. He'd done this to all of them? To Meera? Until now, I'd managed to hold myself together, but now the tears came. I needed to give her a hug. To tell her that help was coming and everything would be okay. But I couldn't even call her name because her cell was near the guard, and he'd hear me.

Elsa began reciting names, and she hadn't been lying about the number of them.

Helene Kuenstler.

Sarah Dennis.

Chelsea Appel.

Musi Lopez.

Ariss Raybourn.

Sheryl List.

Kerensa Stoffel.

Agata Łukasik.

Maryam S... Maryam S...

She started sobbing when she couldn't remember the surname. Many of the victims sounded like tourists rather than locals—had Cass recruited more hostel owners like Silvio as part of his vile scheme?

And what was I meant to do tonight? I'd signed up to be kidnapped, not raped. I suppose... I suppose I should have thought of that, but I'd been so determined to help Meera and the other girls that I hadn't stopped to consider the possibility. If I'd known, would I still have come? Would I have put myself through the ordeal with the knowledge that I'd prevent other girls from suffering the same fate? I thought that maybe I would. Brax would probably have put his foot down, though.

Brax.

Where was he?

How much did he know?

I could see Jerry keeping him in the dark, citing operational security or something. She seemed like a woman who held her cards close to her chest. How would he react when he found out what had happened? Would he be angry with me for allowing it? I hoped he'd be sympathetic. I'd really, really need his support when this was over.

Saige Sigal.

Deana Carman.

Moira Crace.

Kirsty Webb.

Jessica Thieleman.

Layla Cooper.

Kelli Haupt.

Emma McDonald.

Would the list ever end?

The moon was high in the sky when he came for me. Not Cass himself, but another guard, a younger one than the phone-obsessed ogre in the barn. This guy was big too, not fat, but muscular. I considered trying to run, to escape into the surrounding forest, but he'd handcuffed me again, and he kept a firm grip on my arm as he forced me in front of him along the dimly lit path to the house.

I might not have been able to run, but I could talk. Did he speak any English?

"How can you work for this man? Do you know what he's going to do to me?"

No response.

"He's going to rape me. He's a monster, and if you stand

by and let it happen, that makes you a monster too. Do you have a wife? A sister? A daughter?"

Probably not. He didn't answer, and what kind of man would do this to a woman? A freaking psycho. I tried a different tack.

"How much is he paying you? I'll pay you double if you walk me to the gate instead of the house. If you had even a fragment of a conscience, you'd let me go."

That got a dry laugh. So he did understand; he simply didn't care.

"Don't you have a mind of your own? Or do you just blindly follow orders?" Seeing as he was still pushing me along, I had to assume his answers were "no" and "yes" respectively. "What about a god? Aren't you worried how you'll be judged after you die?"

This time, I got a grunt and a miracle.

His grip released.

A second later, the handcuffs clicked as they were removed.

Holy hell—a reminder of his religion, that was what had finally gotten through to him? He still didn't speak, and I almost didn't dare to turn around. What if he changed his mind? Should I run? Which way was the gate? And what about Meera?

"Th-th-thank you."

"Despite what people might say, I'm not a monster."

Wait… That was a woman's voice.

I turned to find Jerry standing there with a syringe in her hand. At least, I was almost certain it was Jerry. The voice was familiar, but her face was covered by a ski mask and she was wearing goggles over her eyes. She poked at the lifeless form of the guard with a booted foot.

"Team from Jez." Her voice was quiet and oh-so calm. "I've taken out a guy between the barn and the house. Indi's with me, over."

313

"Is he dead?" I asked.

I'd seen plenty of bodies before, inside and out, but I'd never seen anyone die outside of a hospital setting. Somehow, I couldn't bring myself to care.

"Just sleeping. Were you serious about the rape?"

"The girl in the next cell says Cass—he's the boss—likes to sample the merchandise. She fought back, and he injured her leg."

"How many girls are left in the barn? We're estimating seven."

"Eight, I think. Plus one guard, sometimes two. The guard in there at the moment spends most of the time watching videos on his phone. Can you get the girls out? Please say you can get them out."

"I need to move this asshole."

Jerry took the guy by his armpits and began dragging him toward the trees. I grabbed the feet and helped. He weighed a ton.

"The other girls?" I asked once we'd dumped him behind a sturdy trunk.

She didn't answer right away, but finally, she nodded. "Cass is expecting you, but you're not going. We don't have a choice." Another pause. "Team from Jez. Casa Nova forced our hand. One guard down, and I confirm, I have Indi. Once she's safe, we go in, over." A pause. "Fifteen minutes." Then she focused on me again. "Are you hurt?"

"No, but Meera—"

"You're the priority right now. I'll take you off the property, and Chase will pick you up. You *will* stay where I put you. Do you understand?"

What could I do but nod? I was way, way out of my depth here, and I had no wish to get handcuffed again.

"I understand."

"How are the other women secured?"

"They're in stables in the barn."

"Loose inside? Or are they chained? Cuffed? Tied up?"

"I was loose inside, and so was Elsa next to me. I think the others are too."

"What about the doors? Padlocked? Bolted?"

"Bolted from the outside." I screwed my eyes shut, trying to remember. "Two bolts, one in the middle of the door and one at the bottom, and the bars go all the way to the ceiling. The guard is at the far end. You'll rescue them?"

"We'll see."

"Elsa's injured. She can't—"

"Start walking. And if you don't do as you're told, I have plenty more syringes of the good stuff."

"You don't have to threaten me."

Sometimes, I really didn't like Jerry very much.

"Shh."

"Please, help Elsa? She doesn't have anyone else, and I promised she'd be okay. I *promised* that—"

"For fuck's sake, just shut up."

CHAPTER 43
BRAX

What was a man meant to do when his girlfriend had been kidnapped and his ex-fuck buddy had headed off to rescue her after giving the strict instruction of "Don't do anything stupid, asshole"? Dawson was a part of the operation too, as were the two hired hands, and although Brax had known Dawson for many years, he'd never before seen the hard-as-granite look that had been in his old friend's eyes as he left the house. Brax wasn't sure whether to be comforted or alarmed by it. Ari had gone along to act as lookout, and Brax hoped that she and Dawson would be voices of reason if Jerry decided to do anything, well, Jerry-like.

Brax had tried answering work emails—which was arguably a breach of Jerry's order because he could barely write a coherent sentence—before giving up and picking at a plate of pasta that Chase had made. Chase seemed to be the logistics man. While the others had staked out Casa Nova's lair, he'd stocked the new rental property with food, topped off the gas tanks in the two SUVs that remained at the house, and made sure everyone had clean laundry.

He wore an earpiece, and every so often, he'd say a few

words to whoever was listening. At least everything seemed quiet. And Brax began to understand why Alexa had chosen Chase as her companion—the man was unflappable. He exuded a calmness that would have benefitted her greatly. In Blackstone House, she'd always been jumpy, nervous, an agoraphobe who hated to leave the safety of the basement, although she disliked being labelled as such. Brax knew she travelled now, and he suspected her new-found adventurous streak was partially due to Chase's influence.

Chase was ironing now, and the TV played quietly in the background, tuned to the Portuguese equivalent of CNN. It must have been a slow news day—although Brax couldn't understand what the anchor was saying, the story seemed to be about guinea pigs.

He craved a stiff drink, but he also needed to stay alert in case anything happened. Was there a gym here? Maybe he could work out his frustrations on a treadmill? Priest had left with the two Blackwood men over four hours ago, and there'd been no real updates since then. The newcomers had shown up in yet another SUV stuffed with even more equipment, and when Brax asked what it was for, one of the men just smiled and shrugged. Brax had assumed he didn't speak English until he heard him having a perfectly fluent conversation with Priest five minutes later.

Brax hated being kept in the dark. Which was ironic, considering the name of his clubs, but that was a different—

Why was Chase turning off the iron? That shirt was only half-finished.

"Is there a problem?"

A shrug. "There's been an adjustment to the timeline."

"Why? What adjustment?"

"I don't know the details, but I have to make a pickup."

"A pickup? What kind of a pickup?"

A pause. A *long* pause. "Indi."

"Is she okay? Is she—"

"As I said, I don't have the details. Can you put the ironing board away? We'll be back soon."

"Fuck the ironing board. I'm coming with you."

"That's not part of the plan."

"Then fuck the plan too."

"I can't take you into the middle of an operation."

"Fine, I'll drive myself."

There were two SUVs outside in the driveway, but where were the damn keys? Brax had seen them on the counter earlier, but now they were gone.

"Looking for these?"

Chase held up a key in each hand. That man had been spending too much time with Alexa.

"In that case, I'll walk."

Or run. Casa Nova was five miles away, but if Indi was in trouble, Brax wouldn't leave her to face it alone. And a cab was out of the question.

"I can't let you do that."

"Really? How are you going to stop me?"

Chase was a personal assistant. Yes, he might have been an inch taller than Brax, but Brax worked out in the gym at Nyx every day he was home, and he wasn't in bad shape. But he made the mistake of blinking, and when he opened his eyes, he was face down on the floor with his arm twisted behind his back. Damn, that hurt. Chase had been spending too much time with Jerry as well.

"Haven't you ever been in love with a woman?" Brax asked, his cheek squashed against the tile.

"No."

"A man?"

The merest hesitation. "No."

Brax suspected Chase was lying about that.

"If Alexa was in a bad situation, wouldn't you want to be there to help?"

"Not if it risked making the situation worse." But it turned out that Alexa was eavesdropping on the conversation. "She says you have to stay in the car. If you get out, she'll never fix your shit again—that's a direct quote. And…she'll also put a picture of your tattoo on the billboard down the street from Nyx."

Of course she would. Brax didn't doubt it.

"I'll stay in the car, I swear. I just need to see Indi."

CHAPTER 44
THE ASSISTANT

When Jerry returned to the devil's playground, I'd expected war to break out. Gunfire, explosions, the works. But instead, there was silence, and perhaps that was worse?

What was going on? Were the other girls safe?

Thorns scratched at my back as I pressed deeper into the undergrowth. The road was just a few yards away, and Jerry had told me to wait here for Chase, but what if something went wrong? The trek across the estate had been a terrifying stop-start journey, with Jerry pausing to listen every few seconds before dragging me forward again, her grip tight around my wrist. She'd carried a gun in her other hand. I didn't know much about firearms, but I'd watched enough movies to know it was a shotgun.

We'd been near the gate when a guard appeared from the darkness, his features a mix of light and shadow as he stepped under one of the ornate lamp posts that illuminated the driveway. Cass's men must have realised there was a problem because he was carrying a gun too, a pistol that he raised in our direction when I tripped and sent a stone skittering across the path. Hell! I froze, but Jerry didn't. She raised the shotgun, and there was a *crack* as she fired with no hesitation. My heart lurched into my throat, and I steeled myself for the explosion of flesh and blood, but instead of blossoming into a scarlet mess, the guard dropped and convulsed. What the…?

"Electrified slug," she whispered. "Five hundred volts."

She darted forward and injected him from another syringe before cuffing his wrists and ankles with plastic ties and dragging him into the gloom. The whole process took seconds.

"Why are you just standing there?" she asked. "Move."

I moved.

And now I was hiding, hoping for the best but fearing the worst.

The distant purr of an engine sent my pulse into a frenzy. Was this Chase? Or backup for Cass? How many men were on the estate? I'd only seen five in the barn—three guards, the driver, and Cass himself—but there could be fifty. Fifty against Jerry, Tulsa, and Priest.

Another sound… A quiet *whomp-whomp-whomp* I didn't recognise. And then a sound I did—the snap of a twig. My heart skipped. Should I run? What were my other options? Hiding and hoping? Being scared to death? That was literally a thing. I'd learned about it in school. A surge in adrenaline could cause arrhythmia followed by stress-induced cardiomyopathy.

The footsteps came closer, and I couldn't stay where I was. I couldn't sit and wait to be murdered by a band of psychos.

I ran.

I ran toward the road, short of breath as my heart pounded against my ribcage. Fear took over, and I didn't know where I was going, only that I needed to get away from the nightmare behind me.

Then pain.

Pain as a dark-coloured vehicle rounded the bend and

clipped my elbow. I spun away and fell, my knees scraping along the asphalt thanks to the stupid dress I'd been made to wear. My chin hit the ground and the impact snapped my head back. I lay there dazed for a second.

Have to get away.

A car door opened.

And then I heard the sweetest sound in the world.

"Indi!"

Brax. He scooped me up, and I clung to him as he bundled me into the back seat of the car and slammed the door.

"Are you all right? Indi? Are you hurt?"

My knees were bleeding, probably my face too, but in that moment, the pain barely registered.

"I'm okay."

Brax had me. I was safe. Chase was driving, and he accelerated along the road, then stopped just as quickly. Why? Why was he stopping? The *whomp-whomp-whomp* grew louder, almost deafening, and Chase cursed as a helicopter flew overhead.

"Is that him?" Brax asked.

"Yeah. Guess the sick freak spent his ill-gotten gains on an expensive toy."

Did he mean Cass? Cass was getting away? I didn't have time to consider the implications because the back door opened again and someone shoved Meera in beside me. Then Elsa got bundled into the front, crying out as she landed. I grabbed Meera's hand as Chase skidded the car around, and a second later, we zoomed off in the opposite direction.

"Meera." I wrapped my arms around her, and then the tears came. Tears for all we'd been through and tears of relief that it was over. She hugged me right back, and I knew I'd have a heck of a lot of explaining to do. But it could wait. It could all wait.

The helicopter was way ahead of us now, a black silhouette against the purple sky. Stars twinkled, and as it passed in front of the full moon, it would have made a spectacular picture if not for the fact that a sadistic son of a bitch was escaping. Would anyone be able to find him again? Alexa? Jerry? The police?

The five of us were thrown forward as Chase braked sharply, and Brax grabbed my arm to stop me from falling off the seat. Dammit, I should have worn a seat belt. Having seen the aftermath of more car crashes than I cared to remember, I was always lecturing people about that.

"What's happening?" Brax asked Chase.

"If you have a phone, turn it off."

"Why?"

"We're going dark. You have an analogue watch?"

"Yes, but—"

"Count me two minutes."

"But…" Brax decided against asking questions. "Okay."

It was too dark to see the hands of Brax's watch, but he held it up to his ear, close enough for me to hear the quiet ticking. The only other sounds were Elsa's sobbing, an owl hooting outside, and the distant rotors of Cass's helicopter.

Then…then the rotors changed in pitch.

The helicopter began to lose altitude.

"Two minutes," Brax said. "What the hell happened?"

"It's in the Lord's hands now."

"The helicopter's going to crash?"

"Maybe. Once they lose power, they can auto-rotate down if the pilot's good enough."

Chase turned his phone back on, then started the car again. The helicopter kept going, but it was getting lower and lower, and I couldn't hear the engine anymore. A vehicle sped past us, another SUV, but Chase didn't seem alarmed.

"Friend or foe?" Brax asked.

"Friend. In a minute or two, I need to assist with a search. It shouldn't take long—we have approximate coordinates."

"A search for what?"

"A dead drone."

"Is that something to do with the issue the helicopter appears to be having?"

"No comment."

This time, our pace was more sedate, and for the first time since the walk to the main house, I was able to breathe properly. The worst was over. Meera was alive. Brax was still with me, and I hoped he knew what to do next because my brain had turned to mush.

"Is anyone physically hurt?" Chase asked. "Do we need a doctor?"

I was a freaking doctor, but I could barely tell my gluteus maximus from my iliac crest at that moment.

"Elsa needs to go to a hospital. She has a leg injury. Meera, are you okay? I mean, I know you're not, but…"

"No doctor. I can't… I don't want anyone touching me."

A month ago, if someone had told me that people like Jerry and Tulsa existed, women who did questionable things while giving the legal system the finger, I'd have been appalled. But now? Now, if they'd handed me a pair of scissors, preferably blunt ones, I'd have removed Cass's genitals myself and taken pleasure in it. My beautiful, vivacious friend had been stolen and replaced with a shell of her former self.

The car stopped again, this time near a pasture, and Chase climbed out.

"Give me a hand?" he asked Brax.

I didn't want him to go, not when I still felt so fragile, but we had to work as a team. He must have understood because he leaned in and kissed my hair.

"I love you. And when I come back, we can start the rest of our life."

"Please hurry."

Then we were alone again, and I kept checking out of the windows in case a bunch of Cass's men materialised from the darkness. Logically, I knew Brax and Chase wouldn't have left us if there were any danger, but the fear was still very real.

"Who are these people?" Elsa whispered.

I wasn't sure how much I was allowed to tell her. "They're friends."

"You brought them here?"

"Yes."

Meera hugged me tighter. "I thought nobody would come. *He* said the cops didn't care."

"But *I* care, and I finally found a man who does too."

"That's Brax? That's your boss?"

"He's been amazing. Even after I lied to him about everything, he helped me, and…and…" The events of the past few days overwhelmed me, and I blinked back tears. "I don't know what the future holds, but I do know I want him to be in it."

"I just want to go home."

"Back to Massachusetts? Or to Rhode Island?"

She stiffened. "I…I'm not sure. My parents… What am I gonna tell my parents?"

"We'll worry about that later. First, let's focus on getting through today, okay?" In Brax's absence, I had to be the strong one. "Elsa, where are you from?"

"Alabama. But there's n-n-nothing for me to go back to." She gave a sniffle. "Just…just a man who ruined my life and a whole lot of bad memories."

Another challenge.

"We'll deal with that after you've recovered, okay? What happened to your leg? You said Cass threw you against a fireplace?"

"I f-f-fell and landed on the hearth, and I heard something crack in my thigh."

She'd fractured her femur? If that was true, it was a serious injury that usually required surgical intervention.

"How long ago?"

"Almost a month, I think? It was hard to keep track of time in that place." She began sobbing again. "I thought I'd die there."

"Hey, hey, it's okay." I reached between the seats and squeezed her hand. "You're safe."

As soon as the words left my mouth, the trunk opened, and I jumped out of my skin. But when I twisted in the seat, it was just Brax and Chase coming back. *Way to give a girl a heart attack.* They were carrying the mangled remains of the drone, and it had some kind of electronic contraption duct-taped underneath it.

"What is that thing?"

Chase dodged the question. "You didn't see this, and we were never here."

I was still curious, but I could live with not knowing. The important word there? *Live.* I was still alive, and so was Meera. Against all the odds, we'd succeeded on this rescue mission. The healing process would be long and bumpy, but we'd get through it together.

CHAPTER 45
THE ASSISTANT

Two days later, we were still in Portugal putting the pieces together, both the broken fragments of our lives and the clues from Cássio Novo's business dealings. At least Elsa had received medical treatment now. A contact of Priest's had arranged a room in a private hospital, and today, she'd undergone the operation to fix her femoral malunion. They'd had to perform an osteotomy—which effectively meant rebreaking her leg—and insert a rod into the bone's medullary cavity. She'd stay in the facility for another week at least, and then she'd start the long road to recovery. Three months for the bone to heal, followed by physio and a gradual return to normal life.

Whatever that was.

Brax had offered all of us a place to stay—me, Meera, and Elsa—but we'd made no decisions about our long-term future. Although he said he loved me, he'd distanced himself since the rescue, spending most of his time on the phone while I comforted Meera and visited Elsa. Was he giving us space, or had he come to the conclusion that I brought nothing but trouble into his life?

As for Meera, she'd barely left her room in the farmhouse.

This afternoon, we were sitting on the king-sized bed together, Meera bundled up under the quilt because she'd been chilled to the bone overnight in the stables, and she still shivered every few minutes from the memory.

"That reporter's on again," Meera said.

She fixed her gaze on the TV, and I unmuted the sound, even though I had no idea what the reporter was saying. The pretty brunette was speaking from outside Novo's gates. Meera had learned basic Portuguese, so she understood some of it.

"Is there anything new?" I asked.

Jerry and her team had managed to overrun the estate without a single casualty. When the police arrived, they'd found the six remaining women huddled together in one stable while Cássio Novo's men, all nine of them, were drugged and hog-tied in another. As for Novo himself, he'd survived the helicopter's crash landing with a concussion and a broken leg, only for Jerry and Tulsa to catch up with him. They'd handcuffed him to a tree along with the groggy pilot. Two more men had appeared from somewhere—a security company, Brax said—and one of them was friendly with a guy in the Polícia Judiciária, which was the National Police Agency that dealt with serious crimes in Portugal. Kidnapping and trafficking certainly counted. And it was a good thing we hadn't gone to the local police because it turned out that one of Novo's men had a brother who worked there. Whether anyone could prove the guy had been aware of what went on at Novo's estate was a question that would only be answered in time.

At this moment, specialists were combing through computers found in Novo's home while trying to navigate the depths of the dark web. Elsa and I had both been interviewed with a lawyer present, and Elsa had listed all the names she could remember for further investigation. There were over a hundred of them. The detective heading up the investigation warned us it would be a long haul.

As for Jerry, Tulsa, and Priest, they'd skipped town before anyone could ask them questions. Since they'd loaded up the car with surfboards, I had to assume they were heading to a beach someplace. Brax had refused to discuss their involvement with anyone in authority, and I'd played dumb too. We owed them everything. And since Novo's gang had been left alive and relatively unscathed—Novo had lost several teeth, apparently—the police didn't seem overly concerned about our silence. Irritated, yes, but the lawyers said they wouldn't try charging us with anything.

Reporters had quickly picked up on the story, and there was a crowd of them camped outside Novo's gates. So far, we'd kept our presence under the radar, and the farmhouse had stayed blessedly quiet.

"A source says there's been a breakthrough with Novo's records," Meera said. "They hope that maybe they'll be able to find some of the other women."

I hated to think of where they might be now. Sold to the highest bidder, forced into lives they hated. Or early deaths. I shuddered, and Meera touched my arm.

"It'll be okay."

"Shouldn't I be the one saying that?"

She managed a tiny smile, the first since we'd found her, and I felt a flicker of hope.

"I don't even know where to start with fixing my life." Meera picked at a loose thread on the quilt. "Alfie's been trying to call me."

Her phone had reappeared at the house yesterday, courtesy of Chase.

"You can't seriously be thinking of taking him back?"

She snorted. "I sent a text telling him to go to hell."

"Good."

"I'm off men forever. No more dicks." That smile grew a little wider. "Unless Brax has a brother?"

There was a glimmer of the old Meera, and boy, was I relieved to see it.

"Shut up!"

She began humming "Here Comes the Bride," and I groaned.

"It won't happen. He just got divorced last week, and I doubt he'll ever want to get married again."

"Wait, he actually got divorced?"

"I've seen the papers."

"Wow. At least he's not one of those assholes who messes around with you and then goes back to his wife."

"That was never going to happen—she's been a thorn in his side for years. But if I stay with him, that means I can't get married either."

"What do you mean, *if* you stay with him?"

"I can't hide forever. When my family finds me, they'll try to make me go home."

"Tell them to get lost. You have a job and a boyfriend now. Did you and Brax…?"

I knew exactly what she was asking, and my cheeks burned as I nodded.

"And?"

"Meera! Don't ask me that." But maybe the question was a good thing? Was talking about sex part of the healing process? Novo had raped Meera the day she arrived at the estate, she'd admitted that much, but she'd cried when the police tried to ask her more questions. "It was mind blowing."

"I'm glad you finally found a good one."

"But my father won't leave me alone unless I have a ring on my finger. He still sees me as property, plus he does business with Karam's family."

He wouldn't want to lose face with a work associate,

which was clearly more important than his daughter's future happiness.

"Brax won't let him interfere."

"You think?"

"Have you seen the way he looks at you? Just tell him you're worried."

"Maybe."

If he gave me bad news, I wasn't sure I could take it right now.

"Maybe?"

"I have to go and see Elsa."

"Don't mess this up."

"I'm trying, but I've never been in a relationship before, and I'm so unprepared. I just assumed that I'd marry a man my parents chose and spend the rest of my life taking Xanax."

Meera rolled her eyes. "Talk to him."

"Are you going to talk to your parents?"

She sank farther under the quilt, and I realised I'd said the wrong thing.

"They keep leaving messages. I wish I could tell them what happened, but I don't want to hurt them, and if they find out that I've spent the past year lying, that I ran off with Alfie and then got kidnapped, then they'll never trust me again. And yeah, yeah, I know I deserve that. But I just want to be able to go back home for Christmas and Thanksgiving and not have to deal with their disappointment."

"So you're going to keep all this a secret?"

"What benefit would telling them have? Nothing can change the past, and I want us to keep a good relationship. At least I broke up with Alfie, right? Now I just need to learn to live with what Cass did to me, and I have to believe that'll get easier with time."

How could I argue with her logic? If I were in her position, I sure wouldn't want to tell my parents either. And while she'd never had the closest relationship with her family, they got along okay, and I understood why she'd want to maintain the status quo.

"You can always talk to me."

She wrapped me up in a fierce hug. "You're the best friend I could ever have."

"Ditto."

"Then listen to me and talk to Brax."

"I will."

Later.

I'd talk to him later.

"How's Elsa?" Brax asked, looking up from his laptop when I ventured back into the kitchen. He'd been on the phone earlier, so Chase had driven me to the hospital.

"The surgeon said the operation went well. Physically, she should make a good recovery in time, although that leg will always be slightly shorter than the other."

"And mentally?"

"When we get back to the US, she'll need a good therapist."

"I'll ask around for recommendations." Brax rose and walked toward me. He looked tired this evening. He'd abandoned his contacts in favour of glasses, and his eyes had lost their usual brightness. "And how are you, Indi?"

Was this it? The big discussion I'd been putting off for as long as possible?

"We should talk."

"We should."

Even though we'd shared a bed each night since the kidnapping, Brax had made no attempt to touch me intimately, just curled around me as we slept. I'd felt safe, protected, but he'd left me even more confused than ever as to where I stood. Now he cupped a hand around the back of my neck and kissed my forehead. No, that didn't clear things up.

"I love you," I blurted. Wow, that was articulate.

"But?"

"But what?"

"It feels as though there's a 'but' coming."

"But...but I've turned your world upside down. Your friends' worlds too. And it won't stop. When I return to the US, it'll only be a matter of time before my father and brothers track me to LA."

"I'll hire you a bodyguard."

Brax would really do that?

"You didn't sign up for a girlfriend with this much baggage. And if I don't have a ring on my finger, they'll never leave me alone."

"Then I'll put a ring on your finger."

"Exactly. It really would be best if I..." Hold on. Wait a second. "What did you just say?"

"I'll put a ring on your finger."

"Like a wedding ring? One that comes with a marriage certificate?"

"There *will* be a prenup, and this time, it'll be very much in my favour. But if a ring is what it takes to stop you from worrying, then yes, I'll marry you."

"But...but I thought after Carissa..."

"You're not Carissa. And I hate the idea of losing you far more than I hate the idea of getting hitched again." Another soft kiss, this time on my lips. "It's your call. You deserve happiness."

I burst into tears, but this time, they were happy ones. Brax looked horrified as he fished in his pocket for a handkerchief.

"Is the idea of being Mrs. Vale that bad?"

"No, it's good. Unbelievably good." I wiped my eyes with

a sleeve and threw my arms around him. My legs too. "My answer's yes. Of course it's yes. And I don't want a thing in the prenup. Make sure it says that—not a single thing." Brax had protected me, and now I had to protect him right back. "Apart from you, obviously. I want you. And now I'm babbling."

This time, his kiss was deeper, and there was heat behind it. Not just a little warmth, but a freaking volcano. All the fears I'd been bottling up erupted into passion as I kissed him back.

"I love you. I love you, I love you, I love you."

"I love you too, Mrs. Almost-Vale. But you're wearing too many clothes."

"Then take them off."

His cock began to harden, and as he strode toward the stairs with me in his arms, it rubbed me in exactly the right place. I wasn't sure how I'd gotten this lucky, but I definitely needed to pay a visit to Vegas.

CHAPTER 46
BRAX

"Grey, I need a favour."

"Only the second time you've spoken with me in seven and a half years, and you already need a favour?"

"Can you draft a prenup for me?"

There was a long pause as Greyson Meyer took in this latest piece of information.

"Is this a joke? Tell me you're not getting married again?"

"It's not a joke, but it is a long story."

"Should I pour myself a drink?"

"I'll do the same."

Indi was sleeping soundly for the first time in days—aided by two orgasms—and Meera's door was closed, so Brax had taken the opportunity to spend a quiet moment downstairs. The house was silent. Chase had gone out for dinner alone, an arrangement he appeared quite comfortable with. If he lived permanently with Alexa, it was probably a regular occurrence. Brax couldn't imagine her spending much time in a busy restaurant. Although she'd definitely fork out for delivery—hell, if she had a craving for Chinese food, she probably got the dishes couriered in from Shanghai.

But enough about Alexa tonight.

Brax was engaged.

And strangely, the prospect of being Mr. Indali Vale didn't fill him with dread.

Chase's efforts had extended to stocking the drinks cabinet, and Brax poured himself a glass of Scotch, two fingers on the rocks. He still enjoyed a tipple, but since Indi had come onto the scene, he hadn't felt the same desire to drown his sorrows every night. Love was far more addictive than alcohol.

As he sipped, he summarised the events of the last few weeks—how he'd fallen for Meera, who'd turned out not to be Meera at all, and then ended up entangled in a sex-trafficking plot. Grey gave a low whistle when Brax mentioned Jerry's involvement.

"I always wondered what happened to her. Guess it's not a huge surprise that she hooked up with Alexa. They share the same lack of ethics."

"I've learned to be grateful for that."

Grey chuckled. "Same. How do you think I found out my opponent in the primary was fucking the babysitter?"

"That was Alexa?"

"There were photos, so now I'm wondering whether Jerry was involved too."

"I thought it was strange how the guy suddenly decided to 'spend more time with his family.'"

"If he'd done that in the first place, maybe he wouldn't have gotten into trouble. So, you're really trading the old ball and chain for a new model?"

"That's not how it is."

Brax told Grey about Indi's family, about the man she'd been engaged to and her father's outdated beliefs. What kind of man would insist that his daughter marry a man she disliked? It was hardly a recipe for lasting happiness.

"So it's a pity marriage?" Grey asked.

"Fuck you. I said I love her."

"Just checking."

"It's true we haven't been acquainted for long, and there's still a lot we don't know about each other, which is why I need a watertight prenup. But I hope this will last."

"What do you want in the agreement?"

"If we divorce, Indi gets a million dollars in cash. Nothing else."

Another whistle. "A million bucks? That's generous."

"It's an insurance policy. If this doesn't work out, I don't want her to stay because I'm her meal ticket. A million bucks would give her a fresh start. If she stays in spite of that, then I'll know it's out of love."

"Interesting logic."

Plus that amount was back-of-the-couch change for Brax.

"Will you draft the agreement? I have an attorney on retainer, but..." Brax sighed. "But despite our differences, there's nobody I'd trust more than you to do this."

"I'll do it. And yes, we've had our differences, but if you need a best man this time around, let me know."

"You'd step up?"

"Alexa says Indi is a marked improvement on Carissa. And I figure that any woman who voluntarily gets kidnapped in order to rescue a friend can't be that bad. Could you imagine Carissa doing that? She'd have typed a post on social media that somehow made it all about her, and then headed out for dinner."

The sad thing was, that was true. Brax had married Carissa at a low point in his life, grateful that she'd stuck by him in the aftermath of Ruby's murder when Justin's fiancée had run for the hills, and she'd repaid him by making his life hell for years. Indi was different. She wanted the freedom to choose her own career, not a free ride.

"I'll take you up on the offer if you're available next week."

"Next week? That fast?"

"Why wait? The sooner we make this official, the sooner she can tell her father to go to hell."

"I'll be there. Any idea of the location?"

"Vegas. We can stop there on the way back."

If her father or one of her brothers had followed the breadcrumbs to California, Brax wanted to be married by the time he and Indi arrived home. If she liked the idea of a fancier ceremony later, they could do that, but he wanted her off the market.

Indi was his, his to have and fucking hold, and he wasn't letting her go.

Brax's next call went to Luisa.

"I know you retired, my darling, but I'm in desperate need of some organisational help…"

CHAPTER 47
THE ASSISTANT

"Tomorrow? You want to get married *tomorrow*?"

Brax watched me over the rim of his coffee mug. "You don't?"

Meera burst out laughing. The kidnapping had changed her, and perhaps she'd never fully regain her old carefree personality, but the past week had made a big difference. Moving south to our original rental property three days ago had helped. She'd needed the physical distance between us and Novo's estate. They'd found two bodies buried beside the barn now, and none of us doubted that Elsa would have suffered that same fate if she'd stayed.

Thanks to her, they had names, at least, and the victims would be laid to rest in a more dignified manner soon.

Plus the first of the missing women had been found. First and second, actually—aided by the massive amount of publicity the case was generating, Emma McDonald had been recognised by a neighbour who'd spotted her hanging out laundry after her photo was published online by her parents. She'd been bought by a businessman from Marseilles who'd wanted a sex slave-slash-housekeeper. He was in jail now. And Saige Sigal had been thrown out of a car on the highway in England, presumably by a purchaser who'd feared the same fate.

In the past twenty-four hours, a specialist cyber team had also gained access to Novo's records, so it was only a matter of time before more victims were freed. And by "specialist cyber team," I meant Alexa. Dawson and Ari had been at Novo's estate on the night of the rescue, and they'd "borrowed" his laptop before the Polícia Judiciária arrived.

As for Elsa, she was just getting started on the road to recovery. Her leg might heal in months, but the mental scars would take much longer. She'd barely spoken on the drive to our temporary home, and she hadn't said much more since our arrival. Those pretty emerald eyes of hers were haunted. But the agonising pain she'd suffered for months had eased, and she'd agreed to speak to the therapist Brax had found once we settled in LA, which gave me hope that, in time, she'd recover. She and Meera would both stay with Brax and me at Nyx for the first few weeks. The conversation about The Dark had been awkward. Meera already knew, and Elsa's eyes had nearly popped out of her head when I explained the bare bones of what lurked in the basement. But they both understood that although sex was involved, Nyx was nothing like Novo's operation. Brax provided a healthy outlet for willing participants to act on their desires, that was all. Having roommates wasn't quite how I'd envisioned starting off married life, but Brax was being remarkably understanding about the situation.

I was getting married.

Tomorrow.

Holy shit.

"But...but how will we plan a wedding in twenty-four hours?"

"Most of the arrangements have already been made. All you have to do is pick out a white dress and whatever flowers you want."

Meera raised her hand. "Nuh-uh. A red dress."

Now Brax looked puzzled. "A red dress?"

"In our culture, people wear white to funerals. Red is the best colour for weddings. My mom wore a red dress when she married my dad."

"Red symbolises purity, love, commitment, strength, and bravery," I explained.

"Seems I have a lot to learn. You should definitely wear red."

I reached for his hand. "We'll make this work."

"We will."

"Aw, you guys… Save the sappy stuff for tomorrow, okay? Is there any more coffee?"

"Do you need a stylist?" Elsa asked, her voice soft. "Before I went travelling, I trained to do hair and make-up."

"Brax?" I asked.

"I think we booked someone, but I can cancel."

"No, don't cancel," Meera told him. "Elsa needs her hair done too. We're gonna be bridesmaids, right?"

Of course they were. There was nobody I'd rather have beside me—an old friend and a new one. Elsa was the opposite of Meera, so quiet and reserved, but she was easy to get along with. I nodded because I couldn't speak through the lump in my throat.

"What about the bachelorette party?" Meera asked.

A groan escaped. "We can live without a stripper."

"Urgh, I didn't want a stripper anyway. I was thinking of a spa day or a movie night. Or a cooking class. You totally need a cooking class. Hey, Brax, did you know she burns everything?"

"Shhh!"

Brax just gave a one-shouldered shrug. "There's a chef downstairs."

"He's a keeper. Can we go to a spa? What about one of those flotation pools? Elsa could do that, right?"

"Seeing as this whole event is being organised on a tight timeline out of necessity, why don't you go to a spa after we've tied the knot?" Brax suggested. "Find somewhere you like, and I'll hire a new assistant who can make the arrangements."

Hey, wait a second... "You're firing me?"

"You're going to be a doctor, my queen. You can't do both jobs."

Meera put both hands over her heart. "Definitely a keeper." I absolutely knew that. "Uh, are you taking applications for the assistant position? Because I need a new job."

"It's yours if you want it."

"Really?"

"Everyone thinks you already work for me, your parents included, so it seems as if that would be the most straightforward solution all around. But I'd like to add to your duties—until now, I haven't given much thought to sustainability within Vale Holdings, and with your qualifications, you could probably offer some advice."

"Like, greenify the company?"

"Exactly."

"I've never worked in an office before, but I could try. I mean, I know the theory."

"Then it's a deal. I'm sure you won't want to sit behind a desk forever, but take a few months to get back on your feet, and then you can look for something that will work better for you long-term."

Another problem solved. Another step in the healing process for Meera. And I couldn't wait for the next chapter in my life to begin.

I thought the wedding would be a tacky affair surrounded by slot machines and a fake Elvis, just the two of us plus Meera and Elsa as witnesses, but I was totally wrong. At four o'clock in the afternoon, I found myself in a hidden tropical oasis, part of the gardens at the Black Diamond Hotel. A personal shopper had brought a selection of dresses to the hotel suite Brax had arranged for us to get ready in, and while off-the-rack red wedding dresses weren't common in the US, I managed to pick out a beautiful bridesmaid dress that was perfect for the job. Meera and Elsa wore matching knee-length dresses, green to symbolise our new beginning, and a henna artist had painted works of art on all of us. Plus another gift from Brax arrived before the ceremony—a gold, ruby, and diamond necklace in the shape of a heart. I welled up, and Elsa sighed as she fixed my make-up yet again.

And when I got downstairs, I found we had guests. Priest, Jerry, Chase, and Tulsa were there, and someone had set up a webcam so Alexa could watch too. And Brax's mom had flown in with a nurse. I'd only met her that one time, and I had a brief moment of fear that she'd think we were rushing into this—because let's face it, we were—and assume I was only marrying her son for his money. But she greeted me with a warm hug.

"You look lovely, my darling."

"Thank you." I wiped away more tears. Elsa was definitely going to huff at me.

"And my son looks happy. I've never seen him smile so much, not when he was with— Well, we'll avoid mentioning her name."

"I'm thrilled you're here. And I hope we'll see more of you in the coming months."

"I'd like that."

And I also hoped that someday, my mom would escape her unhappy marriage too, but only she could make the decision to leave. I'd be there waiting if she did. Maybe when

I found my feet in this new life with Brax, I'd feel brave enough to contact her, to tell her there was more to life than being a rich man's slave.

A lady Leon's age passed me a tissue. "Don't ruin your make-up, *querida*. This is a good day."

I nodded, my eyes still damp. "It is. Uh, do we know each other?"

"I'm Luisa. I used to be Brax's assistant before I moved back to Mexico."

"Oh, he told me about you. Did you help with"—I waved a hand at the flowers—"all of this?"

"Somebody has to keep that man organised."

A quiet snort escaped. "Coffee at one hundred and forty degrees?"

"If he doesn't behave, give him decaf."

Yes, I liked Luisa.

Brax's old roommates showed up as well. Zach came with Ari, and Dawson brought Violet Miller. Plus Violet's friend Lauren was there with her fiancé—Lauren worked for Brax as well, and I recognised her from the restaurant at Nyx. Others' faces were familiar from photos Brax had shown me—Justin Norquist and Nolan de Luca. And when I walked down the aisle on Priest's arm, I spotted Greyson Meyer standing next to my soon-to-be husband in the best-man position.

Blessedly absent? My entire family.

Our vows were short and oh-so sweet. I promised to be true to Brax in good times and in bad, in sickness and in health. To love and honour him forever and always. It would be the easiest promise I'd ever had to keep. Our rings were plain, a blank canvas to build a relationship upon, but our kiss was anything but boring. We kind of forgot there was an audience until they began whistling, and then my cheeks matched my dress.

Now I was Indali Vale for real.

Dinner was served in a ballroom, and we were

surrounded by our friends and yet more flowers. If a year ago, someone had told me I'd marry a sometimes bossy, always sexy millionaire with a movie star, a champion surfer, a congressman, and several black-ops lunatics in attendance, I'd have laughed them all the way to the psych ward. But there I was, and I wouldn't have wanted it any other way.

Love took centre stage that day, and love was all that mattered.

CHAPTER 48
THE ASSISTANT

We flew back to LA the next day, and thank goodness Brax had chartered a private jet because I overslept. He'd shattered me, but purely in a good way, over and over and over again. The Blackstone crew were still at the hotel, everyone except for Jerry, anyway. Chase said there had been "an incident" the night before, and all hands were needed to clean up afterward. I dreaded to think. The last time I saw her, she'd been dancing with a dark-haired guy she'd picked up when she went to the bathroom, so hopefully whatever had happened wasn't too serious.

Brax said that until the murder, he'd been happy living in Blackstone House, and now I understood why. His old roommates were an eclectic bunch but interesting and fun to be around, even Grey, who usually looked so serious in public. I hoped we'd see more of them. We'd meet Nolan again, for sure—he'd offered us a stay at his vineyard as a wedding gift, plus two dozen bottles of wine from the latest vintage, and I was looking forward to taking a trip to the Sierra Nevada Mountains.

But for now, it was back to reality.

"Oh, hell," I gasped as the limo pulled up outside Nyx. Brax couldn't possibly take a cab like a normal person, so he'd hired a vehicle fit for a movie star. Actually, scratch that —Violet was a movie star, and she'd mentioned that she drove a Prius.

"Oh, hell," Meera echoed.

Elsa pressed her face against the window. "What's wrong? Wow, is that the place?"

Two families were waiting for us—mine and Meera's. My father and both brothers stood stony-faced outside Nyx's doors while Meera's mom clutched her husband's arm for support.

"You still didn't call your parents, did you?" I asked her.

"I sent a text." And Meera thought that would be enough? Sheesh. "I said everything was fine."

"Is that your father?" Brax asked me.

I nodded.

"And your brothers?"

"Yes."

"Want me to handle it?"

"That's not fair. This is my mess."

"It would be my absolute pleasure to send those three packing."

"Are you sure?"

"I'm positive."

"I love you."

"Forever and always."

Then my wonderful husband climbed out of the car and offered me a hand. I grabbed it like a lifeline, desperate to borrow some of his strength. Behind us, Meera helped Elsa to stand and made sure she had her crutches. They were still decorated with green velvet ribbon from the wedding. Lauren had hitched a ride back with us, and she hurried inside, heading for the elevator.

"Can I help?" Brax asked, keeping his voice neutral. Disinterested, even.

My father stepped forward, his disgust all too evident as he looked at our joined hands. "I'm here to take my daughter home."

"Your daughter? Do you mean my wife?"

It was the first time I'd seen my father speechless. His mouth opened and closed again before he found his tongue.

"Indali can't be married to you. She's engaged to another man."

"The way I understand it, you tried to marry her off to a jackass, and she decided to forge her own path instead."

"I was a witness," Meera said. "They're totally married."

"So was I," Elsa added. "It was such a beautiful ceremony."

My father made a weird gurgling sound and balled up his fists, and I ran through the possibilities in my head. Cardiac arrest? Aortic aneurysm? No...just anger. He turned the colour of a ripe tomato, and his eyes glittered with fury.

"You want a picture for your mantel?" Brax asked. "We can mail one."

"You'll pay for this."

"I don't doubt it. She costs me a fortune in jewellery, isn't that right, my darling? But she's worth every cent. Can I offer you a ride to the airport? My driver's about to leave." He turned to Meera's parents, who'd been watching wide-eyed. They knew a little about the difficulties I'd had with my parents. I'd stayed with them several times over the years, mostly when I couldn't face going home to Springfield. "And you must be Mr. and Mrs. Adams? Meera's told me so much about you, all good, of course."

Brax had dismissed my father so politely, so effectively, that he didn't know what to say. But my older brother refused to give up.

"You can't just marry her. You didn't ask us for permission."

Brax turned back. "That's because we live in twenty-first-century America. The only person whose permission I needed was hers."

And I'd gladly given it.

My younger brother stepped in. This was a real family affair, wasn't it? "She has to come back to Springfield. There's a warrant out for her arrest." His voice was smug, and his tone said "Gotcha." "She's a thief."

Now Brax's expression turned from congenial to hard. "No, you're the one who has to return to Springfield. Your captain would like a word. You abused your professional position to frame your sister for a crime she didn't commit, and if you'd bothered to show up to work today instead of wasting your time here, you'd know the charges have been dismissed."

Vimal was smart enough to realise that he was way, way out of his depth, and he took a step back.

"It was a misunderstanding."

"Bullshit. You know what? Take a cab to the airport. We're done here." Brax turned back to Meera's parents. "Would you like to join us for dinner? I'm sure you and Meera have a lot to catch up on."

They looked at each other, and her dad nodded. "We'd appreciate that."

"You've brought shame on our family," my father hissed. "You're dead to us."

Do you know what I felt at his words? Not sadness, not anger, but relief.

Relief that I could finally live the life I wanted instead of one chosen for me. I didn't shed a tear as my father marched off along the street, trailed by Raj and Vimal.

Meera's mom had a hundred questions, I could tell, but she started with the obvious one. "Indi, you married Meera's boss? She didn't mention that the two of you were seeing each other."

Brax answered for me. "Meera introduced us, and we hit it off from the start."

Okay, so the hitting part had come from the side mirror of his Porsche, but he wasn't lying.

"Mom, it was a whirlwind romance. Isn't that cute?" Meera gave each of her parents a hug. "Sorry I forgot to call. Indi and I took a last-minute trip to Europe, and there was the time difference, and then the wedding…"

"We were just worried about you. Your phone was turned off."

"It keeps doing that. I think the battery's faulty."

The doorman held the door patiently, and we all trooped inside. The chandelier twinkled above, and Mrs. Adams's look of awe reminded me how stunning Nyx's decor was. I only hoped she didn't look too closely overhead—if she paused to study the crystals, she might realise they were somewhat phallic. Fortunately, Brax quickly herded her into the elevator while the staff fetched our luggage from the limo.

And I breathed deeply for the first time in years.

Brax and I were a team. Partners, the way a marriage should be, not king and subject, not master and slave. We'd support each other in every way possible.

Our secrets were safe.

And so was my heart.

WHAT'S NEXT?

My next book will be a Blackwood novella, *Out of Their Elements*...

When Jenna Olsen took a waitressing job at The Brotherhood of Thieves, she was looking for a fresh start, not a hot commando. But there he is at table twenty, being all gentlemanly and distracting.

Gage Reader doesn't need a woman in his life. Work is his focus, not the jumpy server from his favourite bar, and he's good at his job. But when a shadow from Jenna's past shows up, he just can't help getting involved...

For more details:
www.elise-noble.com/out-of-their-elements

And the next book in the Blackstone House series will be Jerry's story, *Hard Luck*...

Never lose your heart to a man, Jerry Knight's mom always told her. They mess with your sanity. Jerry's too busy saving the world to get tangled up in a relationship anyway, but

351

there's nothing wrong with a one-night stand. Unless of course you bump into a hit squad while doing the walk of shame...

You make your own luck, Cole Gallagher's father always told him. Success comes from hard work. But after he crosses paths with a certain enigmatic brunette, he begins to wonder whether his Uncle Eamon's lucky shamrock might be more than a weed after all.

Jerry doesn't do rest and she doesn't do relaxation, but when a stroke of bad luck leaves her in the Caribbean with nothing to do but Cole—on a boat—she's forced outside her comfort zone. Weeks of doing nothing. It's her worst nightmare. And as for Cole, he's exactly the kind of man her mom warned her about.

Fortunately, some new acquaintances decide to liven up the trip, and Jerry soon finds herself in a game of cat and mouse with a crew of determined criminals. Cole isn't quite so happy about the situation, but who cares? He's nothing more than a pretty face and a little light entertainment. Isn't he?

For more details:
www.elise-noble.com/hard-luck

If you enjoyed *Hard Limits*, please consider leaving a review.

For an author, every review is incredibly important. Not only do they make us feel warm and fuzzy inside, readers consider them when making their decision whether or not to buy a book. Even a line saying you enjoyed the book or what your favourite part was helps a lot.

WANT TO STALK ME?

For updates on my new releases, giveaways, and other random stuff, you can sign up for my newsletter on my website:
www.elise-noble.com

If you're on Facebook, you might also like to join Team Blackwood for exclusive giveaways, sneak previews, and book-related chat. Be the first to find out about new stories, and you might even see your name or one of your suggestions make it into print!

And if you'd like to read my books for FREE, you can also find details of how to join my advance review team.

Would you like to join Team Blackwood?

www.elise-noble.com / team-blackwood

 facebook.com / EliseNobleAuthor
twitter.com / EliseANoble
 instagram.com / elise_noble

ALSO BY ELISE NOBLE

The Devil and the Deep Blue Sea (2023)

Blackwood Elements

Oxygen

Lithium

Carbon

Rhodium

Platinum

Lead

Copper

Bronze

Nickel

Hydrogen

Out of Their Elements (novella) (2023)

Blackwood UK

Joker in the Pack

Cherry on Top

Roses are Dead

Shallow Graves

Indigo Rain

Pass the Parcel (TBA)

Blackwood Casefiles

Stolen Hearts

Burning Love (TBA)

Baldwin's Shore

Dirty Little Secrets

Secrets, Lies, and Family Ties

Buried Secrets

Secret Weapon (Crossover with Blackwood Security)

A Secret to Die For (2023)

Secrets of the Past (TBA)

Blackstone House

Hard Lines

Blurred Lines (novella)

Hard Tide

Hard Limits

Hard Luck (TBA)

Hard Code (TBA)

The Electi

Cursed

Spooked

Possessed

Demented

Judged

The Planes

A Vampire in Vegas

A Devil in the Dark (TBA)

The Trouble Series

Trouble in Paradise

Nothing but Trouble

24 Hours of Trouble

Standalone

Life

Coco du Ciel

A Very Happy Christmas (novella)

Twisted (short stories)

Books with clean versions available (no swearing and no on-the-page sex)

Pitch Black

Into the Black

Forever Black

Gold Rush

Gray is My Heart

Audiobooks

Black is My Heart (Diamond & Snow - Prequel)

Pitch Black

Into the Black

Forever Black

Gold Rush

Gray is My Heart

Neon (novella)

Printed in Great Britain
by Amazon

21116933R10212